Outlaws of the Marsh

Outlaws of the Marsh

Written by Shi Nai'an and Luo Guanzhong
Translated by Sidney Shapiro

UNWIN PAPERBACKS
Sydney London Boston

This edition first published in Great Britain and Australia by
UNWIN PAPERBACKS 1986.

UNWIN PAPERBACKS
40 Museum Street, London WC1A 1LU, United Kingdom

UNWIN PAPERBACKS
Park Lane, Hemel Hempstead, Herts HP2 4TE, United Kingdom

ALLEN AND UNWIN AUSTRALIA PTY. LTD.
8 Napier Street, North Sydney, NSW 2060, Australia

ALLEN AND UNWIN NEW ZEALAND PTY. LTD.
60 Cambridge Terrace, Wellington, New Zealand

© 1986 The Commercial Press, Ltd. Hong Kong Branch

This edition is for sale in the world outside United States,
Hong Kong and Southeast Asia.

National Library of Australia
Cataloguing-in-publication entry
Outlaws of The Marsh.
ISBN 0 04 820027 1 (PBK)

I. Shi Nai'an, ca. 1290-1365. II. Luo Guanzhong, ca. 1330-1400.
III. Sidney Shapiro, 1915-   . IV. Title
Shui Hu Zhuan. English
895.1' 34.

Printed by
C & C JOINT PRINTING CO., (H.K.) LTD.
75, Pau Chung Street, Kowloon, Hong Kong

Preface to the Abridged Version

One of the best known and best loved of the ancient Chinese novels which have come down through the ages, *Outlaws of the Marsh* is set mainly in the final years of Hui Zong, a Song Dynasty emperor who reigned from 1101 to 1125. It tells why and how one hundred some-odd men and women banded together on a marsh-girt mountain in what today is Shandong Province, became leaders of an outlaw army of thousands and fought brave and resourceful battles against pompous, heartless tyrants.

Historians confirm that the story is derived from fact. Some of the events actually happened, some of the persons actually existed. Their rebellious deeds struck a responsive chord in the oppressed masses and gradually evolved into folk legends. Professional story-tellers further dramatized and embellished them in performances at market fairs and amusement centers.

The present consensus among Chinese scholars is that in the fourteenth century two men, Shi Nai'an and Luo Guanzhong, took this raw material and created a novel. Since its original publication, it has appeared in numerous editions ranging from seventy to 124 chapters, the denouement sometimes changing with the political temper of the ruling monarch. (The seventy-chapter edition ends with the outlaws still being hunted. Other editions have them going over to the emperor and themselves becoming the hunters — of other rebels.) Disputes over the authorship, and the authenticity and dates of the various editions, continue to this day.

We may leave this to the specialists. What matters is that the novel now known as *Shui Hu Zhuan* (literally *Marsh Chronicles*), and which we have entitled *Outlaws of the Marsh*, is a remarkable literary *tour de force*. In spite of its enormous cast, all of the characters come across as distinct personalities, convincingly and in depth. The many episodes are closely meshed as integral parts of the whole, and offer an intimate portrayal of the people and their society.

Outlaws of the Marsh has fascinated Chinese readers, young and old, for six hundred years. It has been adapted for stage and screen, for puppet theater, for picture books. Children know the tales by heart. It has been commented upon by scores of eminent scholars. In several countries, such as Japan, it has long been appreciated, in translation, and has exercised a considerable influence.

An English translation based on a combination of the 70 and 100 chapter editions appeared under the aegis of the Foreign Languages Press, Beijing, in 1980. It tells for the first time in English the story of the outlaws in its entirety. Only the "poems" introducing each chapter have been cut. Little better than doggerel, they ruin the suspense by revealing what is about to follow. We have also pared down some of the redundancy and cumbersome detail.

Other than that, we tried to be as faithful to the content as possible, even when this fidelity results in factual inaccuracy. Fourteenth century dress, weapons, government offices, for example, have been superimposed by the authors in some instances on the twelfth. Their native Jiangsu Province colloquialisms are put in the mouths of Shandong Province characters. Locations of towns, time sequences, are sometimes wrong.

Moreover, many official titles and departments, arms, costumes, household implements, ceremonies, religious matters, puns, jokes, literary allusions . . . have no direct equivalent in the English language. Only approximations were possible, at best.

Yet what ordinarily would have been the most difficult part of translating a foreign classic — giving the "feel" of an ancient people in a distant country, conveying a sense of the style of the original — has in this instance not been too much of a problem. The reason lies in the development of the Chinese language. Centuries of feudalism, Confucian morality, limited internal mobility and communications, the very late advent of modern technology and foreign influences, tended to leave modes of expression relatively undisturbed. The spoken language of Song times was somewhat similar to what is heard in many parts of China, even today. One is struck, in reading the novel, by the "modernity" of the dialogue. It is the concepts, the life-style, that are archaic and strange. A fairly straightforward English, therefore, not too sharp or slangy, was adopted — balanced by the knowledge that we are dealing with twelfth century Chinese individuals, each of different temperament, degree of education and station in life.

Our 100 chapter edition, illustrated by original Ming Dynasty woodcuts and handsomely bound in three volumes, has been very well received. Now, to make *Outlaws of the Marsh* more conveniently available to a broad general readership, we have produced this abridged version, in paperback, adorned by sixteen of the Ming woodcuts.

Although of course shorter than the full-length novel, the new edition presents the famous favorite episodes in all of their excitement and rich detailed colour. We know you will savor and enjoy these tales that have thrilled so many people for so many centuries in so many lands.

SIDNEY SHAPIRO
September, 1985
Beijing

CONTENTS

CHAPTER 1
Major Lu Pummels the Lord of the West

Shi Jin followed the road leading to Yanan Prefecture. He ate and drank when hungry and thirsty, he stopped only at night and set out again the next day at dawn. He travelled in this manner, alone, for more than half a month until he arrived in Weizhou.

"This is also a border garrison," he said to himself. "Maybe my teacher, Instructor Wang, is here."

He entered the town. It was a bustling place, with several streets and market-places. On a street corner he saw a small tea-house. He went in and sat down.

A waiter approached him. "What kind of tea would you like, sir?"

"I'll have a cup of steeped."

The waiter brought his order and placed it on the table before him.

"Where is the town's garrison command?" asked Shi Jin.

"It's that place just up ahead."

"Do you know whether they have an arms instructor from the Eastern Capital, a man called Wang Jin?"

"The garrison has many arms instructors. There are three or four named Wang. But I don't know whether any of them is Wang Jin."

While the waiter was talking, a big fellow who looked like an army officer strode in. His head was bound in a bandanna with figured swastikas, buckled in the back with twisted gold rings from Taiyuan. A raven-black plaited sash bound his parrot-green warrior's gown at the waist. On his feet were yellow boots embossed with four welts of brown leather in hawk talon design. He had large ears, a straight nose and a broad mouth. A full beard framed his round face. He was six feet tall and had a girth of ten spans.

When the new-comer had taken a seat, the waiter said to Shi Jin: "That's the major. You can ask him about Wang Jin. He knows all the arms instructors."

Shi Jin rose quickly and bowed. "May I invite you to some tea, sir? Please join me."

The officer saw that Shi Jin was a big stalwart fellow who seemed a man of valor. He walked over and returned his greeting. Then the two sat down together.

"May I be so bold as to ask your name, sir?" Shi Jin queried.

"I'm called Lu Da. I'm a major in this garrison. And who are you, brother?"

"My name is Shi Jin. I'm from Huayin County in Huazhou Prefecture. My teacher, Wang Jin, used to be an arms instructor in the Mighty Imperial Guards in the Eastern Capital. Could you tell me, sir, whether he's here in this garrison?"

"Say, aren't you Young Master Shi from Shi Family Village, the fellow they call Nine Dragons?"

Shi Jin bowed. "I am that humble person."

Lu Da returned his courtesy. " 'Meeting a man of fame is better than just hearing his name.' Is your teacher the Wang Jin who got in wrong with Marshal Gao in the Eastern Capital?"

"The same."

"I've heard of him, but he's not here. They say he's with Old General Zhong in the Yanan garrison. Weizhou is a small post. Young General Zhong is our commander. Brother Wang is not with us. So you're Young Master Shi. I've heard a lot of good things about you. Come out and have a few drinks with me."

He took Shi Jin by the hand. As they were leaving the tea-house, Lu Da called over his shoulder: "Charge the tea to me."

"It doesn't matter, Major," replied the waiter. "Just go along."

Lu Da and Shi Jin strolled down the street arm in arm. Before they had gone fifty paces they saw many people gathered around an open plot of ground.

"Let's take a look," Shi Jin suggested.

They pushed through the crowd. There in the center was a man holding a dozen or so staves. Various packets of salves and ointments, with prices marked, were arrayed on a platter on the ground. The man was a medicine pedlar who attracted customers by putting on a show with weapons.

Shi Jin recognized him. It was his first arms instructor, Li Zhong, nicknamed the Tiger-Fighting General.

"Teacher," called Shi Jin. "I haven't seen you in ages."

"What are you doing here, young brother?" Li Zhong cried.

"Since you're Young Master Shi's teacher," said Lu Da, "come and have a few cups with us."

"Gladly, just as soon as I've sold some of these medicines and earned some money."

"Who's got time to wait? Come on, if you're coming."

"Mine is a hand-to-mouth existence, Major. Go ahead. I'll catch up with you later. . . . Young brother, you go on first with the major."

Lu Da was very irritated. He roughly shoved the spectators aside. "Haul your ass holes out of here or I'll beat you to a pulp," he bellowed.

The crowd, recognizing him, hastily scattered. Li Zhong was angry, but he dared not protest. Lu Da was obviously much too fierce. "How impatient you are," Li said with a placating smile. He gathered up his arms and medicines, gave them to a friend for safe-keeping, and set off with Shi Jin and the major.

They turned this way and that through the streets until they came to a famous tavern run by a family named Pan at the foot of a bridge. From a pole sticking out over the tavern door a pennant fluttered in the breeze indicating that liquor was sold on the premises. They went upstairs and selected a clean room. Lu Da took the host's seat, Li Zhong sat opposite, while Shi Jin seated himself at the side.

The waiter, who knew Lu Da, greeted them respectfully. "How much wine do you want, Major?" he asked.

"We'll start with four measures."

The waiter laid out dishes to go with the wine. "What would you like to eat, sir?"

"Questions, questions," Lu Da exploded. "Bring whatever you've got, add up the bill and I'll pay! Must you gab so?"

The waiter went downstairs. Soon he returned and heated the wine. He covered the table with platters of meat and other food.

Each of the three men downed several cups. They talked of this and that, comparing methods in feats at arms. Just as their conversation was at its liveliest, they heard the sound of sobbing in the next room. The irascible Lu Da immediately became enraged. He snatched plates and dishes and smashed them on the floor. The waiter, alarmed, rushed up the stairs. He found Lu Da fuming.

"If there's anything you want, sir, just give the order and I'll bring it," he said, with a bow.

"Who wants anything? I think you know who I am. Yet you have the brass to allow people to bawl in the next room and disturb us while we dine. I haven't underpaid you, have I?"

"Don't be angry, sir. I would never permit anyone to disturb you. The people weeping are a man and his daughter who sing in the taverns. They didn't know you and your friends were drinking here. They can't help lamenting their bitter fate."

"There's something peculiar going on. Bring them here to me."

In a few minutes the waiter returned with a girl of about eighteen, followed by a man in his late fifties. Both carried wooden clappers. Though not very pretty, the girl was rather appealing. Wiping her eyes, she made three curtsies. The old man also greeted the diners.

"Where are you from?" asked Lu Da. "Why do you weep?"

"I will tell you our story, sir," the girl replied. "We are from the Eastern Capital. My parents and I came to visit a relative, but when we arrived we learned he had left Weizhou for the Southern Capital.[1] My mother fell ill in the inn and died. My father and I were having a hard time. Master Zheng, who is called the Lord of the West, saw me and wanted me for a concubine. He sent people to wheedle and threaten, and finally signed a contract promising my father three thousand strings of cash for me.

"The contract was real but the promise was false. In less than three months his wife, a hard woman, drove me out of the house. What's more, Master Zheng ordered the innkeeper to demand that we 'return' his three thousand strings of cash. We never received a penny of his money. How could we repay him? My father is weak. He couldn't argue with a rich and powerful man like Zheng. We didn't know what to do. My father taught me many ballads when I was a child and we began making rounds of the taverns, singing. We give Zheng most of what little we earned each day, saving a little for our travelling expenses so that we can go home.

"But the last few days the taverns haven't had much business, so we couldn't pay. We're afraid Zheng will come asking for it and abuse us. Ours is a hard lot, and we've no place to seek redress. That's why we've been weeping. We hadn't meant to disturb you, sir. Please forgive us."

"What's your family name?" asked Lu Da. "Which inn are you staying at? Where does Master Zheng, that Lord of the West, live?"

The old man replied: "Our name is Jin. I am the second among my brothers. My daughter is called Jade Lotus. Master Zheng is the butcher who sells meat at the foot of Zhuangyuan Bridge. His nickname is Lord of the West. My daughter and

---

[1] Present-day Shangqiu in Henan Province.

I live in the Lu Family Inn just up ahead inside the town's East Gate."

"Bah," said Lu Da contemptuously. "So Master Zheng is only Zheng the pig-sticker, the dirty rogue who runs a butcher shop under the patronage of Young General Zhong, our garrison commander. And he cheats and bullies too, does he?"

He turned to Li Zhong and Shi Jin. "You two wait here while I beat the varlet to death. I'll be right back."

They grabbed him. "Calm yourself, brother," they pleaded. "Let's talk this over again later." They finally managed to restrain him.

"Come here, old man," Lu Da said to the father. "I'll give you some money. Tomorrow you can go back to the Eastern Capital. How about it?"

"If you can help us return home you'll be giving us a new lease on life," said father and daughter. "But we're afraid the innkeeper won't let us go. Master Zheng has ordered him to collect our payments."

"Don't worry about that," said Lu Da. "I'll take care of the innkeeper." He pulled out five ounces of silver and placed them on the table. To Shi Jin he said: "This is all I've brought today. If you have any silver, lend it to me. I'll give it back tomorrow."

"It doesn't matter, brother. .No need to repay." Shi Jin extracted a silver bar weighing ten ounces from his bundle and put it down beside Lu Da's money.

The major looked at Li Zhong. "You lend me some too."

Li Zhong produced two ounces of silver.

Lu Da was annoyed at the smallness of the offering. "Big-hearted, aren't you?" he snorted. He handed the fifteen ounces of silver to the old man. "This will cover your travelling expenses for you and your daughter. Go to the inn and pack your things," he directed. "Tomorrow at dawn I'll come and see you off. Just let that innkeeper try and stop you!"

Old Jin and his daughter thanked him and departed. Lu Da returned the two ounces to Li Zhong.

After the three men finished two more measures of wine they went down the stairs. "I'll pay you tomorrow, host," called Lu Da.

"Just go along," the owner of the tavern said. "You can drink here on credit any time, sir. Our only fear is you won't come."

The three left the Pan Family Tavern. On the street they separated. Shi Jin and Li Zhong went to their respective inns.

Lu Da returned to his quarters near the garrison and angrily went to bed without any supper. His landlord didn't dare ask what was wrong.

Old Jin returned to his inn with the fifteen ounces of silver. He settled his daughter down, went to a place far outside the town and hired a cart. Then he returned to the inn, packed their belongings and paid their rent, fuel and rice bills. After that they could only wait for the morrow.

The night passed without incident. Father and daughter rose at dawn, lit a fire and cooked breakfast. When they finished eating, they collected their utensils. The sky was just turning light. Lu Da strode into the inn.

"Boy," he called, "which room is Old Jin's?"

"Uncle Jin," the attendant shouted, "Major Lu Da is here to see you." The old man opened his door. "Ah, Major, please come in and sit a while."

"Sit, nothing," retorted Lu Da. "If you're going, go. What are you waiting for?"

Old Jin summoned his daughter and raised his carrying-pole to his shoulder. He thanked Lu Da and started for the inn gate. The attendant stopped him.

"Where are you going, Uncle Jin?"

"Does he owe you any rent?" Lu Da demanded.

"He paid up last night. But Master Zheng has ordered me to collect the money he laid out for Jin's daughter."

"I'll return the butcher's money in person. Let the old man go."

The attendant refused. Lu Da slapped him across the face with such force that blood gushed from his mouth. The punch that followed knocked out two of his front teeth. Crawling to his feet, the attendant scuttled to the interior of the inn and hid himself.

Of course the innkeeper dared not intervene.

Jin and his daughter quickly departed from the inn, then left the town to get the cart the old man had hired the day before.

Lu Da, afraid the attendant might still try to stop them, sat himself down on a stool in the inn and remained there for four hours. Only when he was confident that the old man was far away did he leave the inn. He went directly to the Zhuangyuan Bridge.

There Zheng had a two-room butcher shop with two chopping blocks. Four or five sides of pork were hanging on display. Zheng sat behind a counter by the door, keeping an eye on his ten or so assistants as they cut and sold meat.

Lu Da came to the door. "Butcher Zheng," he shouted.

Zheng recognized him. He came out rapidly from behind the counter and greeted him with respect. "Major, a pleasure." He directed an assistant to bring a bench. "Please be seated, sir."

Lu Da sat down. "The garrison commander has ordered me to buy ten catties of lean meat, chopped fine, to be used for filling. There mustn't be a speck of fat in it."

"Right," said Zheng. He turned to his assistants. "Pick out a good cut and chop up ten catties."

"I don't want those dirty oafs touching it," said Lu Da. "You do it yourself."

"Certainly," said Zheng. "Glad to." He selected a cut of ten catties of lean meat and started mincing.

The attendant from the inn, his head bound in a white handkerchief, arrived to tell Zheng about Old Jin. But when he saw Lu Da seated at the door, he was afraid to come any closer. He stood under the eaves of a house, observing the proceedings cautiously from a distance.

魯提轄拳打
鎮關西

After chopping for an hour, Zheng wrapped the minced meat in a lotus leaf. "Shall I have it delivered, sir?" he asked.

"Delivered, nothing. What's your hurry? Now cut up ten catties of fat meat. There mustn't be a speck of lean in it. This is also for filling."

"The lean can be put in dumplings, but what good is the fat?"

Lu Da glared. "When the commander gives an order, who dares question him?"

"As long as you can use it I'll chop it for you." Zheng selected a cut of ten catties of fat meat and began mincing. By the time he wrapped it in a lotus leaf the morning had gone and it was the hour for lunch.

The inn attendant dared not approach. Even other customers were afraid to draw near.

"Shall I have this delivered to the garrison command for you, sir?" asked Zheng.

"Now I want ten catties of gristle, chopped fine, also to be used for filling, and I don't want to see any meat in it."

Zheng laughed awkwardly. "Are you making fun of me?"

Lu Da leaped up, one package of chopped meat in each hand, and scowled at the butcher. "That's exactly what I'm doing — making fun of you." He flung the contents of the packages full in Zheng's face.

The shower of meat stung the butcher into a rage. From the soles of his feet, fury surged into his forehead. An irrepressible flame blazed in his heart. He grabbed a paring knife from the butcher's block and jumped down from the shop steps. Lu Da was waiting for him in the middle of the street.

None of the dozen or so clerks from the neighboring shops dared to mediate. Passers-by stood frozen in their tracks on both sides of the street. The attendant from the inn was struck dumb.

The knife in his right hand, Zheng reached for Lu Da with his left. Lu Da seized the outstretched hand, closed in and sent the butcher sprawling with a swift kick in the groin.

Another step forward and he put his foot on Zheng's chest. Raising a fist like a vinegar keg, Lu Da thundered: "I was roving inspector of five western military districts under Old General Zhong. People might very well call me Lord of the West. But you're just a meat slicing butcher, a low cur. Where do you come off giving yourself such a title? And who gave you the right to force and cheat Jin's daughter Jade Lotus?"

He landed a punch on Zheng's nose that flattened it to one side and brought the blood flowing like the sauces in a condiments shop — salty, sour and spicy. Zheng struggled vainly to rise. The knife fell from his hand. "A good blow," he cried.

"Mother-raping thief," said the major. "How dare you talk back?" He punched the butcher on the eyebrow, splitting the lid so that the eyeball protruded. Red, black and purple gore flowed like swatches of cloth in a draper's shop.

The spectators were all afraid of Lu Da. None of them ventured to intervene.

Vanquished, Zheng begged to be spared.

"You scurvy knave," the major exclaimed scornfully. "If you had shown any guts I might have let you off. But since you're so lily-livered, I won't." He struck the butcher a heavy blow on the temple. Zheng's head rang like the clanging of gongs, bells and cymbals in a big memorial service. The butcher lay stretched on the ground. Breath was coming out of his mouth, but none was going in. He didn't move.

Lu Da pretended to be incensed. "Playing dead, eh? I'll hit you a few more!" He had observed that Zheng's face was changing color. "I only wanted to give the varlet a beating," he said to himself. "Who would have thought that three blows would kill him? They're sure to hold me for trial, and I've nobody to bring me food in prison. I'd better get out of here."

He rose and strode away, pausing briefly to look back, shake his finger at Zheng's corpse and shout: "Go on playing dead. I'll settle with you later."

Neither the butcher's assistants nor the clerks in the neighboring shops had the courage to stop him.

Lu Da returned to his quarters and hastily packed. He took only some travelling clothes and a bit of silver. His old garments and heavier things he left behind. Carrying a staff as a weapon, he sped out of the South Gate like a whisp of smoke.

CHAPTER 2
Sagacious Lu Puts Mount Wutai in an Uproar

After leaving Weizhou, Lu Da hurried pellmell east and west, passing through several prefectural towns. With him it was a case of:

Any food when you're hungry,
When you're cold rags save life;
Any road when you're frightened,
When you're poor any wife.

He dashed about in a panic, with no idea where to go.

After many days of wandering, he arrived in Yanmen, a county seat in the prefecture of Daizhou. It was a bustling town with many people and thriving markets. Carts and horses filled the streets, which were lined by shops conducting trade and commerce of every type. Although only a county seat, it was more prosperous than a prefectural capital.

On a street corner he saw a crowd gathered in front of a proclamation. Someone was reading it aloud. Illiterate himself, he pushed forward to listen. This is what he heard:

By order of the military commander of Taiyuan, this county hereby publishes the following notice from Weizhou: Wanted — the killer of Butcher Zheng. Name — Lu Da, former major in the Weizhou garrison command. Any man who conceals him or gives him food and shelter shall be deemed equally guilty. Whoever arrests and brings him forward, or offers information leading to his arrest, shall receive a reward of one thousand strings of cash. . . .

As Lu Da stood listening, someone threw his arms around him from behind and cried: "What are you doing here, brother Zhang?" He pulled Lu Da away from the street corner.

Lu Da turned to see who was hustling him away. It was none other than Old Jin from the Weizhou tavern, the man he had rescued. The old fellow didn't stop pulling till they reached an isolated spot. Then he said:

"You're too rash, benefactor. That notice offers a thousand strings of cash for your capture. How could you stand there looking at it? If I hadn't spotted you, you might have been nabbed by the police. Your age, description and place of origin are all there."

"To tell you the truth, when I went to the foot of the Zhuangyuan Bridge that day to see Zheng the butcher about your affair, I killed the churl with three blows of the fist, and had to flee. I've been knocking about for forty or fifty days now, and just happened to wander into this town. I thought you were returning to the Eastern Capital. What are you doing here?"

"After you saved me, benefactor, I found a cart. Originally I intended to go back to the Eastern Capital, but I was afraid that rogue would catch up and you wouldn't be around to rescue us. So I changed my mind and headed north. On the road I met an old neighbor from the capital who was coming here on business. He took me and my daughter along. He was good enough to find her a match. She's now the mistress of a wealthy man, Squire Zhao. The squire has provided her with a house. Thanks to you, benefactor, we now have plenty to eat and wear. My daughter has often spoken to the squire of your kindness. He is also fond of jousting. He's said many times he'd like to meet you, but that was never possible before. You must come and stay with us a few days. We can talk about what you should do next."

Lu Da and Old Jin walked less than half a *li* when they came to the door of a house. The old man pushed aside the bamboo curtain and called: "Daughter, our benefactor is here."

The girl emerged, neatly made up and attractively dressed. She begged Lu Da to be seated in the center of the room. Then, as if offering votive candles, she kowtowed before him six times. "If you hadn't rescued us, benefactor," she said, "we'd never possess what we have today." She invited him upstairs to the parlor.

"Don't bother," said Lu Da. "I must be going."

"Now that you're here, benefactor, of course we can't let you leave," said the old man. He took Lu Da's staff and bundles and ushered him up the stairs. To his daughter he said: "Keep our benefactor company. I'll arrange about dinner."

"Don't go to a lot of trouble," said Lu Da. "Anything will do."

"Even if I gave my life I could never repay your benevolence," said Old Jin. "A little simple food — it's not worth mentioning."

The three drank till almost nightfall. Suddenly they heard a commotion outside. Lu Da opened the window and looked. Some twenty to thirty men, all armed with staves, were gathered in front of the house. "Bring him down," they were shouting. A gentleman on a horse cried: "Don't let the rascal get away!"

Lu Da realized that he was in danger. He snatched up a stool and started down the stairs. Old Jin, waving his hands, rushed down ahead of him, exclaiming: "Nobody move!" He ran over to the man on horseback and said a few words. The mounted gentleman laughed. He ordered his band to disperse.

When the men had gone, the gentleman got off his horse and entered the house. Old Jin asked Lu Da to come down. The gentleman bowed as Lu Da descended the stairs.

" 'Meeting a man of fame is better than just hearing his name.' Please accept my homage, righteous Major."

"Who is this gentleman?" Lu Da asked Old Jin. "We don't know each other. Why should he be so respectful?"

"This is Squire Zhao, my daughter's lord. Someone told him that a young man I had brought to his house was upstairs, drinking. So he got some of his vassals and came to fight. When I explained, he sent them away."

"So that was it," said Lu Da. "You could hardly blame him."

Squire Zhao invited Lu Da to the upper chamber. Old Jin reset the table, and once more prepared food and drink. Zhao ushered the major to the seat of honor. Lu Da refused.

"How could I presume?"

"A small mark of my respect. I have heard much of the major's heroism. What great good fortune that I could meet you today."

"Though I'm just a crude fellow who's committed a capital offence, the squire doesn't scorn my lowliness and is willing to make my acquaintance. If there's any way I can be of service, you have only to speak."

Squire Zhao was very pleased. He asked all about the fight with Zheng the butcher. They talked of this and that, discussed jousting with arms, and drank far into the night. Then everyone retired.

The following morning Zhao said: "I'm afraid this place isn't very safe. Why not come and stay at my manor a while?"

"Where is it?" asked Lu Da.

"A little over ten *li* from here, near a village called Seven Treasures."

"All right."

Lu Da stayed at the manor for six or seven days. He and the squire were chatting in the study one day when Old Jin hastily entered. He looked to see that no one else was around, then said to Lu Da: "You mustn't think me overly cautious, benefactor. But ever since the night the squire and his vassals raised such a row in the street because you were drinking upstairs, people have been suspicious. Word has spread that you were there. Yesterday three or four policemen were questioning the neighbors. I'm worried that they'll come here and arrest you. It would be awful if anything should happen to you, benefactor."

"In that case," said Lu Da, "I'd better be on my way."

"Things might turn out badly if I kept you here, Major," the squire admitted. "Yet if I don't, I'll lose a lot of face. I have another idea. It's foolproof and will give you complete protection. But maybe you won't be willing."

"I'm a man with a death penalty waiting for him. I'll do anything to find refuge."

"That's fine. Where the Wenshu Buddha used to meditate on Mount Wutai, some thirty-odd *li* from here, a monastery was erected. They have nearly seven hundred monks. The abbot is my friend. My ancestors were patrons of the monastery and contributed to its upkeep. I have promised to sponsor a novice, and have bought a blank certificate, but have not yet found a suitable man. If you agree to join the Buddhist order, Major, I'll pay all expenses. Would you be willing to shave off your hair and become a monk?"

Lu Da thought to himself: "Who could I go to for protection if I were to leave here today? I'd better accept his offer." Aloud he said: "I'll become a monk if you sponsor me, Squire. I rely entirely on your kindness."

And so it was decided. That night, clothing, expense money and silks were prepared. Everyone rose early the next morning. Lu Da and the squire set out for Mount Wutai, accompanied by vassals carrying the gifts and luggage. They reached the foot of the mountain before mid-morning. Squire Zhao and Lu Da went up in sedan-chairs, sending a vassal on ahead to announce them.

At the monastery gate, they found the deacon and supervisor waiting to welcome them. They got out of their sedan-chairs and rested in a small pavilion while the abbot was notified. He soon emerged with his assistant and the elder. Squire Zhao and Lu Da hurried forward and bowed. The abbot placed the palms of his hands together before his chest in Buddhist greeting.

"It's good of you to travel this long distance, patron," he said.

"There is a small matter I'd like to trouble you about," said the squire.

"Please come into the abbey and have some tea."

Lu Da followed Squire Zhao to the hall. The abbot invited the squire to take the seat for guests. Lu Da sat down on a couch facing the abbot. The squire leaned over and whispered to him: "You're here to become a monk. How can you sit opposite the abbot?"

"I didn't know," said Lu Da. He rose and stood beside Squire Zhao.

The elder, the prior, the abbot's assistant, the supervisor, the deacon, the reception monk, and the scribe arranged themselves in two rows, according to rank, on the east and west sides of the hall.

Zhao's vassals left the sedan-chairs in a suitable place and carried into the hall several boxes which they laid before the abbot.

"Why have you brought gifts again?" asked the abbot. "You've already made so many donations."

"Only a few small things," replied Squire Zhao. "They don't merit any thanks."

Some lay brothers and novices took them away.

Squire Zhao stood up. "I have something to ask of you, Great Abbot. It has long been my desire to sponsor a new member for this monastery. Although I have had the certificate ready for some time, until today I have not been able to do so. This cousin here is named Lu. He formerly was a military officer, but because of many difficulties he wants to have done with mundane affairs and become a monk. I earnestly hope Your Eminence will exercise mercy and compassion and, as a favor to me, accept this man into your order. I will pay all expenses. I shall be very happy if you consent."

"Gladly," said the abbot. "This will add lustre to our monastery. Please have some tea."

A novice served tea. After all had drunk, he removed the cups. The abbot consulted with the elder and the prior on the ceremony for receiving Lu Da into the order, then instructed the supervisor and deacon to prepare a vegetarian meal.

"That man hasn't the makings of a monk," the elder said to the other monks, privately. "See what fierce eyes he has!"

"Get them out of here a while," they requested the Receiver of Guests. "We want to talk to the abbot."

The reception monk invited Squire Zhao and Lu Da to rest in the visitors' hostel. They departed, and the elder and the others approached the abbot.

"That new applicant is a savage-looking brute," they said. "If we accept him, he's sure to cause trouble."

"He's a cousin of Squire Zhao, our patron. How can we refuse? Hold your doubts while I look into the matter." The abbot lit a stick of incense and sat cross-legged on a couch. Muttering an incantation, he went into a trance. By the time the incense was consumed, he returned.

"You can go ahead with the ordination," said the abbot. "This man represents a star in Heaven. His heart is honest. Even though his appearance is savage and his life has been troubled, he will eventually become purified and attain sainthood. None of you is his equal. Mark my words. Let no one dissent."

"The abbot is only covering up his faults," the elder said to the others. "But we'll have to do as he says. We can only advise. If he won't listen, that's up to him."

Squire Zhao and the others were invited to dine in the abbey. When they had finished, the supervisor presented a list of what Lu Da would need as a monk — special shoes, clothing, hat, cape and kneeling cushion. The squire gave some silver and asked that the monastery buy the necessary materials and make them up.

A day or two later all was ready. The abbot selected a propitious day and hour, and ordered that the bells be rung and the drums beaten. Everyone assembled in the preaching hall. Draped in their capes, nearly six hundred monks placed the palms of their hands together in an obeisance to the abbot sitting on his dais, then separated into two groups. Squire Zhao, bearing gifts of silver ingots and fine cloth and carrying a stick of incense, approached the dais and bowed.

The purpose of the ceremony was announced. A novice led Lu Da to the abbot's dais. The prior told him to remove his hat, divided his hair into nine parts and knotted them. The barber shaved them all off. He reached with his razor for Lu Da's beard.

"Leave me that, at least," the major exclaimed.

The monks couldn't repress their laughter.

"Hear me," the abbot said sternly from his dais. "Leave not a single blade of grass, let the six roots of desire be torn out. All must be shaven clean away, lest they manifest themselves again," he intoned. "Off with it," he ordered.

The barber quickly finished the job. Presenting the certificate to the abbot, the elder requested him to select a name by which Lu Da should be known in the Buddhist order.

"A spark from the soul is worth more than a thousand pieces of gold," the abbot chanted. "Our Buddhist Way is great and wide. Let him be called Sagacious."

The scribe filled out the certificate and handed it to Sagacious Lu. At the abbot's direction he was given his monk's garments and told to put them on. Then he was led to the dais. The abbot placed his hand on Lu's head and instructed him in the rules of conduct.

"Take refuge in Buddha, the Law and the Monastic Order. These are the three refuges. Do not kill, steal, fornicate, drink or lie. These are the five precepts."

Lu Da didn't know he was supposed to answer "I shall" to each of the first three and "I shall not" to each of the last five.

"I'll remember," he said.

Everyone laughed.

Squire Zhao invited all present into the assembly hall where he burned incense and offered a vegetarian feast to the Buddhist gods. He gave gifts to every member of the monastery staff, high or low. The deacon introduced Sagacious to various members of the monastery, then conducted him to the rear building where the monks meditated. Nothing further happened that night.

The next day, Squire Zhao decided to leave. He said goodbye to the abbot, who tried in vain to keep him. After breakfast, all the monks went with him as far as the monastery gate. Squire Zhao placed his palms together and said, "Abbot, teachers, be compassionate. My young cousin Lu is a crude, direct fellow. If he forgets his manners or says anything offensive or breaks any rules, please forgive him, as a favor to me."

"Don't worry, Squire," said the abbot. "I shall teach him gradually to recite the prayers and scriptures, perform services, and practise meditation."

"In the days to come I will show my gratitude," promised the squire. He called Lu over to a pine tree and spoke to him in a low voice: "Your life must be different from now on, brother. Be restrained in all things, under no circumstances be proud. Otherwise, it will be hard for us to see each other again. Take good care of yourself. I'll send you warm clothing from time to time."

"No need to tell me, brother," said Lu. "I'll behave."

The squire took his leave of the abbot and the monks, got into his sedan-chair and set off down the mountain for home. His vassals followed, carrying the other, now empty, sedan-chair and boxes. The abbot and the monks returned to the monastery.

When Lu got back to the meditation room, he threw himself down on his bed and went to sleep. The monks meditating on either side shook him into wakefulness.

"You can't do that," they said. "Now that you're a monk, you're supposed to learn how to sit and meditate."

"If I want to sleep, what's it to you?" Lu demanded.

"Evil!" exclaimed the monks.

"What's this talk about eels? It's turtles I like to eat."

."Oh, bitter!"

"There's nothing bitter about them. Turtle belly is fat and sweet. They make very good eating."

The monks gave up. They let him sleep.

The next day they wanted to complain to the abbot. But the elder advised against it. He said: "The abbot is only covering up his faults when he says he will attain sainthood and that none of us is his equal. But there's nothing we can do about it. Just don't bother with him."

The monks went back. Since no one reprimanded him, Sagacious sprawled out on his bed every night and slept snoring thunderously. When he had to relieve himself he made a terrible racket getting up. He pissed and crapped behind one of the halls. His filth was all over the place.

The abbot's assistant reported the matter. "That Lu has no manners. He's not in the least like a man who's left the material world. How can we keep a fellow like that in the monastery?"

"Nonsense," retorted the abbot. "Don't forget our donor's request. Sagacious will change later on."

No one dared argue.

And so, Sagacious Lu remained in the monastery on Mount Wutai. Before he knew it, four or five months had passed. It was early winter and Lu's mind, which had been quiescent for a long time, began to stir. One clear day he put on his black cloth cassock, fastened his raven-dark girdle, changed into monk's shoes, and strode from the monastery.

Halfway down the mountain he halted to rest in a pavilion. He sat down on a low "goose neck" bench and said to himself with a curse: "In the old days I had good meat and drink every day. But now that I'm a monk I'm shrivelling up from starvation. Squire Zhao hasn't sent me anything to eat for a long time. My mouth is absolutely tasteless. If only I could get some wine."

He saw in the distance a man carrying two covered buckets on a shoulder-pole. A ladle in his hand, the man trudged up the slope singing this song:

Before Mount Nine Li an old battlefield lies,
There cowherds find ancient spears and knives,
As a breeze stirs the waters of the Wu River broad,
We recall Lady Yu's farewell to her lord.

Lu watched him approach. The man entered the pavilion and put down his load.

"Hey, fellow, what have you got in those buckets?" Lu asked.

"Good wine."

"How much a bucket?"

"Are you serious, monk, or are you just kidding?"

"Why should I kid you?"

"This wine is for the monastery's cooks, janitors, sedan-chair carriers, caretakers, and field laborers — no one else. The abbot has warned me that if I sell to a monk he'll take back the money and house the monastery loaned me for my winery. I don't dare sell you any of this."

"You really won't?"

"Not if you kill me!"

"I won't kill you, but I will buy some of your wine."

The man didn't like the look of things. He picked up his carrying-pole and started to walk away. Lu dashed out of the pavilion after him, seized the pole with both hands, and kicked the fellow in the groin. The man clapped both hands to his injured parts and dropped to a squatting position. He couldn't straighten up for some time.

Sagacious Lu carried both buckets to the pavilion. He picked the ladle off the ground, removed the covers, and began drinking. Before long, one of the buckets was empty.

"Come around to the monastery tomorrow and I'll pay you," he said.

The man had just recovered from his pain. If the abbot found out, it would mean an end to his livelihood. How could he seek payment from Lu at the monastery? Swallowing his anger, he separated the remaining wine into two half-buckets.

Then he shouldered the load, took the ladle and flew down the mountain.

Lu sat in the pavilion a long time. The wine had gone to his head. He left the pavilion, sat down beneath a pine tree and again rested for quite a spell. The wine was taking increasing effect. He pulled his arms out of his cassock and tied the empty sleeves around his waist. His tattooed back bare, he strode up the mountain, swinging his arms.

The monastery gate-keepers had been watching him from afar. They came forward when he approached and barred his way with their split bamboo staves.

"You're supposed to be a disciple of Buddha," they barked. "How dare you come here in this besotted condition? You must be blind. Haven't you seen the notice? Any monk who breaks the rules and drinks gets forty blows of the split bamboo and is expelled from the monastery. Any gate-keeper who lets a drunken man enter gets ten blows. Go back down the mountain, quickly, if you want to save yourself a beating."

In the first place, Lu was a new monk, in the second, his temper hadn't changed. Glaring, he shouted: "Mother-screwing thieves! So you want to beat me? I'll smash you!"

The situation looked bad. One of the gate-keepers sped back inside and reported to the supervisor, while the other tried to keep Sagacious out with his staff. Lu flipped it aside and gave him a staggering slap in the face. As the man struggled to recover, Lu followed with a punch that knocked him groaning to the ground.

"I'll let you off this time, varlet," said Sagacious. He walked unsteadily into the monastery.

The supervisor had summoned the caretakers, cooks, janitors and sedan-chair carriers — nearly thirty men. Now, armed with staves, they poured out of the western cloister and rushed to meet Lu. The ex-major strode towards them with a thunderous roar. They didn't know he had been an army officer. He sprang at them so fiercely they fled in confusion into the sutra hall and closed the latticed door. Sagacious charged up the steps. With one punch and one kick he smashed the door open. The trapped men raised their staves and came out fighting.

The abbot, who had been notified by the supervisor, hurried to the scene with four or five attendants.

"Sagacious," he shouted, "I forbid you to misbehave."

Lu was drunk, but he recognized the abbot. He cast aside his staff, advanced and greeted him.

"I had a couple of bowls of wine, but I did nothing to provoke these fellows," said Sagacious. "They came with a gang and attacked me."

"If you have any respect for me," said the abbot, "you'll go to your quarters at once and sleep it off. We'll talk about this tomorrow."

"It's only my respect for you that stops me from lambasting those scabby donkeys!"

The abbot told his assistant to help Lu to the monks' hall. He collapsed on his bed and slept, snoring loudly.

A crowd of monks surrounded the abbot. "We told you so," they said. "Now you see what's happened? How can we keep a wildcat like that in our monastery? He upsets our pure way of life."

"It's true he's a bit unruly," the abbot admitted, "but he'll become a saint later on. At present, we can do nothing. We must forgive him, for the sake of our donor, Squire Zhao. I'll give him a good lecture tomorrow, and that will be the end of it."

The monks laughed coldly. "Our abbot isn't very bright," they said among themselves. All retired to their respective abodes.

The next morning the abbot sent his assistant to the monks' quarters to summon Sagacious Lu. He was still asleep. The assistant waited while he got up and put on his cassock. Suddenly, Lu dashed out, barefoot. The surprised assistant followed. He found Lu pissing behind the temple. The assistant couldn't help laughing. He waited till Lu had finished, then said:

"The abbot wants to see you."

Lu went with him to the cleric's room.

"Although you originally were a military man," said the abbot, "I ordained you because of Squire Zhao's sponsorship. I instructed you: Do not kill, steal, fornicate, drink or lie. These are the five precepts by which all monks are bound. First of all, no monk is allowed to drink. But yesterday evening you came back drunk and beat up the gate-keepers, broke the vermilion latticed door of the sutra hall and drove out the cooks and janitors, shouting and yelling all the while. How could you behave so disgracefully?"

Lu knelt before him. "I'll never do such things again."

"You're a monk now," the abbot continued. "How could you violate our rule against drinking and upset our pure way of life? If it weren't for the sake of your sponsor Squire Zhao I'd expel you from the monastery. Don't you ever act like that again."

Lu placed his palms together. "I wouldn't dare," he asserted fervently.

The abbot ordered breakfast for him and, with many kindly words, exhorted him to reform. He gave Lu a cassock of fine cloth and a pair of monk's shoes, and told him to return to his quarters.

Topers should never drink their fill. "Wine can spur action, or ruin everything," as the old saying goes. If drinking makes the timid brave, what does it do to the bold and impetuous?

For three or four months after his drunken riot Lu didn't venture to leave the monastery. Then one day the weather suddenly turned warm. It was the second lunar month. Lu came out of his quarters, strolled through the monastery gate and stood gazing in admiration at the beauty of Mount Wutai. From the foot of the mountain the breeze brought the sound of the clanging of metal. Sagacious returned to his quarters, got some silver and put it inside his cassock near his chest. Then he ambled down the slope.

He passed through an archway inscribed with the words: "Wutai, a Blessed Place". Before him he saw a market town of six or seven hundred families. Meat, vegetables, wine and flour were on sale.

"What am I waiting for?" Lu said to himself. "If I had known there was a place like this, instead of snatching that fellow's bucket I would have come down and bought my own wine. I've been holding back so long that it hurts. Let's see what sort of food they have on sale here."

Again he heard the clang of metal.

Next to a building with the sign "Father and Son Inn" was an ironsmith's shop. The sound was coming from there. Lu walked over. Three men were beating iron.

"Got any good steel, master smith?" he asked the eldest of them.

The man was a little frightened at the sight of Lu's face, with newly sprouted bristles sticking out wildly all over. He ceased his hammering and said: "Please have a seat, Reverend. What kind of work do you want done?"

"I need a Buddhist staff and a monk's knife. Do you have any first-rate metal?"

"I do indeed. How heavy a staff and knife do you want? We'll make them according to your requirements."

"The staff should be a hundred catties."

"Much too heavy," the smith laughed. "I could make it for you, but you'd never be able to wield it. Even Guan Gong's[1] halberd wasn't more than eighty-one catties!"

"I'm every bit as good as Guan Gong," Sagacious burst out impatiently. "He was only a man, too."

"I mean well, Reverend. Even forty-five catties would be very heavy."

"You say Guan Gong's halberd was eighty-one catties? Make me a staff of that weight, then."

"Too thick, Reverend. It would look ugly, and be clumsy to use. Take my advice, let me make you a sixty-two catty Buddhist staff of burnished metal. Of course, if it's too heavy,

---

[1] Guan Gong, a famous general of the Three Kingdoms period (220-280).

don't blame me. For the knife, as I said, we don't need any specifications. I'll use the best steel."

"How much for the two?"

"We don't bargain. You can have them at rock-bottom — five ounces of silver for both."

"It's a deal. If you do a good job, I'll give you more."

The smith accepted the silver. "We'll start right away."

"I have some small change here. Come out and have a bowl of wine with me."

"Excuse me, Reverend. I must get on with my work. I can't keep you company."

Sagacious Lu left the ironsmith's. Before he had gone thirty paces, he saw a wine shop banner sticking out from the eaves of a house. He raised the hanging door screen, entered the shop, sat down, and pounded on the table.

"Bring wine," he shouted.

The proprietor came up to him. "Forgive me, Reverend. My shop and investment money all are borrowed from the monastery. The abbot has a rule for us tavern keepers. If any of us sells wine to a monk, he takes back the money and drives us out of our premises. Don't hold it against me."

"All I want is a little wine. I won't say I bought it here."

"Impossible. Please try some place else. I'm sorry."

Lu rose to his feet. "If another place serves me, I'll have something to say to you later!"

He left the wine shop and walked on. Soon he saw another wine flag suspended over a doorway. He went in, sat down and called:

"Wine, host. Be quick."

"How can you be so ignorant, Reverend?" the tavern keeper demanded. "You must know the abbot's rules. Do you want to ruin me?"

Sagacious insisted on being served, but the tavern keeper was adamant. Lu had no choice but to leave. He went to four or five more wine shops. All refused to serve him.

"If I don't think of something, I'll never get any wine," he said to himself. At the far end of the market-place he saw amid blossoming apricot trees a small house from which a bundle of broom straw was hanging. He came closer and found it was a little wine shop. Lu went in and sat down by the window.

"Host," he called, "bring wine for a wandering monk."

The rustic owner came over and scrutinized him. "Where are you from, Reverend?"

"I'm a travelling monk who's just passing through. I want some wine."

"If you're from the Mount Wutai monastery, I'm not allowed to sell you any."

"I'm not. Now bring on the wine."

Lu's appearance and manner of speaking struck the rustic owner as odd. "How much do you want?"

"Never mind about that. Just keep bringing it by the bowl-ful."

Lu consumed ten big bowls of wine. "Have you any meat?" he asked. "I want a platter."

"I had some beef earlier in the day," said the proprietor, "but it's all sold out."

Sagacious caught a whiff of the fragrance of cooking meat. He went into the yard and found a dog boiling in an earthen-ware pot by the compound wall.

"You've got dog meat," he said. "Why won't you sell me any?"

"I thought as a monk you wouldn't eat it, so I didn't ask."

"I've plenty of money here." Lu pulled out some silver and handed it over. "Bring me half."

The proprietor cut off half the dog carcass and placed it on the table with a small dish of garlic sauce. Lu tore into it delightedly with both hands. At the same time he consumed another ten bowls of wine. He found the wine very agreeable and kept calling for more. The shop owner was dumbfounded.

"That's enough, monk," he urged.

Lu glared at him. "I'm paying for what I drink. Who's asking you to interfere?"

"How much more do you want?"

魯智深大鬧五臺山

"Bring me another bucketful."

The host had no choice but to comply. Before long, Sagacious had downed this, too. A dog's leg that he hadn't finished he put inside his cassock.

"Hold on to the extra silver," he said as he was leaving. "I'll be back for more tomorrow."

The frightened proprietor could only helplessly gape. He watched as Lu headed towards Mount Wutai.

Halfway up the slope, Lu sat down in the pavilion and rested. The wine began to take effect. Leaping up, he cried: "I haven't had a good workout in a long time. I'm getting stiff and creaky in the joints. What I need is a little exercise."

Lu came out of the pavilion. He gripped the end of each sleeve in the opposite hand and swung his arms vigorously up and down, left and right, with increasing force. One arm accidentally struck against a post of the pavilion. There was loud crack as the post snapped. Half the pavilion collapsed.

Two gate-keepers heard the noise and climbed to a high vantage point for a look. They saw Lu staggering up the slope.

"Woe," they exclaimed. "That brute is soused again!"

They closed the gate and barred it. Peering through a crack, they watched Lu advance. When he found the gate locked, he drummed on it with his fists. But the gate-keepers didn't dare let him in.

Lu pounded a while, in vain. Suddenly he noticed a Buddhist guardian idol on the left side of the gate.

"Hey, you big worthless fellow," Lu shouted. "Instead of helping me knock on the gate, you raise your fist and try to scare me! I'm not afraid of you!"

He jumped on the pedestal and ripped up the railing as easily as pulling scallions. Grabbing a broken post, he flailed it against the idol's leg, bringing down a shower of gilt and plaster.

"Woe," cried the gate-keepers. They ran to inform the abbot.

Lu paused, then turned and observed the guardian idol on the right.

"How dare you open your big mouth and laugh at me?" he yelled. He leaped on the pedestal and struck the idol's leg two hard blows. The figure toppled to the ground with a thunderous crash.

Lu laughed uproariously, holding the broken post in his hand.

When the gate-keepers notified the abbot he merely said: "Don't provoke him. Go back to your gate."

At that moment, the elder, the supervisor, the deacon, and other responsible monks entered the hall. "That wildcat is very drunk," they said. "He's wrecked the mid-slope pavilion and the guardian idols at the gate. How can we put up with this?"

"Since ancient times it's been known that 'Even a king shuns a drunkard.' All the more necessary for me to avoid them," replied the abbot. "If he's broken idols, we'll ask his sponsor Squire Zhao to make us new ones. Zhao can repair the pavilion too. Let Sagacious do as he wishes."

"Those guardian idols are the lords of the gate," the monks protested. "You can't change them around just like that."

"Never mind the gate idols," retorted the abbot. "Even if they were the idols of the leading Buddhas themselves that were destroyed, there'd be nothing we could do about it. Stay out of his way. Didn't you see how savage he was the other day?"

"What a muddle-headed abbot," the monks muttered as they left the hall. "Don't open that gate," they instructed the gate-keepers. "Just stand inside and listen."

"If you mother-screwing scabby donkeys don't let me in," bellowed Sagacious, "I'll set fire to this stinking monastery and burn it down!"

"Remove the bar and let the beast in," the monks hastily called to the gate-keepers. "If we don't, he's really liable to do it!"

The gate-keepers tiptoed up to the gate, pulled the bolt, then flew back and hid themselves. The other monks scattered.

Lu pushed hard against the gate with both hands. Unexpectedly, it gave way, and he stumbled in and fell flat on his face. He crawled to his feet, rubbed his head, and hurried to his quarters.

He pushed aside the door curtain and plunged into the meditation room. The monks, who were sitting cross-legged on their pallets, looked up, startled. They immediately lowered their heads. On reaching his own pallet, Sagacious noisily vomited. The stench was frightful. "Virtue be praised," cried the monks, holding their noses.

Lu clambered onto his pallet and opened his cassock and girdle, ripping them in the process. The dog's leg dropped to the floor. "Good," said Sagacious. "I was just getting hungry." He picked it up and began to eat.

The monks hid their faces behind their sleeves. Those nearest him stayed as far out of his way as possible. Lu tore off a piece of dog meat and offered it to the monk on his left.

"Try it," he recommended.

The man pressed his sleeve ends tightly against his lips.

"Don't you want any?" asked Lu. He shoved the meat at the man on his right. The fellow tried to slip off his pallet and escape, but Sagacious seized him by the ear and crammed the meat into his mouth.

Four or five monks on the opposite side of the room jumped up and hurried over. They pleaded with Lu to desist. He flung aside his dog's haunch and drummed his knuckles on their shaven pates. The whole meditation room was thrown into an uproar. Monks got their cassocks and bowls from the closets and quickly left. There was a general exodus. The elder couldn't stop them.

Cheerfully, Sagacious fought his way out. Most of the monks fled to the cloisters. This time the supervisor and deacon didn't notify the abbot, but summoned all the monks on duty, including every caretaker, cook, janitor and sedan-chair carrier they could muster — nearly two hundred men in all. These bound their heads with bandannas, armed themselves with clubs and staves, and marched on the monks' hall.

Lu let out a roar when he saw them. Not having any weapon he ran into the meditation room, knocked over the altar table in the front of the idol of Buddha, tore off two of the table legs, and charged out again.

He came at the attackers so fiercely that they hastily retreated to the cloisters. Sagacious advanced, flourishing his table legs. His adversaries closed in on him from both sides. Lu was furious. He feinted east and struck west, he feinted south and thumped north. Only those furthest away escaped his cudgels.

Right to the door of the preaching hall the battle raged. Then the voice of the abbot rang out: "Sagacious, stop that fighting! You, too, you monks!"

The attackers had suffered several dozen injured. They were glad to fall back when the abbot appeared. Lu threw down his table legs.

"Abbot, help me," he cried. By now he was eight-tenths sober.

"Sagacious, you're giving me too much trouble," said the cleric. "The last time you got drunk and raised a rumpus I wrote your sponsor Squire Zhao about it and he sent a letter of apology. Now you've disgraced yourself again, upset our pure way of life, wrecked the pavilion and damaged two idols. All this we can overlook. But you drove the monks from the meditation room, and that's a major crime. Wenshu Buddha meditated where our monastery stands today. For centuries these hallowed grounds have known only tranquillity and the fragrance of incense. It's no place for a dirty fellow like you. The next few days, you stay with me in the abbot's hall. I'll arrange for you to be transferred elsewhere."

The former major went with the abbot to his residence. The cleric told the supervisor to send the monks back to their meditations. Those who had been injured were to go and rest. Sagacious spent the night in the abbot's hall.

The next morning the abbot consulted with the elder. They decided to give Lu some money and send him on. But first it was necessary to notify Squire Zhao. The abbot wrote a letter and dispatched it to his manor with two messengers, who were instructed to wait for his reply.

Zhao was quite upset by the abbot's missive. In his answer he hailed the cleric respectfully and said: "I will pay for the repair of the broken gate guardians and the pavilion. Lu must go wherever the abbot sends him."

The abbot then directed his assistant to prepare a black cloth cassock, a pair of monk's shoes, and ten ounces of silver, and to summon Lu.

"Sagacious," said the abbot, "the last time you got drunk and made a disturbance in the monks' hall, you didn't know any better. This time you got drunk again, broke the guardian idols, wrecked the pavilion, and caused a riot in the hall of meditation. That's a serious crime. You've also injured many of our monks. Our monastery is a peaceful place. Your conduct is very bad. As a courtesy to Squire Zhao I'm giving you a letter of introduction to another place where you can stay. It's impossible for us to keep you here. In the Eastern Capital a Buddhist brother of mine, called the Lucid Teacher, is the abbot of the Great Xiangguo Monastery. Take this letter to him and ask him to find you a job. Last night I had a vision and composed a four-line prophetic verse to guide your destiny. You must remember these words."

Kneeling before him, Lu said: "I'd like to hear the prophecy."

The abbot intoned: "Take action in the forest, prosper in the mountains, flourish amid the waters, but halt at the river."

Sagacious kowtowed to the abbot nine times, shouldered his knapsack, tied bundles round his waist, and placed the letter in a pocket. He bid farewell to the abbot and the monks, left Mount Wutai, put up in the inn next door to the ironsmith and waited for his staff and sword. The monks were glad to be rid of him. The abbot told the lay brothers to clean up the wreckage of the guardian idols and the pavilion. A few days later Squire Zhao brought some money personally and had the idols and pavilion repaired.

CHAPTER 3
Lin Chong Enters White Tiger Inner Sanctum by Mistake

After eight or nine days on the road Sagacious Lu sighted the Eastern Capital. Lu entered the city. He found it a noisy, bustling place. In the center of town he apologetically asked a passer-by: "Could you tell me where the Great Xiangguo Monastery is?"

"There, ahead, by the bridge."

Sagacious, carrying his staff, went on to the monastery. He looked it over, east and west, then proceeded to the guest-house. A servant went in to announce him. Soon the reception monk came out. He was somewhat startled by Lu's fierce appearance, the iron staff in his hand, the sword at his waist and the pack upon his back.

"Where are you from, brother?" he asked.

"I'm from Mount Wutai," said Sagacious. "I have a letter from my abbot, requesting Lucid Teacher, the venerable abbot of this monastery, to give me a position as a working monk."

"In that case, please come with me."

Sagacious followed him to the abbot's hall, opened his bundle and took out the letter.

"How is it you don't know the ceremony, brother?" the reception monk asked. "The abbot will be here in a minute. Remove your knife, bring out your robe and mat, and light the incense of faith so that you can do homage to the abbot."

"Why didn't you say so before?" demanded Sagacious. He took off his knife, and pulled a stick of incense and a mat and his robe out of his rucksack. But he didn't know what to do with them. The reception monk placed Lu's robe over his shoulders and told him to put the mat on the floor.

A moment later the abbot, Lucid Teacher, appeared. The reception monk stepped forward and said: "This monk comes from Mount Wutai with a letter to you from his abbot."

"It's been a long time since my brother on Mount Wutai has written," said Lucid Teacher.

"Quick, brother," whispered the reception monk. "Pay your respects to our abbot."

Lu didn't know where to put his stick of incense. The reception monk couldn't help laughing. He placed it in an incense burner. Sagacious kowtowed three times. The reception monk stopped him and presented his letter to the abbot.

Lucid Teacher opened the letter and read it. The letter set forth in detail why Sagacious had become a monk and the reason he had been sent down from Mount Wutai to the monastery in the Eastern Capital. "We pray you will exercise benevolence and give him a working post," the missive concluded. "Please do not refuse. This monk will have great attainments later on."

When he finished reading, the abbot said: "You've come a long way. Rest in the monk's quarters. They will give you something to eat."

Sagacious thanked him. He collected his mat, bundle, staff and sword, and followed a novice out.

The abbot summoned both sections of his clergy. When they had all assembled in his hall he said: "My brother abbot on Mount Wutai really has no discretion. This monk he's sent used to be an officer in a border garrison. He shaved off his hair only because he killed a man. Twice he caused riots in the monks' quarters of the Wutai monastery. He made no end of trouble. My brother abbot couldn't cope with him, so he's shoved him off on me. Shall I reject him? My brother's plea is so insistent that I can't very well refuse. But if I keep him here, he's liable to play havoc with our rules and put us in a terrible state."

"Even though he's one of our brothers," said the reception monk, "he doesn't look at all like a man who's renounced the world. How can we keep him?"

"I've thought of something," said the deacon. "Outside Sour Date Gate we have a vegetable garden behind the compound for retired working monks, don't we? The soldiers of the garrison and those twenty-odd knaves living nearby are always despoiling it. They even graze sheep and horses there. It's quite a mess. The old monk in charge doesn't dare interfere. Why not let this fellow take over? At least he wouldn't be afraid of them."

"That's a good idea," said the abbot. He instructed his assistant: "When that brother in the guest-room of the monks' hall has finished eating, bring him here."

The assistant went out. He soon returned with Sagacious.

"My brother abbot has recommended that you join us," said Lucid Teacher. "Our monastery has a large vegetable garden outside Sour Date Gate, next door to the Temple of the Sacred Mountain. I will put you in charge. Every day the men tending the garden must deliver to us ten loads of vegetables. The rest will belong to you."

"I was sent by my abbot to become a member of the abbey here," said Lu. "Even if you don't make me a supervisor or deacon, how can you put me in charge of a vegetable garden?"

"You don't understand, brother," the elder interjected. "You've only just arrived. You haven't shown any special merit. How can you be appointed deacon? Overseeing the garden is also an important job."

"I'm not looking after any vegetable garden," cried Sagacious. "I won't be anything but a supervisor or deacon!"

"Let me explain," said the reception monk. "We have various kinds of members. I, for instance, am the reception monk. My job is to receive guests and visiting monks. Posts like prior, personal assistant to the abbot, scribe and elder, are special jobs. They're not easy to get. The supervisor, deacon, director and manager are custodians of the monastery's property. You've just come. How can you be given such a high post? We also have jobs like master of the sutras, master of the halls, master of the rooms, master of alms begging, and master of the bath house. These positions are held by middle-ranking members.

"And then we have the keepers — keeper of the kitchen, of the tea, of the vegetable garden, of the toilets. These are all overseers' jobs, comparatively low in rank. If you keep the garden well for a year, brother, you'll be raised to keeper of the pagoda. If you do that well for a year, you'll be made master of the bath house. Only after still another year's good work might you be appointed supervisor."

"So that's how it is," said Lu. "As long as there's a chance for advancement, I'll start work tomorrow."

Lucid Teacher let him remain for the day in the abbot's hall. A notice of appointment was written and posted in the compound for retired working monks, effective the following day.

The next morning Lucid Teacher sat on his dais and issued the formal appointment of Sagacious Lu to the post of keeper of the vegetable garden. Sagacious accepted the document, bid the abbot farewell, shouldered his pack, hung his knife at his waist, and took up his staff. With two monks as escorts, he went directly to the compound to assume his duties.

In the neighborhood of the monastery's vegetable fields were twenty or thirty rogues and gamblers. They made their living by selling the vegetables they stole from the monastery's fields. That day, when a few of them went to raid the fields, they saw a notice posted on the gate of the overseer's compound. It read:

> *The monastery has appointed the monk Sagacious Lu overseer of these vegetable fields. Starting tomorrow, he shall be in charge. Those having no business here are strictly forbidden to enter.*

The rascals called a conference of the entire gang. "The monastery has sent a monk called Sagacious Lu to take charge of the vegetable fields," they said. "He's new to the job.

This is a good chance to pick a quarrel and beat him up. Teach the lout to respect us."

"I have an idea," one of them said. "He doesn't know us; how can we pick a quarrel? Let's lure him to the edge of the ordure pit instead, as if to congratulate him, then grab his legs and toss him in head over heels. It will be a nice little joke."

"Good. Good," approved the scoundrels. After making their plans, they went to seek the monk.

As to Sagacious Lu, on arriving at the overseer's compound, he put his pack and luggage in the house, leaned his staff against the wall and hung up his knife. The lay brothers who worked in the fields all came to greet him and he was handed the keys. The two monks who had escorted him there and the monk he was succeeding as overseer bid him farewell and returned to the monastery.

Sagacious then made a tour of the vegetable fields. He saw coming towards him twenty or thirty scamps bearing a platter of pastries and ceremonial wine.

Among the twenty to thirty knaves who lived outside Sour Date Gate, two were leaders. One was Rat Crossing the Street Zhang the Third. The other was Snake in the Grass Li the Fourth. These two were in the lead as the gang advanced. Sagacious naturally walked forward to meet them.

The gang halted at the edge of the ordure pit and chorused: "We've come to congratulate you on your new post."

"Since you're neighbors," said Sagacious, "come into the compound and sit a while."

Zhang and Li dropped to their knees respectfully. They hoped that the monk would approach to raise them courteously to their feet. Then they could go into action.

Noticing this, Sagacious grew suspicious. "This gang is a queer-looking lot, and they're not willing to come forward. Can they be planning to dump me?" he wondered. "The louts think they can pluck the tiger's whiskers. Well, I'll go to them, and show them how I use my hands and feet."

Sagacious strode up to the gang. Still kneeling, Zhang and

Li cried: "We younger brothers have come especially to pay our respects," and each reached to grab one of the monk's legs.

But before they could even lay a finger on him, Sagacious lashed out with his right foot and kicked Li into the ordure pit. Zhang rose to flee, but a quick thrust of the monk's left leg and the two rascals were floundering in the foul mess together.

Startled, the rest of the gang gaped, then turned to run.

"Whoever moves goes into the pit," bellowed Sagacious.

The scoundrels froze, not daring to take a step.

Zhang and Li now raised their heads out of the ordure. The pit seemed bottomless, and they were covered with excrement. Maggots clung to their hair. Standing in the filth, they wailed: "Reverend, forgive us!"

"Help those two dogs out, you oafs," Sagacious shouted to the gang, "and I'll forgive you all."

The rogues quickly hauled their leaders from the pit and helped them over to a gourd arbour. The two stank to high heaven.

Sagacious roared with laughter. "Fools! Go and wash off in the pond. Then I want to talk to all of you."

After the two gang leaders had cleansed themselves, some of their men removed their own clothing to give them a change of garments.

"Come into the compound," Sagacious ordered. "We're going to have a talk."

He sat down in their midst, pointed his finger at them and scoffed, "You ragamuffins! Did you think you could fool me? How could pricks like you ever hope to make sport of me?"

Zhang, Li and the whole gang dropped to their knees. "Our families have lived here for generations," they said, "supporting themselves by gambling and begging and robbing these vegetable fields. The monastery paid people several times to drive us away, but no one could handle us. Where are you from, Reverend? Such a terrific fellow! We've never seen you at the monastery before. From now on, we'll be happy to serve you."

"I'm from Yanan Prefecture, west of the Pass. I used to be a major, under his excellency the garrison commander Old General Zhong. But because I killed many men, I took refuge in a monastery and became a monk. Before coming here, I was on Mount Wutai. My family name is Lu. On entering the Buddhist order I was given the name Sagacious. Even if surrounded by an army of thousands, I could hack my way out. What do you twenty or thirty amount to!"

The knaves loudly and respectfully voiced their agreement with these sentiments. They thanked the monk for his mercifulness and withdrew. Sagacious went into the house, put his things in order, then went to bed.

The next day, after talking the matter over, the rogues scraped some money together and bought ten bottles of wine. Leading a live pig, they called on Sagacious and invited him to join them in a feast. A table was laid in the overseer's compound. Sagacious sat at the head of the table, with the twenty to thirty rascals lining both sides. Everyone drank.

"Why are you spending so much money?" the monk asked.

"We're lucky," they replied. "Now that you are here, you can be our master."

Sagacious was very pleased. Wine flowed freely and the party grew lively. There was singing and talking and applause and laughter. Just as the merriment was at its height, crows were heard cawing outside the gate.

Some of the men piously clacked their teeth and they intoned together: "Red lips rise to the sky, white tongue enters the earth."

"What are you making such a blasted racket about?" demanded Sagacious.

The vagabonds replied: "When crows caw, it means there's going to be a quarrel."

"Rot!" said the monk.

One of the lay brothers who tilled the monastery's fields laughed and said, "In the willow tree beside the wall there's a new crow's nest. The birds caw from dawn to dusk."

"Let's get a ladder and destroy the nest," said some.

"I'll do it," volunteered several of the others.

Feeling his wine, Sagacious went out with the crowd to take a look. Sure enough, there was a crow's nest in the willow tree.

"Get a ladder and tear the nest down," said the men. "Then our ears can have a little peace and quiet."

"I'll climb up and do the job," boasted Li, "and I don't need any ladder."

Sagacious looked the situation over, walked up to the tree and removed his cassock. He bent and grasped the lower part of the trunk with his right hand, while his left hand seized it higher up, then gave a tremendous wrench — and pulled the tree from the ground, roots and all!

The knaves dropped to their knees, crying: "The master is no ordinary mortal! He's truly one of the *Lohans*! If he didn't have ten million catties of strength, how could he have uprooted that tree?"

"It was nothing at all," Lu said. "One of these days I'll show you how to handle weapons."

That night the vagabonds departed. But they came again the next day, and every day thereafter, bringing meat and wine to feast Sagacious, for they positively worshipped him. They begged the monk to demonstrate his skill with weapons.

After several days of this, Sagacious thought to himself: "These fellows have been treating me day after day. I ought to give them a banquet in return." He sent a few lay brothers into the city to buy several platters of fruit and five or six buckets of wine, and he killed a pig and slaughtered a sheep. It was then the end of the third lunar month.

"The weather's getting warm," said Sagacious. He had mats spread beneath the green ash tree and invited the rascals to sit around and feast outdoors.

Wine was served in large bowls and meat in big chunks.

When everyone had eaten his fill, the fruit was brought out and more wine. Soon the feasters were thoroughly sated.

"The past few days you've demonstrated your strength, master," said the rogues, "but you still haven't shown us your skill with weapons. It would be fine if you could give us a performance."

"All right," said Sagacious. He went into the house and brought out his solid iron Buddhist staff, five feet long from end to end and weighing sixty-two catties.

His audience was amazed. "Only a man with the strength of a water buffalo in his arms could handle such a weapon," they cried.

Sagacious took up the staff and flourished it effortlessly, making it whistle through the air. The vagabonds cheered and applauded.

Just as the monk was warming up, a gentleman appeared at a gap in the compound wall. "Truly remarkable," he commended. Sagacious stopped his exercise and turned to see who had spoken.

The gentleman wore a black muslin cap with its two corners gathered together; a pair of interlinked circlets of white jade held the knot of hair at the back of his head. He was dressed in a green officer's robe of flowered silk, bound at the waist by a girdle made of double strips of beaver and fastened by a silver clasp shaped like a tortoise back. His feet were shod in square-toed black boots. In his hand he carried a folding Chengdu fan. About thirty-five years old, he had a head like a panther, round eyes, a chin sharp as a swallow's beak, whiskers like a tiger, and was very tall.

"Indeed remarkable," he said. "What excellent skill."

"If he approves, it certainly must be good," said the vagabonds.

"Who is that officer?" queried Sagacious.

"An arms instructor of the Mighty Imperial Guards. His name is Lin Chong."

"Invite him in. I'd like to meet him."

Hearing this, the arms instructor leaped in through the gap

in the wall. The two men greeted each other and sat down
beneath the ash tree.

"Where are you from, brother monk?" asked Lin. "What
is your name?"

"I'm Lu Da, from west of the Pass. Because I killed many
men, I had to become a monk. In my youth, I spent some
time in the Eastern Capital. I know your honorable father,
Major Lin."

Lin Chong was very pleased, and adopted Sagacious as his
sworn brother on the spot.

"What brings you here today, Arms Instructor?" asked
Sagacious.

"My wife and I just arrived at the Temple of the Sacred
Mountain next door to burn incense. Hearing the cheers of your
audience, I looked over and was intrigued by your performance.
I told my wife and her maidservant, Jin Er, to burn the incense
without me, that I would wait for them by the gap in the wall.
I didn't think I would actually have the honor to meet you,
brother."

"When I first came here I didn't know anybody," said
Sagacious. "Then I became acquainted with these brothers and
we gather together every day. Today, you have thought well
enough of me to make me your sworn brother. That makes me
very happy." He ordered the lay brothers to bring more wine.

Just as they were finishing their third round, the maidservant
Jin Er, agitated and red in the face, rushed up to the gap in
the wall and cried: "Hurry, master! Our lady is having trouble
with a man in the temple!"

"Where?" Lin Chong demanded hastily.

"As we were coming down the stairs of the Five Peaks
Pavilion, a low fellow suddenly blocked her way. He won't let
her pass."

Lin Chong quickly took his leave of Sagacious. "I'll see you
again, brother. Forgive me!" He leaped through the gap in
the wall and raced with Jin Er back to the temple.

When he reached the Five Peaks Pavilion he saw several

idlers carrying crossbows, blowpipes and limed sticks gathered below the stair railing. They were watching a young man who was standing on the stairway with his back to them, blocking the path of Lin Chong's wife.

"Let's go upstairs," the young man was urging her. "I want to talk to you."

Blushing, the lady said, "What right do you have to make sport of a respectable woman in times of peace and order!"

Lin pushed forward, seized the young man by the shoulder and spun him around. "I'll teach you to insult a good man's wife," he shouted, raising his fist. Then he recognized Young Master Gao, adopted son of Marshal Gao Qiu, commander of the Imperial Guards.

When Gao Qiu first rose to high office he had no son to help him run his numerous affairs. And so he adopted the son of his uncle, Gao the Third. Since the boy was not only his cousin but now also his foster son, Marshal Gao loved him to excess.

The young scoundrel made full use of his foster father's influence in the Eastern Capital. His favorite pastime was despoiling other men's wives. Fearful of his powerful connections, none of the husbands dared speak out against him. He became known as the "King of Lechers".

When Lin Chong saw that he was Young Master Gao, the strength left his arms.

"This has nothing to do with you, Lin Chong," said Gao. "Who asked you to interfere!" He didn't realize that the lady was Lin Chong's wife. Had he known, the thing would never have happened. Seeing Lin Chong's hesitancy, he spoke boldly.

The commotion drew a crowd of idlers. "Don't be angry, Arms Instructor," one said. "The young master didn't recognize her. It was all a mistake."

Lin Chong's rage hadn't fully abated, and he glared at the rake with burning eyes. Some of the crowd soothed Lin Chong while others persuaded Gao to leave the temple grounds, get on his horse and depart.

Lin Chong was turning to go with his wife and Jin Er, the maidservant, when Sagacious, iron staff in hand, came charging into the temple compound with huge strides, leading his twenty to thirty vagabonds.

"Where are you going, brother?" asked Lin Chong.

"I've come to help you fight," said Sagacious.

"The man turned out to be the son of our Marshal Gao. He hadn't recognized my wife and behaved discourteously. I was going to give the lout a good drubbing, but then I thought it would make the marshal lose too much face," Lin Chong explained. "You know the old saying, 'Fear not officials — except those who officiate over you!' After all, I'm on his payroll. I decided to let the young rascal off this time."

"You may be afraid of the marshal, but he doesn't scare me a bit," shouted Sagacious. "If I ever run into that young whelp of his I'll give him three hundred licks of my iron staff."

Lin Chong saw that Sagacious was drunk and he said: "You're quite right, of course, brother. It was only because everybody urged me that I let him go."

"The next time you have any trouble, just call me and I'll take care of it!"

The knaves supported the tipsy Sagacious under the arms. "Let's go back, Reverend," they said. "You can deal with young Gao later."

Iron staff in hand, Sagacious said politely to Lin Chong's lady: "Your pardon, sister-in-law. Please don't laugh at me." And to Lin Chong he said: "Until tomorrow, brother." Then he and the vagabonds departed.

Lin Chong, his wife and Jin Er returned home. The arms instructor was angry and depressed.

As for Young Master Gao, when he had drifted into the temple leading his band of idle cronies and met Lin Chong's wife, he had become sorely enamored. After Lin Chong drove him off, he returned unhappily to the marshal's residence.

A few days later, his ne'er-do-well friends called. But they found him so fretful and irritable that they went away.

One of these idlers was an attendant named Fu An, better known as Dried Pecker Head. He suspected what was troubling Young Master Gao, and later went alone to the residence. The young rake was sitting abstracted in the study.

Fu An drew near and said: "You've been rather pale lately, Young Master. You seldom smile. Something must be bothering you."

"How do you know?"

"I'm just guessing."

"Can you guess what it is?"

"Lin Chong's wife. How's that for a guess?"

The Young Master laughed. "Not bad. The problem is I don't know how to get her."

"Nothing to it. You're afraid to provoke Lin Chong because he's a big powerful fellow. But you needn't worry. He's under the marshal's command and is being well provided for. Would he dare to offend? The least that could happen to him is exile, the worst is death. Now I've got a little scheme that will put his wife right into your hands."

"I've met many beautiful women. Why should I love only her? My heart is bewitched, I'm not happy. If you have a scheme that will work, I'll reward you generously."

"One of your trusted men, Captain Lu Qian, is Lin Chong's best friend. Tomorrow, prepare a feast in a quiet nook upstairs in Lu Qian's house. Have Lu invite Lin out for some drinking. Let Lu take him to a secluded room on the upper floor of the Fan Pavilion Tavern. I'll go to Lin's wife and say: 'Your husband has been drinking in Lu Qian's house and has been stricken by a sudden illness. He's collapsed. You'd better hurry and look after him.' Then I'll bring her over to Lu's place, where you'll be waiting. Women are as changeable as water. When she sees what a handsome romantic sort you are, Young Master, and you deluge her with sweet words, she won't be able to resist. What do you think of my plan?"

"Excellent," Gao applauded. "Have Captain Lu Qian summoned here tonight."

It so happened that Lu Qian lived only one street away from the Gao residence. He agreed to the scheme immediately. He felt he had no alternative. As long as it would please the Young Master, he was willing to forget his friendship with the arms instructor.

To get back to Lin Chong. For several days he had been brooding at home. One morning he heard someone shouting at his front door: "Is the arms instructor in?"

Lin Chong went to the door, and there was Lu Qian.

"What brings you here, Brother Lu?" Lin asked quickly.

"I'm concerned about you. Why haven't I seen you on the streets these past few days, brother?"

"My mind is troubled. I don't feel like going out."

"Come and have a few cups with me and forget about your trouble."

"First sit a while and have some tea."

After the two finished their tea, they rose.

"Sister-in-law," Lu Qian called to Lin Chong's wife who was in the next room, "I'm taking Brother Lin over to my place for a few cups of wine."

The lady hurried to the door curtain and pushed it aside. "Don't let him drink too much, brother," she admonished. "Send him home early."

The two men strolled down the street. "Let's not go to my house, brother," Lu Qian said. "We can have our drinks in the Fan Pavilion."

They went to the tavern. They selected a small room and ordered two bottles of good wine and some tidbits to go with it. For a time they chatted idly. Lin Chong sighed.

"What's wrong, brother?" asked Lu Qian.

"You don't know what's happened. I have talents but no intelligent superior to recognize them. I serve under little men from whom I have to take a lot of dirty nonsense."

"There are several arms instructors in the Imperial Guards, but none can compare with you. The marshal regards you very highly. Who would dare to molest you?"

Lin Chong told Lu Qian about his encounter with Young Master Gao a few days before.

"The Young Master didn't realize she was your wife," Lu Qian said soothingly. "It's not serious. Forget it. Let's drink."

Lin Chong downed eight or nine cups. Soon he had to relieve himself. He got up and said, "I have to wash my hands." He went down the stairs, left the tavern, and attended to his business in a small lane to the east. As he was coming out, he met Jin Er.

"I've been looking all over for you, master," said the maidservant. "So you're here!"

"What's up?" asked Lin Chong hastily.

"You had only been gone a little while when a man came rushing over to our house and said to the mistress, 'I'm a neighbor of Captain Lu. While drinking with him, the arms instructor suddenly gasped for breath and fell to the floor, You'd better go and look after him.' Our lady begged Dame Wang next door to take care of our house, then she and I hurried with the man to a place one street past the marshal's residence. When we got upstairs we saw a table laden with food and drink, but there was no sign of you, master.

"As we turned to leave, that young fellow who pestered the mistress at the temple the other day came out and leered: 'Stay a while, lady. Your true husband is here!' I flew down the stairs. Our mistress was screaming for help. I couldn't find you anywhere. Finally I met Doctor Zhang, the medicine vendor, and he told me: 'I just saw the arms instructor and another man going into the tavern.' So I hurried over here. Master, go quickly!"

Shocked, Lin Chong without waiting for Jin Er, ran at triple speed to Lu Qian's house and raced up the stairs. The door was locked. He could hear his lady exclaiming: "In times of peace and order how dare you hold a good man's wife prisoner!" Young Master Gao was entreating: "Have pity on me, mistress. Even a woman of iron and stone shouldn't be so cold-hearted!"

"Wife, open the door," thundered Lin Chong.

Hearing her husband's voice, Mistress Lin rushed to comply. The terrified Young Master Gao pushed open a window, climbed out and fled along the top of a wall. He was gone before Lin Chong entered the room.

"Did that dog violate you?" demanded the arms instructor.

"No," replied his wife.

In a fury, Lin Chong smashed Lu Qian's furniture to bits, then led his wife down the stairs. As they came out of the house, frightened neighbors on both sides of the street hastily shut their doors tight. Jin Er was waiting for them outside. The three of them went home together.

Lin Chong armed himself with a sharp knife and sped directly to the tavern in search of Lu Qian. But his treacherous friend was gone. Lin Chong went to Lu Qian's house and waited outside the door all night. But Lu Qian did not return. Finally the arms instructor went home.

"He didn't harm me. Don't do anything foolish," his wife urged.

"Who would have thought that Lu Qian is such a scoundrel," fumed Lin Chong. "Calling me 'brother' while plotting against me all the time. Even if I can't catch that Young Master I won't let Lu Qian off!"

His wife pleaded desperately with him to remain at home.

Meanwhile, Lu Qian hid in the marshal's residence, afraid to return to his own house. For three successive days, the arms instructor waited for him outside the residence gate, but the traitor didn't dare show himself. Lin Chong's appearance was so menacing, no one had the courage to question him.

On the fourth day since they parted, Sagacious came to Lin Chong's home. "Where have you been keeping yourself these past few days, Arms Instructor?" the monk asked.

"I've been too busy to call on you, brother," replied Lin Chong apologetically. "Since you've honored me with a visit to my humble home, I ought to offer you a few cups of wine. But we don't have anything decent to drink in the house. Why not go out for a stroll together and have a cup or two in the market place?"

"Excellent," said Sagacious.

They went out and drank together all day and arranged to meet again on the morrow. Thereafter, Lin drank with Sagacious every day. In time, he gradually set the other matter aside.

As to Young Master Gao, after he received that fright in Lu Qian's house and had to flee over the wall, he became ill and took to his bed. He didn't dare say anything to the marshal about what had happened. Lu Qian and Fu An called on the Young Master at the residence. They found him pale and in low spirits.

"Why are you so unhappy, Young Master?" asked Lu Qian.

"I won't try to fool you two," Gao replied. "Now that I've failed in both attempts to get Lin's wife, and had that awful scare in addition, I feel worse than ever. If I pass out of this world in three months or half a year, you needn't be surprised."

"Be of good cheer," the sycophants urged. "Unless she suddenly hangs herself, we guarantee to get you that woman, come what may."

At that moment the old chamberlain entered to see how the Young Master was faring. Lu Qian and Fu An withdrew and held a private consultation. "There's only one way . . ." they agreed. After the chamberlain had concluded his call and emerged, they invited him to a quiet corner.

"There's only one way the Young Master can get well," they said. "We must let the marshal know and have him order the death of Lin Chong. Then the Young Master will be able to get Lin's wife and he'll recover. Otherwise, he's sure to die."

"That's easy,' replied the old chamberlain. "I'll inform the marshal this evening."

"We already have a plan," said the two. "We only await word from you."

That night, the old chamberlain saw the marshal. "I've discovered what's wrong with the Young Master," he said. "It's Lin Chong's wife."

"When did he ever see the woman?" asked Gao Qiu.

"On the twenty-eighth of last month, at the Temple of the Sacred Mountain. Today is a little over a month," said the old chamberlain, and he told the marshal what Lu Qian had in mind.

"H'mm, Lin Chong's wife, eh? The question is how to put Lin Chong out of the way," mused the marshal. "Let me think. I can't let my son lose his life just for the sake of Lin Chong."

"Lu Qian and Fu An have a plan."

"So? Bring them in here and we'll talk it over."

The old chamberlain summoned Lu Qian and Fu An into the marshal's hall. They hailed Gao respectfully.

"Do you two have a plan that can cure my son's ailment? If so, I'll raise you both in rank."

Lu Qian stepped forward. "Gracious lord, it can be done only thus and thus and thus. . . ."

"Very well," said the marshal. "You may take action tomorrow." Of this we need say no more.

To get back to Lin Chong. He drank every day with Sagacious Lu and finally forgot about the matter.

One day, as the two friends were nearing a lane, they saw a big fellow standing on a corner, a cap with gathered ends on his head and dressed in an old military robe. He was holding a fine sword in his hand, with a tuft of grass tied to it indicating that it was for sale.

"No one recognizes its value," he was muttering. "What a pity for my precious sword!"

Lin Chong paid no attention and continued walking and chatting with Sagacious. The man trailed behind them, saying: "A splendid sword. It's a shame no one appreciates it!"

Lin Chong and Sagacious were still engrossed in their conversation. The man followed them.

"A big city like the Eastern Capital and not a single person knows the worth of military weapons," he cried.

At this, Lin Chong looked around. The fellow whipped the sword out of its sheath. It gleamed dazzlingly in the sun.

Lin Chong was fated for trouble. He said abruptly: "Let me see it."

The fellow handed him the sword. Lin Chong took the weapon and he and Sagacious examined it.

Astonished, the arms instructor exclaimed: "An excellent blade! How much do you want for it?"

"The price is three thousand strings of cash, but I'll take two."

"It's well worth two thousand, but you won't find anyone who'll give that much. If you're willing to accept one thousand, I'll buy it from you."

"I need money quickly. If you really want the sword I'll knock off five hundred and let you have it for fifteen hundred."

"A thousand is the best I can do."

The fellow sighed. "It's selling gold at the price of iron. All right, all right, but not one copper less."

"Come home with me and I'll give you the money," said Lin Chong. He turned to Sagacious, "Wait for me in the tea-house, brother. I'll join you soon."

"No," said the monk, "I must go back. I'll see you tomorrow."

After taking leave of Sagacious, Lin Chong brought the sword-seller to his home, counted out the purchase price in silver and gave it to him.

"Where did you get this blade?" the arms instructor asked.

"It was handed down to me from my ancestors. Because my family became impoverished I had no choice. I had to sell it."

"What's the name of your family?"

"If I were to tell you, I'd die of shame."

Lin Chong asked no more. The fellow took the money and departed.

Lin Chong turned the sword this way and that. "Truly a beautiful weapon. Marshal Gao is supposed to have a fine sword but he won't show it to anyone. Though I've asked to see it several times, he's never been willing to bring it out.

Today I've bought a fine sword too. One of these days I'll compare blades with him."

The arms instructor didn't let the sword out of his hand all evening. Late that night he finally hung it on the wall, but he was up before daybreak and took the blade down again to admire it.

Some time before noon two lieutenants came to his gate and cried: "Arms Instructor Lin, an order from the marshal. He's heard that you've bought a fine sword and wants you to bring it to compare with his. The marshal is waiting for you in the residence."

"Who is the big-mouthed gossip that reported the news so fast?" wondered Lin Chong.

The lieutenants waited while Lin Chong got dressed. He took his sword and accompanied them.

On the way he said: "I haven't seen you at the residence before."

"We've only recently been transferred," they replied.

Soon they arrived at the residence. In the reception room, Lin Chong halted.

"The marshal is waiting in the rear hall," said the lieutenants.

Lin Chong went with them around a screen wall into the rear hall. But there was still no sign of the marshal, and Lin Chong halted once more.

"The marshal is awaiting the arms instructor in the rearmost court. He directed us to bring you there," said the lieutenants.

Lin followed them through two or three more gateways until they came to a courtyard lined on all sides by green railings.

The lieutenants led him to the entrance of a large hall and said: "Please wait out here, Arms Instructor, while we report to the marshal. We won't be long."

Lin Chong stood before the eaves of a porch while the two lieutenants went inside. A time long enough to drink a cup of tea passed, but they did not return. Growing suspicious, the arms instructor pushed aside a hanging awning, poked his head in and looked. There, above the door, was a placard with four words written in green: "White Tiger Inner Sanctum".

"This is where the highest military affairs are discussed," thought Lin Chong, startled. "How dare I go in there!"

He turned hastily. Behind him he heard the tread of boots, the steps ringing sharply. Another man had entered the courtyard. The arms instructor recognized him. It was none other than Marshal Gao. Lin Chong proffered his sword with both hands, and greeted him respectfully.

"Lin Chong," the marshal barked. "I didn't summon you. How dare you force your way into the White Tiger Inner Sanctum! Don't you know the law? And carrying a weapon! You must have come to kill me! People told me that you were seen waiting outside the Residence two or three day ago with a knife in your hand. Your intentions are surely evil!"

Bowing, Lin Chong replied, "Benevolent lord, two of your lieutenants brought me here saying you wanted to compare your sword with mine."

"Where are they?" cried the marshal.

"They just went into the hall, sir."

"Lies! Lies! No lieutenants would dare enter my official halls. Ho, guards! Seize this lout!"

Before the order had left the marshal's mouth, from the buildings flanking the sides of the courtyard over thirty stalwarts came rushing out and knocked Lin Chong to the ground.

"As an arms instructor of the Imperial Guards, you must know the law," the marshal raged. "Why else would you enter the Inner Sanctum with a sharp sword in your hand if not to murder me?"

He ordered his men to take Lin Chong out and execute him. Lin Chong loudly exclaimed that he was innocent.

The marshal directed his guards: "Take him to Kaifeng Prefecture. Ask Prefect Teng to examine him and investigate the case. Get the truth out of him, then have him executed. Label the sword as an official exhibit and take it along."

Bearing the marshal's order, the guards escorted Lin Chong to Kaifeng Prefecture. It happened that the prefect was still holding court, and Marshal Gao's emissary brought Lin Chong to the prefect's hall and knelt at the foot of the dais. The prefect's secretary relayed the emissary's message from Gao Qiu and placed the labelled sword down in front of Lin Chong.

"Lin Chong," said the prefect, "you're an arms instructor in the Imperial Guards. You must know the law. How could you enter the Inner Sanctum holding a sword? That's an offence punishable by death."

"Benevolent lord, you reflect the truth like a mirror. Lin Chong has been grievously wronged! Although I'm only a crude and stupid military man, I'm not exactly ignorant of the law. How would I presume to enter the Inner Sanctum? The reason I went there was this: On the twenty-eighth of last month I took my wife to the Temple of the Sacred Mountain to burn incense. There I caught Marshal Gao's son trying to seduce her. I berated him and drove him away. Next, he had Captain Lu Qian trick me into going out to drink and got Fu An to lure my wife to Captain Lu's home, where he tried to ravish her. This too I discovered and wrecked Lu Qian's furniture. Though Young Master Gao failed to despoil her, I have witnesses to both attempts.

"Yesterday, I bought this sword. Today, Marshal Gao sent two lieutenants to summon me. They said he wanted me to bring my sword to compare it with his. And so I went with them to the Inner Sanctum. After they went inside, Marshal Gao suddenly entered the courtyard. It's all a plot to destroy me. Please help me, Your Honor!"

After hearing Lin Chong's story, the prefect ordered that a receipt-of-prisoner be issued, a wooden rack locked around the arms instructor's neck, and that he be held in custody. Lin Chong's family sent food to him in jail and gave tips to the keepers. His father-in-law, Arms Instructor Zhang, also called at the prison. He spent quite a bit, bribing high and low.

It happened that in the prefecture there was a scribe named Sun Ding. Because he was extremely just and kindly and always willing to help people, he was known as Sun the Buddha.

Learning the facts of the case, he diplomatically informed the prefect what he had discovered.

"Lin Chong has been wronged," he said. "You must help him."

"But Marshal Gao has confirmed that he committed a crime. He insists that I convict Lin Chong for entering the Inner Sanctum, sword in hand, with the intention of murdering him. What can I do?"

"Is Kaifeng Prefecture ruled by the imperial court or the family of Marshal Gao?"

"Don't talk nonsense!"

"Everyone knows Gao Qiu uses his position tyrannically. There's nothing he won't do. Whoever offends him, even in the slightest, he sends to Kaifeng Prefecture. If he wants a man killed, we kill him. If he wants him hacked, we hack him. We've become a mere subdivision of his family."

"How can I make things easy for Lin Chong? What sort of sentence should I pass?"

"From Lin Chong's story, it's plain that he's innocent, although we haven't been able to find those two lieutenants. Why not have him confess to entering the Inner Sanctum improperly wearing a sword at his waist, sentence him to twenty strokes of the bamboo, tattoo him and exile him to some distant military district?"

After considering this, Prefect Teng went to see Marshal Gao and urged him to agree to such a confession from Lin Chong. Knowing that reason was against him, and since the prefect seemed reluctant to co-operate, the marshal was forced to consent.

The very same day, the prefect called court into session. He had Lin Chong summoned, the rack removed and twenty blows of the bamboo administered. The prefect directed the tattooer to place the mark of a criminal on Lin Chong's cheek. Then he calculated the distance and decided upon Cangzhou as Lin's place of exile. In full court, a hinged wooden rack of seven and a half catties was placed around the arms instructor's neck and nailed fast, and prefectural seals were affixed. The prefect issued a deportation order and designated two guards to escort the prisoner to his destination.

CHAPTER 4
Sagacious Lu Makes a Shambles of Wild Boar Forest

The two guards Dong Chao and Xue Ba locked Lin Chong in a guard house, and returned to their homes to pack some things for their journey. As Dong Chao was tying a bundle together, a waiter from the tavern at the head of the lane came in.

"Sir, a gentleman wishes to speak with you in our tavern."

"Who is he?"

"I don't know. He only told me to invite you over."

Dong Chao went with the waiter to a room in the tavern. He found a man wearing a hat decorated with Buddhist swastikas and dressed in a black silk tunic. On his feet were black boots and plain stockings. When Dong Chao entered, the man quickly rose and clasped hands in greeting.

"Please be seated," he said.

"I have not had the privilege of meeting Your Honor before," said Dong Chao. "How can I serve you?"

"Please sit down. You'll know shortly."

Dong Chao took a chair on the opposite side of the table. The waiter brought wine cups and food and fruit and laid them out.

"Where does Xue the guard live?" the man asked.

"In that lane ahead," replied Dong Chao.

The man called the waiter and asked him for Xue's exact address. "Invite him here to meet me," he instructed.

In less time than it takes to drink a cup of tea, the waiter returned with Xue Ba.

"This gentleman has invited us for a talk," Dong Chao explained.

"May I ask your name, sir?" queried Xue Ba.

"You'll know very soon," replied the man. "First let us drink."

The three took their seats and the waiter served the wine. After they had consumed several cups, the man drew from his sleeve ten ounces of gold and placed them on the table.

"Five ounces for each of you," he said. "There is a small matter I want to trouble you about."

"But we don't know Your Honor. Why should you give us gold?" they asked.

"Aren't you going to Cangzhou?"

"We're taking Lin Chong there under orders of the Kaifeng prefect," said Dong Chao.

"It's precisely for that reason that I must bother you two. I am Marshal Gao's trusted Captain Lu Qian."

Dong Chao and Xue Ba immediately greeted him with profound respect. "How can insignificant men like us presume to sit at the same table with Your Honor," they cried.

"As you know, Lin Chong has incurred the marshal's displeasure. The marshal has ordered me to present you with these ten ounces of gold. He hopes you will finish off Lin Chong in some secluded place along the road — it needn't be too far — and bring back a certification of his death from the local authorities. If Kaifeng Prefecture causes any difficulty, the marshal will take care of it personally. You needn't worry about that."

"I'm afraid it's not possible," said Dong Chao. "The official order of Kaifeng Prefecture directs that we deliver Lin Chong alive, not that we kill him. He's not an old man. How could we explain his death? We'd surely get into trouble. I'm afraid it can't be done."

"Dong, old fellow," said Xue Ba, "listen to me. If Marshal Gao ordered us to die, we would have to obey, to say nothing of a case like this, when he sends this gentleman with gold.

Say no more. I'll share it with you and that's that. If we do
this little favor, we'll be looked after in the future. On the
road to Cangzhou there's a big pine forest, a wild evil place.
Come what may, we'll finish him off there."

Xue Ba took the gold and said, "You can rely on us, Your
Honor. At the latest on the fifth stage of the journey, at the
earliest the second, the thing will be done."

Very pleased, Lu Qian exclaimed: "Xue Ba is truly straightforward and to the point. When the deed is accomplished,
bring back the golden print on Lin Chong's face as proof. I
will then reward you both with another ten ounces of gold. I
shall be waiting for good news. Be sure not to delay."

In Song times, prisoners who were to be exiled were always
tattooed on the face. To make it sound better, the mark was
called "the golden print".

The three finished their wine, Lu Qian paid the bill, then
all left the tavern and went their separate ways.

Dong Chao and Xue Ba, after dividing the gold, returned
to their homes and finished packing. Then they took their
official staves, called for Lin Chong at the guard house, and
set out from the city. They travelled more than thirty *li* before
calling a halt. In Song days, guards escorting a prisoner did
not have to pay for lodging in public inns. Xue and Dong
brought Lin Chong to an inn, and they stayed the night.

At dawn the next morning, the guards lit a fire and made
breakfast, and the three continued their journey to Cangzhou.
It was the height of summer and the weather was scorching.
Lin Chong had not suffered much when he was beaten. But
now a few days had passed, and the fiery heat irritated his
wounds. He walked painfully, with dragging steps.

"Stupid clod," Xue Ba said. "It's over two thousand *li* from
here to Cangzhou. Who knows when we'll get there, at the
rate you're going!"

"I was buffeted a bit in the marshal's compound, and then,
the other day, I was beaten with bamboos. My wounds are
paining me in this awful heat," Lin Chong explained. "Please,

sirs, don't be impatient."

"Just take your time," said Dong Chao. "Never mind his grumbling."

Xue Ba kept complaining and cursing all along the road. "It's our misfortune to have run into a wretched demon like you," he berated Lin Chong.

As the day was drawing to a close, the three again put up at a village inn. Entering the door, the guards rested their staves and removed their packs. Lin Chong also dropped his luggage bundle. Before the guards could say anything, he took out some pieces of silver and told the attendant to bring wine, meat and rice, and set the table. Lin then invited the guards to dine with him.

Dong Chao and Xue Ba ordered still more wine, plying Lin Chong with it until he fell over on his side, wooden rack and all. Xue Ba then boiled a large pot of water. When it was bubbling hot he poured it into a basin.

"Wash your feet, Arms Instructor," he said. "You'll sleep better."

Lin Chong struggled to a sitting position, but he couldn't lean forward because of the rack.

"I'll wash them for you," Xue Ba offered.

"How could I impose upon you?" Lin Chong hastily replied.

"Men travelling together shouldn't be ceremonious over such details," said Xue Ba.

Lin Chong didn't realize it was a plot. He stretched out his legs. Xue Ba seized them and plunged them into the boiling water.

"*Aiya!*" exclaimed Lin Chong, hurriedly pulling his feet out. They had turned red and swollen. "I mustn't trouble you!" he cried.

"Plenty·of prisoners have looked after guards, but how often do you see a guard serving a prisoner?" said Xue Ba. "With the best of intentions I wash his feet, but he has the nerve to complain — the water's too cold, the water's too hot. . . . If this isn't returning evil for good I don't know what is!"

He grumbled and swore half the night.

Not daring to reply, Lin Chong could only fall over and lie on his side.

The two guards poured out the boiling water, filled the basin afresh, then went to wash their feet outside.

They slept until the fourth watch, rising while the rest of the inn was still in bed. Xue Ba heated some water to wash with, and cooked breakfast. Lin Chong, dizzy, was unable to eat and barely able to walk. Xue Ba threatened him with his staff. Dong Chao untied from his belt a pair of new straw sandals with loops and bindings of woven hemp. He told Lin Chong to put them on. Lin Chong's scalded feet were covered with blisters. He wanted his old soft sandals, but they were nowhere to be found. He had to put the new ones on.

The waiter added up the bill and the guards led Lin Chong from the inn. It was by now the fifth watch.

Before Lin Chong had gone more than two or three *li*, the blisters on his feet, broken by the new straw sandals, bled freely. He could hardly drag himself along and he groaned ceaselessly.

"Walk! Faster!" shouted Xue Ba. "Keep moving or I'll help you with this staff."

"Have pity on me, good officer," Lin Chong pleaded. "Would I dare slow down deliberately and delay our journey? It's because my feet are killing me. I can't walk."

"You can lean on me," said Dong Chao. He supported Lin Chong. But since the arms instructor walked with difficulty, they covered only four or five *li*.

It became obvious that Lin Chong really couldn't go much farther. They saw ahead of them a wild evil wood shrouded in mist. Known as Wild Boar Forest, it was the first dangerous place on the road from Kaifeng to Cangzhou. During the Song Dynasty, those who had grudges against prisoners being sent into exile often bribed their escorts to murder them there. Who can say how many good men lost their lives in that wood?

Now, the two guards led Lin Chong straight into the forest.

"In the whole fifth watch we haven't even walked ten *li*," said Dong Chao. "We'll never reach Cangzhou at this rate."

"I'm tired," said Xue Ba. "Let's rest here."

The three men walked deeper into the forest, then removed their packs and placed them at the foot of a tree. Lin Chong groaned. With his back against a tree trunk he slid to the ground.

"Having to wait for you every time we take a step has worn me out too," said Dong Chao. "I want to sleep a while, then we'll go on."

They rested their staves and lay down beside a tree. But no sooner had they closed their eyes than they leaped up with an exclamation.

"What's wrong, good officers?" asked Lin Chong.

"We were just about to sleep when we remembered that there are no doors and locks here. We're afraid you'll run off. We're worried, so we can't sleep in peace."

"I'm a respectable man. Since I've already been convicted, I'd never run away."

"Who can believe that?" scoffed Dong Chao. "The only way we can really feel secure is to tie you up."

"If that's what you good officers want, how can I refuse?"

Xue Ba took a rope from his waist and bound Lin Chong hand and foot and tied him, together with the rack, tightly to the tree. Then he and Dong Chao sprang up, whirled around, seized their staves and advanced on Lin Chong.

"Killing you isn't our idea," they said. "The other day Captain Lu Qian informed us of the order of Marshal Gao. We're to finish you off here and return immediately with the golden print. Even if we travelled a few more days, it would still be your death march. Doing the job here, we can get back that much earlier. Don't blame us two brothers. We're only carrying out orders. We have no choice. You must know: A year from this day will be the first anniversary of your death! We've been given a time limit. We must return quickly with our report."

When Lin Chong heard this, his tears fell like rain. "Officers," he cried, "there's never been any enmity between us. Spare me, and I'll never forget you in this world or the next!"

"Empty talk," said Dong Chao. "You can't be saved!"

Xue Ba raised his official staff and swung it fiercely at Lin Chong's head. But quicker than words can tell, from behind the pine tree came a thunderous roar as a solid iron rod shot forward, intercepted the staff and sent it flying into the sky. Then out leaped a big fat monk.

"I've been listening quite a while," he yelled. Dressed in a black cassock, he was wearing a knife and carried a Buddhist staff which he brandished at the two guards.

Lin Chong, who had just opened his eyes, recognized Sagacious Lu, and he hastily cried: "Brother! Stay your hand. I have something to say!"

Sagacious lowered his iron staff. The guards gaped at him, too frightened to move.

"It's not their doing," said Lin Chong. "Marshal Gao, through Captain Lu Qian, gave them orders to destroy me. How could they refuse? It would be wrong to kill them!"

Unsheathing his knife, Sagacious cut the arms instructor's bonds and helped him to his feet.

"Brother," he said, "I've been worried about you ever since that day we parted, when you bought the sword. After you were convicted, I had no way to rescue you. I heard that you were being exiled to Cangzhou, and I sought you outside Kaifeng Prefecture, but in vain. Someone said that you had been locked in a guard house. Then I learned that a waiter had gone to the two guards, saying: 'A gentleman wishes to speak to you in the tavern,' and I became suspicious. I was afraid these oafs would try to harm you along the road, so I followed.

"When these knaves brought you to the inn, I put up there too. I heard them plotting in whispers. When they tricked you and scalded your feet in the boiling water, I wanted to kill them on the spot. But there were too many guests at the inn and I was afraid I couldn't carry it off. I knew the rogues were up to something dirty. I was very worried.

"You set out before dawn at the fifth watch. I hurried ahead to the forest and waited to kill the two wretches here. They intended to harm you, so I ought to destroy them."

花和尚大鬧野豬林

"Since you've saved me, brother, there's no need to kill them," urged Lin Chong.

"Scurvy knaves," bellowed Sagacious. "If it weren't for my brother here, I'd pound you both into mincemeat! Only because he asks it, I'll spare your lives." He put his knife away and shouted: "Support my brother, and be quick about it! Come with me!" Taking his staff, he set off.

How dared they refuse? "Save us, Instructor Lin," the guards pleaded. They again shouldered their packs and took up their staves. Supporting Lin Chong and carrying his bundle, they followed the monk out of the forest.

After walking three or four *li*, they saw a little tavern at the entrance to a village. All four went in and sat down. They ordered five or six catties of meat, two jugs of wine and some griddle cakes. The waiter laid the table and served the wine.

"May we presume to inquire," the guards said to Sagacious, "in what monastery you reside, Reverend?"

Sagacious chuckled. "Why do you ask, scoundrels? So that you can tell Marshal Gao how to harm me? Others may fear him, I don't! If I meet that wretch I'll give him three hundred licks of my iron staff!"

The guards dared say no more.

The four finished the meat and wine, got their luggage in order, paid the bill and left the village.

"Where are you planning to go, brother?" asked Lin Chong.

" 'To kill a man you must draw blood, to rescue a man you must see him to safety.' I still don't feel at ease about you, brother. I'm going to escort you all the way to Cangzhou."

The two guards secretly groaned: "Woe! That ruins our scheme! What will we say when we get back?" But they could only continue the journey, docilely obeying the monk's orders.

They marched for seventeen or eighteen days, with the monk never relaxing his watch over the two guards. Soon they were only about seventy *li* from Cangzhou. It was a well-travelled road the rest of the way, with no desolate stretches. After inquiring to make sure of this, Sagacious led the party into a pine grove to rest.

"Brother," he said to Lin Chong, "from here to Cangzhou is not far. There are plenty of people on the road and no deserted places. I've already checked on it. I'll part with you here. Some day we'll meet again."

"Go back, brother. Let my father-in-law know I'm all right," said Lin Chong. "If I live, I'll repay you for your gracious protection in full."

Sagacious took out a score or more ounces of silver and gave them to Lin Chong, then handed two or three ounces to the guards.

"Scurvy knaves! Originally I was going to cut your heads off along the road. Out of courtesy to my brother I've spared your paltry lives. The journey is nearly over. Don't get any evil ideas!"

"Would we dare? It was all Marshal Gao's doing," they replied, and accepted the silver.

As they turned to leave, Sagacious glared and shouted: "Wretches! Are your heads harder than this pine tree?"

"We humble servants have heads only of the flesh and skin our parents gave us, wrapped around a few bones."

Sagacious raised his iron staff and struck the tree a mighty blow, cutting a gash two inches deep. The pine folded over neatly and fell.

"Scurvy knaves," roared the monk. "If you get any wrong ideas, I'll clout your heads like I did this pine!"

Dragging his iron staff and swinging his other arm, Sagacious walked off, calling: "Take care of yourself, brother."

The two guards stuck out their tongues in astonishment. It was some time before they remembered to retract them.

CHAPTER 5
Lin Chong Shelters from the Snowstorm in the Mountain Spirit Temple

Lin Chong and the guards departed for Cangzhou. They arrived about noon and sent the luggage bearers back. The guards went directly to the prefecture and presented their order of exile to an official, who immediately brought Lin Chong before the prefect. Accepting custody of the arms instructor, the prefect issued a receipt and wrote out an order committing Lin Chong to prison. The guards bade Lin farewell and departed for the Eastern Capital. Lin Chong was placed in a room by himself and directed to await registration.

He was brooding alone in his room when a turnkey shouted: "The warden orders that new prisoner Lin Chong report to the warden's hall to be registered."

Lin Chong went directly to the hall.

"You are a new prisoner," said the warden. "The first emperor of Song has bequeathed to us the ancient regulation: 'One hundred blows must be administered to every prisoner newly sent into exile.' Guards! Get him ready!"

"Your humble servant caught a bad cold during his journey here, and still hasn't recovered," said Lin Chong. "I request that the beating be postponed."

"He's not at all well," said the head keeper. "Please have pity on him."

"Since the symptoms of his illness are still evident, perhaps we can put this off for the time being," said the warden. "We can beat him when he regains his health."

"Today, the time is up of that prisoner who has been taking care of the garrison prison temple. Why not let Lin Chong replace him," suggested the head keeper.

The warden promptly wrote out an order and the head keeper accompanied Lin Chong back to his room, where he collected his belongings, then led him to the temple.

"I'm being very considerate to you, Arms Instructor Lin, getting you this job," said the head keeper. "It's the easiest work in the garrison prison. All you have to do is burn incense and sweep the floor once in the morning and once again in the evening. You'll soon see that we don't let up on other prisoners from morning till night. As for those without money, we throw them into the dungeon where they pray for life and long for death, both in vain."

"Thanks for your protection," said Lin Chong. He gave the head keeper another few ounces of silver. "There's one more matter I must trouble you about, brother. Could you have this rack taken from my neck?"

"Just leave it to me," said the head keeper as he tucked the money away. He hurried to the warden and relayed the plea. The rack was removed.

From then on, Lin Chong slept and ate in the temple. Every day, he did nothing except burn incense and sweep the floor. Before he knew it, forty or fifty days had gone by. The warden and the head keeper, having been bribed, were always very cordial. He was left free to come and go as he pleased, with no restrictions.

To make a long story short, one day around noon as winter was drawing near, Lin Chong was strolling outside the garrison gates.

Suddenly, he heard someone behind him call: "Arms Instructor Lin, what are you doing here?"

Lin Chong turned around and saw the tavern waiter Li Xiao-er. When they first became acquainted in the Eastern Capital, Lin had helped him financially several times. Later, Xiao-er stole money from the tavern keeper and was arrested. He was going to be sent to the prefect but Lin Chong spoke up in his behalf, and he did not have to stand trial. Lin also paid back the money for him and he was released. Although Xiao-er could no longer find work in the capital, thanks to the travelling expenses which Lin gave him, he was able to seek employment elsewhere. Today, unexpectedly, they met again in Cangzhou.

"What are you doing here, Brother Xiao-er?" asked Lin Chong.

Xiao-er kowtowed and replied, "After you saved me, benefactor, and gave me travelling money, I looked everywhere for a job, but in vain. Finally, I wandered into Cangzhou. Here, a tavern keeper named Wang took me on as his assistant. Because I was a hard worker and could make tasty dishes and sauces, the customers praised me and business improved. The tavern keeper had a daughter, and he gave her to me in marriage and adopted me into his household. Now, both he and my mother-in-law are dead. Only my wife and I are left. We run a tavern in front of the garrison. I was just passing by on my way to collect some bills. What are you doing here, benefactor?"

Lin pointed to the mark on his face. "Because I crossed the will of Marshal Gao, he conspired against me and had me convicted and exiled to this place. At present, I look after the garrison prison temple. I don't know what they'll do with me in the future. I never expected to meet you here."

Xiao-er brought Lin Chong to his home, invited him to be seated, and called his wife in to greet him. Both husband and wife said happily: "We have no close relatives. Your coming here today, benefactor, is like a gift from heaven!"

"I'm an exile," said Lin. "Won't associating with me sully your name?"

"How can you talk like that?' said Xiao-er. "Everyone know your excellent reputation. Be sure to bring all your washing and mending to my wife."

He entertained Lin Chong with food and drink and that night saw him back to the garrison temple. The following morning, he came again to invite Lin to his home.

From then on, Xiao-er and Lin called on each other frequently. Xiao-er often sent tea or soup to Lin in the garrison.

Moved by the couple's respect and devotion, Lin gave them money from time to time to use in their business.

To skip the idle chatter, time passed quickly. Winter came. All of Lin Chong's padded winter garments were stitched and mended by Xiao-er's wife. One day, while Xiao-er was cooking in the entry, a man slipped in and sat down inside at one of the tables. Then another fellow furtively entered. The first man was an army officer, by the looks of him. The second seemed more like an attendant. He also hurried in and sat down.

Xiao-er went up to them. "Wine?" he queried.

The officer handed Xiao-er an ounce of silver. "Take this on account. Bring us three or four jugs of good wine. When our guests come, serve some food and tidbits. You choose the dishes. You needn't ask me."

"You've invited guests, sir?"

"I must trouble you to go to the garrison prison and invite the warden and the head keeper here for a chat. If they question you, just say: 'A gentleman requests that you come and discuss certain matters. He is looking forward to your arrival.' "

Xiao-er assented and left. At the garrison, he first relayed the request to the head keeper then, together, they extended the invitation to the warden, after which all three went to the tavern. The gentleman, the warden and the head keeper exchanged greetings.

"We haven't met before," said the warden. "May we ask your name, sir?"

"I have a letter of introduction here, which I will give you shortly," replied the man. "But first let's have some wine."

Xiao-er quickly opened the jugs and served the food. The gentleman called for a ceremonial tray of wine goblets. After filling and handing them out, he invited his guests to be seated. Xiao-er dashed back and forth like a shuttle, serving without cease. The gentleman's attendant took care of the warming of the wine. A dozen rounds were drunk, more tidbits to go with the wine were ordered.

"My attendant will warm the wine," the gentleman said to

Xiao-er. "You needn't come unless we call you. We want to talk privately."

Xiao-er said: "Very well, sir," and left the room. Outside the door, he conferred with his wife.

"There's something fishy about those two."

"What do you mean?"

"They've both got Eastern Capital accents and neither of them knows the warden. When I went in with those tidbits just now, I heard the head keeper murmur something about 'Marshal Gao'. Wasn't he the one who harmed Instructor Lin? I'll stay here at the door and keep an eye on them. You go and listen on the other side of the partition wall."

"Why not bring Instructor Lin here from the garrison and see if he recognizes them?"

"You don't know what a terrible temper he has. He's liable to commit murder and burn the place down. If I called him and that gentleman turned out to be the Captain Lu he mentioned the other day, Lin would never let him escape alive. If anything happened here, you and I would be involved. You'd better go and listen. We'll decide what to do later."

"Very well," said the wife. She went and listened for a time. Then she returned and said: "They're whispering with their heads together and I couldn't hear much. But I saw that fellow who looks like an officer take something wrapped in a white cloth from his attendant and give it to the warden and head keeper. Maybe there's money in it. I heard the head keeper say: 'Leave everything to us. We'll finish him off, come what may.' "

Just then, from the inner room a voice shouted: "Bring the soup." Xiao-er hastened to comply. As he entered, he saw that the warden had a letter in his hand. Xiao-er served the soup, then brought some more dishes of food.

The feast continued for another hour. After the bill was paid, the warden and head keeper departed first. The other two, heads stealthily lowered, then also left.

Shortly afterwards, Lin Chong entered the tavern. "Brother Xiao-er," he said, "I hope you're prospering."

"Please sit down, benefactor," Xiao-er begged hastily. "I was just about to look for you. I must tell you something very important."

"What is it?" asked Lin Chong.

Xiao-er led him to the inner room, invited him to be seated, and told him all about his recent customers. "I don't know who these fellows are," he said in conclusion, "but I don't trust them. I'm afraid they want to harm you, benefactor."

"What do they look like?" asked Lin.

"One is of average build, fair, clean shaven, about thirty or so. The other fellow isn't very tall either. He has a ruddy complexion."

Startled, Lin Chong cried, "That man of thirty must be Captain Lu Qian! The filthy thief, how dare he come here to harm me! If I get hold of him I'll smash him to a jelly!"

"The main thing is to be on your guard," said Xiao-er. " 'Take care not to choke when you eat, or trip when you walk,' as the old saying goes."

Lin Chong left Xiao-er's home in a towering rage. On the street, he bought a sharp dagger. Carrying it on his person, he made a search of all the streets and lanes. Xiao-er and his wife were in a cold sweat.

At daybreak the following morning, Lin rose, washed his face and rinsed his mouth, then took up the dagger and again prowled through all the streets and lanes both in the city and on the outskirts. He patrolled all day, even searching the prison and the garrison, but nothing was stirring.

Returning to Xiao-er's place, he said: "Nothing happened today either."

"Benefactor," said Xiao-er, "let's hope it stays that way! But remain on your guard."

Lin went back to the garrison prison temple, where he spent the night. He walked the streets for four or five days, without success. His temper gradually began to cool.

On the sixth day, the warden summoned Lin Chong into his hall and said: "You've been here for some time now. Fifteen *li* outside the city's East Gate is a large army fodder depot. Every month you can collect fees from the people delivering the fodder. An old army man is in charge. I've decided to give you the job and have him replace you in the garrison prison temple. Out at the depot you'll be able to earn a little spending money. Go there with the head keeper and take over."

"I'll do that, sir," said Lin.

He first left the garrison and went directly to Xiao-er's house. Lin told the couple the news.

"Today, the warden is sending me to take charge of the army fodder depot. What do you think?"

"It's a better place than the garrison prison temple," replied Xiao-er. "You can earn some regular fees out there. Usually, no one gets that post without paying a bribe."

"Not only haven't they harmed me, but they've given me this good job instead. I don't know what to make of it."

"Why be suspicious, benefactor? As long as nothing happens, that's fine. The only trouble is you'll be living quite far from us. After a while, I'll come and see you, when I have time." Xiao-er pressed Lin Chong to join him in several rounds of drinks.

To make a long story short, the two separated and Lin Chong returned to the garrison prison temple. He packed his belongings, put his dagger in his belt, took up a spear and set out with the head keeper for the fodder depot.

It was a bitterly cold winter day. The sky was overcast, and they walked in the teeth of a rising wind amid thickly swirling snowflakes. Since there was no place along the road to buy drinks, Lin and the keeper soon reached the depot.

Surrounded by an earthen wall, the depot had a gate with two doors. They pushed them open and entered the compound. They saw a thatched building of seven or eight sections, which was serving as a store-house for fodder. All around were piles of hay. In the center stood a small thatched shack. Inside, they found the old soldier huddled over a fire.

"This is Lin Chong," the head keeper said to him. "The warden has sent him to replace you. You are to go back to take care of the garrison prison temple. You can hand over your duties."

The old soldier gave Lin Chong the keys and said: "The stuff in the store-house is under official seal. And those haystacks there are all numbered."

He took Lin around and counted the stacks, then brought him back to the shack and gathered his belongings. As he was leaving, he said: "I'll give you my brazier, my pot, my bowls and my dishes."

"I have such things in the temple too," said Lin. "You can have mine."

The old soldier pointed to a gourd bottle hanging on the wall. He said: "If you want to buy wine, there's a little market-place two or three *li* east down the road." Then he and the head keeper departed for the prison.

As to Lin Chong, he placed his bundle and bedding on the bed and sat down to replenish the fire in the earthen brazier. There was some charcoal in a corner of the room, and Lin used a few sticks of them. He looked around the shack. It was very dilapidated and shook with every gust of wind.

"How can I pass the winter here?" thought Lin. "When the storm stops I must bring a mason out from the city to repair this place."

Although he hugged the fire, he still felt cold. "The old soldier said there was a little market-place two *li* from here," he recalled. "Why don't I go and buy some wine?"

He took some money from his bundle, tied the gourd bottle to the end of his spear, covered the brazier, put on his broad-brimmed felt hat, took the keys and shut the door of the shack behind him. Coming through the compound gate, he closed and locked it. Then, carrying the keys, he headed east. The snow-covered ground was a mass of tiny white jade flakes. Lin Chong trudged forward with the north wind on his back. It was snowing very hard.

He had gone less than half a *li* when he observed an ancient temple. Lin Chong pressed his palms together before his forehead and bowed. "May the gods protect me. I must come here one of these days and burn some paper money in sacrifice."

Lin continued on his way. Ahead, he saw a cluster of houses. He halted, and peered through the storm. The buildings were enclosed by a fence. A clump of broom straw hanging outside one of them indicated that this was a tavern. Lin went inside.

"Where are you from, sir?" the host asked.

"Do you recognize this gourd bottle?" Lin Chong countered.

The man looked at it and said: "It belongs to the old soldier at the fodder depot."

"That's right," said Lin.

"So you're the new custodian," said the host. "Please be seated, brother. It's a bitterly cold day. Let me treat you to a few goblets, by way of welcome."

He served a platter of sliced beef, heated a pot of wine and invited Lin to help himself. Lin bought some more beef, drank a few cups, then had the gourd filled with wine. He wrapped up the two orders of beef, left a few pieces of silver, tied the gourd bottle to the end of his spear and placed the beef inside his shirt.

"Thanks for your trouble," said Lin. He went out through the fence gate and started back against the wind. Now that night had come, the snow was falling harder than ever.

Plodding through the snow in the teeth of the north wind, Lin Chong hurried back to the fodder depot. When he unlocked the doors and entered the compound, he uttered a cry of dismay. Actually, the gods who see everything and protect the good and virtuous were saving Lin Chong's life with that snowstorm. The thatched shack had collapsed under the weight of the snow.

"What am I going to do?" Lin wondered.

He put his spear and gourd down in the snow. Worried that the embers in the brazier might set the place on fire, he pulled open a section of the wall of the fallen shack, pushed himself halfway in and felt around. But the embers had been extinguished by the melted snow. Lin groped around on the bed till he found his quilt and pulled it out, emerging again into the dark night.

"I've no place to build a fire," he pondered. "How am I going to manage?" Then he remembered the ancient temple, half a *li* down the road. "I can spend the night there," he thought. "When daylight comes, I'll decide what to do."

He rolled up his quilt, shouldered his spear with the wine gourd dangling from one end, closed the compound gate once more, locked it, and proceeded to the temple. Entering, he shut the door and propped against it a big stone which he had noticed lying to one side. He walked further into the temple and saw on a platform an idol of a mountain spirit with golden armor, flanked by a Nether Region judge and a small demon, one on each side. In a corner was a pile of paper. Lin Chong inspected the whole temple but could find neither occupants nor anyone in charge.

Lin placed his spear and gourd bottle on the pile of paper and untied his quilt. He removed his broad-brimmed felt hat, shook the snow from his clothes and peeled off his white tunic which was half soaked, then put it together with his hat on the altar table. He covered himself to the waist with the quilt and drank from the gourd bottle from time to time, helping the cold wine down with slices of the beef he had been carrying.

Suddenly, he heard a loud crackling outside. He leaped to his feet and peered through a vent in the wall. The fodder depot was in flames and burning fiercely. Lin grabbed his spear. He was about to open the door and dash to the fire when he heard men's voices. Lin leaned against the door and listened. The footsteps of three men came directly to the temple.

The men pushed the temple door, but the big stone held it fast and they couldn't open it. They stood under the eaves watching the fire.

"Not a bad plan, eh?" one of them said.

"We're much indebted to the warden and to you, Head Keeper," someone replied. "When I return to the capital and report to the marshal, he undoubtedly will make you both big officials. Now Arms Instructor Zhang has no excuse to refuse."

"We've taken care of Lin Chong properly this time," said a third. "Young Master Gao is sure to recover."

"We tried to arrange the match three or four times," said a voice. "We told that lout Zhang: 'Your son-in-law is dead,' but he wouldn't give in. Young Master Gao's ailment kept getting worse. And so the marshal sent us specially to beg you two gentlemen to help. Today, we've succeeded at last."

"I climbed over the wall and set a score of haystacks afire. I'd like to see him get away!"

"The depot is almost completely destroyed."

"Even if he escapes with his life, burning down a military fodder depot is a crime punishable by death."

"Let's go back to the city."

"Wait a little longer. If we bring a couple of his bones with us to the capital, the marshal and the Young Master will praise us for doing the job thoroughly."

Lin Chong recognized them by their voices. One was the head keeper, another was Captain Lu Qian, the third was Fu An.

"Heaven took pity on me," thought Lin. "If that thatched shack hadn't collapsed, I'd have been roasted to death by these villains!"

Softly, he pulled the stone away from the door. Clutching his spear, Lin Chong pushed the door open.

"Where do you think you're going, knaves!" he roared.

The three, who had just been leaving, froze, too shocked to move.

Lin raised his arm and speared the head keeper to the ground.

"Spare me!" cried Captain Lu, weak with terror.

Fu An had run only a score of paces when Lin Chong caught up. With one thrust, Lin plunged the spear into his back, and he also fell.

Lin turned. He saw Captain Lu starting to flee. Before

Lu had gone three paces, Lin Chong shouted: "Halt, treacherous thief!" He grabbed Lu by the front of his tunic and threw him flat on his back in the snow.

Lin jabbed his spear into the ground, put one foot on Lu's chest, whipped out his dagger and held it against the captain's face.

"Filthy wretch," he grated. "I never wronged you. How can you have injured me so? Truly, 'Killing can be forgiven, but never deception!'"

"This wasn't my idea," Lu pleaded. "The marshal ordered me to do it! I didn't dare refuse!"

"Treacherous knave," cried Lin. "We were friends since childhood, yet today you come to destroy me! How can you excuse yourself? Have à taste of this knife!"

He ripped open Lu's clothes, stabbed the blade into his heart and twisted. Blood spurted everywhere. Lin tore out his heart and liver.

He saw the head keeper struggling to his feet to run. Lin seized him in a flash. "Now I know what an evil scoundrel you are," he shouted. "Take that!" He cut off the keeper's head and tied it to the end of his spear.

Next, he went back to Fu An and Lu Qian and cut off their heads too. He put away his knife, tied the three heads together by the hair, carried them into the temple and placed them on the altar in front of the mountain spirit idol. Then he put on his white tunic, tied his waist sash, clapped the broad-brimmed felt hat on his head and finished off the cold wine in the gourd bottle.

Lin tossed his quilt and the bottle aside, took up his spear, left the temple and started east. He had gone only four or five *li* when he saw people from a neighboring village hastening with water buckets and pikes to put out the blaze.

"Hurry and save the place," Lin Chong called to them. "I'm going to report the fire to the officials!"

Spear in hand, he walked on rapidly.

CHAPTER 6
Wu Yong by a Ruse Captures the Birthday Gifts

After buying birthday gifts valued at a hundred thousand strings of cash, Governor Liang in Daming, the Northern Capital, chose a date to start them on their way.

The following day, as he was sitting in the rear hall, his wife, Madame Cai, asked him: "When will the birthday gifts go off, Your Excellency?"

"Tomorrow or the day after. I've bought everything I want. There's only one thing that's troubling me."

"What is it?"

"Last year I purchased a hundred thousand strings of cash worth of jewels and art objects and sent them to the Eastern Capital, but because I didn't pick the right men they were seized by bandits on the road. To this day the robbers haven't been caught. At present I don't know of anyone really competent in my retinue. That is what's troubling me."

Madame Cai pointed to a man standing at the foot of the steps. "Haven't you often said that this fellow is quite remarkable? Why not entrust him with the mission? He can see it through."

The man she indicated was Yang Zhi, the Blue-Faced Beast. Liang was pleased. He summoned Yang Zhi into the hall.

"I had forgotten you," Liang said. "If you can safely deliver the birthday gifts for me, I'll have you raised in rank."

Yang Zhi clasped his hands together respectfully. "Since that is what Your Excellency wishes, I must of course comply. How shall the convoy be composed, and when shall it set forth?"

"I'm ordering the prefectural government to supply ten extra-large carts, and will send ten service personnel from the city guard to escort them. Each cart will carry a yellow banner reading: 'Convoy of Birthday Gifts to the Premier'. In addition, I will have one strong soldier follow each of the carts. You can leave within the next three days."

"It's not that I'm unwilling, but I really can't do it. Please give the mission to some brave and skilful person."

"It's my desire to raise you in rank. Along with the birthday gift documents, I intend to include a letter to the Premier, strongly recommending you. You'll return with his nomination for an official post. Why do you refuse to go?"

"Your servant has heard that the gifts were robbed last year, Excellency, and that the bandits still have not been caught. There are many brigands on the road these days. From here to the Eastern Capital there is no water route; you have to go entirely by land. Purple Gold Mountain, Two-Dragon Mountain, Peach Blossom Mountain, Umbrella Mountain, Yellow Earth Ridge, White Sand Valley, Wild Cloud Ford, and Red Pine Forest — all must be crossed, and all are infested with bandits. No merchant dares travel through them alone. If the bandits know we're carrying a precious cargo, of course they'll want to seize it. We'll just be throwing our lives away. That is why I can't go."

"In that case I'll simply provide you with a larger military escort."

"Even if you gave me ten thousand men, it wouldn't solve anything, Your Excellency. Those craven oafs would run as soon as they heard the bandits coming."

"Do you mean to say that the birthday gifts can't be delivered?"

"If you'll grant your servant one request, I will undertake the mission."

"Since I'm willing to entrust you with it, why not? State your wish."

"As I see it, Your Excellency, we shouldn't use any carts.

Pack the gifts into containers to be carried, disguised as merchandise, on shoulder-poles. Let the ten strong soldiers serve as porters. I'll need only one more person, also dressed as a merchant, to go as my assistant. We'll travel quietly day and night until we reach the Eastern Capital and deliver the goods. That way we'll be able to do it."

"It shall be as you wish. I'll write a letter strongly recommending you for an official appointment."

"My profoundest thanks, Excellency, for your gracious kindness."

That same day Yang Zhi made up the loads and picked his soldiers. The following day he was again summoned to the rear hall. Governor Liang came out and asked: "Yang Zhi, when will you be ready to leave?"

"We would like to start tomorrow morning, Your Excellency. I'm just waiting for the official documents."

"My wife has some gifts for her women relatives. I want you to take them along too. I'm afraid you won't know your way around the Premier's chancellery, so I'm sending with you Chief Steward Xie and two captains of the guards."

"I won't be able to go then, Excellency."

"Why not? The gifts are all packed in containers."

"I was made responsible for ten loads of gifts, and the soldiers were put in my charge. If I told them to march early, they'd march early. If I said late, then late it would be. They'd spend the night where I directed, and rest when I ordered it. Everything would be up to me. But now you also want to send the chief steward and two captains. The steward is one of madame's men, the husband of her old wet-nurse when she was an infant in the Premier's chancellery. If he disagreed with me on the road how could I argue? Yet the blame would be mine if the mission failed."

"That's easy. I'll tell him and the captains to do whatever you say."

"In that case, your servant is willing to accept the mission. May I be severely punished if I fail."

The governor was delighted. "I haven't decided to promote you in vain. You're a very sensible fellow." Summoning Chief Steward Xie and the two captains to the hall he gave them official orders: "Major Yang Zhi has accepted a mission to deliver birthday gifts — eleven loads of jewels and art objects — to the Premier's chancellery in the Eastern Capital. He is fully responsible. You three are to accompany him. During the journey he alone will decide whether to start early or late, where to spend the night, and when to rest. None of you is to cross him. You already know what madame wants done. Be cautious and prudent, leave soon and return quickly, don't let anything go wrong."

The old chief steward promised to obey the governor's injunctions.

Before dawn the next morning the loads were lined up outside the main hall. The chief steward and the captains brought another batch of valuables — making a total of eleven loads. Eleven strong soldiers of the guard were selected and disguised as porters. Yang Zhi was wearing a broad-brimmed hat and a black silk tunic. His feet were shod in hemp sandals tied with laces of cord. At his waist was a sword, and he carried a halberd in his hand.

The old steward was also dressed as a merchant. The two captains were disguised as lackeys. Each carried a halberd and a rattan switch. Governor Liang handed over the official documents. After all had eaten their fill, they formally took their leave in front of the hall. Liang watched the soldiers raise the carrying-poles to their shoulders and set forth. Together with Yang Zhi, the old steward and the two captains, a total of fifteen men left the governor's compound. Marching out of the Northern Capital's city gate, they proceeded down the highway in the direction of the Eastern Capital.

It was then the middle of the fifth lunar month. Although the skies were clear, walking was difficult in the broiling sun. Determined to deliver the gifts in time for the Premier's birthday on the fifteenth of the sixth lunar month, Yang Zhi pushed the march on briskly. During the first week after the convoy left the Northern Capital, they set out every day before dawn to take advantage of the morning cool, and rested in the heat of noon.

By the sixth or seventh day, dwellings were few and far between, travellers had thinned out, and the road began climbing into the mountains. Yang Zhi now started the marches well after sunrise and didn't stop until late in the afternoon. The eleven guards were all carrying heavy loads and the weather was hot. Walking was a severe effort. Whenever they saw a grove they wanted to rest, but Yang Zhi drove them on. If they halted, the least he did was curse them, and often he flogged them with his switch, forcing them to continue.

The two captains, although they bore on their backs only light luggage, gasped for breath and kept falling to the rear. Yang Zhi berated them harshly.

"How can you two be so ignorant? I'm responsible for this mission. Instead of helping me beat the porters, all you do is drag behind. This road is no place to dally!"

"It's not that we want to go slowly," said the captains. "We just can't move any faster in this heat. A few days ago we always set out early when it was cool, but now we march only during the hottest hours of the day. Can't you tell the difference between fair conditions and foul?"

"You're talking farts, not words! A few days ago we were in a good part of the country, now we're in a very ticklish place. We must march in broad daylight. Who dares to set out while it's still dark?"

The captains said no more. But they thought to themselves: "That rogue swears at people whenever he likes!"

His halberd in one hand, his switch in the other, Yang Zhi urged on the convoy. The two captains sat beneath a tree and waited for the chief steward to catch up.

"That murderous Yang Zhi is only a major in his excellency's guard," they complained to the old man. "What right has he to act so mighty?"

"The governor ordered us not to cross him. That's why I haven't said anything. These past few days I too have found him hard to bear. But we must be patient."

"His excellency was only trying to make him feel good. You're the chief steward. Why don't you take over?"

"We must be patient with him," the old steward repeated.

That day they again marched until late afternoon. Then they stopped at an inn. Sweat was raining from the eleven porters. Groaning and sighing, they addressed the steward:

"Unfortunately we're soldiers of the guard, and have to go where we're ordered. For the past two days we've been carrying these heavy loads -in the burning sun, instead of starting early when it's cool. For anything at all, we're given a taste of the switch! We're flesh and blood too. Why should we be treated so cruelly?"

"Don't complain," the steward urged them. "When we get to the Eastern Capital, I'll reward you personally."

"Of course we wouldn't have said anything, Chief Steward," they replied, "if we had someone like you looking after us."

Another night passed. The following morning everyone rose before daylight, hoping to march early while it was still cool. But Yang Zhi jumped up and roared: "Where do you think you're going? Back to bed! I'll call you when it's time to leave!"

"We don't set out early," muttered the guards, "and in the heat of the day when we can't walk, he beats us!"

Swearing, Yang Zhi yelled: "What do you clods understand!" He threatened them with his rattan switch. The soldiers had no choice but to swallow their complaints and return to bed.

After the sun had risen and everyone finished a leisurely breakfast, the convoy resumed its march. Yang Zhi pushed on at a rapid pace, with no pauses for rest in the shade. The eleven guards grumbled constantly, and the two captains made no end of peevish observations to the chief steward. Although the old man did not reply, in his heart he was very irritated with the leader of the expedition.

To make a long story short, after marching for fifteen days there wasn't a man in the convoy who didn't hate Yang Zhi. On the fourth day of the sixth month they again rose late and slowly cooked breakfast. Then they set out. Even before noon the sun was a fiery red ball on high. There wasn't a cloud in sight. It was really hot. Now they were travelling along winding mountain trails. Towering peaks looked down on them from all sides. After marching about twenty *li* the porters were longing to relax in the shade of a willow grove. Yang Zhi lashed them with his switch.

"Move on," he shouted. "I'll teach you to rest before it's time!"

The guards looked up. There wasn't even half a cloud in the sky. The heat was simply unbearable. Yang Zhi hurried the convoy along a path fringing the mountain. It was about noon then, and the stones were so hot they burned the porters' feet. Walking was extremely painful.

"A scorching day like this," groaned the guards. "You're killing us!"

"Hurry up," Yang Zhi urged. "First cross that ridge ahead, then we'll see."

The column of fifteen men hastened on until they mounted the earthen ridge. Then the porters lowered their carrying-poles and threw themselves down beneath the pine trees.

"A fine place you've picked for cooling off," Yang Zhi ranted. "Get up, quick! We've got to push on!"

"Even if you cut us into eight pieces, we can't move another step!" retorted the soldiers.

Yang Zhi seized his switch and lashed them over the head and shoulders. But by the time he beat one to his feet another lay down again. He could do nothing with them. It was at this time that the old steward and the two captains climbed panting to the top of the ridge and sat down beneath a pine, gasping for breath. The old man saw Yang Zhi belaboring the porters.

"It's really much too hot to march, Major," he said. "Forgive them."

"You don't understand, Chief Steward. This is Yellow Earth Ridge, a favorite haunt of bandits. Even in peaceful times they robbed here in broad daylight, to say nothing of what they do in times like these! Stopping here is very dangerous."

"That's what you always say," countered the two captains. "You just use those stories to scare people!"

"Let the porters rest a bit," the steward urged. "We'll start again after noon, what do you say?"

"Impossible. Where's your judgment? For seven or eight *li* around the ridge there isn't a single house. Who dares rest in the shade in a place like this?" Yang Zhi retorted.

"You go on with the porters first, then," said the steward. "I've got to sit a while."

Yang Zhi picked up his rattan switch and roared at the soldiers: "Any man who doesn't march gets twenty blows of this!"

They all noisily protested. "Major," one of them cried, "while you walk empty-handed we're carrying well over a hundred catties apiece! You act as if we weren't even human! If the governor himself were in charge of this convoy, he'd at least let us say a word or two. You have no feeling at all! The only thing you know is to storm and rage!"

"Wretched animal! A beating is all his kind understands!" Yang Zhi rained blows on the man with his rattan switch.

"Stop, Major!" shouted the steward. "Listen to me. In my days in the Premier's chancellery I met thousands of officers, and every one of them treated me with deference! I don't mean to be rude, but it seems to me that an officer under sentence of death whom His Excellency has pitied and made a major of the guard — a post no bigger than a mustard seed — shouldn't be so pompous! Even if I were only a village elder, to say nothing of the governor's chief steward, you ought to heed my advice! Always beating the porters — what sort of conduct is that?"

"You're a city dweller, Steward, born and raised in official residences. What do you know of the hardships of the road?"

"I've been as far as Sichuan, Guangdong and Guangxi, but I've never seen anyone who behaved like you!"

"You can't compare today with times of peace!"

"You deserve to have your tongue cut out if you say such things! What's unpeaceful about today?"

Yang Zhi was going to reply when he saw a shadowy figure poke his head out of a grove opposite and peer at them. "What did I tell you?" he shouted. "Isn't that a bad fellow over there?" Flinging aside his switch, he seized his halberd and charged into the grove, shouting: "Insolent villain! How dare you spy on our convoy?"

In the grove he found a line of seven wheel-barrows and six men, buff naked, resting in the shade. One of them, a fellow with a scarlet birthmark on the side of his temple, grabbed a halberd when he saw Yang Zhi advancing. The seven men cried in alarm: "*Aiya*!" and leaped to their feet.

"Who are you?" Yang Zhi yelled.

"Who are you?" the seven countered.

"Aren't you robbers?"

"That's what we should be asking you! We're only small merchants. We haven't any money to give you!"

"So you're merchants. And I suppose I'm rich!"

"Who are you, really?"

"Tell me first where you're from."

"We seven are from Haozhou. We're bringing dates to sell in the Eastern Capital. At first we hesitated to pass this way because many people say that bandits often rob merchants on Yellow Earth Ridge. But then we said to ourselves: 'All we've got are some dates and nothing of any value.' So we decided to cross. Since the weather is so hot, we thought we'd rest in this grove till the cool of evening. When we heard you fellows coming up the rise we were afraid you might be bandits, so we sent this brother for a look."

"So that's how it is — only ordinary merchants! I thought he was a robber when I saw him watching us, so I hurried in here to investigate."

"Please have some dates, sir," said the seven.

"No, thanks," replied Yang Zhi. Halberd in hand, he returned to the convoy.

"Since there are bandits around, we'd better leave," said the chief steward, who was seated beneath a tree.

"I thought they were bandits, but they're only date merchants," Yang Zhi explained.

"According to you," the old steward remarked, "these fellows were all desperadoes!"

"No need to quarrel," said Yang Zhi. "I only want everything to go well. You men can rest. We'll march on after it cools down a bit."

The guards smiled. Yang Zhi stabbed the point of his halberd into the ground, then he too sat down beneath a tree to rest and cool off.

In less time than it takes to eat half a bowl of rice, another man appeared in the distance. Carrying two buckets on the ends of a shoulder-pole, he sang as he mounted the ridge:

> *Beneath a red sun that burns like fire,*
> *Half scorched in the fields is the grain.*
> *Poor peasant hearts with worry are scalded,*
> *While the rich themselves idly fan!*

Still singing, he walked to the edge of the pine grove, rested his buckets and sat down in the shade of a tree.

"What have you got in those buckets?" the soldiers asked him.

"White wine."

"Where are you going with it?"

"To the village, to sell."

"How much a bucket?"

"Five strings of cash — not a copper less."

The soldiers talked it over. "We're hot and thirsty. Why not buy some? It will ease the heat in our bodies." They began chipping in.

"What are you fellows up to?" Yang Zhi shouted, when he noticed what they were doing.

"We're going to buy a little wine."

Yang Zhi flailed them with the shaft of his halberd. "What

gall! How dare you buy wine without asking me?"

"Always raising a stinking fuss over nothing! It's our money! What is it to you if we buy wine? You beat us for that, too!"

"What do you stupid clodhoppers know anyhow? All you can think of is guzzling! But not a thought do you give to all the tricks that are pulled on the road! Do you know how many good men have been toppled by drugs?"

The wine vendor looked at Yang Zhi and laughed coldly. "You don't know much yourself, master merchant. I wasn't going to sell you any in the first place. What a dirty thing to say about a man's wine!"

As they were quarrelling, the date merchants emerged from the grove, halberds in hand. "What's the trouble?" they asked.

"I was carrying this wine across the ridge to sell in the village and stopped to cool off when these fellows asked if they could buy some," the vendor said. "I didn't let them have any. Then this gentleman claimed my wine was drugged. Is he trying to be funny, or what?"

"*Pei!*" snorted the seven. "We thought robbers had come, at least! So that's what all the row was about. Suppose he did say it — so what? We were just thinking of having some wine ourselves. If they're suspicious, sell a bucket to us. We'll drink it."

"No, no! Nothing doing!" said the vendor.

"We didn't say anything against you, you dull clod," cried the seven. "We'll give you the same price you'd get in the village. If you sell to us, what's the difference? You'll be doing a good deed, like handing out tea on a hot day, and quenching our thirst at the same time!"

"I don't mind selling you a bucket, but they said my wine is bad. Besides, I don't have any dipper."

"You take things too seriously. What do you care what they said? We have our own dippers."

Two of the date merchants brought out two coconut ladles from one of the wheel-barrows, while a third scooped up a big handful of dates. Then the seven gathered around the bucket and removed its cover. Ladling out the wine in turn, they drank, while munching the dates. Before long the bucket was empty.

"We haven't asked you the price yet," said the seven.

"I never bargain," the vendor asserted. "Exactly five strings of cash per bucket — ten strings for the load."

"Five strings you say, then five strings it shall be. But give us one free scoop out of the other bucket."

"Can't be done. My prices are fixed."

While one of the date merchants paid him the money, another opened the cover of the second bucket, ladled up some wine and started to drink it. The vendor hurried towards him, but the man ran into the pine grove with the half consumed dipper of wine. As the vendor hastened after him, another merchant emerged from the grove with another ladle. He dipped this into the bucket and raised it to his lips. The vendor rushed over, seized the ladle, and dumped its contents back into the bucket. Replacing the cover, he flung the ladle to the ground.

"You look like a proper man — why don't you act like one?" he fumed. "Is that any way to behave?"

When the soldiers saw this, their throats felt even drier. All were longing for a drink. "Put in a word for us, old grandpa," one of them begged the chief steward. "Those date merchants drank a bucket of his wine. Why shouldn't we buy the other and wet our throats? We're hot and thirsty, and have nothing else to drink. There's no place to get water on this ridge. Do us a favor, old grandpa!"

The old steward heard them out. He felt like having a drink himself. So he conferred with Yang Zhi.

"Those date merchants have already finished a bucket of that vendor's wine. Only one bucket is left. Why not let them buy some wine and ward off heat stroke? There really isn't any place on this ridge to get water."

Yang Zhi thought to himself: "I watched those birds finish off his first bucket, and drink half a ladleful from the second. The wine must be all right. I've been beating our porters for hours. Maybe I ought to let them buy a few drinks."

Aloud, he said: "Since the chief steward suggests it, you rogues can have some wine. Then we'll march on."

The soldiers chipped in and raised the price of a bucket. But the vendor refused them. "I'm not selling, I'm not selling!" he said angrily. "This wine is drugged!"

"Don't be like that, brother," the soldiers said with placating smiles. "Is it worth making such a fuss?"

"I'm not selling," said the vendor, "so don't hang around!"

The date merchants intervened. "Stupid oaf!" they berated him. "What if that fellow said the wrong thing? You're much too serious. You've even tried to take it out on us. Anyhow, it has nothing to do with these porters. Sell them some wine and be done with it!"

"And give him a chance to cast suspicion on me for no reason at all?" the vendor demanded.

The date merchants pushed him aside and handed the bucket to the soldiers, who removed the cover. Having no ladles, they apologetically asked the merchants if they could borrow theirs.

"Have some dates, also, to go with your wine," said the merchants.

"You're very kind."

"No need to be polite. We're all travellers together. What do a hundred or so dates matter?"

The soldiers thanked them. The first two ladles of wine they presented to Yang Zhi and the chief steward. Yang Zhi refused, but the old man drank his. The next two ladlefuls were consumed by the two captains. Then the soldiers swarmed around the bucket and imbibed heartily.

Yang Zhi wavered. The soldiers showed no ill effects. Besides, the weather was hot and his throat was parched. Scooping up half a ladle of wine, he drank it while munching on a few dates.

"Those date merchants drank a couple of ladlefuls out of this bucket, so you had less wine," the vendor said to the soldiers. "You can pay me half a string of cash less."

The soldiers gave him his money. The vendor took it, then, carrying his shoulder-pole and empty buckets, he swung off down the ridge, again singing a folk song.

Standing on the edge of the pine grove, the seven date mer-

吳用智取生辰綱

chants pointed at the fifteen men of the convoy and said: "Down you go! Down you go!" The fifteen, weak in the knees and heavy in the head, stared at each other as, one by one, they sank to the ground. Then the seven merchants pushed the seven wheel-barrows out of the grove and dumped the dates. Placing the eleven loads of jewels and art objects into the barrows, they covered them over.

"Sorry to trouble you," they called, and trundled off down the ridge.

Yang Zhi, too weak to move, could only groan inwardly. The fifteen couldn't get up. They had only been able to goggle helplessly while the seven had loaded the barrows with the precious cargo. They were paralyzed, bereft of speech.

Now I ask you — who were those seven men? None other than Chao Gai, Wu Yong, Gongsun Sheng, Liu Tang and the three Ruan brothers. And the wine vendor was Bai Sheng, nicknamed Daylight Rat. And how was the wine drugged? When the buckets were carried up the ridge, they contained pure wine. After the seven finished the first bucket, Liu Tang removed the cover from the second and deliberately drank half a ladleful so as to dull the others' suspicions. Next, inside the grove, Wu Yong poured the drug into the other ladle. Then he came out and spilled it into the wine while taking a "free scoop". As he pretended to drink, Bai Sheng grabbed the ladle and dumped the wine back in the bucket.

That was the ruse. Planned entirely by Wu Yong, it can be called "Capturing the Birthday Gifts by a Ruse".

Yang Zhi had not drunk much, and he recovered first. Crawling to his feet, he could hardly stand. He looked at the other fourteen. Saliva was running from the corners of their mouths. None of them could move.

"You've made me lose the birthday gifts," Yang Zhi muttered in angry despair. "How can I ever face Governor Liang again? These convoy documents are worthless now!" He tore them up. "I've become a man without a home or country. Where can I go? Better that I should die right here on this ridge!" Clutching his tunic, he staggered to the edge of the ridge and prepared to jump. But he came to his senses and halted just in time.

"My parents who bore me gave me this fine appearance and handsome physique," he thought. "From childhood I learned all the eighteen arts of armed combat. This is no way to die. I can at least wait until I am captured, then decide."

He gazed at his fourteen companions. They could only stare at him, unable to move. Yang Zhi swore. "It's all because you wretches wouldn't listen to me that this has happened. Now I'm involved!" He picked up his halberd that lay by the stump of a tree, buckled on his sword, and looked all around. There was nothing else that belonged to him. He sighed, and went down the ridge.

Not until the second watch did the fourteen revive. One by one, they crawled to their feet, uttering strings of lamentations.

"You didn't take Yang Zhi's good advice," said the old steward. "You've ruined me!"

"What's done is done, old sir," the others replied. "We'd better come to an understanding."

"Do you have any suggestions?"

"The fault is ours. But as the old saying goes: 'When fire licks your clothes you beat it out, when there's a hornet in your tunic open it quick.' If Yang Zhi were here, we'd have nothing to say. But since he's gone, no one knows where, why not put the blame on him? We can go back and say to Governor Liang: 'He abused and beat and cursed us all along the road, he drove us till we were too exhausted to stir another step. Yang Zhi was in cahoots with the robbers. They drugged us, bound us hand and foot, and made off with the treasure.' "

"That's an idea. We'll report the theft to the local district authorities the first thing tomorrow, and leave the two captains of the guards behind to help in the capture of the robbers. The rest of us will travel day and night till we reach the Northern Capital. We'll tell the governor what we agreed upon, and he will inform the Premier in writing and direct Jizhou Prefecture to apprehend the brigands, and that will be that."

Early the next day the steward and his company advised the Jizhou officials of the robbery. Of that we'll say no more.

We'll talk instead of Yang Zhi who, halberd in hand, gloomily left Yellow Earth Ridge. He travelled southward half the night, then rested in a grove. "I've got no money and there's no one around here I know," he brooded. "What am I going to do?"

By then the sky was just turning light, and he set out again to take advantage of the cool. After covering another twenty *li*, he stopped in front of a tavern.

"If I don't have some wine," he said to himself, "I'll never be able to carry on."

He went in and sat down. The tables and benches were made of mulberry wood. Yang Zhi leaned his halberd against the wall. A woman, who was beside a stove, came over and spoke to him.

"Can I cook something for you, sir?"

"First let me have two measures of wine. Then cook me some rice. If you have meat, I'll have some of that, too. Add it up later and I'll pay the whole thing together."

The woman called a young fellow to pour the wine. She cooked the rice, fried some meat, and set them before Yang Zhi. When he finished eating, he rose, took his halberd and headed for the door.

"You haven't paid yet," the woman said.

"I'll pay you when I come back. Just credit me for now."

The young fellow who had poured the wine rushed after him and grabbed his arm. With one blow Yang Zhi knocked him to the ground. The woman began to wail. Yang continued on his way. He heard another voice shouting at him from behind.

"Where do you think you're going, rogue!"

He turned and saw running towards him a big bare-chested fellow, dragging a staff.

"So he's after me," thought Yang. "Well, that's his bad luck!"

Yang halted. Still further behind was the young waiter armed with a pitchfork and two or three vassals carrying cudgels, all racing towards him at flying speed.

"If I can finish off this first one, the rest won't dare come any nearer," he thought. Gripping his halberd, he charged forward to give combat.

The man, twirling his staff, met him head on. They fought twenty or thirty rounds. Of course the man was no match for Yang Zhi. He could only parry and dodge. The young fellow and the vassals were about to join in the fray when the staff-wielder jumped from the combat circle.

"Nobody move," he shouted. "You, big fellow with the halberd, what's your name?"

Yang Zhi smote his chest. "It is and always has been Yang Zhi, the Blue-Faced Beast! I haven't changed my name!"

"Not Yang Zhi, military aide in the palace of the Eastern Capital?"

"How do you know I'm Military Aide Yang?"

The man cast down his staff and fell on his knees. "I have eyes but didn't recognize Mount Taishan!"

Yang raised him to his feet. "And who are you, sir?"

"I'm from the prefecture of Kaifeng, originally, and I was a pupil of Arms Instructor Lin Chong in the Imperial Guards. My name is Cao Zheng. My family have been butchers for generations. I know how to slaughter, draw sinews, cut bones, remove entrails and skin carcases. For this reason I'm known as the Demon Carver. A rich man in my district gave me five thousand strings of cash and sent me here to Shandong to do some business for him. I lost his entire capital. After that, I couldn't go back, and I married a local country girl and moved in with her family. She's the one you saw at the stove. The boy with the pitchfork is her younger brother. When we fought just now I recognized your moves. They were the same as my teacher, Arms Instructor Lin. I knew I couldn't beat you."

"So you were one of Lin's pupils. Your teacher was ruined by Marshal Gao, and had to take to the hills. He's in Liangshan Marsh, today."

"I've heard that, also. I didn't know whether it was true or not. Please come to my home, Military Aide, and rest a while."

Yang Zhi returned with Cao Zheng to the tavern. The host requested Yang to be seated. He told his wife and the young man to bow to their guest, and to bring him food and wine.

While they were drinking, Cao Zheng asked: "What brings you here, Military Aide?"

Yang related in detail how he lost the birthday gifts he was convoying for Governor Liang.

"In that case, why not remain with me for a time?" Cao Zheng proposed. "Then we can discuss what to do."

"That's very kind of you," said Yang. "But the police are liable to catch up with me. I'd better not stay too long."

"If my place won't do, not far from here, on Two-Dragon Mountain in Qingzhou Prefecture, is a monastery known as the Precious Pearl. It's nestled in the mountains and has only one path leading to it. The monk in charge has given up religious life and let his hair grow. All the other monks have done the same. It's said that he's formed a gang of four or five hundred robbers. His name is Deng Long, and he's known as the Golden-Eyed Tiger. If you're determined to become an outlaw, you might do well to join him."

"Since there is such a place, why shouldn't I take it over and make it my refuge?"

Yang Zhi spent the night at Cao Zheng's house. The next morning he borrowed some travelling money, picked up his halberd, bid farewell to his host, and set out for Two-Dragon Mountain.

He travelled all day. Towards evening, he came in sight of a high mountain. "I'll sleep in this grove tonight," he said to himself, "and climb up tomorrow."

When he entered the grove he received a shock. Seated in the cool of a pine was a big fat monk, stripped to the buff. His back was elaborately tattooed. The monk, on seeing Yang Zhi, grabbed a staff that was beneath the tree and leaped to his feet.

"Hey, prick," he shouted. "Where are you from?"

"He has a west of the Pass accent," thought Yang Zhi. "We're from the same part of the country. I'll ask him." Aloud, he called: "Tell me where you're from, monk."

Instead of replying, the monk came charging forward, twirling his staff.

"That surly bald pate!" Yang swore under his breath. "I'll let out some of my anger on his hide!"

He rushed at his foe, halberd in hand. They battled up and down the grove, man to man, until they had fought forty or fifty rounds, with neither the victor. The monk executed a feint and jumped from the combat circle.

"Rest!" he roared. Both men stayed their hands.

"Where was there ever such a monk?" Yang said to himself admiringly. "He's really good. His skill is terrific! I can just barely outfight him."

"You blue-faced fellow," yelled the monk. "Who are you?"

"I am Yang Zhi, a military aide from the Eastern Capital."

The monk laughed. "Who would have thought we'd meet here!"

"May I presume to ask your name, sir monk? "

"I used to be a major in the Yenan garrison under Old General Zhong. Then I killed the Lord of the West with three blows of my fist and had to shave my head and become a monk on Mount Wutai. Because of the decorations on my back, everyone calls me the Tattooed Monk Sagacious Lu."

Yang Zhi smiled. "So we're both natives of the same place. I've heard a lot about you in the fraternity of gallant men. But I thought you were at the Great Xiangguo Monastery. What are you doing here?"

"It's a long story. When I was in charge of the monastery's vegetable garden, Marshal Gao wanted to have Lin Chong killed. I wouldn't stand for such injustice. I went with Lin all the way to Cangzhou, and saved his life. The two escorts went back and reported to that lout Gao that Sagacious Lu of the Great Xiangguo Monastery had rescued Lin just as they were about to murder him in Wild Boar Forest and had gone with them right up to Cangzhou, and that was why they couldn't finish him off. The mother-raper was furious. He made the abbot dismiss me and was sending men to arrest me. But I was tipped off by a gang of rascals and was able to foil the rogue. I burned down the vegetable garden buildings and took to the road, but nowhere could I find a refuge.

"In Mengzhou Prefecture I stopped at a tavern in Cross-roads Rise and was nearly done in by the tavern keeper's wife. She drugged my wine and I collapsed in a stupor. Luckily, her husband came home early. He was amazed at my appearance, my staff and my sword, and quickly gave me a drink that revived me. After I told him my name he kept me at his house for several days and made me his sworn brother. He and his wife are famous in the gallant fraternity. He is known as Zhang Qing the Vegetable Gardener. She is Sun the Witch. Both are considerate and bold.

"After four or five days at their place I heard that I would be safe in the Precious Pearl Monastery on Two-Dragon Mountain, and I went there, intending to join Deng Long's band. But the wretch wouldn't have me. I fought him, and he saw he was no match for me, so he fled up the mountain, closing and bolting the three big gates at its foot. There is no other way up. No matter how I cursed the prick he wouldn't come down and fight. I was stymied and enraged, and then you, brother, came along!"

Yang Zhi was very pleased. The two bowed to each other there in the grove and sat together the entire night. Yang told in detail how he tried to sell his sword and killed Niu Er, and how he lost the birthday gifts. He related also what Cao Zheng had said.

"Here we are, but Deng Long has closed the gates. How can we get him to come down?" mused Yang. "Let's go to Cao Zheng's house and talk it over."

The two left the grove together and returned to the tavern. Yang Zhi introduced Sagacious Lu. Cao Zheng hastily poured out wine, and they discussed how to take Two-Dragon Mountain.

"If he's really shut the gates," said the tavern keeper, "an army of ten thousand couldn't get up there, to say nothing of just you two. The stronghold can only be conquered by guile, not by force."

"That prick," said Sagacious. "When I went to join him, he met me outside the gates. Because he refused to keep me, we fought, and I floored him with a kick in the groin. Before I could kill him, his gang hauled him up the mountain and locked the frigging gates. No matter how I cursed him, he wouldn't come down and fight!"

"Since it's such a good place," said Yang Zhi, "why don't you and I go all-out and take it?"

"We must have a plan for getting up there, first," said Lu, "or we won't be able to come to grips with him."

"I have an idea, but I don't know whether you two will approve," said Cao Zheng.

"Let's hear it," said Yang.

"You, Military Aide, will have to change your clothes, and dress like a local peasant. I will take the staff and sword of the reverend, here. My wife's younger brother and few stalwarts will go with us to the foot of the mountain, and there we'll bind the reverend. I'll attend to that personally, using nothing but slip-knots. Then I'll shout up and say: 'We're from the neighboring tavern. This monk drank so much he got tipsy, but he refused to pay. He kept muttering that he was going to muster his men and attack your stronghold. We took advantage of his drunkenness to tie him up and present him to your chieftain.'

"Those clods will certainly let us up the mountain. When we get into the stronghold and are brought before Deng Long, the reverend can slip his bonds and I will hand him his staff. Once you two good fellows get to work, Deng Long will be finished. With him out of the way, his underlings won't dare resist. What do you think of my idea?"

"Shrewd, shrewd," said Lu and Yang.

That night all ate and drank and prepared dry rations for the coming expedition. They rose at the fifth watch the following morning and ate their fill. Lu stored his pack and luggage in Cao's house. Then the three men, plus the wife's younger brother and six or seven peasants set out for Two-Dragon Mountain. They reached the grove after noon and changed their clothes. Sagacious Lu was bound tightly by two of the peasants, but the knots were false. Yang put on a straw sun hat and a tattered cloth shirt. He retained his halberd, but held it shaft forward. Cao Zheng carried the monk's staff. The others, who walked closely front and rear, were armed with cudgels.

They halted outside the first gate. It was bristling with bows and lime flagons and ballista stones. When the guards at the gate saw the trussed-up monk, they sent a messenger flying to the summit to report.

Not long after, two junior officers came down to the gate and demanded: "Who are you people? What do you want here? Where did you get that monk?"

"We're from that village below. I run a small tavern," Cao Zheng replied. "This fat monk came and drank himself silly, and then refused to pay. He kept saying: 'I'm going to get a thousand men from Liangshan Marsh and blast that Two-Dragon Mountain, and wipe out this village of yours too!' I plied him with good wine until he was dead drunk, and then tied the rogue up and brought him here to hand over to your chieftain as a token of our filial respect. It will save our village from disaster."

The junior officers were delighted. "Excellent," they said. "Just wait here a little." They returned to the stronghold and reported that the monk had been captured.

Deng Long was overjoyed. "Bring him up," he cried. "I'll eat the scoundrel's heart and liver with my wine to slake a bit of my hatred!"

The brigands were ordered to open the gates and send up the prisoner. Yang Zhi and Cao Zheng, escorting the bound Sagacious Lu, climbed the trail. With its three gates at three perilous passes, the stronghold was a formidable place. Wrapped in the embrace of tall peaks was the monastery. Only a single path wound between the majestic heights. The three gates were guarded by throwing-logs and ballista stones, powerful bows and sharp arrows, and a dense proliferation of bamboo spears.

After passing through the three gates, they came to the Precious Pearl Monastery. A three-doored temple stood on a mirror-smooth clearing, all enclosed in a strong wooden palisade. Seven outlaws stood at the entry arch before the building. They swore when they saw Sagacious Lu.

"You hurt our chieftain, you scabby donkey! Now, you've been taken and he's going to cut you slowly to bits!"

Lu didn't utter a sound as they brought him into the temple. The idol had been removed from its pedestal and replaced by an armchair covered by a tiger skin. Spear-carrying guards stood on either side.

A few minutes later Deng Long entered, supported by two bandits, and seated himself on his throne. Cao Zheng and Yang Zhi pushed Sagacious Lu forward to the foot of the pedestal.

"Wretch!" cried Deng Long. "The other day you knocked me down! My groin is still swollen and black and blue. Today it's my turn!"

Lu glared at him. "Prick! Don't try to get away!"

The two peasants yanked the rope and the slip-knots vanished. Lu took his staff from Cao Zheng and whirled it like a flurry of clouds. Yang Zhi, casting aside his sun hat, turned his halberd point forward and grasped its shaft. Cao Zheng brandished a cudgel. Together, the group charged.

Deng Long struggled to escape, but Lu's staff swiftly split his skull and pulverized the throne. Yang Zhi ran his halberd through four or five of the bandits.

"Surrender, all of you!" yelled Cao Zheng. "If you don't, we'll kill every last one of you!"

The five or six hundred brigands before and behind the monastery and the handful of junior officers were frightened stiff. They all submitted. Men were directed to carry Deng Long's body to the rear of the mountain and burn it. An inventory was taken of the food supplies, the buildings were set in order, and an inspection was made of the items stored in the back of the monastery. Then meat and wine were called for. Lu and Yang became the stronghold's leaders, and they feasted in celebration. The bandits, who all swore fealty, remained under the direct control of the junior officers.

Cao Zheng bid farewell to the two bold fellows and returned home with the peasants. Of them we'll say no more.

CHAPTER 7
Song Jiang Secretly Helps Ward Chief Chao Flee

The old steward and the soldiers who had convoyed the birthday gifts travelled daily from dawn to dusk until they reached the Northern Capital. They reported directly to Governor Liang at his mansion. Kneeling before him, they confessed their criminal blunder.

"You've had a hard time on the road. I'm thankful to you," said Liang. And he asked: "Where is Major Yang Zhi?"

"He's unspeakable!" they cried. "An audacious, ungrateful thief! Five or six days after we left here, we arrived at Yellow Earth Ridge. It was very hot, and we rested in the cool of a grove. Who would have believed that Yang Zhi was in league with seven robbers, disguised as date merchants! He had arranged to meet them, and they were waiting there in the grove with seven laden carts. He also had a fellow carrying wine come and rest on the ridge. We bought wine from him, but it was drugged, and we fell down in a stupor. Then they tied us up, and Yang and the seven robbers loaded the birthday gifts onto the carts, together with their luggage, and trundled them all away! We reported the crime to Jizhou Prefecture and left the two captains to help the authorities apprehend the culprits. The rest of us hurried day and night to report back to Your Excellency."

Liang was shocked. "That thieving exile! A convicted felon who thanks to my efforts was raised to respectability! How could he be such an ingrate! If I ever get hold of him I'll smash him to bits!"

He had his scribe write a document which he immediately dispatched to Jizhou. He also sent an urgent letter to his father-in-law, the Premier in the Eastern Capital, relating what had transpired.

We'll not speak of the messenger to Jizhou, but rather of the emissary to the Eastern Capital. He was received by the Premier and presented the letter. Cai read it, aghast.

"What brash devils those robbers are!" he exclaimed. "Last year they stole the birthday gifts my son-in-law sent me, and they haven't been caught to this day. Now they've robbed me again. Something must be done or we'll never be able to maintain order!"

He issued a directive and dispatched an officer of his court to deliver it, at all possible speed, to the prefect of Jizhou, calling for the immediate arrest of the culprits, and demanding a formal reply.

For some days the prefect had been despondently mulling over the order he had received from Governor Liang of Daming, the Northern Capital. Now, the gate-keeper came in and announced: "An officer from Premier Cai of the Eastern Capital is here with an urgent directive for Your Excellency."

The prefect was startled. "It must be about the birthday gifts," he thought. He hastily summoned court and received the officer. "I've already been notified by Governor Liang's stewards," he said, "and have sent my police to apprehend the criminals. But we haven't discovered a trace. A few days ago, the governor made another query, and I again sent my police out with strict orders to investigate and arrest, but so far they haven't caught them. I'll reply personally to the Premier the moment we hear anything."

"I'm very close to the Premier," the officer said. "He sent me here specially to make sure we get them. Just before I left, he told me that I was to stay here until you've apprehended every one of them — the seven date merchants, the wine seller, and the fugitive officer Yang Zhi. He set a time limit of ten days within which to arrest and deliver them to the Eastern Capital. If you fail to do so, I'm afraid you'll be sent into exile

on the remote Shamen Island! It will also be difficult for me
to return to the Premier's presence, in fact my life will be in
jeopardy. If Your Excellency doesn't believe me, please read
this order."

The prefect was greatly alarmed after reading the document.
He immediately summoned his police officials. A man came
forward and hailed him respectfully.

"Who are you?" asked the prefect.

"Ho Tao, police inspector of third district."

"Are you in charge of that robbery of the birthday gifts on
Yellow Earth Ridge?"

"Yes, Your Excellency. I've been working on the case day
and night. I sent our quickest and most sharp-eyed men to
the ridge to search. But although I've had them beaten several
times, they still haven't found a trace. We're doing our best,
Excellency, but it looks hopeless."

"Rot! 'If the superiors don't press, the underlings loaf.' I
started my career by passing the palace examinations. Becoming a prefect wasn't easy! And now the Premier in the Eastern
Capital has sent an officer with an order giving me ten days to
catch the robbers, on pain of dismissal and exile to Shamen
Island. You're a police inspector, but you're not trying, and
the disaster falls on my head! I'm going to exile you to a
miserable border garrison, so far that even the wild geese can't
reach it!"

The prefect sent for the tattooer and had him write on Ho
Tao's cheek: "Exiled to — prefecture", leaving the name of
the destination blank.

"If you don't catch those crooks," he warned, "you can expect
no mercy!"

Ho Tao left the prefect's court and returned to his station.
He immediately called most of his police to a private room for
a conference. They all sat looking at one another, as silent as
geese with arrow-pierced bills, as mute as gill-hooked fish.

"This is the room that I pay you in," said Ho Tao. "You're
not generally so quiet. Is it because we're having a hard time

solving this case? I'm the one who should be pitied. Don't you see what's written on my face?"

"We're not blocks of wood," said the policemen. "We know you're being pressured from above. It's just that those date merchants must be brigands from some stronghold deep in the mountains in another prefecture. Once they snatched the booty, they surely holed up to celebrate and revel. How can we catch them? Even if we knew where they were, we could only gaze at them from a distance."

Ho Tao had been five-tenths depressed to start with. Now, these words added another five-tenths. He left the station, mounted his horse, rode home, and tied the beast to the trough in the rear of the house. Then he sat and brooded.

"Why are you so dejected?" his wife asked.

"You don't know what's happened," said Ho Tao. "The other day His Excellency issued an order to capture the robbers who stole the eleven loads of birthday gifts Governor Liang was sending his father-in-law Premier Cai. It happened on Yellow Earth Ridge. We don't know who the culprits are and I still haven't caught them. Today, I went to ask for more time, and found that the Premier had sent an officer to wait here for the criminals and bring them back to the Eastern Capital. The prefect asked me about the case and I said: 'There isn't any news, and we haven't caught them yet.' He had an exile tattoo put on my face, leaving only the destination blank. There's no telling how much longer I have to live!"

"What are we going to do?" cried his wife. "This is awful!"

As they were talking, Ho Tao's younger brother, Ho Qing, came to see him.

"What do you want?" Ho Tao demanded. "Why aren't you out gambling? What are you doing here?"

The wife, a clever woman, quickly signalled the young man not to reply, and said: "Won't you come into the kitchen? There's something I want to talk to you about."

Ho Qing went with her into the kitchen and sat down. She served him meat and vegetables, and heated several cups of wine.

"Brother is too overbearing," he complained. "I may have faults, but I'm still his brother! Why is he so high and mighty? He's my brother, isn't he? Would it disgrace him to have a couple of drinks with me?"

"You've no idea how upset he is."

"He's always had plenty of money and goods. What's happened to them? And I haven't been around to bother him. Why should he be upset?"

"You don't know. The other day on Yellow Earth Ridge a gang of date merchants robbed the birthday gifts Governor Liang of the Northern Capital was sending to Premier Cai. The prefect of Jizhou has just received an order from Cai to arrest the robbers within ten days and deliver them to the capital. If he doesn't, he'll be exiled to a distant garrison. Didn't you see what the prefect had tattooed on your brother's face: 'Exiled to — prefecture'? Only the destination has been left blank. If he doesn't catch them soon, he's going to suffer. How can he think of drinking with you? That's why I prepared some food and wine for you in here. He's been very depressed. You mustn't blame him."

"I've heard some rumors that robbers have taken the birthday gifts. Where did it happen?"

"They say it was on Yellow Earth Ridge."

"And what kind of people were the robbers?"

"Brother, you're not drunk. I just told you — seven date merchants."

Ho Qing laughed. "So that's how it was. Since it's known that date merchants did the job. What's there to brood over? Why not just send a few capable men to arrest them?"

"That's easy to say. They can't be found."

"There's nothing to worry about, sister-in-law," Ho Qing smiled. "Brother always welcomes a lot of fair weather friends, but he has no use for his own kin. He's looking for robbers, and his cronies say they can't find them. If he'd drunk a few cups of wine with me from time to time, I might be able to tell him how to go about it."

"Do you really have any clues?"

Ho Qing laughed. "Wait till brother's situation is desperate, then I may have a plan to save him."

He rose to leave. His sister-in-law persuaded him to stay for another few cups of wine.

Meanwhile she hurried into the next room and told her husband. Ho Tao quickly invited his brother to join him.

"Since you know where the robbers have gone," he said with an apologetic smile, "why don't you rescue me?"

"I don't know anything. I was only joking with sister-in-law. How can I rescue you?"

"Good brother, don't be offended by my manner. Think of how good I am to you generally, not of how bad I am on occasion. Save my life!"

"But you have so many sharp-eyed, fast-moving police. There are nearly three hundred men under your command. Aren't they doing their utmost? What can a mere younger brother do?"

"Never mind about them. You've got something up your sleeve. Don't wait for others to be the heroes. Tell me where the robbers have gone and I'll reward you. Let me relax."

"How do I know where they've gone?"

"Don't torment me. Remember we were born of the same mother!"

"No need to panic. When the situation gets really critical, I'll go out and nab the petty culprits myself."

"Ho Qing," said his sister-in-law, "you must rescue him, come what may. It's your duty as a brother. The Premier has issued an order for the arrest of the gang. It's very serious. How can you talk about 'petty culprits'!"

"You know I come only for money for gambling, sister-in-law," Ho Qing said ironically. "Many's the time brother has berated me. Even when he struck or cursed me, I never talked back. And when he feasted, it was always with others. But today I seem to be of some use after all!"

Ho Tao realized there was reason in what Ho Qing said. He hurriedly got a silver ingot weighing ten ounces and placed it on the table. "Take this, brother," he urged. "After we catch the robbers, I guarantee you won't lack for gold or silver, silks or satins."

Ho Qing laughed. "This is certainly a case of 'not burning incense in ordinary times, but embracing the idol's foot in a crisis.' It would be sheer extortion if I accepted your silver now. Take it back. Don't try to bribe me. If you act like this I won't say a word. I'll tell you only because you two have apologized. I'm not impressed by your money."

"My silver is all rewards for cases I've solved," explained Ho Tao. "Naturally, I've always four or five hundred strings of cash on hand. Don't refuse the silver, brother, and tell me — where have those robbers gone?"

Ho Qing slapped his thigh. "I've got them right here in my pocket!"

Ho Tao was astonished. "What do you mean?"

"Never you mind. Just take my word for it. I don't want your silver. You don't have to bribe me. I ask only that you treat me decently."

From a document case at his waist Ho Qing extracted a notebook.

"All the robbers are written down right here!"

"How can that be?"

"To tell the truth, a few days ago I lost again at gambling. I was clean, without a copper. A gambling pal of mine took me to a village called Anle, fifteen *li* outside the North Gate, and I put up at the Wang Family Inn, where I was able to raise a bit of change for the gaming tables. The authorities have issued an order that all inns must keep a register, with proper seals, and that an entry must be made for every guest, stating his name, place of origin, destination, and line of business, and that it must be shown to the local ward chief on demand, once a month. The attendant at the Wang Family Inn is illiterate, and he begged me to keep the register for him for a couple of weeks.

"On the third day of the sixth month, seven date merchants

arrived pushing seven carts. I recognized one of them as Ward Chief Chao of East Bank in Yuncheng County, because I once stayed at his manor with a gambling friend. I took up my brush-pen and asked: 'What is your name, please?' Before he could speak, a fair-faced man with a mustache and goatee quickly answered for him: 'We're all of us named Li. We're from Haozhou Prefecture, and are on our way with dates for the Eastern Capital.'

"Though I was sceptical, I wrote it down. The next day, they left. My host offered to take me gambling in a place in the village. On the way, at a fork in the road, we met a fellow carrying buckets on a shoulder-pole. I didn't know him, but the innkeeper hailed him: 'Where are you going, Master Bai?' 'To a rich man's house in the village. I'm bringing him this load of vinegar,' the man replied. The innkeeper said to me: 'This is Bai Sheng, known as the Daylight Rat. He's also fond of gambling.' I made a mental note of it. Later, when I heard gossip that date merchants had drugged some travellers on Yellow Earth Ridge and stole the birthday gifts, I guessed at once that Ward Chief Chao was involved. Arrest Bai and question him, and you'll get the whole story. Here is my copy of the register."

Ho Tao was delighted. He led his brother in to see the prefect.

"Any developments on that case?" asked the official.

"Some," replied Ho Tao.

The prefect called them into his rear chambers and questioned them carefully. Ho Qing responded in detail. The prefect directed eight policemen to go with the brothers that same night to Anle Village. They compelled the innkeeper to take them to Bai Sheng, and reached the wine seller's house at the third watch. The innkeeper, at their insistence, called Bai Sheng to open the door and strike a light. Bai's wife led them in. They heard Bai Sheng groaning on the bed. The wife said he had a fever but had not been able to sweat. They hauled him from the bed and tied him up. His face was blotched red and white.

"That's a fine thing you did on Yellow Earth Ridge!" they yelled.

Bai Sheng denied everything. They bound his wife, but she also refused to talk. The policemen searched the house. They noticed that the earthen floor beneath the bed was uneven, and started to dig. At a depth of three feet, one of them uttered a cry. Bai Sheng's face turned the color of clay. From the hole in the ground, the diggers extracted a bag of gold and silver.

The police concealed Bai Sheng's head and face in a hood, and took him and his wife and the loot back to Jizhou. It was the fifth watch and the sky was already light when they reached the prefectural office. They brought him before the prefect, tied the ropes around him more securely, and asked him who the brains was behind the robbery. Bai Sheng denied any connection, and refused to name his confederates. They beat him three or four times, till his skin split and blood was pouring from his wounds.

"We already know that the chief culprit is Ward Chief Chao of East Bank, Yuncheng County," shouted the prefect. "There's no use denying it. Name the other six and I'll stop the beating."

Bai Sheng tried to hold out. But soon he couldn't take it any longer. "The leader is Ward Chief Chao," he admitted. "He came with six men and inveigled me into carrying the wine! But I really don't know who the other six are!"

"That's no problem," said the prefect. "All we have to do is take Ward Chief Chao, and we'll find the rest quickly enough."

A twenty-catty rack for condemned criminals was locked around Bai Sheng's neck. His wife, also fettered, was sent to the women's prison. The prefect then issued an order directing Ho Tao to proceed at once with twenty crack policemen to Yuncheng County and request the magistrate to aid in arresting Ward Chief Chao and his six un-named fellow conspirators. Inspector Ho was told to take along the two captains who had accompanied the birthday gift convoy to identify the culprits. But, warned the prefect, he was to proceed quietly and not let news of the raid leak out.

The inspector and his men travelled all night to Yuncheng.

First Ho Tao secretly put up his party at an inn. Then, with two of his policemen and the prefect's order, he presented himself at the gate of the magistrate's compound.

By then it was late morning, and court was in recess. All was still. Ho Tao went into a tea-house across the street and sat down to wait. As he was sipping some steeped tea he had ordered he asked the waiter: "Why is it so quiet outside the magistracy?"

"The morning session is over. The attendants and litigants have all gone off to eat. They haven't come back yet."

"Do you happen to know which clerk is on duty today?"

"Here he comes, now," said the waiter, pointing.

Ho Tao looked. Emerging from the magistracy was a man whose family name was Song. His formal given name was Jiang, his popular given name was Kongming. A third son, he was born in the county's Song Family Village. Because he was short and swarthy, everyone called him Dark Song Jiang. And since he was filial to his parents, and was a chivalrous man, generous to friends, he was also known as the Filial and Gallant Dark Third Master. Above him, his father was still alive, though his mother had died early. Below him was a younger brother Song Jing, known as the Iron Fan who, with their father, the Venerable Song, ran the farm in the village and lived on the fruits of their fields.

Song Jiang was a clerk of the county magistrate's court in Yuncheng. He wrote legibly and well, and was familiar with administrative procedures. Especially fond of playing with weapons, he was adept at many forms of fighting. He made friends only in the gallant fraternity, but he helped anyone, high or low, who sought his aid, providing his guest with food and lodging in the family manor, tirelessly keeping him company, and giving him travelling expenses when he wanted to leave. Song Jiang scattered gold about like dust! He never refused a request for money. He was always making things easy for people, solving their difficulties, settling differences, saving lives. He provided the indigent with funds for coffins and medicines, gave charity to the poor, assisted in emergencies, helped in cases of hardship.

And so he was famed throughout the provinces of Shandong and Hebei, and was known to all as the Timely Rain, for like the rain from the heavens he brought succor to every living thing.

As Song Jiang walked from the magistracy with an attendant, Inspector Ho crossed the street to meet him.

"Won't you join me for some tea, sir Clerk?"

Song Jiang could tell from his appearance that Ho Tao was in the police.

"Where are you from, brother?" he queried courteously.

"If I may have the pleasure of your company in the tea-house we can talk there."

"As you wish, sir."

The two men entered the tea-house and sat down. Song Jiang told the attendant to wait outside. Then he turned to the inspector.

"May I presume to ask brother's name?"

"I am Ho Tao, a mere police inspector of Jizhou Prefecture. May I dare ask your name, sir Clerk?"

"Forgive me for not having recognized you, Inspector. I'm a small official called Song Jiang."

Ho Tao fell to his knees and kowtowed. "I have long known your fame, but never had the honor of meeting you."

"You overwhelm me. Please sit at the head of the table."

"An insignificant person like me — I wouldn't dream of it!"

"As a member of our superior organization and a guest from afar, you must, Inspector."

They argued politely for a few moments. Then Song Jiang took the host's seat and Ho Tao the guest's.

"Waiter," called the clerk, "two cups of tea." The refreshments soon came and both men drank.

"What instructions from above do you bring to our humble county, Inspector?" asked Song Jiang.

"I'll speak frankly. It concerns several important people here."

"It couldn't be about a robbery?"

"I've brought a sealed order. I trust you will help me carry it out."

"How could I do otherwise with an emissary from our superiors? Which robbery does it involve?"

"You're the keeper of the official records, sir Clerk. There's no harm in telling you. On Yellow Earth Ridge, which is under our prefect's jurisdiction, a band of eight robbers drugged fifteen men who were bringing birthday gifts from Governor Liang of Daming, the Northern Capital, to Premier Cai and made off with eleven loads of gold and jewels of an estimated value of a hundred thousand strings of cash. We've caught Bai Sheng, the accomplice. He says the other seven, the actual robbers, are all in this county. The Premier has sent an aide to our prefecture with orders to remain until we've caught them. We hope you'll give us every assistance."

"Of course we'll apprehend the criminals and turn them over. We'd do that on your orders, Inspector, to say nothing of orders from the Premier himself. Who are the seven named by Bai Sheng?"

"The leader is Ward Chief Chao of East Bank. To tell you the truth, we don't know the names of the other six. We beg your utmost diligence."

Song Jiang was shocked. He said to himself: "Chao Gai is one of my dearest friends! This crime he's committed is a capital offense! I must save him. If they capture him he's sure to die!"

Concealing his anxiety, Song Jiang said: "That dirty scoundrel. Everyone in the county hates him. So now he's come to this. We'll make him pay!"

"Please help us apprehend him."

"There won't be any difficulty. 'Easy as catching turtles in a jug. Just stretch out your hand,' as the old saying goes. But you'll have to present your order to the magistrate when the court is in session. He will read it and send men to make the arrest. I'm only a clerk. I couldn't assume responsibility for an important matter like this. What if word leaked out!"

"You're quite right. Please lead me in."

"The magistrate has been busy all morning and he's taking a short rest. If you'll wait a bit, court will be resumed soon. I'll call you."

"I hope you'll help us accomplish our mission, come what may."

"Naturally. That goes without saying. I must go home to attend to a few things. I'll be right back. Please sit and rest a while."

"Go ahead, sir Clerk. I'll wait here for you."

Song Jiang rose and left the booth. "If that gentleman wants any more tea, put it on my account," he said to the waiter. He hurried from the tea-house and told his attendant to remain outside the door. "When the magistrate resumes court, go into the tea-house and tell the officer I'll be back soon," he instructed. "Ask him to please wait a bit."

At his house, Song Jiang saddled his horse and led it out the rear gate. Quirt in hand, he mounted and walked the beast slowly from the county town. Once outside the East Gate, he struck the horse sharply twice with his quirt, and the animal scooted like a rabbit towards East Bank. In less than half a watch Song arrived at Chao Gai's manor. When a vassal saw who it was, he went in and reported.

Chao Gai was drinking wine with Wu Yong, Gongsun Sheng and Liu Tang beneath a grape arbor in the rear garden. The three Ruan brothers had received their share of the loot and returned to Stone Tablet Village. The vassal announced that Clerk Song was at the front gate.

"How many people with him?" asked Chao Gai.

"He's alone, and his horse is in a lather," replied the vassal. "He wants to see you at once."

"Something must be up." Chao Gai hastened out.

Song Jiang hailed the ward chief respectfully, grasped him by the hand and walked to a small building nearby.

"Why have you come in such a hurry, sir Clerk?"

"You know my devotion, brother. I'd lay down my life for you. They've broken the Yellow Earth Ridge case! Bai Sheng has been taken to the prison in Jizhou. He's confessed about you seven. The prefect has sent an Inspector Ho and several men, with orders both from himself and Premier Cai that all seven be apprehended, and naming you as the leader. Thank Heaven the matter fell into my hands! I put the inspector off by saying the magistrate was sleeping, and told him to wait for me in the tea-house opposite the court. Then I came galloping out here to warn you. 'Of all the thirty-six possible solutions, the best one is — leave.' Get out, quickly! Don't delay! I'm going back now to take the inspector and his documents into court. The magistrate will send men this very night. You mustn't delay. If anything goes wrong, I'll be helpless. Don't blame me if I can't save you!"

"Brother," said the startled Chao Gai, "I'll never be able to thank you enough."

"Save your breath. Just concentrate on getting away. Don't linger. I must go back."

"There are seven of us. The three Ruan brothers — Second, Fifth and Seventh — have returned to Stone Tablet Village with their share. The other three are here. You must meet them." Chao Gai led Song Jiang to the rear garden and introduced him.

"Wu Yong. Gongsun Sheng, from Jizhou. Liu Tang, from Donglu."

Song Jiang exchanged a few brief courtesies and turned to leave. "Look after yourself, brother," he urged the ward chief. "Get away quickly. I'm going now." He mounted his horse at the front gate, flailed his quirt, and flew back to the county town.

"Do you know who that was?" Chao Gai asked his three companions.

"What was he in such a hurry about?" countered Wu Yong. "Who is he?"

"This will surprise you, but if he hadn't come all of us would be dead men!"

"Does that mean there's been a leak and our story's got out?" cried the three.

"That brother came to warn us, at the greatest risk to himself.

Bai Sheng has been arrested. He's in Jizhou Prison, and he's named the seven of us! The prefect has sent an Inspector Ho and some men, together with a special order from the Premier, to request Yuncheng County to apprehend us immediately. Fortunately, my friend kept the inspector waiting in a tea-house while he rushed out here. When he gets back the magistrate will issue his orders and send men this very night to arrest us. What shall we do?"

"If he hadn't informed us, we'd all be in the net," said Wu Yong. "Who is our benefactor?"

"A clerk in the magistrate's court, Song Jiang, Defender of Chivalry."

"I've heard of him, but we've never met, though we live not far apart."

The other two asked: "Isn't he the one known among chivalrous men as Song Jiang the Timely Rain?"

Chao Gai nodded. "That's the man. He and I are very close, we're sworn brothers. Teacher Wu hasn't met him, but I can assure you he's worthy of his reputation. Since I became his blood brother I feel that my life hasn't been lived in vain!"

To Wu Yong he said: "Our situation is critical. How can we solve it?"

"There's nothing to discuss. 'Of all the thirty-six possible solutions, the best one is — leave.' "

"That's what Clerk Song said. But where should we go?"

"I'm considering that. I'd say we should get together six or seven shoulder-pole loads of possessions and join the three Ruan brothers in Stone Tablet. First send a man on ahead quietly to let them know we're coming."

"But they're fishermen. How can they accommodate so many of us?"

"You're not thinking carefully, brother. Stone Tablet Village is only a few steps away from Liangshan Marsh. The citadel on the mountain top is thriving. When the officials and police go looking for robbers, they don't dare even glance in its direction. If the search for us gets too hot, we can always join the band."

"A very good idea. But what if they don't want us?"

"We've plenty of gold and silver. If we present them with some they'll accept us all right."

"Since we're all agreed, we'd better get started. Teacher Wu, you and Liu Tang take several vassals and a few loads and go first to the Ruan family and arrange everything. Have them meet us. We'll be coming by land. I and Gongsun will join you as soon as we've settled things here."

Wu Yong and Liu Tang made up the purloined birthday gifts of gold and jewels into half a dozen loads, and directed six vassals to eat a meal. Then, the teacher tucked his bronze chain into his sleeve, Liu Tang took up his halberd, and the group set out for Stone Tablet, shouldering the loads.

The ward chief and the Taoist priest began closing down the manor. They gave money to those vassals who didn't want to go along, and advised them to find other masters. Those who wished to go gathered their possessions and prepared their luggage. Of that we'll say no more.

We'll speak rather of Song Jiang, who galloped back to town and hurried to the tea-house. Inspector Ho was standing outside the door, looking for him.

"Sorry to keep you waiting so long," said the clerk. "A relative from my village kept me tied up talking about family affairs."

"May I trouble you to take me in?"

"Please come this way."

The two men entered the magistracy, where Shi Wenbin was holding court. Song Jiang with the sealed papers in his hand, led Ho Tao to the magistrate's table, and instructed the attendants to put up a "Do Not Disturb" sign.

"Documents from Jizhou Prefecture," he told the magistrate, "brought by Inspector Ho because of the urgency of the robbers' case."

Shi opened the envelope and read the documents. He was shaken. "The Premier has dispatched an aide to wait in the prefecture!" he exclaimed to Song Jiang. "We must send men and catch the criminals!"

"If they go during the day, word is liable to get out. Night would be the best time. Once we take Chao Gai, we'll be able to bag the other six."

"Chao Gai is the ward chief of East Bank and has a very good reputation. I don't understand how he could have become involved in such a business!"

The magistrate summoned his sheriff and two constables. One was called Zhu Tong, and the other Lei Heng. Both were unusual men.

After receiving instructions from the magistrate in the rear chambers, they and the sheriff got on their horses, rode to the garrison and there picked over a hundred men, including ordinary soldiers and walking and mounted archers. When night fell, they all set out with Inspector Ho and the two captains who had originally accompanied the birthday gifts. Every man carried ropes and weapons. The sheriff rode his horse, as did the two constables. They wore swords, bows and arrows, and each held a halberd. Front and rear were platoons of mounted and walking archers. They left the town through the East Gate and proceeded rapidly towards East Bank and the home of Ward Chief Chao.

It was the first watch by the time they reached the village, and they assembled in the Guanyin Temple courtyard.

"Chao Gai's manor is just ahead," said Zhu Tong. "There are roads leading from both its front and rear gates. If we attack from the front, he'll leave by the rear. If we attack from the rear, he'll escape through the front. We must bear in mind that Chao Gai is a remarkable man. We don't know who those other six are, but they're certainly not kindly gentlemen, and they're all desperate. If they decide to fight their way out, with their vassals helping, we'll never be able to stop them. Our only hope is to shout from one direction and attack from another, get them running around in confusion, then make our move.

"I propose that we divide our forces into two groups, with me taking one half and Constable Lei taking the other. I will go quietly with my men, on foot, to the rear gate, and lay an ambush. When you hear us whistle, Constable Lei, you and your group smash in through the front gate. Arrest every man you can lay your hands on."

"That sounds all right," said Lei. "Only, wouldn't it be better if you and the sheriff struck from the front gate while I cut off the rear?"

"You don't understand, brother. There are three possible escape routes from the manor. I've observed them often. I know every path. Even without torches, I could follow them in the dark. You're not familiar with all the places Chao Gai could twist in and out of. If he gets away it'll be no joke."

"You're right, Constable Zhu," said the sheriff. "Take half the men."

"I'll only need about thirty," said Zhu Tong. He picked ten archers and twenty soldiers and departed.

The sheriff again climbed into his saddle, and Lei Heng placed a protective cordon of mounted archers around him. The soldiers were ranged in front. In the light of thirty or so torches, with tined-spears and halberds and hooks, they advanced rapidly in a body towards the manor.

When only half a *li* away, suddenly they saw fire rising from the central building, spreading a thick pall of black smoke and spewing red flames into the sky. Another ten paces and they saw thirty or forty more blazes springing up everywhere around the front and rear gates.

Lei Heng waved his halberd, the soldiers behind him shouted, and they broke through the front gate in a body. Inside, the fires had turned the manor bright as day, but the attackers didn't see a single person. Then, from the rear of the manor they heard yells and shouts, and cries of "Grab them!"

Actually, it had been Zhu Tong's intention from the start to let Chao Gai escape through the rear, and so he told Lei Heng to attack from the front. Lei Heng had the same idea. He too wanted to cover the rear gate and let Chao Gai flee. He had no choice when Zhu Tong insisted that he make a frontal assault, but he only put on a show, creating a lot of noise and running about with the aim of hastening the ward chief's get-away.

By the time Zhu Tong arrived at the rear gate Chao Gai had not yet finished putting his affairs in order. Vassals hastened to report: "The soldiers have come! We must hurry!" Chao Gai ordered them to set fire to the manor. He and Gongsun the Taoist priest, at the head of a dozen or so vassals, brandishing their halberds, dashed through the rear gate.

"Try to stop us and die, get out of our way and live!" they shouted.

"Halt, Ward Chief," Zhu Tong called from the shadows. "I've been waiting here for you a long time!"

Chao Gai paid no attention. He and Gongsun continued slashing furiously with their halberds. Pretending to dodge, Zhu Tong left a hole in the besiegers' line. The ward chief sent Gongsun and the vassals plunging through, and then followed, protecting their rear.

Zhu Tong pulled his foot archers from the manor's rear gate. "There are robbers ahead, catch them!" he yelled. Lei Heng, hearing his shouts, came out of the front gate and also ordered his mounted and foot archers to give chase in various directions. He himself rushed about in the light of the fires, pretending to seek the fugitives.

Zhu Tong got away from his men and ran after Chao Gai, halberd in hand.

"Why are you chasing me, Constable Zhu?" the ward chief called over his shoulder. "I've done no wrong."

Zhu Tong saw there was no one behind him, and he dared to speak freely. "You don't know what I've done for you, Ward Chief. I was afraid Lei Heng would get muddled and not treat you right. So I fooled him into raiding your front gate, while I waited at the rear to ensure your escape. Didn't you see that big breach I just made for you? Liangshan Marsh is your only safe refuge. Don't try any other place."

"I'm deeply grateful to you for rescuing us. Some day I'll repay you."

Behind them came the sound of Lei Heng shouting: "Don't let them get away!"

"There's nothing to be alarmed about," Zhu Tong said to the ward chief. "Keep going. I'll draw them off." He called back: "Three robbers are heading for the east path! After them, Constable Lei!"

Lei Heng and his men hurried east, followed by the soldiers. Zhu Tong continued talking with Chao Gai while feigning to pursue him. The fact is he was protecting the ward chief and seeing him on his way. Chao Gai finally vanished into the night. Zhu Tong pretended to trip. He fell heavily to the ground. The soldiers caught up and raised him to his feet.

"I couldn't see the path in the darkness. I ran off into the fields by mistake," said Zhu Tong. "I slipped and fell. My right ankle is sprained."

"The main culprit got away," said the sheriff. "A pretty kettle of fish!"

"It isn't that I didn't try, but there isn't much I can do in the dark of the moon," said Zhu Tong. "Most of these soldiers are useless. They're afraid to go after the robbers."

The sheriff ordered the soldiers to continue the chase. But the soldiers thought: "Those two constables weren't any use themselves. If they couldn't get close, what good can we do?" They made a desultory show of pursuit, then came back and reported: "In this darkness we can't find which path they've taken."

Lei Heng also returned after running a while. "Zhu Tong and Chao Gai are close friends," he said to himself. "He's probably let him escape. I have no reason to harm him. I also wanted to let him go. Well, now he's gone, before I could prove my good intentions."

"We hadn't a chance of catching them," he said to the sheriff. "Those robbers are fantastic!"

It was already the fourth watch by the time the sheriff and the two constables reached the front of the manor. Inspector Ho observed the soldiers straggling in. After hunting all night they hadn't nabbed a single robber.

He groaned. "What am I going to tell the Jizhou prefect?"

All the sheriff could do was to seize a few of the ward chief's neighbors and take them back to Yuncheng County.

CHAPTER 8
The Men of Liangshan Marsh Make Chao Gai Their Chief

Chao Gai, Gongsun Sheng, the three Ruan brothers and the dozen or more fishermen left the Stone Tablet marshes in six or seven boats and went directly to Lijia Entry, where they found the craft of Wu Yong and Liu Tang, and rejoined them.

They set their vessels in order and went together to the tavern of Zhu Gui the Dry-Land Crocodile. When all had arrived, they said they wanted to join the mountain stronghold. Zhu Gui hastily welcomed them. Wu Yong told him their story. The tavern keeper was very pleased, and greeted them, one by one. He invited them in, begged them to be seated, and ordered the waiter to bring wine.

Then he took a leather-bound bow, fitted a whistling arrow, and shot it into a cove of reeds, opposite. Soon a small boat came out, rowed by one of the brigands. Zhu Gui quickly wrote a letter of introduction, stating the number of men who wished to join, and their names, and gave it to the bandit, instructing him to deliver it to the stronghold. After this he slaughtered sheep to feast his guests.

The next morning Zhu Gui ordered a large boat, and invited the bold fellows on board. Together with the boats which had brought Chao Gai and the others, it set forth for the mountain fortress. After sailing a long time, they came to an inlet. They could hear drums beating and gongs crashing along the shore. Four sentry craft glided out, manned by seven or eight bandits. These recognized Zhu Gui, greeted him respectfully, and returned to their hiding place.

At the Shore of Golden Sands the party disembarked, leaving their families and fishermen to wait by the boats. Several score bandits came down the mountain and led them to the fortress gate. Wang Lun and the other leaders came out to greet them. Chao Gai and his party bowed politely. The bandit chieftain returned the courtesy.

"I am called Wang Lun. The fame of Chao Gai the Heavenly King has long thundered in my ears. It is a pleasure to welcome you to our humble stronghold."

"I am a crude, unlettered fellow seeking refuge, hoping only to be a simple foot soldier under your command. Please do not refuse me."

"You mustn't talk like that. Please come to our small fortress, and we will confer."

All went up the mountain and entered Righteous Fraternity Hall, where Wang Lun insisted that his guests sit on the raised platform. Chao Gai and his six companions stood in a row on the right, while Wang Lun and the other bandit leaders stood in a row on the left. After an exchange of courtesies, they took their seats as hosts and guests. Wang Lun instructed his junior officers, at the foot of the platform, to hail the visitors. When this was done, musicians in an ante-chamber commenced to play. The chieftain ordered a lieutenant to go down the mountain and look after his guests' retinue. These were quartered in a hostel below the gate.

Within the fortress two oxen .were slaughtered, and ten sheep and five pigs, and everyone feasted, to the accompaniment of drums and horns. And as they drank, Chao Gai told the outlaw leaders the entire story.

Wang Lun listened uneasily, deep in thought, and made only brief non-committal replies. They dined until evening, then the brigand chiefs escorted their visitors to the hostel below the stronghold gate, and left them to be waited on by the vassals who had come with them.

Chao Gai was very pleased. "We've committed such serious capital crimes. Where else could we find refuge?" he said to the other six. "If it weren't for the kindness of Chieftain Wang Lun we'd be in a real dilemma. We should always be grateful."

Wu Yong laughed coldly.

"Why are you sceptical, Teacher?" asked Chao Gai. "Tell us what you know."

"You're brave, but too honest, brother. Don't think for a moment Wang Lun will let us stay. You didn't see what was in his heart. You noted only his facial expression and manner."

"What's wrong with that?"

"When we first began dining, he was quite friendly. But after you told him how we killed all those officers and soldiers and the deputy, and released Ho Tao, and how bold the Ruan brothers were, his expression changed. Although he answered you courteously, his heart wasn't in it. If he actually wanted to keep us, he would have already assigned us proper seats.

"Du Qian and Song Wan are a couple of boors. What do they know about how to treat a guest? Lin Chong, on the other hand, was an arms instructor in the Imperial Guards, a big city man, very polished. But right now he can't help himself. He holds only fourth place here. I noticed that he looked dissatisfied when he saw how Wang Lun was answering you. He never took his eyes off him. There was clearly something on his mind. I think he'd like to help us, but he's in a difficult position. I'm going to throw out a few suggestions, and see whether I can't set them against each other."

"We rely completely on your shrewdness, Teacher," said Chao Gai.

The seven men retired for the night.

The next morning it was announced that Arms Instructor Lin was calling.

"He's come to see us," Wu Yong said to Chao Gai. "Just what we wanted!"

The seven men hurried out to greet their visitor and invited him into the parlor.

"We imposed too much on your generosity last night," said Wu Yong. "We must apologize."

"It is I who must apologize. Though I longed to show my

respect, I was not in a position to do so. Please forgive me."

"We have no talent, but we are not blocks of wood. We were most sensible of your kind intentions. We're extremely grateful."

Chao Gai begged Lin Chong to take the seat of highest rank. Lin Chong wouldn't hear of it. He pushed Chao into the chair and seated himself opposite. Wu Yong and the other five sat in a row on the side.

"We have long known of the Arms Instructor's fame," said Chao Gai. "We did not think we would have this opportunity to meet."

"When I was in the Eastern Capital I never failed in courtesy to my friends," said Lin Chong. "I now have had the honor to make your acquaintance, but have been unable to behave as I wished. I come especially to express my regret."

"We sincerely thank you," said Chao Gai.

"Quite some time ago I heard of the Arms Instructor's chivalry in the Eastern Capital," said Wu Yong. "How did you fall out with Gao Qiu, and why did he ruin you? When the army fodder depot was burned in Cangzhou, that also was his doing, wasn't it? And who introduced you to this mountain stronghold?"

"If I told you of the wickedness of that scoundrel Gao Qiu it would make your hair stand on end. And I cannot get revenge! I found refuge here on the recommendation of Lord Chai."

"Not Chai Jin, known in the gallant fraternity as the Small Whirlwind?"

"The very one."

"I have heard much about his righteousness and generosity, how warmly he treats brave men," said Chao Gai. "It is said that he is a descendant of the royal Zhou family. How wonderful it would be to meet him!"

"Lord Chai is famed throughout the land," said Wu Yong. "Surely it was because of your extraordinary skill with weapons, Arms Instructor, that he recommended you here. I am not exaggerating in the least when I say that Wang Lun should have relinquished top leadership to you. This is common opinion and in keeping with Lord Chai's letter."

"Teacher rates me much too highly. I committed a capital crime and found shelter with Lord Chai. He was quite willing to keep me, but I didn't want him to become involved. I came to this mountain of my own volition. Little did I know that it's a dead end! I don't mind having a lower rank, but Wang Lun is hard to get along with. He's not sure of himself, and is often untruthful."

"He seems friendly enough," said Wu Yong. "What makes him so narrow-hearted?"

"Having you gallant heroes join us would be of great mutual benefit, like embroidering flowers on brocade, like rain on dry sprouts. But Wang Lun's very jealous of the talented and able, he's afraid you'll overwhelm him. When you told, last night, how you slaughtered the soldiers and officers, he was upset. He's plainly reluctant to let you stay. That's why he asked you to rest in this outside hostel."

"Since that's how he feels," said Wu Yong, "there's no point in waiting for him to say so. We'll go somewhere else."

"Please don't take it amiss, but I have an idea," said Lin Chong. "I was afraid you bold fellows might be thinking of leaving, so I came early to confer. Why not wait and see how Wang Lun behaves today. If the lout speaks reasonably, not like yesterday, then everything can be discussed. But if he breathes so much as half an improper sentence, just leave the rest to me!"

"Your kind consideration is more than we deserve," said Chao Gai.

"Why should you quarrel with your old brothers for the sake of your new?" asked Wu Yong. "If he'll have us, we'll stay. If not, we'll go."

"No, Teacher!" cried Lin Chong. "As the ancients say: 'The astute and the gallant each cherish their own kind.' That filthy churl! What use is he to anybody? Gallant fellows, you can rely on me." He rose and took his leave. "We shall be meeting soon," he said.

They saw him to the gate, and Lin Chong went back up the mountain.

Not long after, a bandit arrived from the stronghold and said: "Today, our chieftains are inviting you to dine in the waterside pavilion in the fort on the south side."

"Tell them we will be there shortly," said Chao Gai. The bandit departed. "What shall we do, Teacher?" Chao Gai asked Wu Yong.

The teacher smiled. "Don't worry, brother. The stronghold is going to have a change of masters. Lin Chong seems determined to have it out with Wang Lun. If he shows any signs of hesitation, my tongue is sharp enough to prick him into open strife. You all carry concealed weapons. If I stroke my beard, get in and help him."

Chao Gai and the others silently and gladly agreed.

By mid-morning messengers had come four more times to repeat the invitation. Finally, neatly dressed, with weapons hidden on their persons, the seven set out for the feast. Song Wan arrived personally, on horseback, to lead the way, and seven sedan-chairs were provided for the guests. All proceeded directly to the waterside pavilion on the mountain's southern slope, and the seven came down from their conveyances. Wang Lun, Du Qian, Lin Chong and Zhu Gui were waiting to meet them and invite them into the pavilion. Hosts and guests took their seats, to the left and right respectively, on a dais.

Lesser brigands kept on refilling their goblets. When several rounds of wine had been drunk and two courses of food served, Chao Gai proposed to Wang Lun that the seven join the fraternity. But the bandit chieftain casually changed the subject. Wu Yong watched Lin Chong. The arms instructor was glaring at Wang Lun.

They drank until after noon. "Bring them in," Wang Lun said. Three of the bandits went out and soon returned. One of them was carrying five large silver ingots on a platter. Wang Lun rose, goblet in hand, and addressed himself to Chao Gai.

"We are honored that you heroes have assembled with us

here. Unfortunately, our stronghold is only a swampy marsh, not fit for gallants of such stature. We offer these few modest gifts and hope you won't laugh at them. When you have settled in some large suitable fortress, I will personally send men to serve under your command."

"For a long time we have known that this great stronghold welcomed able fighters," Chao Gai replied, "and so we made a beeline here to join. If you won't have us, we shall leave. As to the silver you so graciously offer, we cannot accept it. Not that we are rich, but we do have a bit of travel money. Please take back your splendid gift. We must be on our way."

"Why refuse it? We would be very glad to have you. It's only that we're short of grain and housing. Staying in a place like this would be holding you heroes back. It's not in keeping with your dignity. That's why we are not asking you to remain."

Before the words were out of Wang Lun's mouth, Lin Chong, scowling fiercely, shouted: "When I first came here you tried to put me off by saying you were short of grain and housing! Now you tell brother Chao and his gallant company the same story! What's the big idea?"

"Calm yourself, sir leader," Wu Yong begged. "We shouldn't have come. We've only stirred up bad feeling among you. Chieftain Wang Lun is not driving us away, he's sending us off with travelling expenses. Please don't be angry, any of you. We'll go, and that will be the end of it."

"Wang Lun has a knife behind his smile!" said Lin Chong. "He's a man of pure words but dirty deeds! I'm not going to let him get away with it!"

"Animal!" barked Wang Lun. "You're not drunk. How dare you speak of me like that? Have you no respect for your superiors?"

"You're an impoverished scholar who failed in the government examinations, a man of threadbare learning," Lin Chong scoffed. "What right have you to be stronghold leader?"

"Our coming here has caused this quarrel," Wu Yong said to Chao Gai. "We must get some boats and depart today."

The seven men rose as if to leave the pavilion.

"Stay at least till the end of the banquet," Wang Lun proposed.

With a kick Lin Chong sent the table crashing to one side. He jumped to his feet and pulled a glittering knife from beneath his robe. Wu Yong stroked his beard. Chao Gai and Liu Tang hurried over as if to restrain Wang Lun.

"You mustn't quarrel," they exclaimed.

Wu Yong pretended to be soothing Lin Chong. "Please don't be rash," he urged.

Gongsun Sheng cried to both sides: "Don't destroy your harmony on our account!"

Ruan the Second wrapped his arms around Du Qian, while Fifth enveloped Song Wan, and Seventh did the same to Zhu Qui.

The assembled lesser bandits watched in frightened stupefaction. Lin Chong cursed Wang Lun.

"You're a poor village scholar! If it weren't for Du Qian, you wouldn't even be here! Lord Chai supported you, gave you travelling expenses, befriended you, but when he sent me with a letter of introduction, you did everything to put me off! Now these bold heroes come, and you want to send them down the mountain! Does Mount Liangshan belong to you? You're a thief, jealous of men of talent! What good is there in keeping you alive? You haven't any particular ability. Who are you to lead this stronghold?"

Du Qian, Song Wan and Zhu Gui tried to press forward to help Wang Lun, but they were held so tightly by the Ruan brothers that they couldn't move. The bandit chieftain turned to go. Chao Gai and Liu Tang blocked his path. Wang Lun realized his danger.

"Where are my boon companions?" he cried.

Several bandits who had always been very close to him wanted to come to his rescue, but they were cowed by Lin Chong's fierce manner.

Again Lin cursed the bandit chief, then stabbed him through the heart. Wang Lun collapsed in a heap. Chao Gai and the others each produced a knife. Lin Chong cut off Wang Lun's head and raised it aloft. Terrified, Du Qian, Song Wan and Zhu Gui fell to their knees.

"Let us serve as grooms who hold your whip and stirrup," they begged.

Chao Gai, with polite haste, helped them to their feet. Wu Yong pulled the chair of the highest chieftain from the pool of blood and pushed Lin Chong down into it.

"If anyone disagrees, he will go the way of Wang Lun," he shouted. "From now on Arms Instructor Lin is the leader of Mount Liangshan."

"No, Teacher," exclaimed Lin Chong. "I killed the scoundrel out of loyalty to you gallant heroes! I seek no position for myself. I will be the laughing stock of the whole chivalrous fraternity if I take this seat today. I'd rather die, first! But I have another suggestion. I wonder whether you'll listen to me?"

"Speak," said the others. "Who would dare disagree? Let's hear it."

Lin Chong said: "Although I'm an exile from the Imperial Guards I am able to be with these heroes here today. I turned against Wang Lun because his heart was narrow, because he was jealous of their talents and refused to accept them, not because I wanted his position. I could never have brains and courage enough to destroy the evil ministers surrounding the emperor and repulse their armies. Brother Chao is a gallant, charitable man. He is intelligent and brave. He's famed and admired everywhere. In the spirit of chivalry I propose that he become the leader of this stronghold. What do you say?"

"Very suitable," cried the men.

"No," said Chao Gai. "Since ancient times 'the strong guest must not exceed his host.' Strong I may be, but I've only recently arrived from distant parts. I cannot assume high command."

Lin Chong pushed him into the leader's chair. "This is the time. Don't refuse." To the other brigands he shouted: "If anyone disagrees, let him remember what happened to Wang Lun!"

Courteously he insisted that Chao Gai retain his seat. He

called to the bandits to come to the pavilion and pay homage. He ordered that Wang Lun's body be removed, and that a feast be prepared inside the fortress. He instructed that all the junior officers stationed on the front and rear of the mountain be summoned to the stronghold for a meeting.

Lin Chong and the others helped Chao Gai into a sedan-chair, then all got on their horses and proceeded to Righteous Fraternity Hall, where they dismounted and entered. Chao Gai was seated on the chair of first rank, in the middle. An incense burner was lit in the center of the hall. Lin Chong came forward.

"I'm only a crude fellow who knows a bit about arms. I have no learning or talent, no wisdom or technique. Today we are fortunate enough to be here with you gallant men and our just principles are clear. We cannot be casual about authority, as we were before. Teacher Wu Yong shall be our military adviser, in charge of our fighting forces. He must take the second seat."

Wu Yong replied: "I'm a simple village school teacher, with neither the learning nor the ability to manage affairs. Though I've read something of the military classics by Sun and Wu, I haven't shown even half a grain of talent. How can I accept?"

"The time is at hand," Lin Chong said. "No need for modesty." Wu Yong took the second chair and Lin Chong said: "Master Gongsun, please take the third seat."

"That cannot be," Chao Gai protested. "If you keep giving way like this, I'll withdraw completely."

"You mustn't say that, brother. Master Gongsun is known throughout the gallant fraternity. He's an excellent commander, and even the spirits cannot fathom his tactics. He can summon the wind and the rain. There's no one like him!"

"Though I know a bit of magic," said the Taoist priest, "I haven't any real learning to benefit the world. How dare I become a leader? That place belongs to you."

"We all saw your cleverness today in defeating the enemy," said Lin Chong. "A tripod vessel must have three legs. With

梁山泊義士尊晁蓋

only two it cannot stand. No need to be polite."

Gongsun took the third seat. Lin Chong wanted to yield further, but Chao Gai, Wu Yong and Gongsun wouldn't hear of it. "Because you talked of a tripod needing three legs, we had no choice but to accept the three top positions," they explained. "But we'll all withdraw if you relinquish any further." They firmly seated him in the fourth chair.

"Song and Du should now be seated," said Chao Gai. But Du Qian and Song Wan absolutely refused. They begged Liu Tang, Ruan the Second, Ruan the Fifth and Ruan the Seventh to take the fifth, sixth, seventh and eighth places respectively. Du Qian then accepted the ninth chair, Song Wan the tenth and Zhu Gui the eleventh.

From then on, the positions of the eleven heroes were fixed in Liangshan Marsh. The nearly eight hundred men guarding the mountain front and rear all came and paid their respects, then stood on either side. Chao Gai addressed them.

"Today, Arms Instructor Lin has made me leader of this stronghold and Teacher Wu the military advisor. Master Gongsun also controls military authority. Arms Instructor Lin and the others have over-all charge of the fortress. You lieutenants retain your original commands. Observe your daily duties and guard the palisades and the beaches. Let no mishaps occur. We must all be united in mind and virtue."

He directed that the houses on both sides of the hall be put in order for the two families which had come with them, and ordered that the purloined birthday gifts — the gold and silver and jewels — as well as the valuables he had taken with him from the manor, be brought forth. From these he distributed largesse to the lieutenants and the rank and file brigands.

Oxen and horses were slaughtered as a sacrifice to the gods of Heaven and Earth, and in celebration of the reorganization. The leaders ate and drank far into the night. They feasted in this manner for several days. Then Chao Gai, Wu Yong and the other chieftains checked the granaries, had the fortifications repaired and more weapons made — lances, halberds, bows, arrows, armor and helmets — readied boats large and small, trained their soldiers and boatmen to board vessels and fight, and prepared in general to meet any enemy attack.

CHAPTER 9
Song Jiang Slays Poxi in Fit of Anger

A new prefect was appointed.

After taking office, he sent for the new garrison commander and they discussed a campaign against the mountain stronghold. They would replenish their troops, buy more horses, store fodder and grain, recruit men who were clever and bold. The prefect wrote to the Council of Administration, requesting that neighboring prefectures be directed to give all possible aid. At the same time he issued an order to the counties under him to join in the hunt and keep a close watch on their borders. No more of that need be said.

When the prefectural order was received in Yuncheng, the magistrate directed his clerk Song Jiang to relay the instructions to the county's subordinate townships. Song read the document and was shocked.

"I never dreamed Chao Gai and the others would go so far," he said to himself. "They've robbed the birthday gifts, killed policemen, injured Inspector Ho Tao, annihilated many soldiers and horses, and are holding Huang An in their fortress! For such crimes whole families and relatives to the ninth degree of consanguinity can be executed. They may have been forced into it, but the facts stand. Legally, they have no excuse. If anything should go wrong, they'll be in a terrible fix."

He brooded for a time, then told his assistant Zhang Wenyuan to draw up instructions and make the prefectural order known to the various townships and villages.

Song Jiang left the office. Before he had gone thirty paces, a voice hailed him from behind: "Clerk Song!"

He turned around. There was Mistress Wang, the match-maker, with another woman. "You're in luck," she said to her companion. "This is our charitable clerk."

"What did you want to see me about?" asked Song.

Mistress Wang blocked his way. She pointed at the other woman. "Her family is from the Eastern Capital, they're not local people. Just three of them — her husband Old Yan, her daughter Poxi, and herself. Old Yan used to be a singer, and he taught Poxi many ballads. She's only eighteen, quite pretty, too. They came here to Shandong to join the household of an official they knew, but they couldn't find him. They drifted around and ended up in Yuncheng. But people here don't care much for music and entertainment, and they haven't been able to make a living. They have a flat in a quiet lane behind the magistracy. Yesterday, Old Yan fell ill of the epidemic and died, but his wife has no money to bury him. She doesn't know what to do, and she's asked me to find a man to keep Poxi. 'Where can I find anybody who would be so good at a time like this?' I said. I didn't know where to borrow money for her, either. It looked hopeless. Then I saw you, and I hurried after you with Mistress Yan. Have pity on her. Help her buy a coffin."

"So that's it," said Song Jiang. "You two come with me. I'll borrow a pen and ink at that tavern at the end of the lane and write a note to the coffin shop in the east part of town." And he asked: "Have you living expenses?"

"We can't even afford a coffin," said Mistress Yan. "Where would we find living expenses?"

"Then I'll give you ten ounces of silver."

"You are my parents reborn! I'd gladly serve as a donkey or a horse to repay you!"

"No need to talk like that." Song Jiang gave the widow a silver ingot and departed.

She took the note to the coffin shop, selected a casket, returned home and arranged for the funeral. When it was over, she still had five or six ounces of silver left, which she and her daughter kept for their living expenses. Of that we'll say no more.

One day, Mistress Yan came to thank Song Jiang, and she observed that he had no woman in the house. Later, she asked her neighbor, Mistress Wang, about it.

"Doesn't he have a wife?"

"I know his home is in Song Family Village, but I've never heard any mention of a wife. He works here as county clerk and has only temporary quarters. He's always handing out money for coffins and medicines, and helping people in distress. I doubt if he's married."

"My daughter is a good-looking girl. She can sing and knows all sorts of amusing games. When she was little and we lived in the Eastern Capital she used to wander around the brothels. All the managers thought she was adorable. One or two famous courtesans several times offered to buy her. But I wouldn't agree, because there was only my husband and myself at home and no son to support us in our old age. I never thought Poxi would suffer as a result. When I went to thank Clerk Song the other day I noticed he had no wife around. I wish you'd tell him for me — if he wants a woman, I'll be glad to give him Poxi. He was very charitable to me, with your help. I have no other way to thank him, but this much I can do."

The next day, Mistress Wang went to Song Jiang and broached the subject. At first he refused. But he was no match for the marriage broker's eloquence, and finally he consented. He took a house in the western part of town, bought some furnishings, and installed Poxi and her mother. In less than half a month, Poxi was draped in silks and her hair was studded with precious ornaments. Not long after, even Mistress Yan had a certain amount of finery. Poxi was living in luxury.

In the beginning, Song Jiang slept with her every night. But gradually he came to the house less frequently. Why? Well, Song Jiang was a chivalrous man whose main interest was skill with weapons. Sex had only a moderate appeal. Poxi was a frivolous girl of eighteen or so, in the bloom of youth. She was quite dissatisfied with Song Jiang.

One day he brought his assistant Zhang Wenyuan over to have some wine. Zhang was a handsome young fellow, with dark brows, fine eyes, white teeth and ruby lips. Fond of the houses of pleasures, he was something of a gadabout, and had learned all the romantic mannerisms. Besides which he was an accomplished musician and could play all the stringed instruments and woodwinds.

Poxi, an entertainer who loved to drink and frolic, was attracted to Zhang the moment she laid eyes on him. She kept giving him emotion-laden glances. Zhang, an enthusiastic drinker and ladies' man, of course understood the girl's suggestive signals. Afterwards, he called when Song Jiang was not at home, pretending to be looking for him. Poxi asked him to stay to tea. They talked of this and that, and suddenly they were lovers.

Who could have expected that from then on the two would burn so hotly that Poxi was left without a particle of affection for Song. She spoke harshly to him whenever he called and never sought to dally with him. Song was a soldierly man who cared little for women. So his visits dwindled to once every ten days or half month.

The lovers stuck together like glue. Zhang came every night and left with the dawn. All the neighbors knew about it, and word finally reached Song's ears. He only half believed the report.

"Anyhow," he thought, "she's not a real wife formally chosen by my father and mother. If she's lost interest in me, what do I care? I'll just stop going." More than a month went by and he did not call. Mistress Yan sent an invitation, but he wouldn't go. He claimed he was too busy.

To speak of another matter, on leaving the magistracy one day towards evening, Song Jiang went into the shop across the street and sat down to have some tea. A big fellow, dripping sweat and breathing hard as he walked, was gazing at the magistrate's office. He was wearing a broad-brimmed white felt hat and a silken gown of dark green, with leggings and knee-guards and sandals of hemp, a sword at his waist and a large pack on his back.

The man was clearly hesitant about something. Song Jiang got up and followed. The man had gone about thirty paces when he turned around and stared at Song Jiang. He showed no signs of recognition, but to Song he looked familiar.

"Now where have I seen that fellow before?" he mused. For the moment he couldn't recall.

A gleam of recognition came into the man's eye. He stopped and looked at the clerk, but didn't have the courage to speak.

"What's the matter with the fellow? Why is he staring at me like that?" thought Song Jiang. He too couldn't bring himself to ask.

The man went into a barber shop. "Can you tell me the name of that official outside, brother?" he queried.

"That's Clerk Song Jiang," the barber replied.

Halberd formally in hand, the man approached Song Jiang and hailed him respectfully. "Don't you remember me, sir Clerk?"

"You look very familiar."

"Let's walk a bit, and talk."

Song Jiang led him into a quiet lane.

"That tavern might be better," the man suggested.

The two entered the tavern and went upstairs and sat down in a secluded room. The man rested his halberd, removed his pack and placed it under the table. Then he dropped to his knees and kowtowed.

Song Jiang hastily returned the courtesy. "May I ask your name, sir?" he said.

"Benefactor," the man replied, "how could you have forgotten your younger brother?"

"Who are you? You really do look familiar, but I don't remember."

"I'm Liu Tang, known as the Red-Haired Demon. I had

the honor of meeting you in Ward Chief Chao's manor. You saved our lives."

Song Jiang was startled. "Brother," he cried, "you're very rash. It's lucky no policeman has seen you, or you might be in serious danger!"

"Even if it meant my life, I had to thank you!"

"How are Ward Chief Chao and the others? Who sent you here?"

"Brother Chao is very grateful to you for saving his life. He feels he must express his thanks. He's now the highest leader of our stronghold on Mount Liangshan. Wu Yong is military adviser of our army. Gongsun Sheng also controls military affairs. Lin Chong gave us full support, and destroyed Wang Lun. He, and the three who were originally there — Du Qian, Song Wan and Zhu Gui — plus us seven make a total of eleven leaders. We have a force of nearly eight hundred men, and grain without measure. There is no way we can repay you for your great benevolence, but I have been sent with a letter and a hundred ounces of gold as a token of our thanks to you and Constable Zhu Tong."

Liu Tang opened his pack, produced a letter and gave it to Song Jiang. The clerk read it, then drew a pouch from inside his gown. Liu Tang also took a bundle of gold from the pack and placed it on the table. Song chose only a single gold bar, wrapped it in the letter and put both in the pouch, which he again concealed beneath his gown.

"Cover the gold up, brother," he said. He called a waiter to bring wine, a platter of beef, some vegetable dishes and fruit, and to pour the wine for his guest.

Day was drawing to a close when Liu Tang finished drinking. The waiter went out. Liu Tang again opened the bundle of gold on the table. Song Jiang stopped him.

"Listen to me, brother. You seven have just gone to the mountain stronghold. It's a time when you can use money. I have a family income I get along on. Keep the rest of this gold for me in the fortress. I'll come for it when I need it. You see I'm not refusing — I've taken one bar. Zhu Tong also has family property. You don't have to give him anything. I'll tell him of your good intentions and that will be enough. I won't ask you to stay the night, brother. If you were recognized it would be no joke. Tonight there will be a bright moon and you'll be able to get back to the stronghold. Don't hang around here. Give my best regards to the leaders and say I hope they'll forgive me for not coming to congratulate them in person."

"We shall never be able to repay you, brother, for your enormous kindness, but I have been sent specially with this small token of our appreciation. Ward Chief Chao is our chieftain and Wu Yong is our military adviser. They have ordered me to deliver the gold. How can I take it back? I'll definitely be reprimanded."

"Since your discipline is so strict, I'll write a letter, explaining, which you can give them."

No matter how Liu Tang pleaded, Song Jiang remained unyielding. He had the waiter bring pen and paper, wrote a detailed letter and made Liu Tang place it in his pack. Liu Tang was a straightforward fellow. When he saw that Song Jiang was determined not to accept the gold, he wrapped it up and put it away.

It was getting late. "Since you have a reply, brother," said Liu Tang, "I'll deliver it tonight."

"If I don't keep you, you understand why."

Liu Tang bowed four times. Song Jiang summoned the waiter.

"This gentleman is leaving an ounce of silver. I'll drop in tomorrow to settle accounts."

Liu Tang shouldered his pack, picked up his halberd and followed Song Jiang down the stairs. They walked together from the tavern to the end of the lane. Dusk had fallen and a full moon rode in the sky. Song grasped Liu Tang's hand.

"Be careful, brother. Don't come here again. There are too many police. It's dangerous. I won't see you off any further. We'll say goodbye here."

Liu Tang strode away in the moonlight, heading west. That same night he returned to Liangshan Marsh.

As Song Jiang walked slowly back to his quarters, he thought: "How fortunate that none of the police spotted him! That really would have put the fat in the fire!" Then he mused: "So Chao Gai has turned brigand. And he's doing things in a big way!"

He had made only a couple of turns through the streets when a voice hailed him from behind.

"Where've you been, sir Clerk? I've been looking all over for you."

He looked around, and started in surprise. It was Mistress Yan who hailed him.

She hurried to catch up. "I sent someone with an invitation a long time ago, but you're so important it's hard to get hold of you," she said. "If my baggage of a daughter has said anything to offend you, forgive her for my sake. I've reprimanded the girl, and told her she must apologize. I'm in luck tonight, running into you. We can go back together."

"I'm busy at the magistrate's office. I can't get away. I'll come another time."

"Nothing doing. The girl is at home longing for you. Comfort her a bit. Why must you be this way?"

"I'm really busy. I'll come tomorrow, for sure."

"No, tonight." She pulled him by the sleeve. "Who's provoking you against her? We're dependent on you for the rest of our lives. Whoever is telling you stories, don't believe him. Make up your own mind. If my daughter has done anything wrong, I'm the one to blame. Please come with me."

"Stop insisting. I'm busy and can't get away."

"The magistrate won't punish you if you put your work off a little while. I'm not likely to run into you again. You must come. I've things to tell you when we get home."

Song Jiang was an impetuous fellow, and the old woman clung to him tenaciously. "Let go of my arm," he said. "I'll go."

"Don't run away. An old woman like me could never keep up with you."

"What would I do that for!"

They continued on, side by side. At the door, Song Jiang halted. Mistress Yan pulled him by the hand.

"You've come this far. Why not go in?"

Song Jiang entered and sat down on a bench. The sly old woman, afraid that he would try to escape, sat down beside him.

"Daughter," she called, "your beloved is here."

Poxi was lying on her bed, staring at the lamp and thinking of nothing in particular. She was hoping that Zhang would come. When she heard her mother say: "Your beloved is here," she thought it was the young rake. She got up quickly and fixed her hair.

"That rogue," she muttered. "He made me wait long enough. I'll box his ears!"

She flew down the stairs and peeked through the lattice wall. The glass lamp in the parlor brightly illuminated the figure of Song Jiang. Poxi promptly turned, went back up the stairs and threw herself down on her bed.

Mistress Yan heard her daughter's footsteps come down and then go up again. "Your lover is here, daughter," she shouted. "Why have you gone away?"

From her bed, Poxi replied: "This room isn't so far that he can't reach it! He's not blind! Why doesn't he come up here instead of waiting for me to come down and greet him? Don't gabble so!"

"She's bitter that you stayed away so long," Mistress Yan explained to Song Jiang. "That's why she talks like that." The old woman laughed. "I'll go with you."

Song Jiang felt uncomfortable and awkward. But Mistress Yan was insistent, and he went with her up the stairs.

The girl's room was fairly large. In the outer half was a dressing-table and bench. The inner half contained on one side a carved bed with railings at head and foot and hung with a red silk canopy. There was a clothing rack and a towel at one end of the bed. At the other was a wash-basin. A pewter lampstand rested on gold lacquered table, which was flanked by two matching stools. In the center of the middle wall was a painting of a beautiful girl. Four wooden armchairs stood in a row along the wall opposite the bed.

Mistress Yan pulled Song Jiang into the room, and he sat down on one of the stools near the bed. The old woman went over and pulled her daughter up.

"Sir Clerk is here. He's been staying away because you've offended him. You have a rotten temper, but you think of him often. It hasn't been easy for me to get him to come. Yet instead of getting up and apologizing, you sulk!"

Poxi pushed her hands away. "What are you making such a fuss about? I haven't done anything wrong. If he never comes how can I apologize?"

Song Jiang listened but did not speak. The old woman pulled a chair over beside him and pushed the girl down on it.

"You sit here with him. If you won't apologize, at least behave yourself."

But Poxi refused to sit by Song Jiang. She took a chair opposite. The clerk kept his gaze lowered and remained silent. Poxi averted her face.

" 'Without wine and soysauce how can you lay a feast?' " quipped Mistress Yan. "I've got some good wine. Now all we need is some food and we'll be able to express our apologies. Daughter, keep sir Clerk company. Don't be embarrassed. I'll be right back."

"That old woman has me nailed down tight," thought Song Jiang. "When she goes downstairs, I'll leave!"

But Mistress Yan guessed what he was planning, and bolted the bedroom door from the outside after her.

"The old bawd's out-foxed me," Song Jiang said to himself.

Mistress Yan went downstairs, lit the lamp by the stove, saw that the water was hot, and added a few sticks of wood. She took some change and, at the end of the lane, bought fruit, fresh fish, a tender chicken, and pickled fish. These she brought

home, and put them on plates. After pouring the wine into a
jug, she ladled some into a kettle and heated it on the stove.
She poured the warm spirits into a wine pot. Then she cooked
a few dishes and carried these, along with three cups and three
sets of chopsticks, on a tray upstairs.

She set the tray on the dressing table, opened the bedroom
door, entered, and placed the food and drink on the table of
gold lacquer.

Song Jiang still sat with his head down, Poxi with her face
turned.

"Daughter, pour the wine."

"You two drink. I don't feel like it."

"Your father and I spoiled you since childhood. But you
shouldn't act like this in front of others."

"What if I don't pour the wine? Will his sword come flying
and cut off my head?"

The old woman laughed. "It's all my fault. Sir Clerk is
a gentleman. He won't take umbrage at the likes of you. If
you won't pour the wine at least turn around and drink with
us."

But the girl wouldn't look at Song Jiang, and Mistress Yan
had to toast him herself. He reluctantly drank a cup.

"Don't blame her," the old woman urged with a smile. "I
know there are a lot of rumors. I'll explain everything tomorrow. Some people are envious of you. It burns them up to
see you here. They'll say anything that comes into their heads.
Just empty farts! Don't listen to them. Now, let's drink."

She filled the three cups and said to her daughter: "Quit
acting like a child. Have some wine."

"Leave me alone! I'm full. I couldn't touch another thing."

"Come now, daughter. Drink with your beloved."

Poxi said to herself: "I've given my heart to Zhang. Who
wants to stay with this lout! But if I don't get him drunk I
suppose he'll be wanting things from me." She forced herself
to down half a cup.

Mistress Yan laughed. "My girl is upset. Relax, have a few
drinks and go to bed. Sir Clerk, drink your fill."

Song Jiang couldn't resist her urgings. He drained four or five cups in a row. The old woman also had quite a few. She went downstairs to heat some more wine. She had been annoyed when her daughter refused to drink. Now that the girl had changed her mind she felt much better.

"If we can inveigle him into staying tonight," she thought, "he'll get over being angry. The thing is to hang onto him for a while longer, then we'll see."

By the stove, she drank another three cups. This only increased her craving, and she filled a bowl and downed that, too. Mistress Yan then poured half a kettle of heated wine into the pot and crawled back up the stairs. She found Song Jiang sitting in silence, with lowered gaze. Poxi, her head turned away, was toying with her skirt. The old woman laughed.

"You two aren't made of clay. Why don't you speak? Be a man, sir Clerk. All you have to do is show a little tenderness and whisper a few sweet nothings."

Song Jiang didn't know what to do. He said not a word. To stay or go, both seemed wrong.

"You never come to see me," Poxi thought, "and now you expect me to talk and play around with you as usual. Not a chance!"

Mistress Yan had drunk a lot of wine and she babbled all kinds of nonsense. Gossiping about this one, slandering that, she talked a blue streak.

While this was going on, Tang the Ox went looking for Song Jiang. Tang was a pedlar of pickled meats and vegetables who also managed to do some of hustling on the streets of the county town. Song Jiang often helped him financially. Whenever Tang picked up a bit of useful information about court cases and litigants he let Song Jiang know, and the clerk gave him some money. And so, if Song Jiang ever had need of him, Tang went all out.

On this particular evening Tang had lost at gambling, and he went to the county office to put the touch on Song Jiang. But the clerk was nowhere to be seen.

"Who are you looking for in such great haste, brother?" asked one of Song's neighbors.

"What a thirst I've got. I'm looking for my patron, but he's not around."

"Who is your patron?"

"Clerk of the county court, Song Jiang."

"I saw him going off with Mistress Yan not long ago."

"That daughter of hers is a dirty tramp. She and young Zhang are really hot for each other. The girl's cheating on Song Jiang. He probably got wind of it and stopped going there. Today, the old bawd must have tricked him into paying a visit. I've got no money and my throat is dry. I'll just drop by and borrow enough for a few bowls of wine."

Tang headed for Mistress Yan's house. A lamp was burning and the door was not locked. As he reached the foot of the stairs he heard the old woman laughing wildly in the room above.

He tiptoed up the stairs and peered through a crack in the wall. Song Jiang and Poxi both were gazing downward. The old woman was sitting at the head of the table, jabbering twelve to the dozen. Tang stepped in and greeted each of them courteously. He remained standing near the entry.

"Just in time!" thought Song Jiang. He gestured with pursed lips.

Tang was a clever fellow. He got the signal. "I've been looking all over for you," he said to Song. "And you've been here drinking, snug and peaceful, right along!"

"Has something important happened at the county office?"

"You've forgotten, sir Clerk. It's about that matter that came up this morning. The magistrate is having fits in his chambers. He's sent four or five court attendants looking for you. His Worship is raising the roof. You'd better get going!"

"If it's that important, I suppose I must." Song Jiang stood up and headed for the stairs. Mistress Yan stopped him.

"Don't pretend, sir Clerk. I know he's putting on an act." She whirled to face Tang the Ox. "Tricky rogue! Think you can fool me? You've as much chance as taking the adze from Lu Ban the Great Carpenter! At this hour the magistrate is home drinking and merry-making with his wife. What official business would he bother about tonight? You can't diddle me with your phony stories!"

"The magistrate is really waiting for him. It's very urgent. I wouldn't lie!"

"Dog farts! These old eyes are crystal clear. You saw the clerk signal with his mouth to invent a tale. Instead of encouraging him to stay, you try to lure him away! 'Killing can be forgiven, but never deception,' as the old saying goes."

Mistress Yan jumped up, grabbed Tang by the neck with both hands, and rushed him stumbling down the stairs.

"Get your hands off my neck," Tang yelled.

"You're ruining our business, cutting off our food and clothing! That's as bad as killing a man's parents or his wife! Make any more noise and I'll clobber you, you thieving beggar!"

Tang stepped up to her. "Let's see you hit me!"

Filled with the courage of wine, Mistress Yan slapped Tang so hard he staggered out backwards, taking the bamboo door curtain with him. The old woman, swearing a blue streak, rolled up the curtain, put it inside, closed the double doors and bolted them firmly.

Tang the Ox bawled from the yard: "Dirty whore-monger, if it weren't for Clerk Song I'd smash your house to smithereens! You just wait. If I don't get you on an odd day, I'll get you on an even!" Cursing, he pounded his chest. "If I don't kill you my name isn't Tang!"

Mistress Yan went back up the stairs. "You shouldn't pay any attention to that beggar," she said to Song Jiang. "He came to cadge the price of a couple of drinks. All he does is stir up trouble. A stinking wretch who'll die in the streets dares to come to my door with his quackery!"

Song Jiang was an honest fellow. Now that the old woman had seen through his attempt, he couldn't bring himself to leave.

"Don't hold this against me, sir Clerk. We know how good you are to us. Daughter, drink this cup with sir Clerk. You two haven't seen each other for a long time. I can imagine how eager you are to get to bed. I'll just straighten up a bit in here and go."

She had two more cups with Song Jiang, collected the bowls and dishes, and went downstairs to the kitchen.

"I've heard that this girl and Zhang are hitting it off," the clerk said to himself, "but I'm not sure. There's nothing I've seen with my own eyes. If I go now she'll think I'm a rube. Besides, it's late and I want to sleep. I may as well find out how this girl really feels about me."

The old woman came up the stairs again and called: "It's late. Go to bed, you two."

"Mind your business," snapped Poxi. "Go to bed yourself!"

Mistress Yan laughed and went downstairs, saying: "Rest well, sir Clerk. Enjoy yourself. Take your time getting up in the morning."

She put the kitchen in order, washed her feet, blew out the lamp, and retired.

Song Jiang, sitting on the stool, glanced at the girl and sighed. It was already the second watch. Poxi lay down on the bed, fully clothed. She rested her head on her embroidered pillow, and rolled over facing the wall.

"The trollop goes to sleep without even looking at me," Song Jiang thought irritably. "Her mother wangled me into coming here and plied me with wine. I can't keep my eyes open. It's late. I'd better get some rest."

He removed his head kerchief and put it on the table, took off his tunic and hung it on the clothes rack. The sash around his waist, with its attached dagger and pouch, he draped over the bed rail. Then he pulled off his silk shoes and white socks and lay down with his head towards the girl's feet.

Half a watch later, he heard her snicker. Song Jiang was furious. How could he sleep? " 'Joy regrets night's swift race. Misery hates its leaden pace,' " he thought.

By the time the third watch had gone and the fourth begun, he was completely sober. At the fifth watch he got up, washed his face in the basin with cold water, dressed, tied his kerchief on his head. "Unmannerly slut," he muttered.

Poxi heard him. She hadn't slept either. She turned around.

"You ought to be ashamed!" she retorted.

Swallowing his rage, Song descended the stairs.

Mistress Yan heard his footsteps and called from her bed: "Sleep a little longer, sir Clerk. Wait until daylight before you go. There's no reason to get up at the fifth watch."

Song Jiang did not reply. He unbolted the door.

"If you must go, sir Clerk," said the old woman, "pull the door closed behind you."

Song Jiang did so. Still smoldering, he set out quickly for his quarters. As he was passing the magistracy, he saw down the street a small lampglow. Grandpa Wang, the medicinal broth seller, was coming to the square in front of the county office to catch the morning market.

The old man hailed him. "What are you doing up so early, sir Clerk?"

"I had too much to drink last night. Just now when I awoke I counted the beat of the watch drum wrong."

"The wine surely upset your stomach. I've just the soup for that. Let me give you a bowl."

"All right," said Song Jiang. He sat down on a bench. The old man filled a bowl with thick broth and handed it to him.

As he was sipping it, Song Jiang thought: "I often drink his soups, and he never asks me to pay. Though I promised to buy him a coffin, I still haven't done it."

He remembered the gold Chao Gai had sent and the bar he had selected and put in his pouch. "I'll give him the money now. That will make him happy," he thought.

"Grandpa, I haven't given you the money yet I promised you for your coffin," he said. "I have some gold here which you can have. Buy yourself a coffin and keep it in your home. When you reach a hundred and go to your final rest, I'll pay your funeral expenses."

"You're always so good to me, benefactor, and now you give me money for a coffin. There is no way I can thank you in this life, but in my next incarnation I'll serve you as a donkey or a horse!"

"Don't talk like that." Song Jiang pulled up the edge of his over-vest and felt for his pouch. He uttered a groan and thought: "I must have left it on that creature's bed rail last night. I was so angry I could think only of getting out, and forgot to put on my sash. The gold doesn't matter, but it's wrapped in Chao Gai's letter! I was going to burn it when I was with Liu Tang in the tavern, but I was afraid he'd go back and say I treated his mission lightly. I decided to destroy it when I returned to my quarters, but Mistress Yan nabbed me before I could get there. Then last night I thought I'd burn it in the lamp. But I was afraid the girl would see and so I didn't do it. This morning I left in such a hurry I forgot it! I've often noticed Poxi looking at song sheets, which means she can read a bit. If she gets her hands on that letter, it will be very bad!"

He stood up and said: "Forgive me, grandpa. I meant what I said. But the gold is in my pouch, and I left home so quickly this morning I forgot it. I'll get it now."

"Don't bother," said the old man. "Any time will do."

"You don't understand. I left something important with it. I need them both." Song Jiang set out rapidly for Mistress Yan's house.

Meanwhile, after Poxi heard Song leave, she got up. "That oaf kept me awake all night. Frozen face, hoping I'd apologize and be nice to him. I don't want him! Zhang and I get along fine. Who wants to bother with Song Jiang! If he doesn't come around, so much the better!"

She spread the quilt, took off her tunic and skirt, opened her chemise and stepped out of her slip. In the light of lamp by the bedside she saw the sash hanging on the rail. Poxi laughed.

"That black-faced rogue was so drunk he forgot his sash. I'll give it to my Zhang to wear."

As she lifted it, with dagger and pouch attached, the pouch felt unusually heavy. Poxi opened it and spilled its contents on the table. Out came a gold bar and a letter. She picked up the gold bar, gleaming yellow in the lamplight.

"A gift from heaven," she laughed. "My Zhang has been

getting too thin. Now I can buy him some good things to eat."

She put the bar down and opened the letter. She saw Chao Gai's signature, and what he had written.

"Aha!" she said. "I knew that the bucket went to the well, but here we have the well also coming to the bucket. Song Jiang is all that prevents me and Zhang from becoming man and wife. Today I've got him in the palm of my hand. So he's in cahoots with the bandits in Liangshan Marsh, and they've sent him a hundred ounces of gold. I'll fix him!"

She again wrapped the gold bar in the letter and put it in the pouch. "Even with five demons he won't snatch this away!" she said to herself.

Poxi heard the door downstairs squeak open, and the old woman call from her bed: "Who's there?"

"Me," Song Jiang replied.

"I told you it was too early, sir Clerk, but you wouldn't listen. Now you've come back. Go up and sleep with Poxi. Wait until daylight, then leave if you must."

The clerk made no reply, but mounted the stairs. Hearing that it was Song Jiang, the girl hastily rolled the pouch and dagger in the sash, got under the covers with the bundle, turned facing the wall, and pretended to snore.

Song burst into the room and went straight to the rail of the bed. His belongings were gone. The clerk was in a panic. He controlled his anger over the shabby way the girl had treated him all night and shook her by the shoulder.

"For the sake of my kindness to you before, give me back my pouch."

Poxi continued to feign sleep. Song Jiang shook her again.

"Don't be angry. I'll apologize to you later."

"I've been sleeping peacefully here. Who wakes me so rudely?"

"Quit acting. You know very well it's me."

Poxi turned around. "Oh, Black-Face. What are you saying?"

"I want my pouch."

"Did you put it in my hands? Why ask me for it?"

"I left on the rail at the foot of the bed. Nobody else has been here. You must have taken it."

"A demon's run away with your wits!"

"I behaved badly last night. I'll apologize to you later. But you must return my pouch. Quit fooling around."

"Who's fooling? I never took it!"

"You hadn't undressed before, or covered yourself with the quilt. You must have taken it when you got up and laid out the bedding."

Poxi's lovely brows rose and her starry eyes widened. "Yes, I took it, and I'm not going to give it back. Now have me arrested as a thief!"

"I didn't say you stole it."

"I'm not a thief, I'll have you know!"

Song Jiang's panic was growing. "I've treated you and your mother well. Give it back to me! I've things to do!"

"Always mumbling that I was carrying on with Zhang. He's not your equal in some ways, but at least he isn't a dirty criminal! He doesn't consort with bandits and robbers!"

"My darling sister, keep your voice down! If the neighbors hear, it won't be any joke!"

"If you're afraid people will hear, you shouldn't do such things. I'm going to hold on to that letter! I might return it, but you have to do three things, first."

"I'll do thirty, gladly, to say nothing of three!"

"Maybe you won't agree."

"Anything in my power, I'll do. What do you want from me?"

"First, give back my contract of sale to you, and write another transferring me to Zhang in marriage, with a guarantee that you'll never contest it."

"Agreed."

"Second, all the ornaments in my hair, the clothes on my body, the furnishings in the house, all come from you. Write another promise that you won't ask their return."

"Agreed."

"It's the third thing I'm afraid you'll balk at."

"I've already agreed to two things. Why not a third?"

"I want those hundred ounces of gold Chao Gai sent you from Liangshan Marsh. In exchange, I'll let you off your 'top-magnitude crime', and return your purse and what's in it."

"Your first two demands I've already agreed to. It's true I was sent a hundred ounces of gold, but I refused them, and told the man to take them back. If I still had the gold here I'd gladly present it to you with both hands."

"Fine words! 'Money to an official is like blood to a fly.' They sent you gold and you turned it down? That's a farting lie! Among officials 'What cat doesn't eat meat?' Does the King of Hell let condemned souls go? Who do you think you're kidding? Give me that gold. What does it mean to you? If you're afraid it'll be identified as stolen goods, melt it down first!"

"I'm an honest man, you know that. I wouldn't lie. If you don't believe me, give me three days' time. I'll sell my family belongings and raise the money for you. Let me have my pouch."

The girl laughed coldly. "Tricky, Black-Face, aren't you? Do you think I'm a child? I give you the pouch and letter today, and three days from now you give me gold? Not a chance! With one hand I take the money, with the other I release the goods. Let's have it, quick, and get this over with!"

"I don't have any gold, I tell you!"

"Is that what you're going to say when I accuse you in court this morning!"

At the mention of the word "court", Song Jiang began to burn. He glared at the girl.

"Are you going to give it back or not?"

"Dare I refuse, with you so fierce?" she said sarcastically.

"You really won't give it back?"

"No, a hundred times no! I'll return it to you in the county court!"

Song Jiang grabbed the quilt covering Poxi and yanked it off. She didn't care about her nakedness, but lay huddled with the bundle clutched to her chest. Song recognized the fringe of his sash.

"So that's where it is!"

He seized the bundle with both hands. The girl wouldn't let go. Song hauled for dear life. Poxi clung in a death grip. The clerk gave another hard pull, and the dagger fell out on the mattress. He instinctively pounced on it. The girl looked at the dagger in his hand and screamed.

"Murder! Black-Face wants to kill me!"

It wasn't until then that the idea entered his mind. All his suppressed fury burst forth like a wave. Before Poxi could scream again he pushed her down with his left hand and with his right slit her throat. Fresh blood spurted. Poxi gurgled. Afraid she wouldn't die, Song Jiang slashed with his dagger once more. The girl's head dangled loosely on the pillow.

Song quickly unwound the pouch, extracted the letter and burned it in the lamp flame. He fastened the sash around his waist and went downstairs.

CHAPTER 10
Wu Song Kills a Tiger on Jingyang Ridge

It was late autumn and early winter, Song Jiang and his brother Song Qing moved along briskly. "With whom should we cast in our lot?" they wondered, after covering several stages.

"In the gallant fraternity I have often heard the name Lord Chai, of Henghai County in the prefecture of Cangzhou," Song Qing remarked. "They say he is the direct descendant of the emperors of Later Zhou. Of course, I've never met him. Why don't we put ourselves under his protection? He's chivalrous and generous, they say, and cordially receives all bold fellows and helps men in exile. He's the living incarnation of hospitable Meng Changjun. We ought to join him."

"That's what I've been thinking," Song Jiang responded. "Though we haven't met, he and I have been keeping up a correspondence."

They headed for Cangzhou, crossing mountains and streams, passing county towns and prefectural cities.

After several days the brothers came to the borders of Cangzhou. They asked directions to Lord Chai's manor and, when they arrived there, addressed one of his vassals.

"Is Lord Chai at home?"

"No. He's gone to the eastern manor to collect grain rents."

"How far is it from here?" asked Song Jiang.

"Over forty *li*."

"How do we get there?"

"May I presume to ask your names, sirs?"

"I am Song Jiang, from Yuncheng County."

"Not Clerk Song, known as Timely Rain?"

"The same."

"Lord Chai speaks of you often, and says how sorry he is that you and he have never met. I'll be glad to show you the way."

The vassal led Song Jiang and his brother to the eastern manor. They reached it in less than three watches.

"If you two gentlemen will wait in this pavilion," said the vassal, "I will inform the lord that you are here."

"Good," said Song Jiang.

He and Song Qing entered the mountainside pavilion, rested their halberds, removed their swords and packs, and sat down.

Not long after the vassal departed, the central gate of the manor opened and Lord Chai came running out, followed by four or five attendants. He rushed up to the pavilion and dropped to his kness before Song Jiang.

"If you knew how I've been thinking of you! What heavenly wind brings you here? Nothing in my life have I wanted more. What wonderful luck!"

Song Jiang also fell on his knees and kowtowed. "Though only a distant petty functionary, I've come especially to see you!"

Lord Chai raised him up. "The lamp wick flowered last night, and this morning a magpie called. I didn't realize these were portents of your visit, brother!" His face was wreathed in smiles.

Song Jiang was delighted with the warmth of his reception. He introduced his brother.

"Take Clerk Song's luggage," Lord Chai instructed his servants. "They'll be staying in the west room of the rear hall." He led Song Jiang by the hand into the main hall, where they seated themselves as host and guests.

"If you don't mind my asking, brother," said Lord Chai, "how were you able to find time from your duties in Yuncheng County to come to our insignificant village?"

"For a long time your fame has thundered in my ears, my Lord. Although I received letters from you frequently I never could pay my respects in person because unfortunately my humble office always kept me busy. I'm a man of no talent, and I've done a stupid thing, and now my brother and I must find refuge. We recalled your chivalry and generosity, and we've come here hoping to join you."

Lord Chai smiled. "Don't worry, brother. Even if you committed the gravest crime you'd be safe here. I'm not boasting, but there isn't a police chief or army officer who dares cock an eye at our little manor."

Song Jiang gave a complete account of how he killed Yan Poxi. Again Lord Chai smiled.

"Forget it. Even if you killed an official appointed by the imperial court or robbed the government treasury, I'd have no compunctions about concealing you here."

He invited the two brothers to bathe, and presented them with fresh clothing, kerchiefs, silken shoes and clean stockings. They bathed, put on their new garments, and a vassal brought their original clothes to their room. Lord Chai invited them to the rear hall where wine and tidbits had been prepared.

Their host asked Song Jiang to sit at the head of the table, while he seated himself opposite. Song Qing sat down at the side. A dozen or so ranking vassals and several overseers were also present. By turns they toasted the guests and waited on them, joining in the merriment. Lord Chai repeatedly urged the brothers to drink without restraint. Song Jiang thanked him again and again. By the time they had drunk half their fill, the three were expressing the highest mutual regard and admiration.

Day was drawing to a close, and lamps were lit. "Enough of wine," Song Jiang begged. But Lord Chai wouldn't hear of it. They continued drinking until the first watch. Song Jiang rose to relieve himself. His host directed a vassal to light his way with a lantern to the end of the eastern veranda.

"I'll have to miss the next round," said the clerk. He made a wide detour and came out of the front porch, crossed the courtyard diagonally and mounted the veranda running along the eastern wing.

Song Jiang was eight-tenths drunk, and he staggered along, not looking where he walked. A big fellow, chilled by a malarial attack, was on the veranda huddled over some burning embers on a shovel. Song Jiang, head high, stepped on the handle and bounced the embers into the man's face, startling him so that he broke into a sweat. Angrily he rose and grasped Song Jiang by the front of his tunic.

"Who are you, you son of a bitch, that you think you can play games with me!"

Song Jiang was surprised speechless. But the vassal carrying the lantern cried out: "Don't be rude! He's his lordship's most favored guest!"

"Guest, guest, " the man muttered. "I was a guest too, at first, and 'most favored' as well. But Lord Chai listens to the lies of his vassals, and has become distant towards me! How true it is that 'friends don't last forever'!"

He pulled back his fist to hit Song Jiang. The vassal dropped his lantern, rushed forward and intervened. But he couldn't separate the two men. Three more bobbing lanterns came flying in their direction.

"I couldn't find you, sir Clerk," said the voice of Lord Chai, as he quickly approached. "What's all the fuss?"

The vassal explained about the shovel. Lord Chai smiled.

"Do you know this illustrious clerk?" he asked the big fellow.

"Illustrious, my foot! Compared to our Clerk Song of Yun-cheng, he's nothing!"

Lord Chai laughed. "Have you met Clerk Song?"

"We've never met, but the whole gallant fraternity has heard of Song the Timely Rain! He's world famous."

"What's he famous for?"

"It would take too long to tell it all, but he's a real hero. What he starts, he finishes! As soon as I get over this illness, I'm going to join him."

"Would you like to meet him?"

"Who wouldn't!"

"Big fellow, he's as far as a hundred and eighty thousand *li*, and as near as right in front of you!" Lord Chai pointed at

Song Jiang. "This is Song the Timely Rain!"

"You're not joking?"

The clerk said: "My name is Song Jiang."

The big fellow stared, then dropped to his knees and kow-towed. "I never dreamed I'd meet you today, brother!"

"I don't deserve such courtesy."

"But I was just very discourteous. I beg your pardon. I 'have eyes but didn't recognize Mount Taishan'!" The man re-mained kneeling.

Song Jiang hastily raised him to his feet. "What is your honorable name, sir?"

Lord Chai supplied the answer. "He is called Wu Song. He's from Qinghe County, and is the second son in his family. He's been here a year."

"I've heard his name many times in the gallant fraternity. I never thought I'd run into him today. How fortunate!"

"Truly a happy circumstance when men of courage meet," said the lord. "Let's sit inside, shall we, and talk."

Song Jiang, very pleased, walked hand in hand with Wu Song to the rear hall, where the clerk introduced him to his brother. Chai Jin asked Wu Song to be seated. Song Jiang requested him to sit at the head of the table, but Wu Song refused. After some minutes of polite argument, Wu Song took the third seat. Chai Jin called for wine and urged his three guests to drink without restraint.

In the lamplight Song Jiang noted with pleasure what a fine figure of a man Wu Song was, and he asked: "How do you happen to be here?"

"I was drunk one day back in Qinghe County and got into a brawl with the keeper of confidential documents in the local government office. With one blow of my fist I knocked him senseless to the ground. I thought I'd killed him, and ran away and took refuge here in Lord Chai's manor. That was over a year ago. Later I learned that the fellow hadn't died, that he revived. I intended to go home and see my older brother, but then I caught this malaria and wasn't able to leave. I had the chills and was warming myself by a fire when you stepped on the handle of that shovel. You gave me such a start that I broke into a sweat. It seems to have cured my illness!"

Song Jiang and Wu Song were constantly in each other's company for a dozen or more days. But Wu Song was homesick. He wanted to go back to Qinghe County and see his older brother. Chai Jin and Song Jiang urged him not to hurry away. But Wu Song said: "I'm concerned about my brother. I haven't heard from him in a long time."

"If you must go," said Song Jiang, "we won't keep you. Come and see us again, if you have the chance."

Wu Song thanked him. Chai Jin gave the young man some money.

"I have caused you a great deal of trouble, my Lord," said Wu Song.

He wrapped his belongings into a pack, tied on his staff and got ready to leave. Chai Jin gave him a farewell feast. Wu Song was wearing a new red silk robe and a broad-brimmed hat of white felt. He shouldered his pack, took up his staff, and bid his friends goodbye.

Wu Song travelled for several days and came to Yanggu County. It was noon and he was a good distance from the county town, and he was hungry and thirsty from walking. Further up the road he saw a tavern. By the doorway hung a pennant reading: *Three bowls and you can't cross the ridge.*

Wu Song went inside, sat down, and rested his staff. "Wine, quickly, host," he called.

The tavern keeper brought three bowls, a pair of chopsticks and a plate of tidbits, placed them on the table, and filled one of the bowls to the brim with wine. Wu Song raised the bowl and drained it.

"This wine has a kick in it! If you've got anything filling, host, I'll buy some to go with the drinks."

"We only have cooked beef."

"Slice me two or three catties of the best part."

The host went back inside and came out with two catties of

beef on a large platter, which he placed before Wu Song. Then he filled another bowl. Wu Song drank it.

"Very good wine!" he said. And he downed another. That was his third bowl. The host poured no more. Wu Song rapped on the table.

"Host, where's the wine?"

"More beef, sir? Coming right up."

"I want beef and wine, both."

"I'll slice some beef for you, but I can't give you any more wine."

"That's screwy! Why not?"

"Didn't you see that pennant hanging by my door *Three bowls and you can't cross the ridge*?" queried the tavern keeper.

"What does it mean?"

"Although our wine is just a village product, it's as fragrant as the old brews. Any traveller who drinks three bowls of it gets drunk and can't cross that ridge there. Hence, the name. No one who stops here ever asks for more than three bowls."

Wu Song smiled. "So that's it. I've had three bowls. Why aren't I drunk?"

"My wine is called 'Seeps Through the Bottle Fragrance'. It's also called 'Collapse Outside the Door'. You don't feel anything at first. But a little later, down you go."

"Poppycock! I'm paying, aren't I? Pour me three more bowls!"

Seeing that the wine had little effect on Wu Song, the tavern keeper again filled three bowls with wine. The big fellow drank them.

"Excellent," he cried. "Host, I'll pay you bowl for bowl. Just keep pouring."

"You'd better take it easy, sir. This wine really knocks people out! And there's no medicine that brings them around!"

"Bullshit! Even if you doped it, I've got a nose, haven't I!"

The tavern keeper couldn't convince him. Again he filled the three bowls.

"Bring me another two catties of beef," said Wu Song.

The host served the sliced meat and poured three more bowls of wine. Wu Song's appetite seemed to improve. He put some silver on the table.

"Look here," he called. "Is this enough for the wine and meat?"

"Plenty," said the tavern keeper. "In fact I owe you some change."

"I don't want any change. Just keep the wine coming."

"There are five or six bowls left. But I doubt that you can finish them."

"Five, six, or even more, I'll drink as many as you've got."

"You're a big hulking fellow. If you fall, how am I going to pick you up?"

"If you have to pick me up, I'm no real man!"

The host continued to stall. Wu Song grew irritated. "I'm paying for what I drink," he said. "Don't make me mad, or I'll smash up your place and turn it ass over tea kettle!"

"This rogue is drunk," thought the tavern keeper. "I'd better not provoke him!"

He served Wu Song six more bowls of wine, a total of eighteen in all.

Wu Song grasped his staff and rose to his feet. "I'm not a bit drunk!" He laughed as he went out the door. "Who says 'Three bowls and you can't cross the ridge'?" He started walking away.

The tavern keeper ran after him. "Where are you going, sir?" he shouted.

Wu Song halted. "What's it to you? I don't owe you anything, do I? What are you yelling about?"

"I mean well. Come back. I want to show you a government proclamation."

"What does it say?"

"There's a fierce tiger with a white forehead and bulging eyes on Jingyang Ridge. It comes out at night, and has already killed nearly thirty strong men. The authorities have ordered hunters to capture it, on pain of being beaten, and have posted this warning at every path leading to the ridge. It says travellers must go in groups and cross only between late morning and early afternoon. At all other times the ridge is closed. No one is permitted to travel alone. It's already late, and I saw you setting off without a word. I don't want you to kill yourself! Why not spend the night at my place, and then tomorrow you can gradually get together a band of twenty or thirty travellers and cross the ridge in safety."

Wu Song laughed. "I'm a Qinghe County man. I've crossed that ridge at least twenty times. I've never seen any tiger. Don't try to scare me with that crap. Even if there is a tiger, I'm not afraid."

"I'm only trying to save you. If you don't believe me, come in and have a look at the proclamation."

"Balls! I'm not scared of any tiger. You want to keep me here so that in the middle of the night you can rob me, kill me! That's why you're trying to frighten me with your tiger story!"

"All right! You take my good for evil and talk to me like that! Don't believe me, then! On your way!" The tavern keeper shook his head and went back inside.

Staff in hand, Wu Song strode off towards Jingyang Ridge. After walking four or five *li* he came to the foot of it. A piece of bark had been peeled from a large tree, and on the white patch words were written. Wu Song could read quite well, and he saw that it was a notice with this inscription: *Of late a tiger on Jingyang Ridge has been killing people. Travellers must form bands and cross only between late morning and early afternoon. Do not take risks.*

Wu Song grinned. "That host is a crafty one. Scares his customers into staying the night. Well, he can't scare me!"

He proceeded up the slope, holding his staff level. It was late afternoon by then, and the red sun was pressing on the mountains in the west. Still primed by all the wine he had consumed, Wu Song continued climbing the ridge. Before he had gone another half *li* he came upon a dilapidated Mountain Spirit Temple. A notice was posted on the door. It read:

*Yanggu County Notice: Lately, a big tiger has been kill-
ing people on Jingyang Ridge. Although all township
leaders, village chiefs and hunters have been ordered to
capture the beast or be beaten, they have so far failed.
Travellers are permitted to cross the ridge only between
late morning and early afternoon, and only in bands. At
other times, and to single travellers at any time, the ridge
is closed, lest the tiger take their lives. Let this be known
to all.*

So there really was a tiger! The notice with its official seal
confirmed that. Wu Song considered returning to the tavern.
But then he said to himself: "If I do that, the host will laugh
at me for a coward. I can't go back." He thought a moment.
"What's there to be afraid of," he exclaimed. "Just keep
climbing and see what happens."

He walked on. The warmth of the wine rose in him, and
he pushed back the felt hat till it was hanging by the string
on his shoulders. Clapping the staff under one arm, he plodded
up the slope. When he looked back at the sun, it was almost
gone. The days are short in late autumn, and the nights are
long. It gets dark early.

"There isn't any tiger," he said to himself. "People just scare
themselves and don't dare come up the mountain."

The wine was burning inside him as he walked. With his
staff in one hand, he unbuttoned his tunic with the other. His
gait was unsteady now, and he staggered into a thicket. Before him was a large smooth rock. He rested his staff against
it, clambered onto its flat surface, and prepared to sleep.

Suddenly a wild gale blew, and when it passed a roar came
from behind the thicket and out bounded a huge tiger. Its
malevolent upward-slanting eyes gleamed beneath a broad
white forehead.

"*Aiya!*" cried Wu Song. He jumped down, seized his staff,
and slipped behind the rock.

Both hungry and thirsty, the big animal clawed the ground

景陽岡武
松打虎

with its front paws a couple of times, sprang high and came hurtling forward. The wine poured out of Wu Song in a cold sweat. Quicker than it takes to say, he dodged, and the huge beast landed beyond him. Tigers can't see behind them, so as its front paws touched the ground it tried to side-swipe Wu Song with its body. Again he dodged, and the tiger missed. With a thunderous roar that shook the ridge, the animal slashed at Wu Song with its iron tail. Once more he swivelled out of the way.

Now this tiger had three methods for getting its victim — spring, swipe and slash. But none of them had worked, and the beast's spirit diminished by half. Again it roared, and whirled around.

Wu Song raised his staff high in a two-handed grip and swung with all his might. There was a loud crackling, and a large branch, leaves and all, tumbled past his face. In his haste, he had struck an old tree instead of the tiger, snapping the staff in two and leaving him holding only the remaining half.

Lashing itself into a roaring fury, the beast charged. Wu Song leaped back ten paces, and the tiger landed in front of him. He threw away the stump of his staff, seized the animal by the ruff and bore down. The tiger struggled frantically, but Wu Song was exerting all his strength, and wouldn't give an inch. He kicked the beast in the face and eyes, again and again. The tiger roared, its wildly scrabbling claws pushing back two piles of yellow earth and digging a pit before it. Wu Song pressed the animal's muzzle into the pit, weakening it further. Still relentlessly clutching the beast by the ruff with his left hand, Wu Song freed his right, big as an iron mallet, and with all his might began to pound.

After sixty or seventy blows the tiger, blood streaming from eyes, mouth, nose and ears, lay motionless, panting weakly. Wu Song got up and searched around under the pine tree until he found the stump of his broken staff. With this he beat the animal till it breathed no more. Then he tossed the staff aside.

"I'd better drag this dead tiger down the mountain," he thought. He tried to lift the beast, lying in a pool of blood,

but couldn't move it. He was exhausted, the strength gone out
of his hands and feet.

Wu Song sat down on the rock and rested. "It's nearly
dark," he thought. "If another tiger comes I won't be able to
fight it. I'd better get off this ridge first, somehow. Then,
tomorrow morning, I can decide what to do."

He collected his broad-brimmed felt hat from beside the rock,
skirted the thicket, and slowly descended the ridge. Wu Song
had travelled less than half a *li* when two tigers leaped out
of the tall dry grass.

"*Aiya!*" he exclaimed. "I'm a goner!"

But there in the shadows the two tigers suddenly stood upright. He looked closely and saw that they were men with
tiger pelts bound tightly around them. Each held a five-pronged
pitchfork. They stared at Wu Song in amazement.

"Have you eaten a crocodile's heart, or a panther's gall, or
a lion's leg, that you're so full of courage?" they cried. "How
dare you cross the ridge at dusk, alone and weaponless? Are
you a man or a demon?"

"Who are you two?" Wu Song demanded.

"We're local hunters."

"What are you doing on this ridge?"

"Don't you know?" the hunters asked in surprise. "There's
a big tiger up here! It comes out at night and preys on people.
It's killed seven or eight of us hunters alone, and more travellers than we can remember! The county magistrate has ordered
the township and village leaders and us hunters to capture it.
But it's so powerful nobody dares go near it! We've been beaten
time and again because of this, but we still can't catch the beast.
Tonight it's our turn to try. We've got a dozen peasants with
us, and we've laid spring-bows with poisoned arrows all over
the place. We were waiting here in ambush when we saw your
big form moving down the ridge. You scared the life out of
us! Who are you, anyway? Have you seen the tiger?"

"I'm a Qinghe County man. My name's Wu, a second son.
I just met the tiger up there beside a thicket. I punched and
kicked it to death."

The hunters gaped. "You're kidding!"

"Look at the blood on my clothes if you don't believe me."

"How did it happen?"

Wu Song told them the whole story. The two hunters listened, joyous and astonished, then shouted for their peasant band. The men soon crowded round, carrying pitchforks, snare-bows, knives and spears.

"Why weren't they with you?" Wu Song asked the hunters.

"The tiger was too fierce. They didn't dare come up." The hunters repeated Wu Song's story to the peasants. None of them believed it.

"Come along with me, then," said Wu Song, "and see for yourselves."

They had flint and steel and struck a fire, and lit six or seven torches. They went with him up the ridge to where the tiger lay dead in a great heap. Everyone was delighted. A man was sent immediately to report to the village chief and the leading family in charge. Five or six peasants trussed up the tiger and carried it down the ridge slung from a pole.

When the party reached the foot of the ridge seventy or eighty people were already waiting, noisy and animated. They formed a procession, with the dead tiger in front, and Wu Song following on an open litter, and marched to the home of the leading family.

Both the head of the family and the village chief were waiting to welcome him at the entrance to the village. The tiger was placed in front of a hall. Another twenty or thirty men — hunters and the heads of prominent township families — also greeted Wu Song.

"What is your name, young stalwart," they asked, "and where are you from?"

"I'm from the neighboring county of Qinghe. My name is Wu Song, and I'm a second son. On my way home from Cangzhou yesterday afternoon I got drunk in a tavern on the other side of the ridge. I climbed the ridge and met the tiger." He told in detail how he fought the beast with fists and feet.

"Truly, a hero," his listeners cried.

The hunters presented him with game and drank his health. Wu Song was exhausted from his battle with the tiger and wanted to sleep. The head of the leading family ordered his vassals to prepare a guest-room for Wu Song's use. He sent word to the county seat the following morning, and had a special litter built so that the tiger could be delivered there.

Wu Song got up at daybreak, washed and rinsed his mouth. His host and the others brought a cooked sheep and two buckets of wine to the front of the hall to feast him. Wu Song put his clothes on, adjusted his head kerchief, and went out and joined them. Raising their cups, they toasted him.

"That tiger killed countless people, and for that reason the hunters were beaten several times," they said. "But you came, young stalwart, and rid us of that calamity, bringing us luck and making the road safe for travel! We owe everything to you!"

"I have no talents. I was only borrowing from your pre-destined good fortune."

Everyone congratulated Wu Song, and they drank all morning. The tiger was placed upon the litter. Members of the prominent families draped Wu Song with silks and flowers. His luggage was placed in safe-keeping, then everyone marched through the village gate. Emissaries of the magistrate had long since been waiting to escort Wu Song to the Yanggu County office. They greeted him, and ordered four vassals to convey him in an open sedan-chair. Decked with silks and flowers, he followed behind the tiger as the procession advanced on Yanggu County.

When the townspeople heard that a brave young fellow had killed the big tiger on Jingyang Ridge, they all turned out, cheering, and swarmed to the county office. From his sedan-chair, Wu Song looked at the noisy throngs crowding every street and lane. Everyone wanted to see the tiger. The magistrate was waiting in a hall inside the county office compound.

Wu Song descended from the sedan-chair, slung the great beast over his shoulders, walked up to the hall, and placed the tiger in the entrance way. The magistrate gazed at the strapping young man, then at the huge striped animal, and he thought: "No one else could have killed that tiger!"

He summoned Wu Song into the hall. Wu Song hailed him respectfully.

"How were you able to kill the beast?" the magistrate asked.

Wu Song told his story. Everyone listened in stupefaction. The magistrate gave him several cups of wine, and rewarded him with one thousand strings of cash contributed by the prominent families.

"It was only because I was basking in Your Excellency's lucky aura that I was able to kill the tiger. I have no ability of my own," said Wu Song. "How can I accept any reward? I've heard that, because of the tiger, Your Excellency punished the hunters several times. I'd like to give the thousand strings of cash to them."

"If that's how you feel, it's up to you."

Wu Song promptly distributed the money among the hunters. The magistrate, impressed by his generosity and honesty, decided to raise him in rank.

"Although you are from Qinghe, it's very close to our Yanggu County," he said. "I'm thinking of making you a constable here. How about it?"

Wu Song dropped to his knees. "If Your Excellency favors me I'll be grateful all my life!"

The magistrate instructed his clerk to draw up the appropriate documents that very day commissioning Wu Song a constable in the police force. All the heads of the leading families came and congratulated him, and drank with him for four or five consecutive days.

"I wanted to go home to Qinghe and see brother," Wu Song said to himself. "Who would have thought I'd wind up a constable in Yanggu!"

Thereafter, he had the affection of his superiors and was

famed throughout the countryside.

Two or three days later, he was leaving the county office in search of amusement when a voice hailed him from behind.

"You've fallen into luck, Constable Wu! Is that why you don't know me any more?"

Wu Song turned around. "*Aiya*," he exclaimed. "What are you doing here?"

Constable Wu fell to his knees and kowtowed, for it was none other than his brother, Wu the Elder. "I haven't seen you for over a year," said Wu Song. "What are you doing here?"

"You were gone a long time. Why didn't you write? Sometimes I reproached you in my heart, and yet I missed you."

"How is that?"

"When I remembered how you used to get drunk in Qinghe Town, and brawl and be hauled into court, and how I used to suffer, waiting for the judge's decision, with never a moment's peace, I thought of you with reproach. Recently I took a wife, but the men of Qinghe are bold, and they kept trying to take advantage, and I've had no one to protect me. If you were home, which of them would have dared to so much as fart? Things got so bad I had to move here to Yanggu and rent a house. That was when I missed you."

These two were born of the same mother. But Wu Song was tall and handsome and enormously strong. Otherwise, how could he have killed the fierce tiger? Wu the Elder was very short, with an ugly face and a ridiculous head. He was known in Qinghe as Three Inches of Mulberry Bark.

Now, it happened that a wealthy family there had a maidservant by the name of Pan Jinlian. In her early twenties, she was quite pretty, and the master of the house began pestering her. Jinlian, or Golden Lotus, didn't want him, and told his wife. He hated her so much for this that he personally provided her with a dowry and married her off to Wu the Elder, free of charge.

Several of Qinghe's dissolute idlers began visiting Wu's house and behaving provocatively. Since nothing about her husband pleased the girl — he was short and grotesque, and had no flair for merry-making whatever — Golden Lotus was quite ready to take a lover. It got so that dandies hanging around outside the door would say openly in front of the timid, law-abiding Wu: "Imagine that luscious piece of meat landing in a dog's jaws!"

The couple couldn't remain in Qinghe. Wu and Golden Lotus moved to Yanggu Town, and rented a house on Purple Stone Street. Every day, Wu went out and peddled buns. He was doing this in front of the county office when he saw Wu Song.

Now he said: "The other day I heard people talking on the street, all excited, about how some stalwart named Wu had killed a tiger on Jingyang Ridge, and how the county magistrate appointed him constable. I was pretty sure it was you. Today, at last, we've met. I won't bother selling any more buns. I'll take you home."

"Where is your house, brother?"

Wu the Elder pointed. "On Purple Stone Street, up ahead."

Wu Song carried his brother's shoulder-pole and hampers and Wu the Elder led the way. They wound through several lanes until they came to Purple Stone Street. The house was beside a tea-shop.

"Wife, open the door," Wu the Elder shouted.

A bamboo curtain was raised, and a woman appeared. "What are you doing home so early?" she asked.

"Your brother-in-law is here. I want you to meet him." Wu the Elder took his carrying-pole and wares inside, then emerged again and said: "Come in, brother, and meet your sister-in-law."

Wu Song raised the curtain and entered.

Wu the Elder said: "This is my younger brother. And what do you think — he's the one who killed the tiger on Jingyang Ridge and was made a constable!"

Golden Lotus clasped her hands in greeting. "I wish you every good fortune."

"Please be seated, sister-in-law." Wu Song dropped to his knees like a collapsing mountain of gold, like a falling pillar of jade, and kowtowed.

Golden Lotus raised him up. "You embarrass me," she courteously protested.

"My respects, sister-in-law."

"I heard from Mistress Wang, next door, that a hero who had killed a tiger was being welcomed at the county office. I wanted to go and see, but I was delayed and got there too late. And all along it was you, brother-in-law! Please come upstairs and sit a while."

The three mounted the stairs and sat down. Golden Lotus looked at her husband. "I'll keep brother-in-law company. You prepare some food and drink so that we can entertain him."

"Fine," said Wu the Elder. "Sit a while, brother. I'll be back soon." He went downstairs.

Golden Lotus gazed at the handsome figure of Wu Song. "He's so big," she thought. "You'd never know they were born of the same mother. If I could have a man like that I wouldn't have lived in vain! With the one I've got I'm cursed for good! Three Inches of Mulberry Bark — three-tenths man and seven-tenths monster. What filthy luck! Wu Song beats up tigers. He must be very strong. . . . And I hear he's not married. Why not get him to move in? Who would have thought I was fated to meet my love here!"

Her face wreathed in smiles she asked: "How long have you been in town?"

"Ten days or more."

"And where are you staying?"

"For the time being in the county office compound."

"That can't be very convenient."

"I live alone. My needs are simple. I have a soldier orderly."

"A man like that can't do things properly. Why don't you move over here? Anything you want to eat or drink I'll be glad to make for you. Much better than having some dirty orderly do it. Even if it's only clear water, when you drink it in this house you have nothing to worry about."

"That's very kind of you."

"Do you have a wife? I'd like to meet her."

"I've never married."

"How old are you?"

"Twenty-five."

"Three years older than me. Where were you before coming to this town?"

"I lived in Cangzhou for over a year. I thought brother was still in Qinghe. I didn't know he had moved here."

"I can't begin to tell you! That man is too honest. I've seen it ever since I married him. People tried to take advantage. We just couldn't remain in Qinghe, so we moved here. If we had a big strong fellow like you staying with us, no one would dare abuse us."

"Brother has always been well-behaved. He's not a rowdy like me."

"Why turn things upside-down?" the girl smiled. "As the old saying goes: 'There's safety only in a stiff backbone.' I make up my mind fast, and act. I hate the slow dawdling types who never give you a direct answer."

"At least he doesn't get into trouble and worry you."

While they were talking, Wu the Elder returned with the food and wine he had bought and put them in the kitchen. He went to the foot of the stairs and called: "Wife, come down and get things ready."

"Where are your manners?" Golden Lotus retorted. "I can't leave brother-in-law just sitting here."

"Don't bother about me," said Wu Song.

"Get Mistress Wang from next door to do it," the girl said to her husband. "Can't you manage even a simple thing like that!"

Wu the Elder asked Mistress Wang over. When the food was ready he carried it up and put it on the table. Besides fish, meat, fruit and vegetables, there was also heated wine. Wu the Elder placed his wife at the head of the table and Wu Song opposite. He himself sat at the side and poured the wine. Golden Lotus raised her cup.

"Forgive our poor fare," she said to Wu Song. "Please drink this one with me."

"Thank you, sister-in-law. No need to be polite."

Wu the Elder was so busy warming the wine and refilling the cups he had no time for anything else. Golden Lotus was all smiles.

"You haven't touched the fish or meat," she cried. She picked choice morsels and put them on Wu Song's plate.

Wu Song was a straightforward fellow who thought of her only as a sister-in-law. She, from her years as a maidservant, had learned how to please in small ways. Wu the Elder, a timid person, knew little about entertaining guests.

After they had downed several cups, Golden Lotus frankly ran her eyes over the younger man's body. Embarrassed, Wu Song kept his head down and avoided her gaze. They finished a dozen or so cups, and he rose to leave.

"Have a few more first," Wu the Elder pleaded.

"This is quite enough," said Wu Song. "I'll be coming to see you again."

His hosts walked with him down the stairs. "You must move over here," Golden Lotus said. "Otherwise, people will laugh at us. After all, you're our own brother." She turned to her husband, "We'll clean out a room for him and have him move in. We don't want the neighbors criticizing."

"You're right," said Wu the Elder. "Move in with us, brother, and I'll be able to hold up my head."

"If that's what you both want, I'll bring my things over tonight."

"Don't forget," said Golden Lotus. "I'll be waiting."

Wu Song said goodbye, left Purple Stone Street and returned to the county office. The magistrate was holding court. Wu Song made a request.

"I have a brother on Purple Stone Street. I'd like to sleep at his place. I could be here the rest of the time, awaiting orders. But I don't want to move without Your Worship's permission."

"Naturally I won't hamper fraternal devotion. Just make sure you get here every morning."

Wu Song thanked the magistrate and went to pack his belongings — his new clothes and the reward money. He had a soldier carry them to his brother's house. Golden Lotus greeted him with such smiling joy you'd think she'd found a treasure in the middle of the night!

Wu the Elder had a carpenter partition off a room for him downstairs, and put in a bed, a table, two stools and a charcoal brazier. Wu Song arranged his belongings and let the soldier go. After a night's sleep, he rose early the next morning. Golden Lotus got up quickly and brought him water to wash and rinse his mouth with. Wu Song performed his ablutions, tied on his head kerchief and left to sign in at the magistracy.

"Come home early for lunch," his sister-in-law called. "Don't eat any place else."

"I'll be back soon," said Wu Song. He attended all morning to business, then returned to the house.

Golden Lotus had washed her hands and done her nails. She looked very neat and trim. She served the food, and the three of them ate at the same table. After the meal Golden Lotus ceremoniously, with both hands, gave Wu Song a cup of tea.

"I'm too much trouble to you," he said. "I don't feel right about it. I'll get a soldier from the county to help."

"How can you treat us like strangers?" the girl protested. "You're not just anyone, you're our own flesh and blood! With a soldier the kitchen would never be clean. I couldn't stand having that kind of lout around!"

"In that case I'll just have to impose on your kindness."

Enough of idle chatter. After Wu Song moved in, he gave his brother silver to buy tea and tidbits and invite the neighbors. They in turn chipped in and bought gifts for Wu Song. Wu the Elder, then felt constrained to invite them to a meal. All of this is by the way. A few days later Wu Song presented his sister-in-law with a piece of silk of beautiful hue suitable for making clothes. She smiled gaily.

"You shouldn't have done it! But since you already have, I suppose I can't refuse. I'll just have to accept."

From then on Wu Song lived in his brother's house, and Wu the Elder continued to peddle buns on the street. Every morning Wu Song signed in at the magistracy and performed his duties. Whenever he returned home, whether early or late, Golden Lotus had food ready. She served him with obvious pleasure. It rather embarrassed him. She was always dropping subtle hints. But Wu Song was a man of solid virtue, and he paid no attention.

To make a long story short, a little more than a month had gone by, and winter was setting in. The wind blew for days, heavy clouds gathered. Then one morning thick snowflakes began to fall. It was still snowing at the first watch that night.

Wu Song left early the next morning to sign in at the magistracy. By noon he still hadn't returned. Golden Lotus sent her husband out to peddle buns, and asked her next-door neighbor Mistress Wang to buy some wine and meat for her. The girl lit the charcoal brazier in Wu Song's room.

"I'm really going to tempt him, today," she said to herself. "I don't believe he can't be aroused...."

She stood alone by the door curtain watching the snow till she saw him coming through the falling flakes of white jade. She raised the curtain and greeted him with a smile.

"Cold?"

"Thanks for your concern." He entered and removed his wide-brimmed felt hat. She took it from him with both hands.

"Don't trouble," he said. He took it back, shook the snow from it and hung it on the wall. He untied the sash from around his waist, divested himself of his outer tunic of parrot-green silk, went into his room and hung it up to dry.

"I've been waiting for you all morning," the girl said. "Why didn't you come home for lunch?"

"A man in the county office invited me. Just now another fellow suggested we drink. But I wasn't in the mood, and came straight home."

"Oh. Warm yourself by the fire."

"Right." He took off his oiled boots, put on a pair of socks and warm shoes, pulled a stool over beside the fire and sat down.

Golden Lotus bolted the front door, closed the back door, brought in wine and food and tidbits and placed them on the table.

"Where has brother gone that he's not back yet?" Wu Song asked.

"Out selling buns, as he does every day. We can have a few cups of wine, just the two of us."

"Hadn't we better wait for him?"

"Why should we?" The girl picked up the cylindrical container that the wine was heating in.

"Don't bother, sister-in-law," said Wu Song. "I'll do it."

"Thank you," said Golden Lotus. She too pulled a stool over to the brazier and sat down. On the table, which was near the fire, was a tray with wine cups. The girl raised a full one and looked at Wu Song.

"Drink it down."

He took the cup from her and drained it. She refilled it. "It's cold today. You'd better have a double."

"As you say." Wu Song finished this one off, too. He poured a cup and handed it to the girl. She drank it, poured more wine from the heating container and placed it in front of him.

Her swelling bosom slightly exposed, her hair hanging down in a soft cloud, Golden Lotus smiled bewitchingly. "Someone told me you're keeping a girl singer in the east part of town. Is it true?"

"You shouldn't listen to such nonsense. I'm not that kind of person."

"I don't believe you. I'm afraid you say one thing and do another."

"Ask my brother, if you don't believe me."

"What does he know? If he knew about things like that, he wouldn't be a seller of buns. Have another drink."

The girl poured him three or four cups in succession, and had the same number herself. Warmed by a rising, uncontrollable passion, she talked more and more freely. Wu Song understood most of what she said. He kept his eyes down.

Golden Lotus went out to get some more wine. When she came back, Wu Song was poking up the fire in the brazier. Holding the container in one hand, she placed the other on his shoulder and squeezed.

"Is that all the clothing you're wearing in this cold weather?" Annoyed, he said nothing. She took the poker from him. "You don't know how to stir up a fire. I'll show you. The idea is to get it good and hot."

Wu Song was frantic with embarrassment. He didn't reply. But the girl was blinded to his state of mind by the urgency of her desire. She put down the poker, poured a cup of wine, drank a mouthful and offered Wu Song the rest.

"Finish this, if you have any feeling for me."

He snatched the cup and flung its contents on the floor.

"Have you no shame!" he cried. He gave her a push that nearly knocked her off her feet. Wu Song glared.

"I'm an upstanding man with teeth and hair who holds his head high, not some wicked immoral animal! Stop this indecent behavior! If I hear any whispering about you, watch out! My eyes may recognize you as a sister-in-law, but my fists won't! Let's not have any more of this!"

Crimson, the girl pulled her stool away. "I was only joking! Why are you making such a fuss? Have you no respect!"

She removed the cups and plates to the kitchen and left Wu Song fuming in his room.

Early in the afternoon Wu the Elder came home, carrying his shoulder-pole and hampers. He pushed the locked door a few times, and Golden Lotus hurriedly opened it. He set down his equipment and followed her into the kitchen. Her eyes were red from weeping.

"Who did you quarrel with?" he asked.

"It's all your fault for being such a softy! Letting people pick on me!"

"Who would dare?"

"You know very well! That nasty brother of yours! He came back in the big snow and I served him wine. When he saw no one was around, he tried to get fresh!"

"My brother isn't like that. He's always been very well behaved. And keep your voice down! If the neighbors hear, they'll laugh at us!"

Wu the Elder turned away from his wife and went to Wu Song's room. "Brother," he said, "you haven't eaten yet. We'll have something together."

Wu Song didn't reply. He thought for several minutes, then removed his shoes and socks, put on his oiled boots, his outer tunic and broad-brimmed felt hat, fastened his waist sash and headed for the door.

"Where are you going?" Wu the Elder called.

Wu Song silently continued upon his way.

Wu the Elder returned to the kitchen. "He wouldn't talk to me. He just went off down that street to the magistracy," Wu the Elder said to his wife. "What's wrong with him?"

"You dolt," cried Golden Lotus. "Is that so hard to figure out? He's ashamed, he can't face you, so he left! I forbid you to let that knave live in this house ever again!"

"We'll be scoffed at if he moves out."

"Idiot! I suppose we won't be scoffed at if he makes passes at me! Live with him if you like! I'm not that kind of a woman! Just give me an annulment paper and you can have him all to yourself!"

Wu the Elder didn't dare open his mouth.

At that moment Wu Song arrived with a soldier and a carrying-pole. He went into his room, packed his belongings, and left again. Wu the Elder ran after him.

"Brother," he said, "why are you moving?"

"Don't ask. If I spoke, it would only be hanging out the sign-board of just what kind of merchandise you've got in there! Let me go!"

Wu the Elder was stricken dumb. Wu Song departed, while Golden Lotus cursed.

"Good riddance! Everyone thought how nice to have a constable who looked after his brother and sister-in-law. Little did they know what a traitor he was! 'The prettiest papayas are emptiest inside.' There never was a truer word. He's moved, thank Heaven and Earth! Now at least we don't have an enemy right under our noses!"

Her husband couldn't understand her rage. Unhappiness began to gnaw at his heart with nagging persistence.

Thereafter Wu Song maintained quarters in the county office compound. Wu the Elder peddled his buns on the street as usual. He wanted to go and see Wu Song, but his wife issued strict injunctions against "provoking" him, so in the end Wu the Elder abandoned the idea.

CHAPTER 11
For Money Mistress Wang Arranges a Seduction

Time flowed by, and soon the snow was gone. Another ten days or so passed. The county magistrate in the two and half years since he had assumed office had accumulated a large hoard of gold and silver. He wanted to send it to a member of his family in the Eastern Capital to hold for him, using part to buy him a higher post. But he needed an able, trustworthy person to deliver the money, so that it wouldn't be robbed in transit. Suddenly, the magistrate thought of Wu Song.

"The very man. A hero like that would be ideal."

He summoned Wu Song and said: "I have a load of gifts and a letter I want to send to a relative in the Eastern Capital. But I'm afraid there may be trouble on the road and need a hero like you to bring them. Do this for me, and don't be afraid of the difficulty. I'll reward you well when you return."

"Your Excellency has raised me in rank. I can't refuse. If you give me this task, of course I'll go. Besides, I've never been to the Eastern Capital. I'd like to see it. Get the things ready, Your Excellency, and I'll leave tomorrow."

The magistrate was very pleased. He favored Wu Song with three cups of wine. Of that we'll say no more.

Wu Song went to his quarters, took some silver, got a soldier, bought a bottle of wine and food and tidbits, and proceeded to Wu the Elder's house on Purple Stone Street. When the older brother returned from bun selling, he found Wu Song sitting outside his door. He told the soldier to go into the kitchen and prepare the meal.

Golden Lotus still had a yen for Wu Song. She saw him arrive with food and wine, and she thought: "The knave must have me on his mind, so he's come back! I'm too much for him! I'll get the story out of him gradually."

She went upstairs, put on fresh make-up, fixed her hair, and changed into more alluring clothes. She greeted Wu Song at the door.

"Have we offended you in some way? You haven't been here for days! I don't understand it. I told your brother to go to you in the county office and apologize, but he couldn't find you. Now, happily, today you've come! But you shouldn't spend money like this!"

"I've something to say," replied Wu Song. "I've come specially to speak to you both."

"Well, then, come upstairs and sit."

The three mounted the stairs and entered the parlor. At Wu Song's insistence, his brother and sister-in-law sat at the head of the table. He moved a stool over and sat at the side. The soldier brought up the meat and wine and placed it before them. Wu Song urged Wu the Elder and Golden Lotus to drink. She kept giving him coy glances, but he concentrated on his wine.

After five rounds, Wu Song had the soldier fill a pledge cup with wine. Holding it, he faced his brother.

"I've been given a mission to the Eastern Capital by our magistrate. I'm leaving tomorrow. I'll be gone for forty or fifty days, maybe two months. There's something I must say, first. You've always been weak and timid, and people may try to take advantage when I'm not around. If you sell ten trays of buns a day usually, from tomorrow on don't sell more than five. Leave the house late and come back early. Don't drink with anybody. And when you get home, lower the curtain and bolt the door. In that way you'll avoid arguments. If anyone insults you, don't quarrel. I'll take care of him when I come back. Pledge me this, brother, with this cup."

Wu the Elder accepted the cup from Wu Song's hand. "What you say is right, and I agree." He drank the wine.

Wu Song poured a second cup and turned to Golden Lotus.

"Sister-in-law is clever. There's no need for me to say much. My brother is a simple, honest fellow. He needs you to look after him. 'Inner force counts more than outward strength,' as the saying goes. With you running the house properly, he'll have nothing to worry about. As the ancients put it: 'When the fence is strong no dogs get in.' "

A flush crept from the girl's ears till her whole face was suffused. She shook her finger at Wu the Elder.

"You filthy thing! What rumors are you spreading — slandering me? I'm as tough and straightforward as any man! A man can stand on my fist, a horse can trot on my arm! I can show my face proudly anywhere! I'm not one of those wives you need be ashamed of. Ever since I married you, not so much as an ant has dared enter your house! What's this about fences not being strong and dogs getting in? Before you talk wild, you'd better be able to prove it! Every dropped brick or tile must come to earth!"

Wu Song smiled. "Since that's how you feel sister-in-law, that's fine. Just make sure your deeds correspond to your words. I'll remember what you've said. I ask you to drink to it."

Golden Lotus thrust the cup aside and ran out of the room. Halfway down the stairs she shouted: "You're so smart. Haven't you heard 'An elder brother's wife deserves the respect you give a mother'? When I married your brother I never even heard of you. You come here, I hardly know you, and you try acting like a father-in-law! Just my luck to run into all this shit!"

Weeping, she went downstairs, putting on a big show of injured innocence.

The brothers drank several more cups of wine, then Wu Song rose to leave.

"Come back soon," said Wu the Elder. "I want to see you again." There were tears in his eyes. Wu Song saw them.

"Don't go out selling buns, brother," he urged. "Stay home. I'll send you money for your expenses."

Wu the Elder walked down the stairs with him and saw him to the door.

"Don't forget what I've told you, brother," Wu Song said.

He returned to the county office compound with the soldier and prepared for the journey. Early the next morning he tied up his pack and went to see the magistrate. The official's cases were already loaded on a cart. The magistrate selected two strong intelligent soldiers, plus two trusted servants to go with Wu Song, and gave them private instructions. Then all bid farewell to the magistrate. Wu Song buckled on his armor and took his halberd. The five of them, guarding the cart, left Yanggu Town for the Eastern Capital.

Our story now divides in two parts. We'll talk of Wu the Elder. His wife reviled him for four full days after Wu Song departed. Wu the Elder took her abuse in silence, and remembered his brother's words. He sold only half as many buns as before and came home early. No sooner did he rest his carrying-pole than he lowered the bamboo curtain, bolted the front door and sat himself down. Golden Lotus fumed with resentment. She shook her finger at him.

"Wretched imbecile! I've never seen a house where they close the bloody door when the sun is only halfway across the sky. People will jeer that we're warding off demons! You just listen to your brother's dirty mouth. You don't care that others may laugh!"

"Let them laugh, let them say what they like. My brother's advice is good. It will prevent all sorts of trouble."

"Dolt! You're a man. Why can't you make up your own mind instead of listening to someone else?"

Wu the Elder waggled his hand firmly. "I'm going to do what Wu Song said. His words are pure gold."

For another two weeks she rowed with him about his unvarying schedule. But then she became accustomed to it, and when he was due to come home she lowered the bamboo curtain and bolted the door herself. Wu the Elder was relieved. "It's much better this way," he said to himself.

Another two or three days passed, and winter was nearly over. There was more sunlight, the weather was slightly warmer. Golden Lotus, expecting her husband home shortly, went to the door with a forked pole to lower the curtain over the entrance way.

But then something happened. A man was passing by. As the old saying goes: "Without coincidence there would be no story." The pole she was holding slipped and landed right on the man's head. Angrily, he halted and turned around, ready to blast. But when he saw the lissome creature standing there, he promptly cooled down. His rage went sailing off to Java, and he smiled.

The girl clasped her hands and curtsied apologetically. "I was careless and you've been hurt!"

Adjusting his head kerchief, the man bowed. "It doesn't matter. Think nothing of it."

Mistress Wang, the girl's neighbor, observed all this through the screen of her tea-shop door. She laughed. "Who told you to walk so close to the eaves of the house," she called. "Serves you right!"

The man smiled. "It's my own fault. I bumped into the lady. I hope she'll forgive me."

Golden Lotus also smiled. "Then you're not angry?"

Again the man laughed. He gave her a sweeping bow. "I wouldn't dare." His eyes roved over her boldly, then he swaggered off with measured pace.

Golden Lotus let down the curtain, took the pole inside, bolted the door, and waited for Wu the Elder's return.

Do you know who that man was? Where he lived? Originally from one of the wealthier Yanggu families, he had come down in the world and opened a drug and medicine shop in front of the county office. He was smooth and cunning, and skilled with fists and stave. Recently, he had grown quite rich again, acting as a go-between in litigation, making deals, passing money, corrupting officials. The whole county treated him with

careful deference. His family name was Ximen, his given name
Qing. Being a first son, he had been known as Ximen the Elder.
But when he again became wealthy, people called him the Right
Honorable Ximen.

Shortly after his encounter with Golden Lotus, Ximen returned, entered Mistress Wang's tea-shop and sat down by the
screen.

"Right Honorable," grinned Mistress Wang, "that was quite
a bow you gave out there."

Ximen chuckled. "Tell me, godmother, whose woman is
that pullet next door?"

"She's the King of Hell's kid sister, daughter of his commanding general. Why do you ask?"

"I'm serious. Give me a straight answer."

"You mean to say you don't know her husband? He peddles
food outside the county office every day."

"Not Xu San who sells date pudding?"

Mistress Wang waved her hand negatively. "No, though
they'd make a good pair. Guess again."

"Li Er the silver carrier?"

"No, though they also would be well matched."

"It couldn't be Lu Xiaoyi with the tattooed arms?"

Mistress Wang grinned. "No. They'd be a fine team, though.
Guess again, Right Honorable."

"Godmother," said Ximen, "I really can't imagine."

Mistress Wang laughed. "This'll kill you. Her old man
is Wu the Elder who sells hot buns!"

Ximen howled and stamped with laughter. "Not Three
Inches of Mulberry Bark?"

"The very same."

Ximen groaned. "Such a delicious morsel landing in a dog's
mouth!"

"A real pity," Mistress Wang agreed. "But life is like that.
'A magnificent steed gets a dolt for a rider, a charming wife
sleeps with an oaf of a husband,' as the saying goes. The marriage god makes some crazy matches."

"What do I owe you for tea?"

"Not much. Let it go. We'll add it up some other time."

"Who is your son working for these days?"

"I hate to tell you. He went up the Huaihe River with a merchant and still hasn't returned. Who knows whether he's alive or dead!"

"How would you like him to work for me?"

Mistress Wang smiled. "If Your Honor were willing to raise him up, that would be fine."

"Wait till he gets back. We'll figure out something."

They chatted a while longer. Ximen thanked Mistress Wang and left. Less than half a watch later, he was sitting by her door screen again, gazing at Wu the Elder's house. Mistress Wang came out from the back of the shop.

"A *mei* plum drink, Right Honorable?"

"Excellent. Make it good and sour."

She soon placed the drink before him respectfully, with both hands. He slowly sipped the concoction, then set the cup down on the table.

"You make very good sour plum drinks, godmother. Do you have a lot in stock?"

Mistress Wang laughed. "I've been making *mei*[1] all my life, but I don't keep anyone here!"

"I was talking about sour plum drinks and you're talking about making matches! There's a big difference."

"Oh. I thought you wanted to know whether I was a good match-maker."

"Since that's your line, godmother, I like you to make a match for me, a first-rate one. I'll reward you well."

"If your wife hears about this she's liable to box my ears!"

"My wife is very tolerant. I already have several concubines at home, but none of them please me. If you know someone suitable, don't hesitate to speak. Even a woman who was married before will do, as long as I find her to my liking."

---

[1] A pun. The words for "plum" and "matches" are both pronounced *mei* in Chinese.

"I came across a good one the other day, but I'm afraid you won't want her."

"If she's really good, you arrange it for me, and I'll thank you."

"A very handsome woman, but a bit mature."

"A year or two's difference in our ages won't matter. How old is she?"

"She was born in the year of the tiger. At New Year's she'll be exactly ninety-three!"

Ximen laughed. "You're mad! Always joking!"

Still chuckling, he stood up and left. Day was drawing to a close. Mistress Wang had just lit the lamp and was getting ready to lock up for the night when Ximen again flitted in and sat down by the door screen, facing the house of Wu the Elder.

"How about a nice 'get together' drink, Right Honorable?" suggested Mistress Wang.

"Fine. I'd like it a bit sweet."

She brought the beverage and handed it to him. He sat a while, drinking, then rose once more.

"Put it on my bill, godmother. I'll pay you tomorrow."

"No hurry. Rest peacefully, and drop in again soon."

Ximen laughed. Nothing further happened that night.

Early the next morning when Mistress Wang opened her door and looked outside, there was Ximen, walking back and forth in front of the shop.

"That stud sets a fast pace," she said to herself. "I'll spread a little sugar on the tip of his nose, just out of reach of his tongue. He's great at wheedling favors in the county office, but I'll show him that he can't get anything from me on the cheap!"

She opened the door wide, started the fire, put the kettle on. Ximen entered immediately and sat down by the door screen, his eyes on the bamboo curtain before Wu the Elder's door. Mistress Wang pretended not to notice, and remained in the rear, fanning the fire.

"Godmother," Ximen called. "Two cups of tea, please,"

"So it's you, Right Honorable," Mistress Wang grinned. "Haven't seen you in days. Have a chair."

She set two cups of strong ginger tea on the table before him.

"Have one with me," Ximen invited.

"I'm not your dearie," the old woman cackled.

Ximen also laughed. "Godmother," he queried, "what do they sell next door?"

"Steaming, dripping, hot, spicy, delicious goodies."

Ximen grinned. "You really are a mad woman!"

"Not a bit of it," laughed Mistress Wang. "But she has a husband."

"I'm serious. They say he makes very good buns. I'd like to order forty or fifty. Do you know whether he's home or not?"

"If it's buns you want, wait till he returns. No need to go to his house."

"You're quite right." Ximen sat a while, drinking his tea. He stood up. "Put it on the bill, godmother."

"Don't worry. I'll do that all right."

Ximen smiled and departed.

Soon afterwards, Mistress Wang, tending her shop, glanced outside. Ximen was again pacing in front of the door. He walked to the east, and gave a look. He walked to the west, and looked again. Seven or eight times he did this, then once more entered the tea-shop.

"A rare visit, Right Honorable!" Mistress Wang hailed him. "It's been a long time!"

Ximen smiled. He took out a piece of silver and handed it to her. "This is for the tea, godmother," he said.

"It doesn't amount to all this much."

"Just hang on to it."

"Got him!" the old woman thought with inner satisfaction. "The stud is really hooked." She put the money away and said: "You look thirsty. A cup of steeped broad-leafed tea — now, that's what you want."

"How did you guess?"

"Easy. I could see it in your expression. 'One look at a man's face tells you whether he's prospering or suffering,' as the old saying goes. Not even the strangest things get by me."

"I have something on my mind this minute. I'll give you five pieces of silver if you can guess what it is."

Mistress Wang grinned. "I don't need three or four guesses. One is enough. Right Honorable, bring your ear down to me. All your coming and going these last two days is because of that person next door. Right?"

Ximen smiled. "Godmother, you're a shrewd woman. To tell you the truth, ever since she beaned me with the pole and I got a good look at her that day, I've been entranced! But I don't know how to get to her. Have you any ideas?"

Mistress Wang laughed uproariously. "Right Honorable, I'll give it to you straight. This tea-shop is just a front — 'the devil playing night watchman'. From the snowy morning on the third day of the sixth month three years ago when I sold my first cup of steeped tea, I've never done much business here. My real trade is in the 'mixed market'."

"What do you mean — 'mixed market'?"

"Mainly, I'm a match-maker. But I'm also a broker, a midwife, a lovers' go-between, and a bawd."

"Godmother, if you can bring this off for me, I'll give you ten pieces of silver to pay for your coffin."

"Listen to me, Right Honorable. These seduction cases are the hardest of all. There are five conditions that have to be met before you can succeed. First, you have to be as handsome as Pan An. Second, you need a tool as big as a donkey's. Third, you must be as rich as Deng Tong. Fourth, you must be as forbearing as a needle plying through cotton wool. Fifth, you've got to spend time. It can be done only if you meet these five requirements."

"Frankly, I think I do. First, while I'm far from a Pan An, I still can get by. Second, I've had a big cock since childhood. Third, my family has a bit of change. Maybe not as much as Deng Tong, but enough. Fourth, I'm very forbearing. Even if she struck me four hundred blows, I'd never return one.

Fifth, I've plenty of time. Otherwise, how could I keep hanging around here? Godmother, you must help me. If we succeed, I'll pay you heavily."

"Right Honorable, although you say you meet the five requirements, there's still another stumbling block."

"What's that?"

"Forgive me if I'm blunt, but these seduction cases are very tricky. Every bit of the money needed must be provided. You mustn't hold back even one penny out of a hundred. You've always been a little tight-fisted. You don't like to throw your money around. That's going to stand in our way."

"We can cure that easily enough. I'll simply do what you say."

"If you're willing to spend the money, Right Honorable, I can arrange a meeting between you and the pullet. But you have to promise me something."

"Anything you want. What's your plan?"

"It's late, today. Come back in three months or half a year and we'll discuss this some more."

Ximen knelt at her feet. "Quit kidding around, godmother," he begged. "You've got to do this for me!"

Mistress Wang chuckled. "Impatient, aren't you? I have a plan, and it's a good one. It may not be foolproof, but it's ninety per cent sure. Now here's what we do: This girl was the goddaughter of a wealthy Qinghe family, and she's a fine seamstress. You go out and buy me a bolt of white brocade, a bolt of blue silk, a bolt of white silk gauze, and ten ounces of good silk floss and have them delivered here. I'll go over to the girl's house and have a cup of tea with her. I'll say: 'A kind gentleman has given me some material for burial garments. Would you please look in your almanac and see what's an auspicious day for me to hire a tailor?' If she doesn't respond, then that's the end. If she says: 'I'll make them for you,' and tells me not to bother about a tailor, then we've scored one point out of ten. I'll ask her over to my place. If she won't come and says: 'Bring the material here,' then that's the end. If she's pleased, and agrees, we've scored point two.

"When she comes, the first day, I'll have some wine and tidbits for her. You stay away. The second day, if she says it's not convenient here, and insists on taking the work home, we're finished. But if she's willing to come again, we've won point three. You stay away that day, too.

"Around noon the third day, I want you to arrive, neat and clean, and stand outside the door and cough as a signal. Then you call: 'Godmother, why haven't I seen you these days?' I'll come out and invite you into the rear room. If when she sees you she runs home, I won't be able to stop her, and that will be the end of it. If she stays put, then we've won point four.

"You sit down, and I'll say to the pullet: 'This is the benefactor who has given me the material. I'm terribly grateful!' I'll praise your many good qualities, and you compliment her on her needlework. If she doesn't respond, it's over. If she replies, that's point five.

"Then I'll say: 'I'm lucky to have this lady do the sewing for me. I'm very grateful to both you benefactors. One gives money, the other gives skill. This lady wouldn't even be here if I hadn't gone out of my way to beg her. Won't you help me, Right Honorable, to show her my thanks?' You take out some silver and ask me to buy her something. If she turns and leaves, I won't be able to stop her, and that will be the end. If she remains, we've won point six.

"I'll start for the door with the money and say to her: 'Please keep this gentleman company for a while.' If she gets up and goes home, there's nothing I can do about it. That will be the end. If she doesn't leave, we'll still be winning. Point seven will belong to us.

"When I return with the things I've bought and put them on the table, I'll say to her: 'Rest a while and have a cup of wine. We can't refuse this gentleman's treat.' If she won't drink with you at the same table and leaves, that's the finish. If she only says she wants to go, but doesn't, that's fine. Point eight will be ours.

"After she's had plenty to drink and you've started a conversation with her, I'll claim there's no more wine, and tell you to buy some more. You ask me to do it. I'll pretend to go, and close the door, leaving you two alone inside. If she gets upset and runs home, that will be the end. But if, after I close the door, she doesn't make any fuss, we've won point nine. We'll need only one point more for the game.

"But that's the tough one, Right Honorable. You'll have to speak to her sweetly. Take it easy. If you make any sudden moves and spoil everything, there's nothing more I can do for you. Brush one of the chopsticks off the table with your sleeve. Bend down as if to pick it up and pinch her foot. If she screams, I'll come charging in to the rescue, and you will have lost, probably for good. If she doesn't make a sound, that will be point ten. Then, and then, she will be all yours! How do you like my plan?"

Ximen was delighted. "Maybe it couldn't get into the emperor's Hall of Fame, but it's excellent!"

"Don't forget my ten ounces of silver!"

" 'Can one forget Dongting Lake while eating its fragrant tangerine peel?' When do we start?"

"I'll have news for you by tonight. I'm going to sound her out today before Wu the Elder gets back. You buy those silks and send them over."

"Put this through for me, godmother, and I won't disappoint you!"

Ximen bid farewell to Mistress Wang, went to the market, bought the brocade, silk, gauze and ten ounces of pure silk floss. He had a family servant wrap and deliver them to the tea-shop, together with five pieces of silver.

Mistress Wang received the silks and money and sent the servant back. Leaving her place via the rear door, she went to Wu's house. Golden Lotus invited her upstairs to sit a while.

"Why don't you ever come over to my place for a cup of tea?" the old woman asked.

"I haven't been feeling well these last few days. I just don't have the energy," the girl replied.

"Do you have an almanac here? I want to pick a good day to hire a tailor."

"What sort of clothes are you making?"

"I'm getting all kinds of aches and ailments in my old age. If anything should happen, I'd like to have my burial garments ready. Fortunately, a wealthy gentleman, seeing my condition, has given me some fine silks and good floss. I've had them at home for over a year, but I can't get them made up. Lately, I've been feeling that my days are numbered. Because it's leap year I wanted to use this extra month to get them done. But my tailor keeps stalling. Says he's too busy, can't come. It's simply awful!"

Golden Lotus laughed. "Maybe you wouldn't like my work, but I'd be glad to make them for you, if you'll let me."

The old woman's face was wreathed in smiles. "If you'd apply your precious hands to them, I would be the gainer, even after death! I've heard of your skill with the needle, but I never had the courage to ask you."

"Why not? I've said I'd do it, and I will. We must get someone to choose a lucky day for you from the almanac, and I'll start."

"You're my lucky star! As long as you'll do it, we don't need any special day. I recall now I asked someone the other day, and he said tomorrow would be a Most Auspicious Day. I forgot, because you don't really need a Most Auspicious Day to cut materials."

"How can you say that? You do for burial garments."

"In that case, fine. Tomorrow's the day. I'll trouble you to come to my humble home."

"That won't be necessary, godmother. Just bring the materials here."

"But I'd love to see you work. Besides, I have no one to watch the shop."

"All right, then. I'll come over after breakfast."

Mistress Wang thanked Golden Lotus profusely and left. That evening she told Ximen what had transpired, and instructed him to return the day after tomorrow.

Nothing happened that night. Early the next morning Mistress Wang cleaned her house, bought some thread, put on the tea kettle, and waited.

Wu the Elder finished his breakfast, took his carrying-pole and hampers of buns, and went out on the street. Golden Lotus rolled up the front door curtain and proceeded through the back door to the house of Mistress Wang. The old woman greeted her with unrestrained joy. She led the girl into the rear room, poured her a cup of strong tea, spread before her shelled pine nuts and walnuts, and urged her to eat. First wiping the table clean, Mistress Wang laid out the silks. The girl measured them, cut the appropriate lengths and began to sew.

"What technique," marvelled the old woman. "In my nearly seventy years I've never seen such fine needlework!"

Golden Lotus continued sewing until noon, when Mistress Wang served her wine and noodles. The girl resumed sewing until it was nearly dark, then gathered the materials together and went home. Wu the Elder was just entering the door with his carrying-pole and empty hampers. The girl opened the door for him and lowered the screen. As he came into the room he noticed that his wife's face was flushed.

"Where have you been drinking?"

"Mistress Wang, next door, asked me to make some burial garments for her. She served me a snack at noon."

"*Aiya*! You mustn't eat her food. We may be wanting a favor from her some day. Come home when it's time to eat. Don't trouble her. Take some money with you, if you go again tomorrow, and treat her to wine in return. 'A close neighbor means more than a distant relative.' Don't forget your manners. If she won't let you treat her, take the materials home and work on them here."

The girl listened. Nothing more was said on the subject that evening.

Mistress Wang's plan for getting Golden Lotus over to her house was set. The next morning after breakfast, Wu the Elder departed, and the old woman promptly called for her. She brought out the materials and, as the girl sewed, served her tea. Of that no more need be said.

When noon approached, Golden Lotus handed Mistress Wang a string of copper coins. "Let's have some wine together, god-mother."

"*Aiya*! Who ever heard of such a thing? I've asked you here to do some work for me. I can't let you spend any money!"

"My husband said if you insist on being polite, I'm to take the work home and do it for you there."

"Wu the Elder is too polite," the old woman said quickly. "Since that's how it is, I suppose I'll have to agree." The last thing she wanted was to disturb the arrangement.

She added some money of her own to what the girl had given her, bought some top quality wine and food, and fruits out of season, and served them solicitously to Golden Lotus. Good reader, observe: Nine out of ten women, no matter how clever they may be, invariably are taken in by small attentions and flattery.

The girl ate and drank, and sewed a bit longer. When it began to grow dark, showered with the thanks of her hostess, she returned home.

To skip the idle chatter: The moment Mistress Wang saw Wu the Elder leave after breakfast the third morning, she went to his rear door and called: "I'm here to bother you again. . . ."

Golden Lotus came down the stairs. "I was just coming over."

The two went to the old woman's rear room, sat down, got out the materials, and the girl commenced to sew. Mistress Wang poured tea, which they both drank.

It was nearly noon. Ximen, unable to wait another day, arrived at the door of the tea-shop on Purple Stone Street. He wore a new kerchief on his head, was smartly dressed, and had brought four or five ounces of silver.

He coughed. "Godmother, where have you been these days?"

The old woman glanced out. "Who's that, calling god-mother?"

"It's me."

Mistress Wang hurried into the shop. She smiled. "I had no idea. So it's you, Right Honorable. You've come just at the right time. Please step inside. I want to show you something." She took him by the sleeve and led him into the rear room. To the girl she said: "This is the gentleman I told you about. The one who gave me the materials."

Ximen greeted Golden Lotus respectfully. She quickly put down her work and curtsied.

"I've had the silks you gave me for a year," Mistress Wang told Ximen, "but I couldn't get them made up. Fortunately, this lady is now doing them for me. Her stitches are as fine as any machine weave! So close and exact! A rare skill! See for yourself, Right Honorable."

Ximen picked up the unfinished garment and gazed at it admiringly. "Remarkable. A fairy touch!"

The girl smiled. "The gentleman is making fun of me."

"Godmother," said Ximen, "may I ask? Whose wife is this lady?"

"Guess."

"How can I?"

Mistress Wang laughed. "She's married to Wu the Elder, next door. Did that pole hurt your head the other day? You've forgotten."

Golden Lotus blushed. "It slipped. I hope the gentleman won't hold it against me."

"Of course not," exclaimed Ximen.

"The Right Honorable is very amiable," Mistress Wang interpolated. "He's not the kind to bear a grudge. A very nice man."

"We hadn't met before the other day," said Ximen. "So she's Wu the Elder's wife. I know him. A competent manager. He conducts his business on the street and never offends anyone, old or young. He earns money and has a good disposition. An unusual person."

"That's Wu the Elder," cried Mistress Wang. "And this lady is the most dutiful of wives."

"He's a useless fellow," said Golden Lotus. "You're laughing at us, sir."

"Not at all, madam," protested Ximen. "The ancients say: 'The pliant rise in the world, the hard invite disaster.' An excellent man like your Wu the Elder 'doesn't lose a drop in ten thousand tons of water'."

"How true," gushed the old woman, beating the drum from the sidelines.

Still uttering compliments, Ximen sat down opposite the girl.

"Do you know who this gentleman is?" asked Mistress Wang.

"No, I don't."

"He's one of the wealthiest men in the county, a friend of the magistrate. He's called the Right Honorable Ximen. He's very rich. He has a medicinal drug shop opposite the county office. His money would overflow the Big Dipper. Rice rots in his granaries. Whatever of his that is yellow is gold, what's white is silver, what's round is pearls, what glitters is jewels. He has rhinoceros horns and elephant tusks. . . ."

With wild exaggeration, Mistress Wang praised Ximen. The girl listened, her head bent over her sewing. Ximen gazed at her, consumed with desire. He couldn't wait to get her alone. The old woman poured tea and put a cup in front of each of them.

"Have some tea with the gentleman," she said to Golden Lotus.

There was a touch of provocation in the girl's glances. Mistress Wang looked at Ximen significantly and touched her face with five fingers of her hand. He understood. Five-tenths of the battle was won.

"If you hadn't come, I wouldn't have presumed to call on you and invite you," Mistress Wang said to him. "But you two were fated to meet, and here, by lucky coincidence. Although 'One person shouldn't impose on two patrons,' as the saying goes, you have spent money, Right Honorable, and this lady is giving her skill. I hate to bother you any further, but don't you think, since she's kind enough to come here, that you might treat her to a little something, on my behalf?"

"How could I be so slow! Here is some money." Ximen took out some pieces of silver and handed them wrapped in a kerchief, to Mistress Wang.

"I can't allow you to do that," said the girl. But she remained seated.

The old woman took the money and went to the door. "Keep Right Honorable company a while," said Mistress Wang.

"You mustn't go to any trouble, godmother," said the girl. She didn't budge.

Ximen and Golden Lotus were strongly drawn to each other. He was frankly staring at her. She, glancing at him from under her lashes, thought him a fine figure of a man, and was already more than half willing. But she kept her head down over her work.

Soon Mistress Wang returned with a cooked fat goose, stewed meat and delicate tidbits. She placed everything on platters and set them on the table.

"Put your sewing away," she said to the girl, "and have a cup of wine."

"You go ahead, godmother. It's not proper for me to join the gentleman," said Golden Lotus. But she didn't leave her seat.

"We're doing this to express my thanks, especially to you. How can you say such a thing?" Mistress Wang laid the dishes on the table. The three sat down, and she poured the wine. Ximen raised his cup.

"Drink hearty, madam," he said to Golden Lotus.

"Thank you, sir," the girl smiled.

"I know you have a real capacity," Mistress Wang said to her. "So don't stint on your drinking."

Ximen picked up his chopsticks. "Godmother, please serve this lady for me."

The old woman selected choice pieces and placed them on Golden Lotus's plate. She poured three rounds of wine in succession, then went out to heat some more.

"May I ask how old you are?" Ximen said to the girl.

"Twenty-three."

"Five years younger than me."

"You're comparing the earth and the sky, sir," the girl said politely.

Mistress Wang came back into the room. "This lady is remarkably clever," she gushed. "Not only does she sew beautifully, but she's read all the classics."

"Where can you find such a girl these days?" said Ximen. "Wu the Elder is certainly fortunate."

"You mustn't think I'm trying to provoke anything," said Mistress Wang, "but with all the women in your household, there isn't one who can compare."

"That's quite true. I can't tell you how hard it's been. I guess I was born unlucky. I've never been able to find a really good one."

"There was nothing wrong with your first wife."

"You can say that again. If she were still alive, my household wouldn't be in such a state. Those women are just mouths waiting to be fed. They don't look after a thing."

"How long ago did your wife die, sir?" the girl asked.

"It's a sad story. Though she came from a poor family, she was very skilful. She did everything for me. She's been gone three years now. My household is in a mess. That's why I spend so much time outside. It only aggravates me when I'm home."

"Do you mind if I'm frank?" said Mistress Wang. "Your first wife wasn't as handy with a needle as this lady is."

"She wasn't as good-looking, either."

Mistress Wang laughed. "Why haven't you ever invited me to tea in that house you have on East Street?"

"You mean where I'm keeping Zhang Xixi, the ballad singer? She's just a singsong girl. I don't care for her much."

"You've had Li Jiaojiao for quite a while."

"Yes. I keep her at home. If she were like this lady here, I'd have raised her to the status of wife long ago."

"If you could find such a girl, would you have any trouble bringing her into the family?"

"Both my parents are dead. I'm my own master. Who would dare to object?"

"I'm only joking. The problem is, there isn't any girl who would please you."

"Who says there isn't? It's just that my marriage luck has been bad. I've never met the right one."

Ximen and the old woman talked for a while in this manner, then Mistress Wang said: "I'm afraid the wine is nearly finished. Can I trouble you to buy another bottle?"

"There are five ounces of silver in my purse. You can have them all. Take what you need and keep the change."

Mistress Wang thanked him and got up, glancing at Golden Lotus. The dram of wine inside the girl was stirring her passions. She and the man were talking freely. Both were aroused. Golden Lotus kept her head down, but she didn't leave. Grinning, Mistress Wang addressed her.

"I'm going out to buy another bottle. Please keep Right Honorable company. There's still some wine in the heating tube. You and he can each have a cup. I'm going all the way down to that shop opposite the county office to get some good wine, so I won't be back for quite a while."

"You needn't go to so much bother," the girl murmured. She remained where she was.

Mistress Wang went out, closed and tied the doors of the rear room, then sat herself down on guard.

Ximen poured wine for Golden Lotus. With his wide sleeve, he swept a pair of chopsticks from the table to the floor. Fate was on the side of his amorous quest — they landed right beside the girl's feet. He bent down as though to pick them up and instead squeezed one of her embroidered satin shoes. Golden Lotus laughed.

"Sir, you mustn't! Are you trying to seduce me?"

Ximen knelt before her. "I want you so!"

Golden Lotus raised him to his feet and threw herself into his arms. There in Mistress Wang's room the two hastily undressed. Sharing the same pillow, they revelled joyously.

After the clouds had spent their rain, and Golden Lotus and

Ximen were about to put on their clothes, Mistress Wang pushed open the doors and came in. She pretended to be very angry.

"Pretty tricks you two have been up to," she cried, startling the lovers. "A fine thing! I asked you here to make me garments," she said to Golden Lotus, "not to play adulterous games! If Wu the Elder finds out, he'll surely blame me! It would be better for me if I told him about it first!"

She started for the door. The girl grabbed her by the skirt. "Godmother, spare me!"

"Not so loud, godmother," Ximen pleaded.

Mistress Wang chuckled. "I'll spare you both on one condition."

"One or a dozen," said Golden Lotus. "I'll promise you anything!"

"From now on, you must fool Wu the Elder and entertain Right Honorable every day without fail, in which case I'll spare you. But if you miss a single day, I'll tell your husband!"

"Whatever you say, godmother."

"And you, Right Honorable Ximen, you know what I want. The matter is a complete success. Don't forget your promise. If you do, I'll tell Wu the Elder!"

"Never fear, godmother. I won't forget."

The three drank until afternoon. Golden Lotus rose. "My husband will be home soon. I have to go."

She returned through the back door and was lowering the front door curtain when Wu arrived.

At that moment Mistress Wang was saying to Ximen: "Well, what do you think of my method?"

"Marvellous! I'm sending you a bar of silver as soon as I get home. You shall have everything I promised!"

" 'My eyes watch for the banners of royal reward, my ears are cocked for the sound of glad tidings.' Don't fail me! I don't want to be 'a funeral singer demanding payment after the burial' !"

Ximen laughed and departed. Of that no more need be said.

From then on, Golden Lotus slipped over to Mistress Wang's

house every day to meet Ximen. They were as close as lacquer, as thick as glue. As the old saying has it: "News of good behavior never gets past the door, but a scandal is heard of a thousand *li* away." In less than half a month, all the neighbors knew. Only Wu remained in ignorance.

CHAPTER 12
The Adulterous Wife Poisons Wu the Elder

There was a boy of fifteen or sixteen in the county town whose family name was Qiao. Because he was sired by an army man in Yunzhou Prefecture, he was given the name Yunge. All that was left of his immediate family, besides himself, was his old father. A clever youngster, he earned a living selling fresh fruit in the various taverns outside the county office. Sometimes Ximen gave him a bit of money.

One day, carrying a basket of snowy pears, he wandered along the streets looking for Ximen.

"I know a place where I think you can find him," a gabby fellow said to the boy.

"Please tell me, uncle. I can earn forty or fifty coppers from him. I need them for my old pa."

"He's hooked up with the wife of Wu the Elder, the bun seller. He's with her every day in Mistress Wang's tea-shop on Purple Stone Street. You'll probably find him there. You're only a child, so go right in."

Yunge thanked the man, went with his basket to Purple Stone Street and entered the tea-shop. Mistress Wang was sitting on a little stool, hand-spinning hemp thread. The boy put down his basket and greeted her.

"My respects, godmother."

"What do you want, Yunge?"

"I'm looking for Right Honorable. I can earn forty or fifty coppers for my old pa."

"Which Right Honorable?"

"You know which one, godmother. He's the one I mean."

"Even if he's a Right Honorable, he must have a name."

"His name has two syllables."

"What are they?"

"Are you kidding? Right Honorable Ximen. I have to speak to him."

The boy started for the rear of the shop. Mistress Wang grabbed him. "Where are you going, young jackanapes? There's such a thing as privacy in a person's home."

"I only want to call him out a minute."

"Frigging monkeyshines! Who says I have any Right Honorable Ximen in there!"

"Don't hog him all to yourself. Let me have a lick of the juice too. Think I don't know?"

"Little ape! What do you know!"

"Stingy as cutting vegetables with a hoof-paring knife in a wooden spoon, aren't you? Don't want to miss a bit. Well, all I have to do is speak out, and that bun-selling man is liable to lose his temper!"

The old woman realized he was on to her, and she flew into a rage. "You young scamp! How dare you come in here farting and blowing!"

"A young scamp is better than an old bawd any time!"

Mistress Wang seized him and gave him two lumps on the noggin.

"What are you thumping me for?" yelled the boy.

"Thieving ape! If you don't keep your voice down, I'll slap you right out of here!"

"Dirty old whore-monger! Hitting me for no reason at all!"

Mistress Wang held Yunge by the back of the neck with one hand and pounded his skull with the other, while she rushed him through the door. She threw the basket after him, sending the pears rolling all over the street.

The boy was no match for her. Cursing and weeping, he picked up his pears. Angrily, he pointed at her shop. "Just wait, old bawd, I'm going to tell him! You'll see if I don't!" He set out in search, basket on his arm.

After turning through a couple of streets, he saw the short man coming towards him, carrying his hampers of buns. Yunge halted.

"It's only a few days since I saw you! What have you been eating that's made you so fat?"

Wu rested his load. "I'm still the same. What's fat about me?"

"I tried to buy some bran the other day, but couldn't find any anywhere. Everyone said you had some in your house."

"I'm not raising geese or ducks. What would I want with bran?"

"How is it then that you're stuffed so fat you don't even steam when you're trussed up by the heels and cooked in the pot?"

"Mocking me, eh, you young scamp! My wife doesn't sleep with other men. Why are you calling me a cuckold duck?"

"She doesn't sleep with other men, she just sleeps with another man!"

Wu clutched the boy. "Who is he?"

Yunge laughed. "All you do is grab me. But would you dare to bite his pecker off?"

"Tell me who he is, little brother, and I'll give you ten hot buns!"

"I don't want your buns. But if you treat me to three cups of wine, I'll talk."

"If it's drink you want, come with me." Wu picked up his carrying-pole and led the boy to a small tavern. He rested his load, took out a few buns, and ordered some meat and a dram of wine, all of which was set before Yunge.

"That's enough wine," said the young rascal, "but I could use a few more slices of meat."

"Tell me about it, little brother!"

"Keep your shirt on. I will just as soon as I've finished eating. Don't let it get you down. I'm going to help you to catch him!"

Wu watched the boy polish off the meat and wine. "Now

will you tell me?" he pressed.

"Feel these bumps on my head, if you want to know!"

"How did you get them?"

"Today I went looking for Ximen Qing with a basket of snowy pears, to get a little money out of him. I couldn't find him anywhere. Then a fellow on the street said: 'He cozies up with Wu's wife in Mistress Wang's tea-shop. He goes there every day.' I was hoping to earn forty or fifty coppers, but that sow bitch Mistress Wang wouldn't let me go in and see him! She pounded my skull and threw me out! That's why I've come looking for you. What I said when we met was only to make you mad. Otherwise you wouldn't have asked me about it."

"Can this really be true?"

"There you go again! A real patsy! Those two are having themselves a time. The minute you leave they get together in Mistress Wang's. And you ask whether it's true or false!"

"Frankly, little brother, I have been suspicious lately. She goes over to Mistress Wang's to sew every day, but when she comes back, her face is flushed. So that's what it is! I'll put my pole and hampers away and go over and catch them in the act. How about it?"

"Where are your brains? You couldn't do it alone. That Mistress Wang is a tough old bitch. You'd never get by her. The three of them must have some signal. They'd hide your wife somewhere as soon as you showed up. And that Ximen Qing is a devil. He could take on twenty like you. You wouldn't catch your wife, and he'd give you a beating. He's rich and influential. He'd probably file a complaint as well, and sue you in court. You don't have any strong backing. He'd finish you off!"

"Everything you say is so, little brother. How am I going to get back at them?"

"That old bitch pummeled me. I want to get back at her, too. Now here's what you do: When you go home tonight, don't blow up, act as if you don't know anything, the same as any other day. Tomorrow, make less buns than usual. I'll be waiting for you at the end of Purple Stone Street. If Ximen has gone in there, I'll call to you. You follow me, carrying your hampers, and wait nearby. I'll go and sass the old bitch. She's sure to sail into me. I'll toss my basket out into the street. That's the signal for you to go charging in. I'll butt the old bitch with my head and hold her off. You rush into the back room and start yelling that you've been wronged.... How's that for an idea?"

"All right! We'll do it! But it's going to be hard on you, little brother. Take these strings of cash and buy some rice for yourself. Wait for me tomorrow morning at the entrance to Purple Stone Street."

The boy accepted the money, and several hot buns, and departed. Wu paid the bill, shouldered his carrying-pole and went out to hawk his wares.

Generally, Golden Lotus scolded and chivied her husband in a hundred ways. But she knew she was being unreasonable, and lately she had been treating him somewhat better. When he returned home that evening, he behaved as usual and said nothing out of the ordinary.

"Have you been drinking?" she asked.

"I had a few cups with another pedlar."

Golden Lotus set the food on the table, and they ate. That night nothing special happened.

The next morning after breakfast Wu prepared only two or three trays of buns to put in his hampers. All the girl's thoughts were of Ximen, and she paid no attention to what her husband was doing. Wu shouldered his carrying-pole and set out. No sooner had he gone than Golden Lotus hurried over to Mistress Wang's to wait for Ximen.

When Wu arrived at the entry to Purple Stone Street, he found Yunge already there with his basket.

"What's happening?" Wu asked.

"It's early yet," said the boy. "You sell some buns for a while. He's almost sure to come. Don't go too far away."

Wu was off and back like a whirling cloud.

"Watch for my basket," the boy reminded him. "When I

fling it out, you rush in.''

Wu stored his pole and hampers in a safe place. Of that we'll say no more.

We'll talk rather of Yunge, and how, with his basket, he entered the tea-shop.

"Old bitch," he cried. "What right did you have to hit me yesterday?"

Mistress Wang's temper had not improved. She jumped to her feet and shouted: "There's nothing between us, young ape! How dare you come cursing me again?"

"You're a bawd, I say, and a whore-mongering old bitch. So what!"

In a fury, Mistress Wang grabbed Yunge and pummeled him.

"Hit me, will you!" yelled the boy. He threw his basket out into the street. Seizing her around the waist, he butted her in the belly. She staggered backwards until brought up short against the wall, the young scamp's head still rammed into her mid-section.

Wu, raising the front of his gown, strode quickly into the tea-shop. Mistress Wang tried frantically to stop him, but the boy held her firmly pinned to the wall.

"Wu the Elder is here!" she loudly exclaimed.

Golden Lotus, in the rear room, became frantic. She ran over and leaned hard against the door. Ximen dived under the bed. Master Wu tried to push the door open, but couldn't budge it.

"Fine goings-on!" he shouted.

The girl, distraught, stood pressing against the door. "You're always shooting off your mouth what a great fighter you are, but in an emergency, you're useless!" she spat at Ximen. "A paper tiger scares you silly!"

This was a plain hint for Ximen to strike Wu down and escape. The recumbent gentleman under the bed, stimulated by these words, crawled out. He pulled open the door and cried: "Don't fight!"

Wu tried to grab him, but Ximen lashed out with his right

foot and caught the short man square in the center of the chest,
knocking him flat on his back. Ximen then fled. Yunge,
seeing that things had gone wrong, pushed the old woman aside
and also ran. The neighbors knew what a tough customer
Ximen was. They dared not intervene.

Mistress Wang raised up Wu the Elder. Blood was flowing
from his mouth, his skin was a waxy yellow. She called Golden
Lotus. The wife emerged from the rear room, scooped a bowl-
ful water and brought him round. She and Mistress Wang,
supporting Wu under the arms, helped him through the back
door and up the stairs of his house, where they put him to bed.
Nothing further happened that night.

The next day Ximen inquired and learned there were no
repercussions, so he met Golden Lotus as usual. They hoped
her husband would die. Wu was ill for five days and couldn't
leave his bed. When he wanted soup or water she wouldn't
give it to him. When he called her she didn't answer. Each
day she made herself up alluringly and went out, returning
always with a rosy face. Wu several times nearly fainted from
sheer rage, but she paid him no heed.

He called her to him and said: "I know what you're up to.
I caught the two of you together. You got your lover to kick
me in the chest, and I'm more dead than alive, yet you two are
still going on with your games! I may die — I'm no match for
you. But don't forget my brother Wu Song! You know what
he's like! Sooner or later he's coming back. Do you think
he's going to let you get away with it? Have pity on me.
Help me recover quickly, and when he comes home I won't say
anything. If you don't treat me right, he'll have something to
say to the both of you!"

Golden Lotus did not reply, but went next door and told
Mistress Wang and Ximen what her husband had said. Ximen
felt his blood run cold. He groaned.

"Constable Wu is the man who killed the tiger on Jingyang
Ridge. He was the boldest fighter in Qinghe County! We've
been having this affair for some time now, and we've been marvellous together in body and in mind. I forgot all about your

husband's brother! What are we going to do? This is a terrible situation!"

Mistress Wang laughed coldly. "I've never seen the like. You're the helmsman and I'm only a passenger, but I'm not worried and you're in a flap!".

"Though it shames me to say it, I don't know how to deal with this sort of thing. Have you any idea how to cover for us?"

"Do you want to be long-term lovers, or short?"

"What do you mean?"

"If you're satisfied with being short-term lovers, separate after today and when Wu recovers, apologize to him. Nothing will be said when Wu Song comes home. When he's sent out on another mission, you can get together again. If you want to be long-term lovers, and not have to be frightened and alarmed every day, I have a clever scheme. Of course, you may not be able to do it."

"Save us, godmother! We want to be long-term lovers!"

"The thing we need for this scheme other households don't have. But yours, thank Heaven, does."

"If you ask for my eyes, I'll gouge them out! What is this thing?"

"The wretch is very ill. Take advantage of his misery to do him in. Get some arsenic from your drug shop, let this lady buy medicine for heart pains, mix the two together and finish the dwarf off. She can have him cremated, so there won't be any traces. When Wu Song comes back, what will he be able to do? You know the old sayings: 'Brother and sister-in-law must keep their distance.' 'Parents pick the first husband, widows choose the second.' A brother-in-law can't interfere. You continue to meet secretly for half a year or so till the mourning period is over, then marry her. You'll be long-term lovers, and merry till the end of your days. What do you think of my plan?"

"It's a frightening crime, godmother! Never mind. We'll do it! All or nothing!"

"Good. Pull it out by the roots and it won't grow again.

Leave any roots and it sprouts once more, come spring. Get
the arsenic, Right Honorable. I'll tell the lady how to use it.
When it's over, you'll have to reward me well."

"Naturally! That goes without saying!"

Not long after, Ximen arrived with the arsenic and gave it
to Mistress Wang. The old woman looked at Golden Lotus.

"I'll teach you how to mix this in the medicine. Didn't Wu
ask you to treat him better? Soften him up with a little kindness. He'll ask you to buy some medicine for his heart. Put
this arsenic in it. When he wakes up at night, pour the mixture
down his throat, then get out of the way. Once it starts working in him, it will split his guts, and he'll shout and scream.
Muffle his cries with a quilt. Don't let anyone hear. Have a
pot of hot water boiling, and soak a rag. He'll bleed from
every opening, he'll bite his lips. When he dies, remove the
quilt and clean away all the blood with the rag. Then into the
coffin, off to the cremation, and not a friggin thing will happen!"

"It sounds all right," said Golden Lotus. "Only I'm afraid
I'll go soft! I won't be able to handle the corpse!"

"That's easy. Just knock on the wall, and I'll come up and
help you."

"Do the job carefully you two," said Ximen. "I'll be back
at dawn tomorrow to hear your report." He stood up and departed.

Mistress Wang crushed the arsenic granules with her fingers
into powder and gave it to Golden Lotus to hide.

The girl crossed over to her own house and went upstairs.
Wu was barely breathing. He seemed to be at death's door.
She sat down on the edge of the bed and pretended to weep.

"Why are you crying?" asked Wu.

Golden Lotus dabbed at her eyes. "I made a mistake and
let that scoundrel beguile me. I never thought he'd kick you!
I've heard about a very good medicine. I'd like to buy it
for you, but I'm afraid you don't trust me, so I haven't dared!"

"Save my life and we'll forget about the whole thing. I won't
hold it against you, and I'll say nothing to Wu Song. Go buy
the medicine quickly! Save me!"

The girl took some coppers, hurried to Mistress Wang's house and sent her out for the medicinal powders. Then she brought the packet upstairs and showed it to Wu.

"This is heart balm," she said. "The doctor in the drug shop says you should take it in the middle of the night and cover your head with two quilts to make you perspire. Tomorrow, you'll be able to get up."

"That's fine! I know it's a lot of trouble, but stay awake till midnight and give me the potion."

"Don't worry about a thing. Just sleep. I'll look after you."

The day drew to a close and darkness gathered. Golden Lotus lit a lamp. Then she went down to the kitchen, set a pot of water on the stove and put a rag in to boil. When she heard the watchman's drum thump three times, she spilled the arsenic powder into a cup, filled a bowl with hot water, and took them both up the stairs. She called to her husband.

"Where did you put the medicine?"

"Here under the sleeping mat, beside my pillow. Mix it quickly and give it to me."

Golden Lotus took the packet of medicinal powders, sprinkled them into the cup so that they covered the arsenic, then added hot water and stirred with a silver pin which she drew from her hair. Raising Wu with her left hand, she held the cup to his lips with her right.

"It's very bitter," he said after the first sip.

"As long as it cures you, what do you care how bitter it is."

He opened his mouth for another sip, and the girl tilted the cup and forced its entire contents down his throat. She let him fall back on his pillow and swiftly got off the bed.

Wu gasped. "My stomach hurts! The pain, the pain! I can't stand it!"

The girl grabbed two quilts from the foot of the bed and flung them over his face.

"I can't breathe!" he cried.

"The doctor says I should make you sweat! You'll get well quicker!"

Before Wu could reply, the girl, afraid he would struggle, leaped onto the bed and knelt astride his body, pressing down on the sides of the quilts with both hands. He gasped, panted till his intestines split asunder. Then he breathed his last and lay still.

Golden Lotus pulled back the quilts. Wu had lacerated his lips with his teeth, he had bled from every orifice. Frightened, the girl jumped down from the bed and rapped on the wall. Mistress Wang heard the signal, came to the back door and coughed. Golden Lotus went downstairs and opened the door.

"Is it done?" asked the old woman.

"It's done all right, but I'm absolutely limp. I can't go on!"

"There's nothing to it. I'll help you."

Mistress Wang rolled up her sleeves, filled a bucket with hot water, put the rag in, and carried them upstairs. Rolling back the quilts, she wiped around Wu's mouth, cleaned up the blood that had spewed from his seven openings, and covered him with his clothes. Slowly, the two women toted him down the stairs. They found an old door and laid him out on it. They combed his hair, tied a kerchief round his head, put on his clothes, shoes and stockings, spread a piece of fine white silk over his face, and covered his body with a clean quilt. Then they went upstairs and set the bedroom in order, and Mistress Wang returned home.

Golden Lotus commenced falsely bewailing the departure of her family supporter. Reader please note, women's lamentations are of three kinds the world over: With both tears and sound it is called crying, with tears and without sound it is called weeping, without tears and with sound it is called wailing. Golden Lotus wailed. By then it was the fifth watch.

The sky was not yet light when Ximen came to hear the news. Mistress Wang related it in detail. Ximen gave her money to buy a coffin and other funerary equipment. He told her to call the girl. Golden Lotus crossed over to Mistress Wang's.

"Wu the Elder is dead," she said. "You're my sole support from now on."

"That goes without saying."

"There's only one more difficulty," said Mistress Wang. "Ho, the local coroner, is a clever man. I'm afraid he may notice something, and not agree to the encoffining."

"Don't worry about that," said Ximen. "I'll have a few words with him. He wouldn't dare go against me."

"You do that, then," said the old woman. "Don't delay."

Ximen promptly left.

By the time the sun was well risen Mistress Wang had bought the coffin, candles and paper ingots, and returned home and cooked some soup and rice for Golden Lotus. They lit a mourning lamp and placed it beside the body. Neighbors came to offer their condolences. The girl covered her powdered face and pretended to weep.

"What illness did Wu the Elder die of?" queried the neighbors.

"He had pains in his heart! They got worse every day! It was hopeless! And last night, at the third watch, he left me!" Golden Lotus sobbed loudly.

The neighbors knew there was something peculiar about his death, but they were afraid to probe too deeply. They gave only the usual advice: "The dead are gone, but the living must carry on. Don't take it so hard."

Hypocritically, the girl thanked them, and the neighbors left.

CHAPTER 13
Wu Song Offers Heads as Memorial Sacrifices

Time quickly passed. More than forty days elapsed. Wu Song carried out the assignment given him by the county magistrate and escorted the cart to the relative's home in the Eastern Capital and delivered the letter and the crates. He spent a few days looking around the busy streets while awaiting the written reply, then returned to Yanggu with his men. The whole mission had taken exactly two months.

It was the end of winter when Wu Song had departed. When he returned it was the start of the third lunar month. He had felt uneasy in his mind all the time he was away, and he was anxious to see his brother. But first he delivered the reply to the magistrate.

The official was very pleased. After reading the letter, which said that the valuables had been delivered safely, he rewarded Wu Song with a large silver ingot, and wined and dined him. That goes without saying.

Wu Song went to his quarters, changed his clothes, shoes and stockings, put on a fresh head kerchief, locked his door, and hurried to Purple Stone Street. Alarmed neighbors on both sides of the thoroughfare broke into a sweat. They said in an undertone: "Here comes trouble! This big stalwart won't just let the matter rest! Something bad is bound to happen!"

Wu Song raised the door curtain and entered. The first thing he saw was the tablet with the inscription: "In Memory of Wu the Elder, My Departed Husband". Shocked, he stared.

"Can I believe my eyes?" he thought. "Sister-in-law," he

called, "I'm back. It's me, Wu Song."

Ximen was frolicking with Golden Lotus upstairs. At the sound of Wu Song's voice he farted with terror and pissed in his pants. He scooted out of the back door and left via Mistress Wang's shop.

"Please have a seat," the girl called. "I'll be right with you." She hadn't worn mourning after poisoning her husband, but had adorned and beautified herself every day and reveled with her lover.

She hastily washed off her make-up, removed her hair ornaments, pinned her wanton locks into a severe bun in the back, and quickly exchanged her red skirt and figured tunic for drab mourning garments. Then, sobbing, she descended the stairs.

"Sister-in-law, don't cry," said Wu Song. "When did my brother die? What was wrong with him? What medicines did he take?"

Weeping, Golden Lotus replied: "About twenty days after you left, he had severe pains in the heart. He was ill for eight or nine days. I prayed, I gave him every kind of medicine, but nothing could cure him and he died! Now I'm miserable and alone!"

Mistress Wang could hear them through the wall. She was afraid Golden Lotus would make a slip, and she came over to help her.

"My brother never had that ailment before," said Wu Song. "How could his heart have killed him?"

'Now, Constable,' interjected Mistress Wang, "don't you know the saying: 'The winds and clouds in the sky are unfathomable. A man's luck changes in an instant'? Who can guarantee against misfortune?"

"If it weren't for godmother, here, I would have been helpless," the girl added. "She was the only one of the neighbors who came to my aid."

"Where is he buried?" asked Wu Song.

"I was all alone. How could I go looking for a suitable burial place? There was no other way to do it. After three days, I had him cremated."

"What was the date of his death?"

"In two more days it will be the end of the Seven Times Seven period."

Wu Song was silent for several minutes. Then he left and returned to his quarters. He unlocked the door, went in, and changed into clean sober garments. He had a soldier make a hempen rope which he tied around his waist and concealed on his person a thick-backed and sharp-edged knife. He took some silver and went out, instructing the soldier to lock the door behind them. In the shops in front of the county office he bought rice and flour and spices, as well as candles and paper replicas of gold and silver ingots. In the evening he went to his brother's house and knocked on the door.

Golden Lotus opened it. Wu Song told the soldier to prepare the sacrificial dishes. He lit the lamp before the memorial tablet and laid out wine and tidbits. By the second watch, all was in readiness. Wu Song dropped to his knees and kowtowed.

"Brother, your soul is near! In life you were weak and timid, and the cause of your death is not clear. If you were abused and murdered, come to me in a dream, and I will avenge you!"

He sprinkled wine on the ground, burned the paper money replicas and cried so heart-brokenly that all the neighbors were moved. Inside, the girl also pretended to weep. Finally, Wu Song gave the sacrificial wine and food to the soldier to drink and eat. He got two mats and ordered the soldier to sleep by the door between the inner and outer rooms. He himself bedded down before the memorial tablet. Golden Lotus went upstairs, bolted the door at the head of the stairs, and retired.

Wu Song tossed and turned, unable to sleep. It was nearly the third watch. He looked over at the soldier. The fellow was snoring away, motionless as the dead. Wu Song sat up and gazed at the dim glass lamp in front of the tablet. He heard three beats of the watchman's drum and three stick taps. Wu Song sighed.

"My brother was a soft mark all his life," he said to himself.

"I still don't know how he died."

Before the words were out of his mouth, an icy vapor twisted out from under the altar table, and swirled through the dimness. The lamp before the altar suddenly went out. The paper money on the wall danced wildly.

Wu Song's hair stood on end. He stared. A figure had emerged from beneath the altar table.

"Brother," it said, "I died a cruel death!"

Wu Song couldn't hear clearly. He moved forward. But the cold vapor had vanished, and the figure was gone. Wu Song fell back in a sitting position on his mat. Was it all a dream? He turned and looked at the soldier. The man was fast asleep.

"There must be something wrong about brother's death!" he thought. "He came to tell me, but my living essence scattered his shade. . . ."

Wu Song decided to say nothing now, and wait for morning.

Gradually the sky lightened. The soldier got up and heated some water, and Wu Song rinsed his mouth and washed. Golden Lotus came down the stairs.

"Brother-in-law, you were restless last night."

"Sister-in-law, what, exactly, did my brother die of?"

"How can you have forgotten? I told you yesterday evening. His heart pains killed him."

"Who prescribed the medicines?"

"I have the prescription here."

"Who bought the coffin?"

"I asked Mistress Wang, next door, to do it."

"Who were the pall-bearers?"

"Men from Coroner Ho. He took care of everything."

"I see. I have to go down to the county office and check in for roll-call."

Wu Song departed with his soldier orderly. When they reached the end of Purple Stone Street he asked: "Do you know Coroner Ho?"

"Don't you remember, Constable? He came to congratulate you when you received your appointment. He lives in a lane off Lion Street."

"Take me there."

The soldier escorted him to Ho's door. "You can go now," said Wu Song. The orderly left. Wu Song raised the door curtain.

"Is Coroner Ho home?" he called.

Ho had just got up. When he heard that it was Wu Song he trembled hand and foot. He couldn't even put his head kerchief on. Hastily he took out the silver and the bones and concealed them on his person. Then he came out and greeted his visitor.

"When did you get back, Constable?"

"I returned yesterday. I'd like a few words with you. Please come with me."

"Certainly. But first let me give you some tea."

"That's not necessary. I don't want any."

The two went to a tavern down the street and sat down. Wu Song ordered two drams of wine. Ho rose politely to his feet.

"I haven't yet given you a welcome-home feast. You really shouldn't be so courteous to me."

"Be seated," said Wu Song shortly.

Ho could guess what was on his mind. The waiter poured the wine. Wu Song drank in silence. Ho broke into a sweat. He tried to make conversation, but Wu Song did not respond.

They consumed several cups. Suddenly, from inside his clothes, Wu Song whipped out the sharp knife and stabbed it into the top of the wooden table. The waiter watched, bug-eyed. Of course no one dared come near. Ho turned a greenish yellow. He was afraid to breathe.

Wu Song rolled up his sleeves and grasped the hilt of the knife.

"I'm a crude fellow. I know only that 'The culprit must pay for his wrong, the debtor for his debt.' You needn't be frightened. Just tell me the truth. I want to know exactly how my brother died. You won't be affected in any way. If I hurt you, I'm no true man! But tell me so much as half a lie and this knife will let daylight into you in four hundred places!

Now, start. What was the condition of my brother's body when you saw it?"

Hands on his knees, Wu Song fixed Ho with a burning stare.

The coroner drew a bag from his sleeve and placed it on the table.

"Calm yourself, Constable. Important evidence is here in this bag!"

Wu Song opened it and looked at the blackened bones and the ten-ounce bar of silver. "Why is this important?"

"I don't know what happened before or after, but on the twenty-second of the first lunar month, Mistress Wang who keeps the tea-shop came to my home to ask me to inspect the body of Wu the Elder for encoffining. On my way I was met at the entrance to Purple Stone Street by Ximen Qing who runs the medicinal drug shop in front of the county office. He insisted that I go with him to a tavern and join him in a bottle of wine. There, he gave me this bar of silver and said: 'Put a cover over everything when inspecting the body.' I knew the fellow was a knave, but he wouldn't let me refuse. I drank the wine, took the silver, and went to Wu the Elder's house. When I raised the shroud I saw dried blood in your brother's nose and ears, and gnawed lacerated lips — all signs of poisoning. I wanted to speak out, but there was no one here to take his part, and his wife had announced that he died of heart pains. So I said nothing, but bit my tongue till it bled and pretended I had been taken by an evil spirit. I was carried home.

"I told my assistants to approve the encoffining, but not to accept a penny on my behalf. On the third day, the body was carried off for cremation. I bought some paper money and followed to pay my respects. I managed to get Mistress Wang and your sister-in-law away from the pyre and secretly took these two pieces of bone and brought them home. They're black and flaky — proof of death by poisoning. On this sheet of paper is the date of the cremation and the names of those who attended. That's my story. You're welcome to check it."

"Who is the adulterer?"

"I don't know. But I've heard that a boy called Yunge,

who sells pears, went to the tea-shop with Wu the Elder to catch them. Everyone on this street has heard about it. If you want the details, ask Yunge."

"Right. Since there is such a person, let's go together."

Wu Song sheathed his knife, paid the bill and went with Ho to Yunge's house. At the front door they saw the boy returning with a willow basket on his arm. He had been out buying rice.

"Do you know who this constable is?" Ho asked him.

"Since the day he killed the tiger! What do you two want with me?" Actually, the lad had already guessed, and he added: "There's only one thing. My father is in his sixties and has no one but me. I can't go playing around with you in a court case."

"Here, little brother." Wu Song handed him five ounces of silver. "Give these to your father, then come with me for a chat."

"This will cover the old man's expenses for four or five months," thought Yunge. "It won't matter if I get tied up in court."

He took the money and rice in to his father and accompanied his callers to a restaurant on another street. They went upstairs. Wu Song ordered food for three and turned to Yunge.

"Although you're still very young, little brother, you're a filial son who supports his family. That silver I gave you is only for expenses. I need your co-operation. When this affair is finished I'll give you another fourteen or fifteen ounces and you'll be able to set up in business. Now tell me in detail: How did you and my brother go about catching the adulterers in the tea-shop?"

"I'll tell you, but you mustn't rage. On the thirteenth of the first lunar month I went looking for Ximen Qing with a basket of snowy pears to earn a bit of change from him. I couldn't find him anywhere. When I asked, I was told: 'He's in Mistress Wang's tea-shop on Purple Stone Street with the wife of Wu the Elder, the bun seller. They're hooked up together. He's there every day.' I went directly to the tea-shop, but that old bitch wouldn't let me set foot in the back room! When I said I knew her secret, she pounded me on the noggin, hustled me out, and threw my basket of pears into the street! I was furious! I went to your brother and told him all about it. He wanted to go and nab them right away. I said: 'That's not practical. Ximen Qing is a tough man with his punches and kicks. If you don't catch them in the act, he'll sue you and you'll be in trouble. I'll meet you at the entrance to the street tomorrow. Don't make too many buns. When I see Ximen enter the tea-shop, I'll go in first. You put your things away and wait. As soon as I toss out my basket, you rush in and nab the adulterers!'

"The next day I went to the tea-shop with a basket of pears and cursed the old bitch. She pitched into me. I flung out my basket, butted her with my head and pinned her against the wall. She couldn't stop your brother when he came charging in because I was holding her, but she yelled: 'Wu the Elder is here!' The two inside closed the door. While Wu was shouting, Ximen suddenly pulled the door open, rushed out, and kicked him to the floor. I saw the wife come out. She tried to raise Wu up, but couldn't. I got out of there, fast! About a week later, I heard that he was dead. I don't know how he died."

"You're telling the truth? You'd better not lie to me!"

"I'd say the same thing in court!"

"That's it, then, little brother."

The three ate, Wu Song paid, and they went down into the street.

"I must be going," said Ho.

"Stay with me," said Wu Song. "I need you two as witnesses."

They accompanied him to the county office, where the magistrate was holding court.

"Do you have a complaint, Constable?" the official asked when he saw Wu Song.

"My brother Wu the Elder was poisoned and murdered by his wife and Ximen Qing, who were cohabiting in adultery.

These two men are witnesses. I request Your Honor to do justice."

The magistrate questioned Ho and Yunge, then discussed the case in private with several county clerks and functionaries. All of these gentlemen, to say nothing of the magistrate himself, were tied up with Ximen. And so they reached a common accord — Don't touch it.

Returning to the courtroom, the magistrate said to Wu Song: "You're a constable in this county. You ought to know the law. Since ancient times the rule of proof has been: 'For adultery catch the pair, for robbery find the loot, for murder produce the body.' Your brother's body is no more, and you didn't catch them in the act. Just the testimony of these two isn't enough to prove murder. You haven't got a case. Don't act rashly. Think it over. We can only do what's appropriate."

From inside his robe, Wu Song brought out the two blackened pieces of bone, the ten-ounce silver bar and the sheet of paper. "Surely Your Honor will see that these are no fabrications."

The magistrate looked at them. "You may rise. I must confer about this. You will be notified. If proper, we'll bring them in for questioning."

Ho and Yunge went with Wu Song to his quarters. Ximen was informed the same day of what was brewing. He quickly sent a crony to dispense silver among various county officials and functionaries.

The next morning Wu Song again appeared before the magistrate and urged him to take action. But the official was greedy for bribes. He returned the bones and the silver and said: "Wu Song, you shouldn't let people provoke you against Ximen Qing. The case isn't at all clear. It's difficult to deal with. As the sages said: 'Even what you see with your own eyes may not be true. How can you believe what is said behind people's backs?' You mustn't be so rash."

Also present was the warden of the prison. "Constable," he said, "in murder cases you need five factors: the body, the wound, the ailment, the instrument, and evidence of presence of the accused. Only then can you investigate."

"Since Your Honor won't accept my complaint," Wu Song said to the magistrate, "I shall have to think of something else."

He gave the silver and the bones to Ho and asked him to keep them for him again. Then he returned to his quarters with the coroner and the boy, and instructed his orderly to feed them.

"Wait here for me," he requested. "I'll be back soon."

Carrying ink and a brush-pen, he left the county office compound with three soldiers, and bought four or five sheets of paper, which he concealed on his person. He ordered two of the soldiers to buy a pig's head, a goose, a chicken, two casks of wine and some fruit, and bring them to his brother's house.

At mid-morning he also arrived with the third soldier. Golden Lotus knew by then that he had failed in his accusation, and no longer feared him. Boldly, she waited to see what he would do.

"Come down, sister-in-law," he called. "I have something to say."

The girl leisurely descended the stairs. "What is it?"

"Tomorrow is the last day of the Seven Times Seven mourning period for my brother. The neighbors have gone to a lot of trouble for you. I have bought some wine to thank them on your behalf."

"What do you want to thank them for?" Golden Lotus demanded nastily.

"Manners must be observed," said Wu Song.

On his instructions, the soldiers lit two large candles and placed them, brightly gleaming, before the altar table. They also lit incense in a burner, hung strings of paper money replicas, piled sacrificial dishes before the spirit tablet, and laid out the wine and edibles for the guests. Wu Song retained one soldier to heat the wine, told two others to arrange a table and some benches in the outer room and then stand guard at the house doors, front and back.

"Sister-in-law," he said, "entertain the guests. I'll invite them in." He went first to Mistress Wang, next door.

"You shouldn't trouble," she said. "There's nothing to thank me for."

"We have good reason. We've caused you a lot of inconvenience. It's only a snack and a little wine. You can't refuse."

Mistress Wang took down her tea-shop sign, locked the front door, and went over through the back yard.

"Sit at the head of the table, sister-in-law," said Wu Song. "Godmother, sit opposite."

The women had heard from Ximen, and they drank wine unconcernedly. "What can he do about it!" they thought.

Wu Song also invited a silversmith neighbor, Yao Wenqing, whose shop was on the other side of the house.

"I'm pretty busy," said Yao. "I won't bother you, Constable."

Wu Song pulled him. "Just a cup of weak wine. It won't be for long. Over at our place."

Yao couldn't get out of it. Wu Song seated him beside Mistress Wang. He went next to two shops across the street. The one which sold paper horses for funeral burning was run by Zhao Zhongming.

"I can't leave my business," said Zhao. "I won't be able to join you."

"Don't be like that. All the other neighbors have come." Wu Song wouldn't take no for an answer. He practically dragged him home. "You're of our father's generation," he said. He seated Zhao next to Golden Lotus.

Then he invited Hu Zhengqing, who sold chilled wine across the street. Hu had once been a small functionary. He could sense that something was wrong and didn't want to come. But Wu Song paid no attention to his excuses. He hauled him over and sat him next to Zhao.

"Who lives on the other side of your shop, godmother?" Wu Song queried.

"Grandpa Zhang. He peddles noodles."

It happened that Zhang was home. He was startled to see Wu Song. "Is there something on your mind, Constable?" he asked.

"Our family has been a nuisance to you neighbors. We'd like you to have a cup of weak wine with us."

"*Aiya*, I've never shown your family any special courtesy," protested the old man. "Why should you invite me?"

"It's not worth mentioning. Please come."

Wu Song hustled Grandpa Zhang over and requested him to sit next to Yao the silversmith.

Why, you might ask, hadn't any of the earlier arrivals left? Because there were soldiers at the doors, front and back, standing guard!

Wu Song had invited four neighbors. These, plus Mistress Wang and Golden Lotus, made a total of six. He pulled over a stool, sat down at the end of the table and directed the soldiers to close the doors, front and back. The soldier who had remained in the rear room now came and poured the wine. Wu Song hailed the assemblage politely.

"Neighbors, forgive my crudeness and drink a few cups with me."

"We never gave you a feast to welcome you home from your journey," the neighbors courteously replied, "and yet you go to so much trouble!"

Wu Song smiled. "It's nothing at all. Please don't laugh at our humble fare."

As the soldier poured the wine, the neighbors could sense something was brewing, but they didn't know what to do about it. After three cups, Hu the chilled-wine merchant stood up. "I'm rather busy . . ." he began.

"You can't leave, now that you're here," Wu Song said loudly. "No matter how busy you are, you'll have to stay."

Hu's heart clanged like fifteen buckets in a single well. "Since he was polite enough to invite me here for wine," he thought, "how can he treat me like this? Why does he refuse to let me go?" Nevertheless, Hu resumed his seat.

"Another round of wine," ordered Wu Song.

The soldier filled the cups for the fourth round. By the time they reached the seventh, the guests were very apprehensive.

"Remove the cups," Wu Song shouted to the soldier. "We'll have more later." Wu Song wiped the table, and the neighbors started to leave. He spread his arms and stopped them.

"Now we're going to talk. Is there someone among you respected neighbors who is able to write?"

"Hu Zhengqing writes extremely well," said Yao the silversmith.

Wu Song addressed Hu courteously. "Permit me to trouble you." He rolled up his sleeves and from inside his garments whipped out his knife. Four fingers clutched the hilt, his thumb pointed at his chest, his eyes glared round and fierce.

"In the presence of you honorable neighbors, 'the culprit must pay for his wrong, the debtor for his debt.' I ask only that you be witnesses!"

With his left hand he grasped his sister-in-law, with his right he indicated Mistress Wang. The four neighbors stared and gaped. At a loss, they looked at each other. None of them dared utter a sound.

"Please don't reproach me," said Wu Song. "There's no need to be alarmed. I'm crude but fearless. My motto is 'An eye for an eye, a tooth for a tooth.' No harm shall come to any of you. I request only that you witness this. But if anyone tries to go, don't be surprised if I change my tune and stick him half a dozen times, or even take his life, though I pay for it with my own!"

Bug-eyed, the neighbors sat petrified.

Wu Song glared at Mistress Wang. "Now listen carefully, you old bitch! You are responsible for my brother's death! I want you to answer my questions!"

He turned and faced Golden Lotus. "Trollop! How did you scheme and kill my brother? Tell the truth and I'll spare you!"

"Brother-in-law, you're acting outrageously! Your brother died of pains in the heart. It had nothing to do with me!"

Before the words were out of her mouth Wu Song rammed the knife into the table, grabbed her hair with his left hand and clutched her bodice with his right. He kicked the table over, lightly lifted her across, placed her on her back before the altar table, and stood on her. Again he seized the knife in his right hand and pointed at Mistress Wang.

"Speak, old bitch! And make sure it's the truth!"

The old woman knew there was no escape. "Don't lose your temper, Constable," she said. "I'll talk!"

Wu Song directed the soldier to bring the pen and paper and ink and lay them on the table. With his knife he indicated Hu the former functionary. "Write this down, please, word for word!"

Hu stammered his consent. He ground the ink, added water, took up the pen, smoothed the paper and said: "Mistress Wang, give us the facts."

"It has nothing to do with me. What shall I say?"

"Old bitch," Wu Song grated. "I know everything! You can't lie your way out of it! If you don't talk, first I'll carve up this harlot, then I'll kill you, old dog!"

He flashed the knife twice close to Golden Lotus's face. The girl was panic-stricken.

"Spare me, brother-in-law! Let me up! I'll speak!"

Wu Song picked her up and set her kneeling before the altar table. "Speak, wanton, and be quick about it!"

Golden Lotus was scared witless. She had no choice but to tell the whole story, starting from the day she beaned Ximen Qing with the curtain pole. How they used the sewing of the burial garments as a means of getting into bed together, how Ximen kicked Wu the Elder, how they arranged to poison him, how Mistress Wang taught them and egged them on — she related everything from beginning to end. Wu Song made her pause after each sentence so that Hu could write it down.

"Treacherous snake," cried Mistress Wang. "You've spilled it all! How can I deny anything? You've put me on the spot!"

The old woman also confessed, and her every word was noted by Hu. Then both women were compelled to impress their thumb prints and make their marks. The four neighbors signed their names and made their marks also.

Wu Song had the soldier tie Mistress Wang's hands behind her back with his sash. He rolled up the confessions and put them inside his robe. Wu Song told the soldier to put a bowl of sacrificial wine before the altar table, then he pushed the two women to their knees in front of the memorial tablet.

"Brother, your spirit is near," Wu Song cried. "Today I shall avenge you!"

He ordered the soldier to light the paper money replicas. Golden Lotus could guess what was coming. She opened her mouth to scream. Wu Song yanked her over backwards by the head, planted a foot on each arm, and tore open her bodice. Quicker than it takes to tell, he plunged the knife into her breast and cut. Then, clenching the knife in his teeth, he ripped her chest open with both hands, pulled out her heart, liver and entrails, and placed them on the memorial tablet. Another slash of the knife, and he cut the girl's head off. Blood gushed all over the floor.

The staring neighbors covered their faces. Terrified by Wu Song's savagery, they could only obey his commands. Wu Song sent the soldier upstairs for a quilt, and wrapped Golden Lotus's head in it. He wiped his knife, stuck it in his boot, washed his hands, and spoke to the four neighbors respectfully.

"I hope you won't mind, but I must ask you to wait upstairs. I will return shortly."

The neighbors exchanged glances. They dared not refuse. They went upstairs and sat down. Wu Song instructed the soldier to take Mistress Wang upstairs too and keep her under guard. He locked the door to the upper story and told the other two soldiers to stand watch below.

With the head of Golden Lotus wrapped in a quilt, Wu Song went directly to Ximen's medicinal drug shop. He hailed the manager.

"Is Right Honorable in?"

"He just left."

"Please walk with me a few steps. I have something to say in private."

The manager recognized Wu Song. He dared not refuse. Wu Song led him to a secluded lane. Suddenly Wu Song's face hardened.

"Do you want to live or die?"

"Constable, I've never done you any harm. . . ."

"If you want to die, don't tell me where Ximen's gone. If you want to live, tell me truly where he's at."

"He just went . . . with an acquaintance to . . . to that big tavern at the foot of Lion Bridge. . . ."

Wu Song turned and strode off. The manager was paralyzed with fright. It was several minutes before he was able to totter back to the medicine shop.

At the Lion Bridge tavern Wu Song asked a waiter: "Who is the Right Honorable Ximen drinking with?"

"An acquaintance. They're upstairs in the room overlooking the street."

Constable Wu charged up the stairs. Through a window in the lattice wall he looked in. Ximen was sitting in the host's place. His guest was seated opposite. Two singsong girls sat one on either side.

Wu Song shook open the quilt and rolled out the bloody head. He picked it up with his left hand, grasped his knife with his right, swept the door curtain aside, plunged into the room, and threw the gory head in Ximen's face.

Ximen saw that it was Wu Song. "*Aiya!*" he exclaimed. He leaped on a bench and swung one leg over the window-sill, intending to flee. But he was too high above the street to jump. Ximen was in a panic.

Quicker than it takes to tell, Wu Song vaulted onto the table and kicked off the cups and dishes. The two singsong girls were petrified. The wealthy guest, hysterically scrambling to get out of the way, fell to the floor.

Because Wu Song was coming at him in a wild rush, Ximen feinted with his hands and lashed out with his right foot. Wu Song dodged, but the kick caught his right hand and sent the knife flying. It dropped clattering to the street. Ximen took heart. He feinted with his right, and threw a swift left jab at Wu Song's chest. Wu Song ducked and came in under it. With his left hand he seized Ximen between the head and

武松鬧殺西門慶

shoulder, with his right he grabbed Ximen's right leg, then lifted him high.

"Down you go!" he shouted.

For Ximen, firstly, he was harassed by the wronged ghost of Wu the Elder. Secondly, he had offended against Heaven's laws. And thirdly, how could he cope with Wu Song's superhuman strength? Head down, feet up, he plummeted into the center of the street and landed on his noggin with a crunch that left him half senseless, startling the passers-by.

Wu Song reached under a stool, picked up Golden Lotus's head, then leaped through the window down into the street. He picked up the fallen knife and approached his foe. Ximen was lying flat, already half dead. Only his eyes moved. Wu Song pressed down on him and with one sweep of the knife cut off his head.

He tied the two heads together by the hair. Holding them in one hand and the knife in the other, he hurried back to Purple Stone Street and shouted for the soldiers to open the door. He placed the heads as sacrifices before the memorial tablet and ceremoniously spilled a bowl of wine onto the floor.

"Brother, your spirit is near," he said, weeping. "Go up to Heaven! I have avenged you! I have killed the adulterous pair! Now I will burn your memorial tablet!"

He told the soldier to ask the neighbors upstairs to come down, and instructed him to bring down Mistress Wang. Again taking up his knife and the two heads, he confronted the neighbors.

"Please listen. I still have something to say."

The four neighbors clasped their hands and stood politely. "Speak, Constable. We are listening."

Wu Song said to the four neighbors: "The crime I committed to avenge my brother was proper and reasonable. Though it may mean my death, I have no regrets. I'm sorry I frightened you. I'm going to give myself up now. I don't know whether I'll live or die. First I'll burn my brother's memorial tablet. May I trouble you to sell my possessions to raise money for my trial? Today I shall surrender to the magistrate. All I want you to do is to testify and tell the truth, regardless of the consequences."

He burned the memorial tablet and the paper ingot replicas, then brought two trunks down from upstairs, opened them and gave their contents to the neighbors. Next, he set out for the magistracy, escorting Mistress Wang and carrying the two heads. The whole county town was in an uproar. Countless watchers lined the streets.

When the magistrate heard who was coming and why, he was shocked. He immediately called his court into session. Wu Song brought Mistress Wang forward and knelt. He placed the murder knife and the two heads before the dais. Wu Song knelt to the left, Mistress Wang knelt in the middle, and the neighbors knelt to the right. Constable Wu took out the confessions which Hu had written down and read them from beginning to end.

The magistrate had the recorder question Mistress Wang. What she answered corresponded with her confession. The four neighbors gave corroborating testimony. Coroner Ho and Yunge were called. They also offered clear evidence.

Guarded by a court officer and the coroner's assistants, all those concerned in the case returned to Purple Stone Street, where the body of Golden Lotus was examined. They went next to the street outside the tavern at Lion Bridge for an inspection of Ximen's corpse. Certificates stating the circumstances surrounding the death were filled out, after which all returned to the county office and the certificates were submitted. The magistrate ordered that long racks be fitted to the necks of Wu Song and Mistress Wang and that they be committed to jail. The witnesses were lodged in the gate house.

The magistrate considered Wu Song a gallant principled man. He remembered the mission Wu Song had undertaken for him to the capital and his various good qualities. He wanted very much to help him. He summoned the court officers.

"That Wu Song is a loyal fellow. We'll change the indictment to this: 'Wu Song, wishing to sacrifice to the memory of his brother, was prevented by his sister-in-law, and for that reason they quarrelled. She tried to knock down the memorial tablet, Wu Song sought to protect it, and they fought, in the course of which he killed her. Ximen Qing, who was her adulterous lover, intervened. The two men battled, evenly matched, all the way to Lion Bridge, and there the lover was killed.' "

The new indictment was read to Wu Song and the others involved. The magistrate wrote an order directing that all concerned be taken under guard to Dongping Prefecture for disposition of the case by the prefect.

Although Yanggu was only a small county it had men who appreciated chivalry. Leading families gave Wu Song donations of silver. Others sent him wine and food and money and rice. Wu Song went to his quarters, packed his luggage and entrusted it to one of his soldiers. He sent Yunge twenty or thirty ounces of silver to use in looking after his father. More than half the men under his command presented Wu Song with meat and wine.

Armed with the transfer order, the county officers in charge wrapped up Coroner Ho's cremation record, the silver Ximen had given him, the charred bones, the confessions and the murder weapon and proceeded with his charges to Dongping Prefecture. By the time they got to the prefectural office a noisy crowd was waiting at the gates.

Chen Wenzhao, the prefect, on hearing of their arrival, immediately called his court into session. An intelligent official, Chen already knew about the matter. He had them brought before him and read the report from Yanggu County. Next, he looked over the record of the testimony and questioned each of the witnesses. He directed the keeper of stores to retain the various exhibits and the murder weapon, had Wu Song's heavy rack exchanged for a light one, and committed him to jail. A heavy rack was placed around Mistress Wang's neck and nailed fast. She was locked in a cell for the condemned.

The county officers were allowed to return. As to Coroner Ho, Yunge and the four neighbors, the prefect said: "These six can go home. Let them stay there until further notice. The wife of the principal Ximen Qing must wait here in the prefecture. When I receive instructions from the imperial authorities I will render a detailed judgment."

The county officers and the six returned to Yanggu. Wu Song remained in jail. Several soldiers brought him food.

Prefect Chen sympathized with Wu Song, and thought him a gallant high-minded person. He frequently sent people to inquire after him. As a result, none of the jailers asked him for a single penny, in fact they brought him food and wine. Chen lightened the charges against Wu Song still further, and sent the case up to the Legal Office of the Imperial Government for examination and decision. At the same time he dispatched a trusted emissary to the capital with confidential letters to friends in the Ministry of Criminal Proceedings.

These discussed the matter with the Legal Office, and then rendered the following decision: *Whereas Mistress Wang stimulated sexual cravings and adulterous desires; and whereas she instigated the woman to poison her husband; and whereas she told the woman to prevent Wu Song from sacrificing to the memory of his brother, as a result of which he killed her; and whereas she provoked the man and woman into indecent behavior: it is therefore decided that Mistress Wang shall be executed by being sliced to death. Wu Song, although he was avenging his brother when he fought and killed the adulterer Ximen Qing, and although he voluntarily surrendered, cannot be completely exonerated. He is to be given forty strokes on the back, tattooed with the mark of the criminal and exiled to a place two thousand li distant. The adulterous couple committed major crimes, but they are dead and no more need be said about them. The other persons involved in the case are free to return to their homes. This decision is to be implemented immediately upon receipt.*

When Prefect Chen read this document he summoned before his court Coroner Ho, Yunge, the four neighbors and the wife of Ximen Qing. Wu Song was brought from jail. The decision from the Imperial Government was read to him. The rack was removed, and he was given forty strokes. The jailers saw to it that only six or seven actually cut his flesh. A seven-and-a-half-catty rack was fastened around his neck and the mark of the criminal was tattooed in two lines on his face. The prefect exiled him to prison in the district town of Mengzhou. The others, in accordance with the decision, were allowed to go home.

Mistress Wang was brought from her cell to hear the verdict of the Imperial Government. The reason for the execution was written on a placard, and the prisoner signed her acknowledgement. She was then tied seated on a wooden "donkey" with three ropes and nailed to it by four long spikes driven through her limbs.

The prefect of Dongping gave his order: "Slice her!"

Mistress Wang and the "donkey" were carried out by strong bearers and paraded through the streets. Terrible drums rumbled, frightful gongs sounded. With the placard in the fore and staff-bearers bringing up the rear, with two sharp knives held aloft and a bunch of paper flowers waving, the procession marched to the center of the city. There Mistress Wang was sliced to death.

Wu Song, wearing a light rack for walking, witnessed the execution. Neighbor Yao gave him the money he had obtained by selling the constable's possessions, bid him farewell and went home. Two guards were assigned by the court to take Wu Song to Mengzhou. The work of the prefect was done.

Wu Song and his guards set out. His orderly gave him the luggage he had been looking after and returned to Yangku. The three men left Dongping Prefecture and proceeded slowly along the winding road to Mengzhou.

Later, Wu Song escaped from Mengzhou Prison and joined the outlaws.

CHAPTER 14
Black Whirlwind Fights White Streak in the Waves

When Song Jiang heard that his father had died of illness, he bid farewell to Chai Jin and hurriedly went home. On his arrival, he was arrested for the killing of Poxi and sentenced to the prison in Jiangzhou (today, Jinjiang in Jiangsu province). There, he became friendly with Dai Zong, the prison superintendent. One day, Dai Zong invited him into town.

Song Jiang and the superintendent left the prison and went into Jiangzhou. They mounted the stairs to the upper storey of a tavern off the street and sat down. They summoned the waiter and ordered wine and tidbits and vegetable dishes. Over the wine, Song Jiang told of the many bold heroes and men he had met on the road. Dai Zong, too, spoke frankly, revealing his relations with Wu Yong.

They talked intimately and without reserve. Before they had finished more than two or three cups of wine they heard a tumult of voices on the floor below. The waiter hurried into their room.

"Superintendent, you're the only one who can handle him," he said to Dai. "There's no other way. Please go and settle this."

"Who's raising all that row down there?"

"It's that brother Li we often see you with, the man called Iron Ox. He's trying to borrow money from the host."

Dai laughed. "That rascal is misbehaving again. I couldn't imagine who you meant." To Song Jiang he said: "Excuse me a minute, brother. I'll bring him up."

Dai went down the stairs and soon returned with a big dark-complected fellow. Song Jiang was taken aback by the man's appearance.

"Who is this brother?" he asked the superintendent.

"One of our prison guards, Li Kui, from Baizhang Village, Yishui County, in Yizhou Prefecture. He's nicknamed Black Whirlwind. In his native parts he's also known as Iron Ox. He had to run away from home because he beat a man to death. He wandered to Jiangzhou and here he's remained, although later there was an amnesty. Because he's nasty when he's drunk, many people are afraid of him. He can wield two battle-axes, and he's good with fists and cudgel. He's on our prison staff."

Li Kui looked Song Jiang over. "Who's this swarthy fellow?" he asked Dai Zong.

The superintendent smiled. "You see what a crude lout he is, sir Clerk. No manners whatsoever."

"I only asked," said Li Kui. "What's crude about that?"

"Instead of saying 'Who is this gentleman?' you said 'Who is this swarthy fellow?' If that isn't crude, what is? Well, I'll tell you who he is. He's the noble brother you've been wanting to join for so long."

"Not Blacky Song Jiang, the Timely Rain from Shandong?"

"Must you be so vulgar?" Dai shouted. "Referring to him like that! Haven't you any sense of rank? Kowtow to him, quickly. What are you waiting for?"

"I will if he's really Song Jiang. But if he's just some idler, I'll be blown if I will. You're not just making sport of me, are you, brother?"

"I am indeed Blacky Song Jiang, of Shandong," Song Jiang assured him.

Li Kui clapped his hands. "My blessed grandfather! Why didn't you say so earlier? Iron Ox is delighted!" He flopped to the ground and kowtowed.

Song Jiang hastily returned the compliment. "Brave brother,

please be seated," he pleaded.

"Come sit beside me and have some wine," said Dai.

"All right, but none of those piddling little cups for me.
I want a large bowl."

"What angered you downstairs?" Song Jiang asked.

"I have a big silver ingot that I pawned for ten ounces of
silver coins," said Li Kui. "I wanted to borrow ten ounces
from the host here to get the bar back, plus a little more for
spending money. But the knave wouldn't lend me a thing.
I was just going to deal with him and smash his premises
when brother Dai called me upstairs."

"You need only ten ounces to redeem your ingot? Aren't
there any interest charges?"

"I've got the interest money. All I need is another ten
ounces."

Song Jiang took out ten coins and gave them to Li Kui.
"Go redeem your ingot," he said. Dai Zong wanted to
intervene, but Song Jiang had already handed the money over.

"Great," said Li Kui. "You two brothers wait here. I'll
repay as soon as I get my ingot. And I'll invite brother Song
outside the town to eat and drink with us."

"Stay a while," said Song Jiang. "Have a few bowls here,
first."

"I'll be right back." Li Kui pushed the door curtain aside
and went downstairs.

"You shouldn't lend him money," Dai Zong said. "I tried
to prevent you, but you were too quick."

"Why not?"

"Li Kui is pretty straight, but he loves to drink and gamble.
Where would he get a big silver ingot! It's just a ruse, and
you fell for it, brother. He must be going to gamble. That's
why he left here so fast. If he wins, he'll return your money.
If he loses, you'll never see a penny of those ten ounces of
silver. I'm ashamed to have been the cause of this."

Song Jiang laughed. "Don't treat me like a stranger, brother. The silver's not worth talking about. Let him lose it. He
seems like a straight-forward loyal fellow."

"He has his good points. He's just too rude and rash. In the Jiangzhou prison when he gets drunk he doesn't bother the inmates, but he beats up the toughest guards. He's caused me no end of trouble. The slightest injustice drives him wild, and he tears into bullies. Everyone in Jiangzhou is afraid of him."

"Let's have another cup or two, and stroll around outside the city."

"I nearly forgot. I want to show you the scenery along the river."

"That will be fine. I'd like to see the beauties of Jiangzhou."

Meanwhile, Li Kui, having obtained some money, thought: "What luck! Brother Song Jiang never met me before, but he lends me ten ounces of silver. He certainly deserves his reputation for righteousness and generosity. What a shame I've lost steadily at gambling these last few days. I haven't a copper to invite him out. I'll gamble with these ten ounces of silver he's given me. If I win a few strings of cash I'll be able to wine and dine him, and that will make me look good."

Li Kui hurried to a gambling den outside the city run by a man called Little Zhang Yi. He threw his ten ounces of silver down on the gambling floor and said: "Let me have the toss coins."

Little Zhang Yi knew he played honestly. "Wait a while, brother," he urged. "You take the next round."

"I want this one."

"Bet from the sidelines which way the coins will fall."

"I don't want to do that. I want to toss them myself. I'm betting five ounces of silver." Li Kui snatched the coins from a man who was waiting to toss. "Who'll cover my bet?"

"I will," said Little Zhang Yi.

"Tails," cried Li Kui, and tossed. The coins came up heads. Little Zhang Yi reached for the money.

"I came here with ten ounces," said Li Kui.

"I'll bet you another five, then," said Little Zhang Yi. "If you get tails, I'll return you the five you just lost."

Li Kui took the coins and tossed. "Tails," he shouted. Again the coins turned up heads.

Little Zhang Yi grinned. "I told you to wait for the next round and not grab the toss coins, but you wouldn't listen. Now you've thrown two heads in a row."

"This silver doesn't belong to me."

"It doesn't matter whose it is. You've lost and that's that."

"Lend it to me, then. I'll pay you back tomorrow."

"Idle chatter! As the old saying has it: 'There's no pity in gambling.' You've lost. What are you making such a fuss about?"

Li Kui hitched up the front of his gown. "Are you going to return me that money or not?"

"Brother Li, you gamble honestly as a rule. Why are you behaving so badly today?"

Li Kui did not reply but picked his money up from the floor and also snatched ten ounces of silver belonging to other gamblers, and put them all in the pocket of his cloth gown. Glaring, he said: "I usually play straight, but today's an exception."

Little Zhang Yi rushed up to wrest back the money. Li Kui made a feint and threw him to the ground. A dozen gamblers swarmed against the big fellow. Li Kui feinted east and struck west, feinted south and struck north. He pounded them till they had no place to hide, then he headed for the gate.

"Where are you going, young man?" the gate-keeper asked.

Li Kui thrust him aside, kicked open the gate and went out, pursued by the other gamblers.

From the gate, they shouted after him: "How can you behave like this, brother Li? Taking our silver!" But they didn't dare come close.

As Li Kui was walking away, a man ran up behind him, seized his arm and shouted: "How dare you grab other people's property, you scoundrel?"

"What friggin business is that of yours?" Li Kui spun around to find himself looking at Dai Zong and, standing to Dai's rear, Song Jiang. A look of embarrassment spread over Li's face.

"Don't blame me, brother. Iron Ox usually plays fair. But I lost your silver and had no money to invite you out. I got excited and behaved badly."

Song Jiang laughed. "Any time you need silver, just ask me. You obviously lost, so give them back their money."

Li Kui had no choice but to take the silver from his pocket and put it in Song Jiang's hand. Song Jiang called Little Zhang Yi over and gave him the money.

"I'll take only what belongs to us," said the gambler. "I don't want the other ten pieces which brother Li lost to me. He's liable to hold it against me."

"Take it all, and don't worry," Song Jiang urged, but the gambler was adamant. "Did he hurt any of you?" Song Jiang asked.

"The game master, the collector and the gate-keeper — he knocked them all down."

"Then let this be their compensation. If you won't accept this for them, I'll go to them myself."

The gambler took the silver, thanked Song Jiang and departed.

"Now," said Song Jiang, "let's have a few cups with brother Li."

"Up ahead beside the river is the Pipa Pavilion," said Dai. "It was once frequented by the Tang poet Bai Juyi. Now it's a tavern. We can have some wine there and admire the river scenery."

"Hadn't we better buy some tidbits in town first, to take along?"

"No need. They serve meals, too."

"In that case, let's go."

The three men proceeded to the Pipa Pavilion. One portion of it overlooked the Xunyang River, the other was used as living quarters for the host. Upstairs were ten or so tables. Dai Zong selected a clean one and invited Song Jiang to be seated. The superintendent sat down opposite, and placed Li Kui at his side. They ordered vegetables, fruit and seafood delicacies to go with the wine. The waiter produced two jugs of "Springtime in Jade Bottles" — a famous Jiangzhou liquor — and removed the clay stoppers.

"A large bowl for me," said Li Kui. "I can't drink out of those little cups."

"Rustic," Dai barked. "I want you to just drink your wine and keep quiet."

"This gentleman and I will use cups," Song Jiang told the waiter. "Give our big brother a large bowl."

The waiter responded and went out. He soon returned with a bowl which he placed in front of Li Kui. He poured the wine and served the tidbits. Li Kui grinned.

"You're really a fine man, brother Song, as everyone says. You understand me. Getting you as a friend is one of the best things that ever happened to me."

Six or seven rounds of drinks were consumed. Song Jiang was pleased with his two companions. After drinking several cups, he suddenly got a craving for hot pepper fish soup.

"Is there any fresh fish around here?" he asked Dai Zong.

"Don't you see all those fishing boats on the river?" Dai responded with a smile. "The whole region is teeming with fish and rice."

"Some hot pepper fish soup would be just right for sobering up."

Dai called the waiter and ordered three servings of fish in hot pepper soup. Not long after, the soup arrived.

"'Beautiful crockery is more satisfying than delicious food'," Song Jiang quoted. "Although this is only a tavern, they certainly have lovely bowls." He picked up his chopsticks. After urging Dai Zong and Li Kui to eat, he tasted the fish and sipped the soup.

Li Kui didn't bother with chopsticks. He pulled the fish out of his bowl with his hand and ate it, bones and all. Song Jiang couldn't help laughing. He took two more sips of soup, then put down his chopsticks and stopped eating.

Dai Zong said: "This is preserved fish, brother. I'm sure it's not to your taste."

"I thought a little fresh fish soup would go well after wine. But this fish isn't really very good."

"I can't eat mine, either. I don't like salted fish."

Li Kui, who had finished his own bowl, said: "If you brothers don't want yours, I'll eat it for you." He scooped the fish out of Song Jiang's bowl with his fingers and consumed it, then did the same with Dai Zong's. He spattered the whole table with soup.

Song Jiang watched Li Kui demolish three bowls of fish soup, including bones. He summoned the waiter.

"I think this brother is still hungry. Bring him two catties of sliced meat. I'll pay when you've added up the bill."

"We've no beef, only mutton. You can have all the fat mutton you want."

Li Kui flung the remnants of his soup in the man's face, slopping his clothes.

"What are you doing?" Dai Zong yelled.

"This sassy villain has the nerve to pretend I eat nothing but beef and won't give me any mutton."

"I only asked," the waiter protested. "I didn't say anything."

"Go slice the meat," said Song Jiang. "I'll pay."

Swallowing his anger, the man sliced two catties of mutton and served it on a platter. Li Kui didn't stand on ceremony. In a twiddle of thumbs, he chomped the whole thing down.

"You're a good man," Song Jiang said admiringly.

"Brother Song can read my friggin mind. Meat's much better than fish."

Dai called the waiter over. "The bowls you served that fish soup in were very nice, but the fish was too salty. Don't you have any fresh fish you can make a pepper soup of for this gentleman here, to cut the effects of the wine?"

"To tell you the truth, sir, that fish was last night's. Today's live catch is still on the boats. But none of it can be sold until the catch-master comes. So we don't have any fresh fish yet."

Li Kui jumped up. "I'll get a couple for brother."

"Don't go," said Dai Zong. "We'll ask the waiter to buy some."

"Those fishermen won't dare refuse me. There's nothing to it."

The superintendent couldn't stop him. Li Kui left. "I hope you'll excuse me, brother," Dai said to Song Jiang, "for introducing you to a man like that. He has absolutely no manners. I'm very embarrassed."

"That's his nature. No one can change it. But I respect his honesty."

The two chatted and joked in the Pipa Pavilion.

Li Kui went down to the river. Eighty or ninety fishing boats were moored in a row to willow trees along the bank. Some of the fishermen were sprawled asleep in the stern, some were mending nets on the bow. Others were bathing in the water. It was the middle of the fifth lunar month, and a red sun was sinking in the west. Of the catch-master there was no sign, and so no fish were on sale.

"You've got fresh fish on board," Li Kui called. "Let me have a couple."

"We can't open the hatches till the catch-master comes. Don't you see all those pedlars waiting on the bank?"

"Who cares about your friggin catch-master. Just let me have two fish."

"We haven't burned the paper ingots yet to pay the gods. How can we open the hatches and give you fish?"

Before the fishermen could stop him, Li Kui jumped onto one of the boats. He didn't understand anything about these craft, and he hauled up a bamboo partition.

"Don't do that," the fishermen on the bank yelled.

Li Kui groped around under the hatch cover, but he couldn't find any fish. The river boats had large openings in the stern which let the water in and kept the fish in the hold alive. The bamboo partition was to prevent them from swimming out. Jiangzhou was supplied with fresh fish through this method. When Li Kui pulled up the partition, all the fish in the boat escaped.

He leaped over to the adjoining craft and hauled up its bamboo partition. Seventy or eighty fishermen rushed on board and attacked Li Kui with bamboo poles. Enraged, he stripped off his gown and stood with only a checkered kerchief covering his loins. He snatched half a dozen of the punting poles with both hands and snapped them like scallions. The startled fishermen left hastily, undid the moorings of their boats and shoved off.

Li Kui, naked as an owl, angrily seized a broken pole and charged up the bank to continue the battle. The pedlars shouldered their carrying-poles and fled in confusion.

In the midst of this turmoil, a man was seen approaching along a path. "You've come at last, master," several persons called. "That big dark fellow has been grabbing fish. He's driven off all the boats."

"Which big dark fellow? How dare he behave like that?"

"There, on the bank, chasing and beating people."

The man sped towards Li Kui, shouting: "Have you eaten a panther's heart or a tiger's gall that you dare mess up my business?"

Li Kui looked at him. He was over six feet tall, about thirty-two or three, with a black mustache and goatee. His head was swathed in blue silk of a swastika pattern, through which a lock of hair protruded bound by a string of heartsblood red. He wore a white cloth gown, tied at the waist by a red sash. On his feet were many-looped hemp sandals with black and white bird's-foot design. He held a weighing scale in one hand.

He had come to sell fish, but when he saw Li Kui knocking people about, he passed his scale to a pedlar and rushed forward. "Who else do you want to beat, scoundrel?" he cried.

Without a word, Li Kui whirled his pole and swung. The man dodged and seized the pole. Li Kui grabbed him by the hair. Three times the man snatched for his legs, hoping to trip him up. But Li Kui had the strength of an ox. He simply held him off and prevented him from grappling. The man pummelled Li Kui's ribs, but the big fellow was unperturbed. When he started kicking, Li Kui pushed his head down and pounded his back like a drum with a fist of iron. He couldn't get away.

Someone ran up behind Li Kui and wrapped his arms around his waist, helped by another man. "You can't do this," they

黑旋風鬪浪裡白跳

exclaimed.

Li Kui turned his head and saw Dai Zong and Song Jiang. He released his grip and the man he had been thumping sped away like a whisp of smoke.

"I told you not to go for fish," Dai scolded. "And here you are, fighting. Suppose you killed him? You have to spend the rest of your life in jail."

"Afraid I'd implicate you? If I killed anyone, I'd bear the whole blame myself."

"Don't talk like that, brother," said Song Jiang. "Put your gown on, and we'll have some wine."

Li Kui retrieved his gown from beneath a willow, slung it over his arm, and set off with Dai and Song. Before they had gone a dozen paces a voice behind them shouted: "Swarthy rascal, you and I are going to have this out."

Li Kui turned. The catch-master, naked except for a breech-clout, had skin as white as snow. He had removed his blue silk head-binding, revealing a topknot of hair tied with string of heartsblood red. He was poling a boat towards the bank.

"Villain who deserves ten thousand slices," he yelled. "If I fear you I'm no man. Whoever runs from this fight is a craven coward."

Li Kui roared with rage, cast his gown aside, and rushed to meet the foe. The man poled his boat a bit closer to the bank, cursing steadily.

"Come ashore, if you're such a man," Li Kui invited.

The catch-master poked Li Kui in the legs with his pole. Furious, the big fellow leaped on board. Quicker than it takes to say, the man set himself and, with a few shoves of the pole, sped the craft like an arrow to the middle of river.

Li Kui knew how to swim, but not very well. He was confused and alarmed. The man stopped his swearing and set the pole down.

"Come on," he said, "let's see who'll be the victor." He seized Li Kui by the arms. "I'm not going to fight you yet. I want you to drink some water, first." With his feet he tipped the boat over, turning it bottom up and dumping both men in the river.

Song Jiang and Dai Zong, who had hurried to the bank, groaned. Nearly five hundred people were also watching from beneath the willows. "The big dark fellow was tricked," they said. "Even if he escapes with his life, he'll get a bellyful of water."

The river parted and Li Kui was lifted up, only to be shoved down under again. The two men battled in the jade waves — one dark to the point of blackness, the other pale as glistening frost. Fiercely interlocked they fought, and the five hundred spectators on the bank raised cheer after cheer.

Li Kui had been ducked so often that his eyes were white. Again he was lifted, again pushed under. He was clearly getting the worst of it. Song Jiang told Dai Zong to ask people to save him.

"Who is that big white fellow?" Dai Zong asked.

"He's our local catch-master," someone replied. "Zhang Shun."

When Song Jiang heard that name, he exclaimed: "Not the one they call White Streak in the Waves?"

"Yes, that's him."

"I have a letter for him back at the prison from his brother Zhang Heng," Song Jiang told the superintendent.

Dai went to the edge of the bank and called: "Brother Zhang, stop fighting. There's a letter for you from your older brother Zhang Heng. That big dark fellow is our friend. Let him go. Come ashore and talk."

Zhang Shun recognized the superintendent. He released Li Kui, hurried to the shore, climbed the bank and greeted Dai respectfully.

"Forgive my bad manners, Superintendent," he said.

"For my sake, rescue that brother of mine and bring him here," Dai pleaded. "There's someone I want you to meet."

Zhang Shun dived into the river and swam swiftly to where Li Kui was floundering about, his head in the water. Zhang grasped him by the hand. His legs treaded water so powerfully he seemed to be walking on land, and the waves only came up to his navel. With one hand he hauled Li Kui towards the shore. The audience on the bank cheered. Song Jiang was stricken dumb with amazement. The two men soon reached the bank. Li Kui, gasping, vomited up a lot of water.

"Please come with me to the Pipa Pavilion where we can talk," said Dai.

Zhang Shun got his gown and put it on. Li Kui did the same, and the four men went to the pavilion.

"Do you know me, brother?" Dai asked Zhang Shun.

"Of course, Superintendent. But it's never been my good fortune to meet you."

Dai pointed at Li Kui. "Did you know him before? Today you two have clashed."

"Naturally I know brother Li. But this is the first time we've matched strength."

"You ducked me plenty," said Li Kui.

"And you really pounded me," Zhang Shun replied.

"You're now brothers who've contended," said Dai. " 'You don't know a man till you've fought him,' as the old saying goes."

"In the future, don't try to start anything with me on land," Li Kui warned.

"I'll just wait for you on the water."

All four men laughed, and mutually apologized for their rudeness. Pointing at Song Jiang, Dai addressed himself to Zhang Shun.

"Do you recognize this brother?"

"No. I've never seen him before."

Li Kui jumped to his feet. "That's Blacky Song Jiang."

"Not Clerk Song of Yuncheng, the Timely Rain from Shandong?"

"Yes, he's brother Song Jiang," Dai confirmed.

Zhang Shun promptly kowtowed. "I've long known your fame, but I never dreamed we'd meet today. Many's the time I've heard brothers in the gallant fraternity tell of your virtues, how you rescue those in danger and help the needy, how righteous you are, how generous."

"You mustn't exaggerate. Not long ago I spent a few days in the home of Li Jun the Turbulent River Dragon, below Jieyang Ridge. Then, because of an encounter with Mu Hong at the Xunyang River, I also met your brother Zhang Heng. He wrote a letter which he asked me to deliver to you. I have it back at the prison. I came here today to the Pipa Pavilion with Superintendent Dai and brother Li to drink some wine and admire the river scenery. I got a sudden craving for fish soup to sober me up, and brother Li volunteered to get the fish. We couldn't stop him. Hearing a great row down by the bank, we sent the waiter to see what was going on. He said the big dark fellow was beating people. We rushed down to stop him. Little did we think that we would meet you, warrior. I have indeed have been blessed by Heaven today. I've made the acquaintance of three bold gallants. Please, let's be seated and have a few cups."

They summoned the waiter to lay the table and bring wine and tidbits.

"If it's fish you want, brother," Zhang Shun said to Song Jiang, "I'll get you some."

"Fine."

"I'll go with you," said Li Kui.

"Not again?" said Dai. "Haven't you drunk enough water?"

Zhang Shun laughed, and took Li Kui's hand. "We'll go for the fish together and see what the response is."

CHAPTER 15
In the Xunyang Pavilion Song Jiang Recites a Rebellious Poem

After resting six or seven days, Song Jiang considered going into town and seeing Dai Zong. Another day passed without any visit from the superintendent. Early the following morning after breakfast Song Jiang took some silver, locked his door, left the prison and strolled into the city. Outside the prefectural office, he asked someone where Superintendent Dai lived.

"He has no wife or children," the man said. "He stays in the Guan Yin Monastery next door to the City Temple."

Song Jiang went there, but Dai's door was locked. He had already gone out.

Next, the clerk sought Li Kui the Black Whirlwind. "He's a headless ghost, that one," several people said. "He hasn't any home, except for the prison. And he has no routine. He'll spend a few days here, a couple of days there. You never know where he's at."

Song Jiang then went looking for the catch-master Zhang Shun. "He lives in a village in the suburbs," he was told. "Even when he sells fish it's by the river bank outside the city. He only comes into town to collect money."

The clerk again left the city, still hoping to find Zhang Shun. But he met no one he could ask. He walked on, alone and depressed. Then he came upon a lovely stretch of river, and was enchanted by the view. He saw ahead a several storied tavern. Beside it, hanging from a tall pole, was a blue banner emblazoned with the words: *The Excellent Cellar by the Xunyang River. Xunyang Pavilion*, the tavern's name, was written large in the calligraphy of poet Su Dongpo on a sign beneath the eaves.

"I heard of Jiangzhou's Xunyang Pavilion back in Yuncheng," Song Jiang mused, "and here it is. Although I'm alone, I mustn't miss this opportunity. I'll go upstairs and relax a while."

On the carved vermilion pillars to either side of the door were two white plaques on which a couplet was written: *Incomparable wine* and *A world-famous place to dine.*

Song Jiang entered, mounted the stairs and sat down in a room overlooking the river. He leaned on the railing and gazed around appreciatively.

A waiter came in. "Are you waiting for others, sir, or are you here by yourself?"

"I was expecting two guests, but they haven't shown up. Bring me a jug of good wine, first, and some fruit and meats. I don't want any fish."

The waiter went downstairs and soon returned with a jug of "Moonlight Breeze on Lovers' Bridge" — a fine liquor, and a tray of vegetable dishes and tidbits to go with it. Then came fat mutton, crispy chicken, lees-steeped goose and fillet of beef, all served on vermillion plates and platters.

Song Jiang was very pleased. "Delicious food well arranged on excellent crockery. Jiangzhou deserves its fame," he thought. "Although I'm here as an exile, I can still admire the scenery. We have a few scenic spots and antique remains at home, but nothing to compare with this."

Seated beside the railing, he drank steadily. Gradually, without being aware of it, he became drunk. In a surge of melancholy, he thought: "I was born in Shandong Province and raised in Yuncheng Town. A clerk by profession, I know many a good fellow in the gallant fraternity, and have earned something of a reputation. But though over thirty, I haven't made my name yet or done anything outstanding. Instead, I've the tattoo of the criminal on my cheek and am living in exile. Who knows when I'll see my old father and brother again!"

The wine went to his head, and he wept, very depressed.

Suddenly, he decided to write a poem. He ordered the waiter to bring brush-pen and ink-stone, then rose and scanned appreciatively the poems which others had written on the white calcimined walls.

"Why not write my poem on the wall, too?" he said to himself. "Some day, when I've earned my place in the world, I'll come here and read it again, and think back on my present misery."

Stimulated by the wine, he ground a thick mixture of ink, soaked his brush-pen in it, and wrote on the white wall:

Since childhood I studied classics and history,
And grew up shrewd and intelligent.
Today, a tiger enduring in the wilderness,
I crouch with tooth and claw, intent.

A criminal's tattoo upon my cheek,
An unwilling exile in far Jiangzhou,
I shall have my revenge some day,
And dye red with blood the Xunyang's flow.

Song Jiang laughed uproariously, delighted with his effort. He drank several more cups of wine. By now he was dancing for joy. Again he took up his pen and added four more lines:

Heart in Shandong, body in Wu,
Drifting, I breathe sighs into the air.
If I achieve my lofty aim,
No rebel chief will with me compare.

At the bottom, in large script he wrote: "by Song Jiang of Yuncheng", and tossed the pen on the table. He intoned the verses to himself, then downed a few more cups of wine. He was very drunk. Song Jiang asked for the bill, paid, and told the waiter to keep the change. Brushing smooth his long sleeves, he staggered down the stairs and returned to the prison. He opened his door and collapsed on the bed.

He slept straight through till the following dawn. When he

awakened he remembered nothing about having written a poem in the Xunyang Pavilion. He had a bad hangover, and lay on his bed all day. Of that no more need be said.

Opposite Jiangzhou, on the other side of the river, was a town called Wuweijun, a desolate place. Living there was a former deputy prefect named Huang Wenbing. Although he'd read a bit of the classics, he was a narrow-hearted sycophant who envied men of ability. Those superior in talent he injured, those inferior he mocked. His speciality was harming people throughout the township.

He knew that Prefect Cai was the son of the premier, and frequently crossed the river to call and ingratiate himself. He hoped that this would lead to an appointment making him an official again. It was Song Jiang's fate to arouse this man and be treated by him as an adversary.

That day Huang Wenbing was sitting idle and bored at home. He called two servants, bought some attractive gifts, crossed the river in his own swift boat, and went to call on the prefect. But Cai was in the midst of an official banquet, and Huang didn't dare interrupt. He returned to the boat, which his servants had moored, by coincidence, below the Xunyang Pavilion.

It was a hot day, and Huang strolled up to the tavern. After looking over the wine cellar, he mounted the stairs to the rooms along the balcony. He glanced at the many poems upon the wall. Some were well-written, others were incoherent nonsense. Huang smiled superciliously.

He then read the verses of Song Jiang. "This is rebellious," he exclaimed. "Who could have written it?" He looked at the signature: "Song Jiang of Yuncheng".

Huang read the poem again: *Since childhood I studied classics and history, / And grew up shrewd and intelligent....* He laughed coldly. "Thinks pretty well of himself!"

He continued: *Today, a tiger enduring in the wilderness, / I crouch with tooth and claw, intent....* Huang cocked his head to one side. "The lout has no sense of fitness."

He read on: *A criminal's tattoo upon my cheek, | An unwilling exile in far Jiangzhou....* Again Huang laughed. "This is no noble-minded person. He's only an exiled prisoner."

Once more he read: *I shall have my revenge some day, | And dye red with blood the Xunyang's flow....* Huang shook his head. "Who does the villain want to wreak vengeance on? And why here? He's only an exile. How much of a stir can he make?"

Heart in Shandong, body in Wu, | Drifting, I breathe sighs into the air.... Huang nodded. "At least those lines make sense."

If I achieve my lofty aim, | No rebel chief will with me compare.... Huang stuck out his tongue and wagged his head. "What brass. An incomparable rebel leader! If that's not a proclamation of revolt I don't know what is!"

Huang read the signature again: "Song Jiang of Yuncheng".

"Where have I heard that name before?" he pondered. "Probably some petty functionary."

He summoned the waiter. "Who wrote this poem?"

"A man who was here last night. He drank a whole jug all by himself."

"What does he look like?"

"He has two lines of tattooing on his cheek. He must be one of the inmates of the city prison. A swarthy, short, fat fellow."

"I see," said Huang. He asked for a pen and ink, copied the poem on a sheet of paper, and placed it inside his clothes. "Don't scrape it off," he cautioned the waiter.

He went down the stairs and returned to the boat, where he spent the night. The next day after breakfast, with the servants bearing the gifts, he again proceeded to the prefecture. Cai had already completed court and had withdrawn to the residence. An officer went in to announce Huang. Before long the man came out and conducted Huang to the rear hall. There, Cai joined him. After some friendly chatter and when the gifts had been presented, both men took their seats.

"I came across the river last night to pay my respects," said Huang, "but Your Excellency was giving a banquet and I didn't want to intrude. So I've come today, instead."

"Such an intimate friend, you could have joined us. I'm sorry I missed you." Cai ordered that tea be served.

After a few sips, Huang asked: "May I be so bold as to enquire whether there has been any word from your honorable father the premier lately?"

"I received a letter from him just a couple of days ago."

"What's the news of the capital?"

"He says the Royal Astrologer in a report to the throne states that an evil star is shining on our land of Wu, and on Zhu, and that there are probably trouble-makers abroad who must be eliminated. What's more, says my father, children on the street are chanting this rhyme: *The destroyer of our country is home and tree; water and work are armed soldiery; stretched in a line are thirty-six; Shandong will put us in a terrible fix.* He advises me to keep a careful watch on my prefecture."

Huang thought a moment. Then he smiled. "I'm not surprised, Excellency." He took from his sleeve the poem he had copied and handed it to Cai. "Here's the reason."

The prefect read it. "A rebellious poem. Where did you get it?"

"I didn't dare to intrude last night, and walked back to the river bank. For want of something better to do, I went into the Xunyang Pavilion to escape the heat. I saw poems idlers had inscribed on the white-washed wall, including this newly written one."

"What sort of person is the author?"

"He's put his name down. Song Jiang of Yuncheng."

"Who is he?"

"He tells us in his poem: *A criminal's tattoo upon my cheek, / An unwilling exile in far Jiangzhou.* He's an exile, a criminal in the city prison."

"What can a fellow like that do?"

"Don't underestimate him, Excellency. He fits in exactly

with the children's rhyme your honorable father mentions in his letter."

"What do you mean?"

"*The destroyer of our country is home and tree.* Put the top of the character for 'home' over the character for 'tree' and you've got the character 'Song'. He's the man who'll pillage our country's money and grain. Then, *Water and work are armed soldiery* — the second line. Place the 'water' radical next to the character for 'work' and you've got 'Jiang', the man who will raise armed soldiers. And it's Song Jiang who's written the rebellious poem. This is a warning from Heaven. How fortunate for the populace!"

"What about *Stretched in a line are thirty-six; Shandong will put us in a terrible fix?*"

"Thirty-six either refers to the year of our emperor's reign, or it's a number of some sort. As for *Shandong will put us in a terrible fix*, Yuncheng County is in Shandong. We've something to coincide with every line of the rhyme."

"Is the fellow still here?"

"When I questioned the waiter last night he said the man wrote the poem the day before yesterday. But it's easy enough to find out. Check the prison register."

"An extremely good idea." Cai ordered an attendant to fetch the register of the city prison from the record room. Cai examined it personally. Sure enough, there was the entry: "Fifth month. One newly exiled prisoner — Song Jiang of Yuncheng County."

"The man in the rhyme. This is very important," said Huang. "If we delay, news that we're on to him may leak out. Better seize him immediately and lock him up. Then we can discuss what to do next."

"Precisely," said the prefect. He convened court and summoned the superintendent of the city's two prisons. Dai Zong presented himself and hailed the prefect respectfully.

"Take some police, go to the city prison and bring Song Jiang of Yuncheng here," Cai ordered. "He's written a rebellious poem in the Xunyang Pavilion. I don't want a moment's delay."

Shocked, Dai Zong silently groaned and left the prefectural office. He mustered a number of prison guards. "Go home and get your weapons and assemble at my quarters next door to the City Temple," he instructed them.

The men departed. Using his magic travel method, Dai sped to the prison's Copying Section and pushed open Song Jiang's door. His friend was there. When the clerk saw Dai enter, he hurried forward to greet him.

"I went into town the other day, but couldn't find you anywhere," Song Jiang said. "I was so bored I walked to the Xunyang Pavilion and finished a bottle of wine all by myself. The effects still haven't worn off."

"Brother," Dai exclaimed, "what sort of poem did you write on the wall?"

"Who knows? I was drunk."

"Just now the prefect summoned me and ordered me to bring men and arrest you for having written a rebellious poem in the Xunyang Pavilion. I was very shaken, but I told my men to wait for me by the City Temple to give me time to let you know first. Brother, what are we going to do? How can we get you out of this?"

Song Jiang scratched his head in perplexity. "I'm a goner," he moaned.

"There is a way, though it may not work," said Dai. "I can't delay any longer. I'll have to bring my police and arrest you. Mess your hair, spill your filth on the floor, roll in it, and pretend to be mad. When I come with my men, speak wildly and act as if you were out of your mind. I'll go back to the prefect and report that you're insane."

"Thank you, brother. Save me, I beg you!"

Dai quickly bid farewell and returned to the city. At the City Temple he assembled his police and proceeded with them to the prison at a rapid pace. "Where is the new exile, Song Jiang?" he shouted with feigned ferocity. He led his men to Song Jiang's room in the Copying Section.

There they found the clerk, his hair in disarray, rolling in his own filth upon the floor.

"Who are you pricks?" Song Jiang demanded.

"Seize the wretch," Dai roared.

Eyes glaring, Song Jiang fought in a frenzy. "I'm the son-in-law of the Jade Emperor of Heaven. He's sent me here with a hundred thousand divine troops to slaughter all of Jiangzhou. The King of Hades leads my advance guard, the Demon General commands my rear. The Jade Emperor has given me a golden seal weighing eight hundred catties. I'm going to kill every friggin one of you!"

"He's crazy," said the policemen. "What's the use of arresting him?"

"You're right," said Dai. "Let's go back and tell them. If we have to take him, we'll come again."

They returned to the prefecture, where Cai was waiting in his court. "Song Jiang has taken leave of his senses," they reported. "He rolls in filth and talks wild. He stinks so badly we didn't dare bring him here."

Cai was about to inquire further when Huang emerged from behind a screen. "Don't believe them," he advised the prefect. "That poem he wrote was not the work of a madman. There's something fishy going on. Bring him in. If he can't walk, carry him."

"You're right," said Cai. He turned to the superintendent. "No more excuses. I want him here."

Orders were orders. Dai groaned inwardly, and led his police once more to the prison. "It's not going well, brother," he whispered. "I'll have to take you along." Song Jiang was placed in a large bamboo cage and carried to the prefectural court.

"Bring the rogue forward," the prefect directed.

Guards brought Song Jiang before the official dais, but he refused to kneel. "How dare you question me," he cried, glaring. "I'm the son-in-law of the Jade Emperor. He's sent me here with a hundred thousand divine troops to slaughter all of Jiangzhou. The King of Hades leads my advance guard, the Demon General commands my rear. The Jade Emperor has given me a golden seal weighing eight hundred catties. Hide before I kill every friggin one of you!"

The prefect was at a loss. Again Huang addressed him. "Summon the warden and the head keeper. Ask them whether he was mad when he arrived, or did this happen only recently. If he was crazy when he came, then it's real. If this condition developed only now, then it's false."

"Very well put," said the prefect. He sent for the warden and the head keeper and questioned them. It was impossible for them to lie.

"He didn't show any signs of madness when he arrived," they admitted. "He only became this way lately."

Cai was furious. He instructed the guards to truss the prisoner up and give him fifty blows. Song Jiang was pounded till he was more dead than alive. His skin burst and his blood was streaming. Dai Zong watched, agonized, unable to help him.

At first Song Jiang continued to babble like a lunatic, but finally he could bear no more. "I wrote a rebellious poem because I was drunk," he cried. "I didn't mean anything by it."

Having obtained a confession, the magistrate directed that a twenty-five-catty rack for capital felons be placed around the prisoner's neck and that he be detained in the big jail. Song Jiang had been beaten so badly he couldn't walk. The rack was nailed fast and he was thrown into a cell for the condemned. Dai secretly ordered the guards to treat him well, and arranged for food to be sent in. Of that we'll say no more.

Cai adjourned court and invited Huang to the rear hall. "Were it not for your far-sightedness," the prefect said, "I might have been fooled by that villain."

"The case is urgent, Excellency. It would be best if you rushed a man to the capital with a letter to your honorable father, reporting how you are dealing with this matter of national importance. Suggest that if he wants the man, alive, you'll send him by prison cart. If he doesn't, or if he's afraid the fellow will escape en route, you'll execute him here and eliminate a great danger. The emperor will also be very pleased with the news."

"There's reason in what you say. I was intending to send a person to the capital with gifts for my father, anyway. I shall mention your contribution in my letter and ask him to request the emperor to put you in charge of a wealthy city, so that you may quickly gain fame and fortune."

"All my life I shall rely on your beneficence, Excellency, and serve you as humbly as any groom."

The prefect wrote the letter and affixed his seal. "Who will you send as a trusted messenger?" Huang asked.

"The superintendent of our two city prisons is a man named Dai Zong. He knows certain charms by which he can cover eight hundred *li* in one day. I'm giving him the mission. He'll make the round trip in ten days."

"If he travels that fast, splendid."

Cai entertained Huang with wine in the rear hall. The next day Huang took his leave of the prefect and returned to Wuweijun.

Cai filled two hampers with gold and jewels and precious baubles, then closed and sealed them. The following day he summoned Dai Zong to the rear hall.

"I have here some gifts and a letter which I want delivered to my father the premier in the Eastern Capital before his birthday, which is on the fifteenth of the sixth lunar month. The date is fast approaching, and only you can get there in time. Don't tell me about difficulties. Travel day and night and bring back a reply and I'll reward you handsomely. I have figured out your itinerary and just how long it should take, using your marvellous travel methods, and shall be awaiting your report. Don't dally on the road. This must not be delayed."

The superintendent couldn't refuse. He accepted the hampers and the letter, bid the prefect farewell, and left to prepare. Then he went to see Song Jiang in his cell.

"You can relax, brother," said Dai. "The prefect is sending me on a mission to the Eastern Capital, with a time limit of ten days. While I'm at the premier's Residence I'll pull a few strings and get you out of this. Li Kui will be responsible for bringing you your food every day. Just be patient a little longer."

"I hope you can save my life, brother."

The superintendent summoned Li Kui and said: "Our brother has written a rebellious poem and has been convicted. We don't know yet what the outcome will be. I'm leaving today on a mission to the Eastern Capital and will be back soon. It's up to you to see to it that he gets his food every day."

"So he wrote a rebellious poem. What friggin difference does that make? Thousands of plotters have become big officials! You just go on to the capital and don't worry about a thing. No one in this prison will dare bother him. I'll return good for good. But if anybody plays rough, I'll take my battle-ax and chop his friggin head off!"

"Be careful, please. If you get drunk our brother is liable to miss his meals."

"If that's what worries you, I won't touch a drop all the while you are gone. I'll look after brother Song Jiang every minute. Why not?"

Dai was very pleased. "That's fine," he said, "if you're really determined."

That day, he set out on his journey. Li Kui indeed gave up drink. He remained in the prison, tending to Song Jiang, never leaving him by so much as a step.

CHAPTER 16
Mount Liangshan Gallants Raid the Execution Grounds

Dai Zong returned to his quarters, put on leggings, hemp sandals, and an apricot-yellow robe bound by a waist sash, into which he tucked his identification plaque. Dai changed his head kerchief and put the letter into his pouch, along with some money for the road. The hampers he carried on either end of a shoulder-pole.

Once outside the city, he attached two charms to each of his legs, murmured some magic words, and set forth. He travelled all day, and put up at an inn in the evening. Removing the charms, he burned simulated gold ingots of paper as a gift to the Emperor of Heaven. Then he retired.

He rose early the next morning, had some food and wine, and left the inn. Again he attached the four charms, shouldered the hampers, and travelled — so rapidly that the wind and rain whistled in his ears, and his feet didn't touch the ground. He stopped only once or twice for a snack along the road.

At the end of the day he again spent the night at an inn. The following morning he got up at the fifth watch, to take advantage of the dawn cool. Attaching the charms, he struck out with the hampers on his shoulder-pole. By mid-morning he had covered nearly three hundred *li* without encountering a single clean tavern.

It was a sticky day in early summer. Dai's clothes were soaked with sweat. He was nearly prostrated from the heat. Hungry and thirsty, he noticed a tavern ahead. It was beside a lake at the edge of a grove. Dai was there in the twiddle of a thumb. The tavern was spotlessly clean, and had twelve red lacquered tables, with benches to match, all in a row beside the windows.

He went in, chose a secluded table, rested his hampers, untied his sash and removed his gown. This he sprayed with water and hung on the window railing to dry. As he sat down, the waiter approached.

"How much wine, sir? Would you like some meat to go with it? We have pork, mutton and beef."

"Go easy on the wine. And bring me some rice."

"Besides wine and rice we sell steamed bread and vermicelli soup."

"I don't want meat. Have you any vegetables?"

"How about some peppery stewed bean-curd?"

"Just right."

The waiter soon returned with bean-curd and two vegetable dishes, and poured out three large bowls of wine. Dai was famished. He quickly finished the wine and bean-curd. He was waiting for rice when the earth and sky began to turn dizzily. His sight fading, Dai fell backwards off the bench.

"He's down," the waiter called.

From within the tavern a man emerged. It was Zhu Gui, the Dry-Land Crocodile, member of the Mount Liangshan stronghold.

"Take his hampers inside and see whether he's got anything on him," Zhu Gui ordered.

Two assistants searched Dai and found a paper packet. They handed it to Zhu Gui. He removed the paper and revealed an envelope inscribed: "Peaceful Family Letter, with the Utmost Respect to His Father from His Son Cai Dezhang.". Zhu Gui tore open the envelope and read the missive from beginning to end. It said:

> Today we have arrested a man who fits the prediction rhyme and who has written a rebellious poem — Song Jiang of Shandong, and are holding him in prison.... We await your orders for his disposition.

Zhu Gui was shocked beyond speech. His assistants were

lifting Dai to carry him into the butchering shed when Zhu Gui noticed a red and green object attached to the sash lying on the bench. He picked it up. It was an official's identification plaque. Etched in silver were the words: "Dai Zong, Superintendent of the Two Prisons, Jiangzhou."

"Wait," Zhu Gui said to the cohorts. "I've often heard our military advisor talk of his friend Dai Zong the Marvellous Traveller from Jiangzhou. Can this be the man? But why is he bearing a letter that will harm Song Jiang? Heaven has sent him into my hands." He instructed his assistants: "Give him the antidote and bring him round. I want to question him."

The assistants poured a mixture into some water, raised Dai up and fed it to him. He soon opened his eyes and struggled to his feet. He saw Zhu Gui with the letter in his hands.

"Who are you?" Dai shouted. "How dare you drug me? And you've opened the letter to the premier. Don't you know what a crime that is?"

Zhu Gui laughed. "So what? What's opening the premier's letter to a man who's opposing the Song emperor?"

Dai was astonished. "Who are you, bold fellow? What is your name?"

"I'm Zhu Gui, the Dry-Land Crocodile, of the gallant band in Liangshan Marsh."

"Since you're one of the leaders, you must know Wu Yong."

"He's our military advisor. He controls all our military operations. How do you know him?"

"He's a very close friend."

"You're not Superintendent Dai, the Marvellous Traveller of Jiangzhou, he so often speaks about?"

"I am."

"When Song Jiang was on his way to exile in Jiangzhou, he stayed at our stronghold, and Wu Yong gave him a letter to you. Why are you helping to take his life?"

"Song Jiang is like a brother to me. He wrote a rebellious poem and I couldn't prevent his arrest. I'm on my way to the capital right now to find a way to save him. I'd never harm Song Jiang."

"You don't believe me?" retorted Zhu Gui. "Take a look at this."

Dai read the letter the prefect had written. He was shocked. He told Zhu Gui how he had met Song Jiang, when he came with the note from Wu Yong, and how Song Jiang got drunk and wrote a rebellious poem in the Xunyang Pavilion.

"In that case, please come with me to the stronghold and talk it over with our leaders," said Zhu Gui. "We've got to rescue Song Jiang."

First he wined and dined Dai Zong. Then he went to the pavilion overlooking the lake and shot a whistling arrow to the opposite cove. A bandit promptly rowed over in a boat. Zhu Gui helped Dai and his hampers on board. They landed at the Shore of Golden Sands and climbed to the fortress. When it was reported to Wu Yong that they were at the gate, he hurried down to greet them.

"It's been a long time," he said to Dai. "What good wind blows you here? Please come up. We'll talk in the stronghold."

Wu Yong introduced him to the other leaders, and Zhu Gui told the reason for Dai's visit: "Song Jiang is in prison."

Chao Gai hastily invited Dai to be seated and asked him how this came about. Dai related in detail the story of Song Jiang and his rebellious poem. Chao Gai was very alarmed. He proposed to the other leaders that they immediately muster men and horses, raid Jiangzhou and bring Song Jiang back to the fortress.

"That's not the way, brother," Wu Yong said. "Jiangzhou's quite far from here. A large body of men and horses would only provoke disaster. 'Disturbing the grass alerts the snake.' It would mean Song Jiang's life. What's needed here is guile, not force. I'm not very clever but I have a little plan by which we can rescue Song Jiang. It involves Superintendent Dai."

"Let's hear it, Military Advisor."

"Dai has to bring back a reply to the letter Prefect Cai is sending to the Eastern Capital. We'll write a false one and turn the tables on them. The reply Superintendent Dai will deliver will say: 'Take no action against the prisoner Song

Jiang. Send him here under appropriate guard. After thorough interrogation we shall execute him and put his head on display and discredit the prediction rhyme.' When Song Jiang is being escorted through this area, our men will snatch him. What do you think of my plan?"

"Suppose he doesn't pass this way? We'll miss our chance," said Chao Gai.

"That's no problem," said Gongsun Sheng. "We'll dispatch scouts near and far to inquire. Whichever path he travels, we'll be waiting for him. One way or another, we'll get him. Our only worry is that they won't convoy him to the capital."

"The plan sounds all right," said Chao Gai, "but who's going to write the reply of Cai Qing the premier?"

"I've thought of that," said Wu Yong. "The four most favored styles of writing today are those of Su Dongpo, Huang Luzhi, Mi Yuanzhang, and Cai Qing. In all of Song, they are considered the most perfect. I have a scholar friend in the town of Jizhou named Xiao Rang. Because his calligraphy is so good, he's known as the Master Hand. He's also skilled with lance, staff, sword and knife. I know for a fact he can write in the style of Cai Qing. We'll have Superintendent Dai go to his house and say: 'The Yue Temple in Tai'an Prefecture needs an inscription written for a monument. Here are fifty ounces of silver for your family's expenses while you're gone.' Dai will bring him here. Later, we'll trick his wife and family into coming up the mountain also, and we'll get Xiao to join our band. How's that?"

"If he can write the reply, that's fine," said Chao Gai. "But we'll need a seal as well."

"There's another friend I have in mind for that. He's the best in the whole central plain, and he also lives in Jizhou. His name is Jin Dajian. He carves writing beautifully in stone and cuts excellent jade seals. What's more, he's a demon with lance and staff. He's known as the Jade-Armed Craftsman because he carves jade so well. Dai will give him fifty ounces of silver and tell him he's needed to engrave the monument. We'll capture him too on the way. We can use men like Jin and Xiao here in our stronghold."

"Very shrewd," commended Chao Gai.

That day a feast was laid for Dai Zong, and in the evening all retired.

The next morning after breakfast, Dai was disguised as a deacon and given two hundred ounces of silver. He tied on his charms, went down the mountain, and was ferried from the Shore of Golden Sands to the opposite side, where he set out for Jizhou. In less than two watches he arrived. He inquired for Xiao Rang the Master Hand.

"He lives in front of the Confucius Temple east of the prefectural office," Dai was told.

The superintendent went to Xiao's door and coughed. "Is Master Xiao at home?" he called.

A scholar emerged and looked at Dai. He'd never seen him before. "Where are you from, Deacon?" he asked. "What can I do for you?"

Dai greeted him courteously. "I am the deacon of Yue Temple in Tai'an. We're repairing our Five Sacred Mountains Building and our local gentry want a monument carved. They've instructed me to give you fifty ounces of silver to care for your family while you're away and to ask you to come with me to our temple to write the inscription. The opening date has already been set and cannot be postponed."

"I only write the words on the stone, nothing more. If you're in a hurry for the monument, you'll need an engraver as well."

"I have another fifty pieces of silver. I intend to invite Jin Dajian the Jade-Armed Craftsman. An auspicious day has already been chosen. Please favor us with your guidance. We'll get Jin and go together."

Xiao Rang accepted the silver and took Dai to call on Jin. They went past the Confucius Temple and Xiao pointed. "That's Jin coming now."

Xiao hailed him and introduced him to Dai. He explained what it was that Dai wanted. "The deacon is giving each of us fifty ounces of silver to go with him," the scholar added.

Jin was pleased at the mention of the money. He and Xiao invited Dai to a tavern for a few cups of wine and some vegetable dishes. Dai gave him the silver for family expenses.

"The necromancer has selected a lucky day," the superintendent said. "I'd like both of you to leave with me at once."

"It's very hot today," said Xiao. "If we go now we won't get very far, and won't reach any place where we can put up for the night. Why not start tomorrow at the fifth watch? Just call for us and we'll go."

Jin concurred. "He's right, you know."

They arranged to leave at dawn, and returned to their homes to prepare. Dai stayed over with Xiao Rang, at the scholar's request.

At dawn the next day Jin, with a bundle of clothes and his tools, called for Xiao and Dai, and they left Jizhou. Before they had gone ten *li* Dai spoke.

"You two masters continue slowly. I mustn't rush you. I'll go on ahead and inform the gentry so that they can come and greet you." He lengthened his stride and hurried forward.

The two craftsmen, their bundles on their backs, proceeded at a leisurely pace. By early afternoon they had covered about eighty *li*. Suddenly, a shrill whistle ahead broke the stillness, and a band of forty or fifty bold fellows leaped out from concealment on the slope. In the lead was Wang the Stumpy Tiger of Clear Winds Mountain.

"Who are you two?" he called. "Where are you going? Take them, children. We'll eat their hearts with our wine!"

"We're on our way to Tai'an to carve a stone monument," said Xiao. "We haven't any valuables. Only these clothes."

"I don't want your valuables or your clothes," shouted Wang. "It's your clever hearts and livers I'm after as a savoury for my drinks!"

Alarmed, Xiao and Jin mustered all their skill with arms. Raising their staves, they charged the Stumpy Tiger. Wang attacked with halberd, and the three fought half a dozen rounds until Wang was forced to turn and flee. The craftsmen were about to pursue when, on the heights, they heard the crash of gongs. From the left came Guardian of the Clouds Song Wan. From the right came Skyscraper Du Qian. Behind was Zheng Tianshou the Fair-Faced Gentleman and over thirty others. They seized Xiao and Jin and dragged them into the forest.

"Don't worry," said the four gallants. "We've been ordered by our chieftain Chao Gai to invite you up the mountain to join our band."

"What use would we be in your stronghold?" said Xiao. "We haven't the strength to strangle a chicken. All we can do is eat."

"In the first place Military Advisor Wu is your friend and, secondly, we know of your skill with weapons," said Du Qian. "That's why we sent Dai Zong to your homes to invite you."

Xiao and Jin looked at each other, speechless. All went together to the tavern of Zhu Gui the Dry-Land Crocodile, where food and drink were served. The same night a boat was called and the party proceeded to Mount Liangshan.

On arrival at the stronghold they were greeted by Chao Gai, Wu Yong and the other chieftains. The two craftsmen were given a feast of welcome and were told about forging the letter from Cai Qing.

"And so we're inviting you two to join us," the leaders concluded, "and become part of our righteous fraternity."

The craftsmen clutched Wu Yong anxiously. "We've no objection to staying here," they said, "but what of our wives and children? When the authorities hear about this they'll surely harm them."

"Set your minds at ease, brothers," Wu Yong said. "Tomorrow morning you'll understand."

That night all drank until it was time to retire.

At daybreak a bandit arrived and reported: "They're here."

"Please go and receive your families," Wu Yong said to Jin and Xiao.

The two men could scarcely believe him. Halfway down the mountain they met sedan-chairs coming up, bearing their wives and children. The two questioned them in astonishment.

"After you left, yesterday," the women related, "these sedan-carriers arrived and said: 'Your husbands are at an inn outside of town suffering from heat stroke. They want you and the children to go there at once and look after them.' But when we left the town they wouldn't let us out of the sedan-chairs, and brought us here."

Both families had been reunited. Xiao and Jin had nothing to say. They abandoned all hope of leaving and went back up the mountain to join the band.

When the families were settled in, Wu Yong conferred with Xiao on the writing of Cai Qing's reply. As to the seal, Jin said: "I've always been the one who's carved all of Cai Qing's seals, both of his official name and his popular name."

They set to work and soon finished the letter. A banquet was laid for Dai Zong, who was given detailed instructions. The superintendent bid all farewell and went down the mountain to the Shore of Golden Sands, where a bandit ferried him across to Zhu Gui's tavern. Dai tied the charms to his legs, took leave of Zhu Gui, and strode forth on his journey.

After seeing Dai off to the ferry point, Wu Yong and the other chieftains returned to the mountain fortress and feasted. Suddenly, while they were drinking, Wu Yong uttered a cry of lamentation. Everyone was mystified.

"What's wrong?" they queried.

"That letter I prepared is the death warrant for Dai Zong and Song Jiang!"

"What's the matter with it?" the chieftains asked in alarm.

"I thought only of one thing and forgot another. There's a terrible error in that reply!"

"I wrote exactly in the style of Cai Qing. Not a word was wrong," said Xiao. "Please tell us, Military Advisor, where was the error?"

"The seal I carved corresponds to Cai's in every detail," said Jin. "How could anyone see any flaw?"

Wu Yong raised two fingers and revealed the mistake to the assembled warriors. "I was careless," he said. "I didn't see it. The seal reads 'Cai Qing, Member of the Hanlin Academy.' That seal will cause Superintendent Dai to stand trial!"

"But that's the seal the premier uses on all his writings and essays," Jin protested. "The one I carved is exactly the same. What's wrong with it?"

"A father writing to his son would never use his formal title. I forgot about that. When Dai returns to Jiangzhou he'll surely be questioned. If the truth comes out, it will be terrible."

"Let's send a man after Dai, quickly, and bring him back," Chao Gai suggested. "We'll re-do the letter."

"He couldn't catch him. Dai is using his magic travel method. He must have covered five hundred *li* by now. We can't delay. Dai and Song Jiang have to be saved."

"How can we save them?" asked Chao Gai. "What's your plan?"

Wu Yong spoke softly in Chao Gai's ear for several minutes, concluding with: "Issue the order quietly among our men. Tell them how to act. Instruct them to move promptly, without fail."

The bold fellows, on receiving their commands, took the implements they needed and went down the mountain that very night. They headed for Jiangzhou. Of that we'll say no more.

Dai returned to Jiangzhou and reported to the prefectural office with the reply within the allotted time. Prefect Cai was very pleased. He rewarded his emissary with three ceremonial beakers of wine. Then he took the letter.

"Did you see the premier?" he asked.

"No," said Dai. "I only stayed one night, then came directly home."

The prefect opened the envelope and read:

I have received all your gifts, intact.... As to that demon Song Jiang, the emperor wants to see him personally. Send him to the capital immediately in a cage cart under a trustworthy guard. Make sure he doesn't get away on the

*road. . . . I have spoken to the emperor about Huang Wen-
bing. He undoubtedly will be given a good appointment.*

Cai was delighted. He presented Dai with a flowery silver
ingot weighing twenty-five ounces. He also ordered that a
cage cart be assembled and discussed the guard to be sent. The
superintendent thanked him and returned to his quarters. He
bought wine and meat and went to see Song Jiang in the prison.
We'll say no more of that.

The prefect urged the builders to hurry with the cart. A day
or two later, all was in readiness to take the prisoner to the
Eastern Capital. The gate-keeper entered and announced that
Huang Wenbing was calling.

Cai received him in the rear hall. Huang had brought wine
and fresh fruit. "You're always so thoughtful," murmured the
prefect. "You really shouldn't."

"Meager gifts from my rustic village," said Huang. "Not
worth mentioning."

"Congratulations on the honors which will soon be yours."

"What makes you say that, Prefect?"

"I received a reply yesterday. The evil-doer Song Jiang is
to be sent to the capital. Your contribution has been reported
to the emperor. You will be given a high position. It's all in
my father's letter."

"I'm deeply grateful for Your Excellency's recommendation.
Your messenger is indeed a marvellous traveller."

"Read the letter yourself, if you don't believe me."

"A private, family letter — I wouldn't have dared ask. But
since you permit me. . . ."

"Why not, a trusted friend like you."

Huang read the letter from start to finish, then turned it
over and looked at the seal on the flap. He observed that it
had been newly cut. Huang shook his head.

"This letter is a fake."

"You must be mistaken. It's my father's own handwriting.
It must be authentic."

"His style is easily copied. Did he put this seal on letters to you in the past?"

"No, he just wrote informally. Probably the seal was near at hand and he reached for it automatically."

"Please don't think I'm being meddlesome, but the letter is a forgery. The styles of writing of Su, Huang, Mi and Cai are very popular these days. Anyone can imitate them. And this seal — it was made when your father became a member of the Hanlin Academy.. He affixed it to all his essays and calligraphy. Many people have seen it. But why would he still be using it today, now that he's risen to the position of premier? In any event, a father writing to his son certainly wouldn't add an official signature seal. The premier possesses infinite wisdom and intelligence. He'd never make a mistake like that. If you don't believe me, Prefect, question the messenger closely. Ask him who he saw at the Residence. If he answers incorrectly, then the letter is false. Forgive me for talking so much. It's only because you've been so kind that I dare to speak."

"That's easy enough. He's never been to the Eastern Capital before. I have only to query him and I'll know whether he's lying."

The prefect told Huang to conceal himself behind a screen, and he convened court. He then sent attendants out in all direction to look for Dai Zong. They were to say the prefect had need of him, and to report at once.

The day he returned, Dai went to see Song Jiang in the prison and spoke softly in his ear, telling him what had transpired. Song Jiang was very pleased. A man invited Dai out for wine the following day, and he was drinking in a tavern when an attendant, who had been looking for him, came in. He conducted Dai to the prefectural court.

"You certainly did a good job of the mission I troubled you with the other day," said Prefect Cai. "I still haven't rewarded you properly."

"When entrusted with a task by Your Excellency, I could only do my best."

"I've been rather busy lately. I haven't had a chance to ask you about it in detail. By which gate did you go into the capital?"

"It was already dark when I got there. I didn't notice."

"Who received you at the gate of the family residence? Where did they put you up?"

"A gate-man took your letter in. A short while later he came out and accepted the hampers. He told me to find an inn for the night. I returned to the Residence at dawn the following morning, and the gate-man handed me a reply. I wanted to be sure to reach Jiangzhou on time, so I didn't bother to ask questions and hurried back."

"Did you notice how old the gate-keeper was? Was he dark and thin, or fair and fat? Tall or short? Did he have a beard?"

"It was dark when I reached the Residence, and the next morning at dawn the light was dim. I couldn't see very clearly. He didn't seem very tall, around medium height. I think he had a bit of a beard."

"Take this man before the court," the prefect shouted angrily.

A dozen prison guards came out from the side and dragged Dai to the front of the dais.

"I've done no wrong," the superintendent cried.

"You death-deserving scoundrel! Our old gate-keeper Wang passed on years ago. His son, who has the job now, is only a beardless youth. He has no right to enter the Residence. Any letters that arrive he gives to Secretary Zhang, who hands them over to Majordomo Li. Only Li can notify the inside and accept presents. If a reply is requested, you have to wait three days. And how could anyone who wasn't a trusted attendant and who didn't question you in detail simply take my gifts? My mind was slow the other day. I let you hoodwink me. The truth, now, where did you get that letter?"

"I didn't know all that. I was confused and in a hurry to come back."

"You're lying. These thieving wretches — if you don't beat them they never confess. Guards, pound this rogue for me, hard!"

The prison guards knew it was hopeless. They couldn't be

concerned for their superintendent's dignity. They tied Dai, held him prone, and beat him till his skin split and his fresh blood flowed. Dai couldn't take it.

"The letter is false," he exclaimed.

"Where did you get it?" the prefect demanded.

"I was passing through Liangshan Marsh when a gang of brigands seized and bound me. They hauled me up the mountain to cut my heart out. When they searched me, they found and read your letter. They decided to keep the hampers and set me free. But I couldn't come home. I wanted to kill myself. They wrote this letter, figuring it would cover me. I was afraid of being punished, so I deceived you, Excellency."

"That may be partly true, but plenty of it is poppycock. You're in cahoots with those Liangshan robbers. You plotted with them to steal my hampers, and now you're telling me this fancy tale. Beat him some more!"

But in spite of the torture Dai would not admit to any connection with the men of Liangshan. Again the prefect had him beaten. Dai stuck to his story.

"Enough," said the prefect. "Put a big rack on him and throw him in jail."

He left the court and summoned Huang. "If it weren't for your shrewdness I'd have committed a serious blunder," he said gratefully.

"Dai is obviously also in league with the Liangshan Marsh bandits," Huang said. "They're organized, and plotting a revolt. It must be nipped in the bud, or it will mean disaster."

"I'm going to take the confessions of Dai Zong and Song Jiang and draw up formal documents. I'll have them both decapitated in the market-place and then send a written report to the higher authorities."

"Extremely wise, Excellency. It will please the imperial court and win you high praise for your meritorious handling of this important matter. It will also forestall the Liangshan bandits from coming to raid the prison."

"You are very far-sighted. I shall write a report personally guaranteeing you and recommending that you be raised in rank."

Prefect Cai entertained Huang, and saw him to the gate of the prefectural compound. Huang returned to Wuweijun.

The next day Cai opened court, summoned the scribe, also named Huang, and said: "Compile all documents on Song Jiang and Dai Zong and add in their confessions. Also write criminal convictions to be posted on the day they are beheaded in the market-place. Since ancient times, rebellious plotters have been executed promptly. Decapitating these two will avert calamity."

Scribe Huang was on very good terms with Superintendent Dai. But he had no way to rescue him, and he groaned inwardly.

"Tomorrow is a national day of mourning," he said, "and the day after is Midsummer Ghosts' Day — you can't execute them then. The following day is a national holiday. Nothing can be done till after the fifth."

Huang had no better plan, he could only delay Dai's death as long as possible. He did this usually for condemned men whenever he could. The prefect agreed with his suggestion and set the execution date for the sixth.

On the morning of the appointed day a crossroads in the market-place was swept to serve as an execution ground. After breakfast soldiers and executioners were mustered — well over five hundred men — and assembled outside the prison gate. At mid-morning the warden went to the prefect and formally requested him to supervise the beheadings. Scribe Huang had no choice but to present the convictions. On each the word "Decapitate" was inscribed, and the announcements were pasted on reed mats.

Although the head keeper and guards in the city prison were friends of Dai Zong and Song Jiang, there was nothing they could do to save them. They could only bemoan their fate.

Everything was in readiness. The prisoners' arms were bound, the hair of each was soaked with gluey paste, twisted up in the shape of a pear and transfixed with a red artificial flower. They were driven before a black-faced idol and fed a bowl of

"Eternal Rest Rice" and a cup of "Permanent Parting Wine". Then they were taken from the shrine. Racks were locked round their necks. Surrounded by sixty or seventy guards, Song Jiang, followed by Dai Zong, were marched out of the prison gate. The two men looked at each other, but they were unable to speak. Song Jiang stamped in futility, Dai Zong hung his head and sighed.

A crowd of nearly two thousand jammed the market-place around the crossroads, which was guarded by a wall of soldiers with spears and staves. Song Jiang was placed facing south, Dai Zong was placed facing north and, still bound, they were forced to sit. All were waiting till three quarters after noon, when the supervisor would come and the executions would take place.

The spectators read the announcements of criminal conviction. They ran as follows:

> *Jiangzhou Prefecture. Criminal Song Jiang. Wrote a rebellious poem, spread evil rumors, and colluded with bandits in Liangshan Marsh to foment a rebellion. Sentenced to be decapitated.*
>
> *Criminal Dai Zong. In order to help Song Jiang, secretly handed over a private letter, colluded with the bandits in Liangshan Marsh and plotted with them to foment a rebellion. Sentenced to be decapitated.*
>
> *Supervisor of executions: Cai, Prefect of Jiangzhou*

The prefect reined his horse to a halt and sat, waiting. From the east side of the market a band of snake charmers pushed their way through the crowd. The soldiers tried to beat them back, but they wouldn't leave. In the midst of this disturbance, a group of medical cure pedlars who gave displays of arms elbowed through the spectators on the west.

"You unmannerly louts," the soldiers shouted at them. "Where do you think you are — shoving like that?"

"Ignorant rustics," the men retorted. "We've travelled all over the country, and nowhere have we been prohibited from looking at people. Even when the emperor has culprits killed in the capital you're allowed to watch. Just because your little town is executing two men you think you're shaking the world. We want to see. What's all the friggin fuss about?"

"Get back there," shouted the prefect. "Don't let them come any closer."

At this moment a convoy of porters, carrying goods on shoulder-poles, arrived from the south.

"Heads are going to be chopped off here," the soldiers yelled. "Go another way."

"We're bringing things to your prefect. How dare you stop us?"

"Even if you were officials from the prefectural office, you'd have to detour!"

The porters set down their burdens, detached their carrying-poles, and stood, holding them, among the spectators.

From the north a troupe of merchants approached, pushing two carts. They insisted on passing through the execution grounds.

"Where do you think you're going?" the soldiers barked.

"We're in a hurry. Let us through."

"Not a chance. Criminals are being knocked off here. If you're in a hurry, take another road."

The merchants laughed. "That's easy enough to say. We're from the capital. We're not familiar with your cruddy roads. We can only stick to the main highway."

The soldiers wouldn't let them go on. The merchants crowded together in a stubborn knot and refused to retreat. Arguments were raging on all four sides of the crossroads. Prefect Cai was unable to quell them. He observed that the merchants had climbed onto their carts and were watching from there.

Not long after, the group of officers on the execution grounds parted and a man stepped forward and announced: "Three quarters past noon."

"Cut off their heads," ordered the prefect.

Soldiers opened the prisoners' racks. Two executioners stood with swords at the ready. Quicker than it takes to say, rioting broke out. One of the merchants pulled a small gong from his tunic. Standing on the cart he struck it sharply three times. On all sides, men went into action.

A hulking dark tiger of a fellow, stark naked, appeared in the upper storey of a tea-house beside the crossroads. Brandishing a battle-ax in each hand, he uttered a heaven-splitting roar, leaped down, hacked the executioners to death, and began carving his way towards the mounted prefect. Soldiers thrust at him with their spears, but nothing could stop his headlong advance. They crowded around Cai and rushed him off to safety.

Daggers suddenly appeared in the hands of the snake charmers on the east side, and they began killing soldiers. The medicine men on the west side, holding spears and staves, let out a yell and charged into the soldiers and guards, slaughtering left and right. On the south, the porters swung their carrying-poles, felling soldiers and spectators indiscriminately. The merchants on the north jumped down from the carts and tipped them over, blocking the road. Two of the merchants darted through the melee and got Song Jiang and Dai Zong on their backs. Some of the remainder produced bows and arrows and started shooting. Others threw stones they had concealed in their clothes. A few waved pennanted signal spears.

The merchants were in fact Chao Gai, Hua Rong, Huang Xin, Lü Fang and Guo Sheng. The medicine men were Yan Shun, Liu Tang, Du Qian and Song Wan. Disguised as porters were Zhu Gui, Stumpy Tiger Wang, Zheng Tianshou and Shi Yong. The snake charmers were actually the three Ruan brothers and Bai Sheng. These leaders from Liangshan Marsh had brought with them more than a hundred men, and all were locked in furious battle.

They saw the big dark fellow laying about him vigorously with his battle-axes. Chao Gai didn't recognize him, but he knew that he had been the first to go into action, and that he was killing more of the foe than anyone.

"Dai Zong mentioned a Black Whirlwind Li Kui, a wild rash fellow who was good friend of Song Jiang," Chao Gai recalled,

and he shouted: "Hey, bold fighter, aren't you the Black Whirl-wind?"

But Li Kui paid no attention, and continued consuming lives with his big axes like a blazing inferno. Chao Gai ordered the men carrying Song Jiang and Dai Zong to follow in the big dark fellow's wake.

By now bodies of soldiers and civilians were sprawled all over the crossroads, and blood flowed in rivulets. Countless more had been felled and wounded. The Liangshan leaders abandoned their carts and merchandise and continued behind the big fellow, fighting their way out of the city. Hua Rong, Huang Xin, Lü Fang and Guo Sheng, covering the rear, sent swarms of arrows in their pursuers. Neither the soldiers nor the people of Jiangzhou dared come too near.

Li Kui slaughtered down to the stream's edge, his whole body spattered with blood. He went on killing along the bank.

Halberd in hand, Chao Gai shouted: "Don't hurt the ordinary people. This has nothing to do with them!"

But the big man wouldn't listen. He cut down victims one after another.

They walked six or seven *li* along the stream outside the city until they saw before them a broad river. Here, all paths came to an end. Chao Gai was very distressed. Only then did Black Whirlwind speak:

"Don't worry. Carry our brothers into that temple."

Ahead, near the river, was a large temple, its double gates tightly locked. Li Kui smashed them open with his battle-axes, and they all went into the courtyard. Ancient junipers and pines blocked out the sunlight. A plaque upon the building was inscribed in letters of gold: *Temple of the White Dragon Spirit.*

Song Jiang and Dai Zong were carried inside and set down. Song Jiang opened his eyes and saw Chao Gai and the others. "Brothers," he exclaimed, weeping, "this must be a dream."

"You wouldn't stay with us on the mountain, brother. That's why you're in such a predicament today," Chao Gai expostulat-ed. "Who is that big swarthy fellow who fights so powerfully?"

"Li Kui the Black Whirlwind. He was ready to spring me out of prison all by himself. But I didn't think we could get away with it, so I didn't agree."

"A remarkable man. He fought harder than any of us, and was absolutely fearless in the face of every enemy weapon."

"Bring fresh clothing for our brothers," Hua Rong called.

While they were changing, Li Kui started down the porch, battle-axes in hand. Song Jiang shouted after him: "Where are you going, brother?"

"Looking for those monks. I'll kill them all. Not only didn't the louts come out to welcome us, they even barred their friggin gates. If I find them, I'll slay them before those gates as a sacrifice!"

"Come over here, first. I want to introduce you to my brother, the chieftain."

Li Kui cast aside his axes and dropped to his knees before Chao Gai. "Forgive Iron Ox's crassness, brother," he entreated. He was also introduced to the others and discovered he and Zhu Gui came from the same township. Both men were exceedingly pleased.

"Brother," Hua Rong said to Chao Gai, "you told us to follow brother Li, and now here we are, with a big river cutting us off, and no boat to take us across. When the soldiers from the city catch up how will we be able to repel them and escape?"

"Never mind," said Li Kui. "I'll fight my way back into the city and chop them into mincemeat, friggin prefect and all!"

Dai Zong had just revived by then, and he cried: "Don't be rash, brother. There are six or seven thousand troops in the city. If you go charging in, you'll be throwing your life away."

Ruan the Seventh said: "I see some boats along the opposite bank. My brothers and I will swim over and haul a few back. How will that be?"

"The best possible idea," said Chao Gai.

Stripping and tying on daggers, the Ruan brothers dived into the river. They had swum about half a *li* when three boats, being rowed with the speed of wind, prows raised, came flying across the surface of the water. On each were a dozen or more men, all with weapons in their hands.

The watchers on the shore grew alarmed. "My fate is bitter," Song Jiang lamented when he heard of the approaching vessels. He hurried out of the temple to look. Seated in the foremost craft was a big fellow holding a five-pronged pitchfork. His hair was twisted up on top of his head and bound by a red cord. He wore a pair of white silk swimming pants, and he was whistling sharply.

It was none other than Zhang Shun. Song Jiang waved his arms and shouted: "Save me, brother!"

Zhang Shun and the others recognized him. "We will," they cried.

Their boats flew towards the shore. The Ruan brothers turned around and swam back. All headed for the bank before the temple.

Zhang Shun was leading a dozen sturdy fellows. Zhang Heng, on the second craft, led Mu Hong, Mu Chun, Xue Yong and ten or more vassals. On the third boat Li Jun was in command of Li Li, Tong Wei, Tong Meng and a dozen salt smugglers. Fully armed, they disembarked and climbed the bank.

To Zhang Shun the sight of Song Jiang was a gift from Heaven. Weeping, he kowtowed and said: "I was beside myself when I heard that you had been tried. But I couldn't think of how to rescue you. Then I heard that Superintendent Dai had been taken, and brother Li Kui had disappeared. I went to my brother Zhang Heng and took him to Squire Mu's manor and called together many of our friends. Today we were going to fight our way into Jiangzhou and snatch you out of prison. I never dreamed that gallant men would have saved you already and brought you here. May I ask which of these heroes is Chao Gai, chieftain of Liangshan Marsh?"

Song Jiang pointed to a man standing to the fore. "That is brother Chao Gai. Let's all go into the temple and be ceremoniously introduced."

The nine leaders of Zhang Shun's party, the seventeen of

Chao Gai's, plus Song Jiang, Dai Zong and Li Kui, a total of twenty-nine, entered the White Dragon Temple.

CHAPTER 17
Song Jiang's First Attack on the Zhu Family Manor

On leaving Qizhou, Yang Xiong, Shi Xiu and Shi Qian the Flea on a Drum travelled steadily, resting at night and continuing the next morning. In a few days they reached the prefecture of Yunzhou. After crossing Fragrant Woods Hollow, they saw before them a high mountain. It was growing dark, and they made for an inn beside a stream. A waiter was in the process of locking up as they reached the gate.

"You must have come a long way to arrive here so late," he said.

"More than a hundred *li*," Flea on a Drum replied.

The waiter let them in and gave them a room. "Would you like a fire?" he asked.

"We'll attend to it ourselves," said the Flea.

"We've no other guests and there are two pots of boiled water on the stove. You're welcome to use them if you wish."

"Have you any meat and wine?"

"We had some meat this morning, but people from neighboring villages bought it all. There's a jug of wine left, but nothing to go with it."

"That'll do. And bring us five measures of rice. We'll cook it here."

The waiter brought the rice to the Flea, who cleaned it and put it on to boil. Shi Xiu laid out his luggage. Yang gave the waiter one of the hairpins in payment for the wine and promised to settle the full account the next day. The waiter fetched the jug and opened it, and placed a few hot vegetable dishes on the table. The Flea carried in a bucket of hot water for Yang and Shi Xiu to wash their hands and feet with.

The wine was poured, and the three asked the waiter to sit down and join them. They drank from four large bowls.

Shi Xiu noticed a dozen good halberds under the eaves.

"Why do you need weapons in this inn?" he asked.

"They belong to the master."

"What sort of person is he?"

"You've been around, sir. Haven't you heard of this place? That big mountain out there is called Lone Dragon Mountain. The high cliff before it is Lone Dragon Cliff. On top of it is my master's residence. All the land around here for thirty *li* belongs to the Zhu Family Manor. Lord Zhu, my master, has three sons. They're known as the Three Zhu Warriors. This manor has five or six hundred families, all tenants, and two halberds have been issued to each family. You're staying in the Zhu Family Inn. Usually, there are several dozen of our men spending the night here. That's why we keep the halberds handy."

"What use are they in an inn?"

"We're not far from Liangshan Marsh. Those bandits might come to rob our grain. We have to be prepared."

"If I gave you some silver would you let me have one of the halberds?"

"Oh, no. Each halberd has its owner's mark. My master would beat me. He's very strict."

Shi Xiu laughed. "I was only kidding. Don't get excited. Have some more wine."

"I can't. I must go to bed. Enjoy yourselves, sir guests. Drink all you want."

The waiter retired. Yang and Shi Xiu had another round.

"Would you like some meat?" the Flea asked them.

"Didn't the waiter say they don't have any?" Yang replied. "Where would you get meat?"

The Flea chuckled. He walked over to the stove and lifted a cooked rooster out of a pot.

"Where does that come from?" asked Yang.

"I went out in back to relieve myself and saw this rooster in a cage. I thought it would go well with your wine, so I quietly killed it by the stream, brought out a bucket of boiling water, cleaned the bird and cooked it. And here it is, ready for you two brothers to eat."

"Still as light-fingered as ever, you villain," said Yang.

The Flea grinned. "I haven't changed my profession."

The three laughed. They tore the bird apart with their hands and ate it, together with the rice they had cooked.

The waiter slept only a little while. Uneasy in his mind, he got up and looked things over, front and back. On the kitchen table he saw feathers and bones. A pot on the stove was half filled with greasy water. He hurried out to the cage in the rear of the inn. It was empty. He hastened into the room where the three men were staying.

"Is that any way to behave?" he demanded. "Why did you steal our rooster and eat it?"

"You're seeing ghosts," scoffed the Flea. "I bought that bird on the road. Who's seen your rooster?"

"Where is it, then?"

"Dragged off by a wildcat, eaten by a weasel, pounced on by a hawk — who knows?"

"That bird was in the cage just a short while ago. If you didn't steal it, who did?"

"Don't wrangle," said Shi Xiu. "We'll pay you whatever it's worth."

"It heralds the dawn. Our inn can't do without it. Even ten ounces of silver wouldn't be money enough. Give me back our bird."

"Who are you trying to extort?" Shi Xiu said angrily. "Just for that I won't give you a penny. What are you going to do about it?"

The waiter laughed. "Regular fire-eaters, aren't you? Our inn is different. We'll drag you up to the manor and try you for being bandits from Liangshan Marsh!"

"Suppose we were? Do you think you could capture us and

claim the reward?" Shi Xiu demanded.

Yang Xiong was also very irate. "With the best of intentions, we were going to give you some money. Now we won't," he said. "Let's see you take us!"

"Thieves, thieves," shouted the waiter.

Four or five big bruisers, stripped to the waist, charged into the room and made for Yang and Shi Xiu. With one blow of the fist each, Shi Xiu knocked them flat. The waiter opened his mouth to yell. The Flea slapped him so hard that his face swelled up and he couldn't utter a sound. The bruisers fled through the rear gate.

"Those louts must be going for help," said Yang. "Let's finish eating, quickly, and get out of here."

The three ate their fill, shouldered their packs, put on comfortable hemp sandals, attached their daggers, and helped themselves to one halberd apiece from the weapons rack.

"A henchman is a henchman," said Shi Xiu. "We can't let any of them off."

He lit a bundle of straw in the stove and set fire to all sides of the inn. Fanned by the wind, the thatched roofs burst into blaze, great tongues of flame leaping into the sky. The three men struck out along the highway.

When they had marched for about two watches, they saw before and behind them innumerable torches. Nearly two hundred men, shouting and yelling, were closing in.

"Keep calm," said Shi Xiu. "We'll take to the small paths."

"No," said Yang Xiong. "Let them come. We'll kill them singly or in pairs. At daybreak, we'll go on."

Before the words were out of his mouth, they were attacked from four sides. Yang was in the lead, Shi Xiu covered the rear, the Flea defended the middle. With halberds they fought the charging vassals, who came at them with staves and spears. The pursuers didn't know what they were letting themselves in for. Yang, wielding his halberd, promptly felled half a dozen. The assault group fled pell-mell. Shi Xiu gave chase and hacked down half a dozen more.

When the other vassals saw this carnage, they decided they

wanted to live, and that this was not a very healthy atmosphere. They turned and ran, with the three in hot pursuit. More shouting rose, and two long hooked poles snaked out of the dry grass, fastened onto the Flea and dragged him into the underbrush. Shi Xiu whirled to go to his rescue. From behind, another two hooked poles shot out. The sharp-eyed Yang Xiong swiftly knocked them aside with his halberd and stabbed into the thicket. There were cries, and the ambushers hastily departed. The two saw them pulling away the Flea, but they had no heart for a fight in the depths of the thicket, and could only let him go.

They finally found a path and went on. The glow of the distant torches provided them with illumination, since the path was bare of trees or shrubbery, and they proceeded along it in an easterly direction.

The vassals, after searching for them in vain, collected their wounded. They brought the Flea, his hands tied behind his back, to the Zhu Family Manor.

Yang and Shi Xiu were still walking at daylight. A village tavern lay ahead.

"Let's buy some wine and food, brother, and ask directions," Shi Xiu suggested.

They entered the tavern, leaned their halberds against the wall, sat down, and ordered food and drink. The waiter served a few vegetable dishes and heated some wine. They were about to start, when a big man came in. His face was broad, his eyes bright, his ears large, his appearance rough and ugly. He wore a tea-brown robe, a head kerchief decorated with swastikas, a white silk waist sash, and oiled leather boots.

"His Excellency wants those loads delivered to the manor right away," he shouted.

The tavern host replied hastily: "Everything's ready. We'll send them over very soon."

The man turned to go. "Hurry it up," he said. He was passing Yang Xiong's and Shi Xiu's table on the way to the door. Yang recognized him.

"Young man, what are you doing here?" Yang called.

"Won't you take a look at me?"

The big fellow stared. Recognition grew in his eyes. "What are you doing here, benefactor?" he exclaimed. He dropped to his knees and kowtowed.

Yang Xiong raised the man to his feet and called Shi Xiu over.

"Who is this brother?" asked Shi Xiu.

"Du Xing is his name. He's from the prefecture of Zhongshan. Because of his crude features everyone calls him Demon Face. Last year he came to Qizhou as a trader. He killed one of the other merchants in his company in a fight, and was brought before the prefect and committed to my prison. I talked with him and found him very knowledgeable about hand-to-hand fighting and jousting with staves. So I used my influence and got him off. I never expected to meet him in this place."

"Are you here on official business, benefactor?" asked Du Xing.

Yang leaned close to his ear. "I killed a man in Qizhou and want to join the band in Liangshan Marsh. We spent last night at the Zhu Family Inn. Shi Qian, who's travelling with us, stole their rooster and we ate it, and the waiter raised a fuss. We got angry and set fire to the inn and ran away in the night. Pursuers caught up with us and we two knocked down several, but a couple of hooked poles reached out of the thicket and dragged Shi Qian away. We barged around until we came here. We were just about to ask for directions when you unexpectedly arrived, brother."

"Don't let it worry you, benefactor. I'll get them to return Shi Qian to you."

"Sit down and have a drink with us."

The three men sat and drank. Du Xing said: "Since leaving Qizhou I benefitted greatly from your kindness. Here, a big official took a liking to me and appointed me his steward. Every day all the thousand and one things in his household are in my hands. He trusts me completely. That's why I have no thought of going home."

"Who is this big official?"

"Before Lone Dragon Mountain are three cliffs, and on each of these is a village. Zhu Family Village is in the center, Hu Family Village is to the west, Li Family Village is to the east. These three villages and their manors have a total of nearly twenty thousand fighting men. Zhu Family Manor is the strongest. It is headed by Lord Zhu, who has three sons, known as the Three Warriors. The eldest is called Dragon, the second is called Tiger, the third is called Tiger Cub. They have an arms instructor, Luan Tingyu, who's known as the Iron Staff. Ten thousand men are no match for him. The manor has nearly two thousand fearless vassals.

"Hu Family Manor, to the west, is headed by Squire Hu. He has a son named Hu Cheng, the Flying Tiger, who is a powerful fighter. He also has a daughter, an extremely courageous girl, known as Ten Feet of Steel because of the two long gleaming swords she wields. She's an excellent horsewoman.

"My master heads the eastern manor. His name is Li Ying, and he's skilled with a steel-flecked iron lance. On his back he carries five concealed throwing knives. He can hit a man at a hundred paces, quicker than you can blink.

"The three villages have a solemn pact. If one is attacked by evil-doers, the others must go to its rescue. They're worried that bold fellows from Liangshan Marsh will raid them for grain, so they've prepared to defend themselves, together. I will take you to meet my master, and we'll request him to write a letter asking for Shi Qian's release."

"Your master Li Ying, isn't he the one known in the gallant fraternity as Heaven Soaring Eagle?" queried Yang Xiong.

"The very same."

Shi Xiu said: "I've heard that Li Ying of Lone Dragon Mountain is a chivalrous fellow. So this is where he's from. They say he's a remarkable fighter, a real man. We'll go to him."

Yang asked the waiter for the bill, but Du Xing insisted on paying. The three left the tavern. Du led them to the Li Family Manor. It was a huge affair. Fronting on a river cove, it was surrounded by whitewashed walls beside which grew hundreds of willows each thicker than two arms could embrace. They crossed a lowered drawbridge to the manor gates and entered. Twenty racks on either side of the outer chamber of the main hall were filled with gleaming weapons.

"Please wait here a moment, brothers," said Du. "I will inform the master that you've come."

Du Xing went inside. Shortly afterwards he emerged with Li Ying. Du brought Yang and Shi into the reception chamber, where they kowtowed. Li Ying returned the courtesy and invited them to be seated. The two visitors and their host politely argued over who should sit where, but finally took their places. Li called for wine.

Again the two visitors kowtowed. They said: "We beseech you, sir, to send a letter to the Zhu Family Manor, asking them to spare the life of Shi Qian. We shall never forget your kindness, now or in the hereafter."

Li Ying summoned the family tutor, dictated a letter, and affixed his seal. He directed his assistant steward to deliver it at once on a fast horse and return with the captive. The man took the missive, mounted, and left. Yang and Shi expressed their thanks.

"You needn't worry," said Li Ying. "When they get my letter, they'll release him."

The two thanked him again. "Please come with me to the rear chamber," said their host. "We can have a few drinks while we're waiting."

They went with him and found that breakfast had been prepared. When they finished eating, tea was served. Li asked them some questions about jousting with spears. Their replies showed they knew what they were talking about, and Li was very pleased.

At mid-morning the assistant steward returned. Li Ying, in the rear chamber, asked: "Where is the man you were sent to fetch?"

"I sent the letter in," said the messenger, "confident they

would let him go. Instead, the three sons came out and were quite unpleasant. They wouldn't answer your letter, and they wouldn't release the man. They're determined to turn him over to the prefectural authorities."

Li Ying was surprised. "Our three villages have a life-and-death alliance. They ought to respect my letter. How can they behave like that? You must have spoken rudely, to provoke such a response." He turned to Du Xing. "Steward, you'd better go yourself. See Lord Zhu personally, and explain the circumstances."

"I will, sir. But I suggest you write a missive in your own hand. Then, they'll have to let him go."

"Very well," said Li Ying. On a flowery sheet of paper he wrote a letter, added his personal seal to the envelope and handed it to Du Xing.

A fast horse was led out from the stable, already saddled and bridled. Whip in hand, Du walked through the manor gates, mounted, struck the animal a sharp blow, and galloped off towards the Zhu Family Manor.

"Don't worry," Li Ying said to his two callers. "When they receive this personal letter, they're sure to let him go quickly."

Yang Xiong and Shi Xiu profusely thanked the squire. He drank wine with them, while waiting in the rear chamber.

Daylight was beginning to fade, and still Du Xing hadn't returned. Li Ying became concerned, and he sent men down the road to meet him. A vassal soon came in and reported:

"Steward Du is approaching."

"Who else is with him?"

"He's galloping back alone."

Li Ying shook his head in wonderment. "Very strange. He isn't usually so dilatory. Why is he slow today?"

He left the hall, followed by Yang and Shi. Du had dismounted and was just entering the manor gates. His face was tight with rage and his teeth were bared. For several minutes he was unable to speak.

"Tell us in detail," said Li Ying. "What happened?"

Du Xing controlled himself with an effort. "I carried your

letter to their third big gate, and found, by coincidence, the three sons sitting there. I hailed them courteously. 'What do you want?' Tiger Cub snarled. I bowed and said: 'My master has sent me with this letter. I respectfully submit it.' His face darkened, and he replied: 'How can your master be so ignorant? The wretch he sent this morning brought a letter asking us for that Liangshan Marsh bandit Shi Qian. We're going to take him before the prefect. Why have you come again?' I said: 'Shi Qian isn't a member of the Liangshan Marsh band. He's a merchant from Qizhou who's come to see my master. There was a misunderstanding and he burned down your inn. My master undertakes to rebuild it. As a courtesy to us, please be lenient and forgive him.' The three brothers shouted: 'We're not going to let him go.' I said: 'Please, sirs, at least read the letter my master has written.' Tiger Cub took it and, without opening it, tore it to shreds. He yelled for his men to throw me out of the manor. He and Tiger said: 'Don't make your betters angry, or we'll' — I wasn't going to tell you this, but those animals really were too crude — 'we'll nab that Li Ying and take him up before the court as a Liangshan Marsh bandit as well!' They yelled for their vassals to lay hands on me, but I jumped on my horse and raced away. I was burning with rage all the way home. What scoundrels! After all these years of close alliance, to behave so churlishly!''

When Li Ying heard this, his fury burst out of control and spurted sky-high. "Vassals," he roared, "bring me my horse!"

"Calm yourself, sir," Yang and Shi pleaded. "Don't spoil the local harmony for our sakes."

But Li would not listen. He put on golden armor with animal-faced discs, chest and back, and over that a voluminous red cape. Behind him, he affixed five throwing knives. He took his steel-flecked spear, donned his phoenix-winged helmet, strode out of the manor gates, and selected three hundred of his toughest vassals. Du Xing also put on armor, got a lance, and mounted. With him were twenty other horsemen. Yang and Shi girded up their robes. Halberds at the ready, they followed

Li Ying's horse as the company advanced rapidly on the Zhu Family Manor.

The sun was sinking in the western hills when they reached Lone Dragon Cliff. They spread out in battle formation. The manor was strategically well situated upon a cliff and surrounded by a broad stream. It was enclosed by three sets of walls, one within the other, each twenty feet high and built of sturdy rock. The front and rear gates of the manor were equipped with drawbridges. Within the walls were huts bristling with weapons. In the gate-house atop the wall were war drums and gongs.

Li Ying reined in his horse in front of the manor. "Three sons of the Zhu Family," he shouted. "How dare you slander me!"

The manor gates opened and out rode fifty or sixty horsemen. In the lead, astride a charcoal roan steed, was Tiger Cub, third son of Lord Zhu. Li Ying shook his finger at the youth.

"The smell of milk hasn't gone from your lips. You've still got baby hair on your head. Your father has a life-and-death alliance with me. We've sworn to defend our villages jointly. When your family is in difficulty and needs men, we give them at once. When it needs materials, we never stint. Today, in good faith, I sent you two letters. Why did you tear them up? Insult me? Why have you committed this outrage?"

"Yes, we have a pact with you to defend our mutual interests," Tiger Cub retorted, "and to grab any bandits from Liangshan Marsh and destroy their mountain lair. How is it you're colluding with them? Are you planning to become a rebel too?"

"Who says Shi Qian is from Liangshan Marsh? You're slandering an innocent man. That's criminal."

"He's already confessed. Your lies aren't any use. They can't conceal the facts. Now, get out of here. If you don't, we'll grab you for a bandit and turn you in as well."

Furious, Li Ying whipped up his horse and charged at Tiger Cub with levelled lance. The youth spurred his own mount forward, and the two fought before Lone Dragon Cliff. To and fro, up and down, nearly eighty rounds they battled. Tiger Cub realized he couldn't vanquish his adversary. He turned his horse and ran. Li Ying gave chase. Tiger Cub rested his lance athwart his animal's neck, fitted an arrow to his bow and drew it to the full. Twisting in the saddle, he aimed and let fly. Li Ying dodged, but the arrow struck him in the shoulder, and he tumbled to the ground. Tiger Cub wheeled his mount and started back, intending to seize him.

Yang Xiong and Shi Xiu uttered a great shout and dashed in the path of the youth's horse with raised halberds. Tiger Cub knew he was no match for them, and again he hurriedly turned his mount. Yang jabbed the horse in the withers, and it reared in pain, nearly unseating its rider. Zhu Family archers, who had followed after the horsemen, began whizzing arrows at Yang and Shi. They had no armor, and had to withdraw. By then, Du Xing had lifted Li Ying to his steed and ridden away. Yang and Shi followed in the wake of the retreating Li Family vassals. The Zhu Family forces pursued them for two or three *li*. But daylight was fading, and they returned to their manor.

Holding Li Ying, Du Xing rode home. At the gate he dismounted and helped his master into the rear chamber. The women of the household came in to attend him. They extracted the arrow, removed his armor, and applied a poultice to the wound.

That night, the men conferred. Yang and Shi said to Du Xing: "That rogue has insulted Li Ying. He's wounded him with an arrow and we haven't rescued Shi Qian. It's all our fault for having involved your master. We two will go to Mount Liangshan and entreat Chao and Song and the other leaders to come and avenge him and rescue Shi Qian." They thanked Li Ying and requested leave to depart.

"It's not that I didn't try, but the odds were too great," said Li Ying. "Please forgive me." He directed Du Xing to present Yang and Shi with gold and silver. They didn't want to accept, but Li Ying said: "We're all in the gallant fraternity. No need for courtesy."

Only then did they take his gifts. They kowtowed and bid him farewell. Du Xing saw them to the edge of the village and pointed out the main road, then returned to the Li Family Manor. Of that we'll say no more.

Yang and Shi pushed on towards Liangshan Marsh. They saw in the distance a newly built tavern, its wine pennant fluttering in the breeze. On arrival, they ordered drinks and asked directions. Actually, this tavern was a lookout place recently added by the men on Mount Liangshan. Shi Yong was in charge. He overheard them asking the waiter how to get to the fortress, and could see that they were no ordinary men. He walked over to their table.

"Where are you two gentlemen from? Why do you want to go up the mountain?" he queried.

"We're from Qizhou," Yang Xiong replied.

Shi Yong suddenly remembered. "Then you must be Shi Xiu."

"No, I'm Yang Xiong. This is Shi Xiu. How do you know his name, brother?"

"We haven't met. But not long ago brother Dai Zong stopped here on his way back from Qizhou and told me a lot about him. Today, you two want to go up the mountain. That's very good news."

The three exchanged courtesies, and Yang and Shi told Shi Yong of their encounter with the Zhu Family. Shi Yong directed the waiter to serve them the best wine. He opened the window of the pavilion overlooking the water, bent his bow, and shot a whistling arrow. Instantly, a bandit rowed a boat over from the reeds in the cove opposite. Shi Yong escorted the two on board and delivered them to Duck's Bill Shore. He had sent a man ahead to report, and now Dai Zong and Yang Lin came down the mountain to welcome them. After courtesies were exchanged, they went together to the stronghold.

When the leaders were informed that more bold fellows had arrived, they convened a meeting in the hall and sat in their chairs of rank. Dai Zong and Yang Lin led in Yang Xiong and Shi Xiu and presented them to Chao and Song and the other leaders. Chao questioned them carefully on their backgrounds. The two told of their skill with arms and of their desire to join the band. The leaders were very pleased, and offered them seats.

After a time Yang Xiong said: "There is a man named Shi Qian who also wants to join. But unfortunately he stole a rooster that heralded the dawn at the Zhu Family Inn and we got into a row. Shi Xiu burned the place down and Shi Qian was captured. Li Ying sent two letters requesting his release, but the three sons of the Zhu Family have refused to let him go. They've vowed to take all the gallants in this stronghold, and they've cursed and reviled you in every way. Those varlets have no sense of fitness whatsoever."

If he hadn't told this, nothing would have happened. But he did, and Chao Gai flew into a rage.

"Children," he shouted to the assembled bandits, "take these two out, cut off their heads, and report back."

Song Jiang hastily intervened. "Calm yourself, brother. These two warriors have come a long distance, and with one thought in mind — to help us. Why do you want them executed?"

"Ever since our bold fellows took over here from Wang Lun, we've always placed chivalry and virtuous behavior towards the people first. Brother after brother has gone down the mountain, but none of them has injured our prestige. All our brothers, new or old, are honorable and chivalrous. These rogues, in the name of the gallants of Liangshan Marsh, stole a rooster and ate it, shaming us by association. They must be decapitated, and their heads displayed at the scene of the crime as a warning. I will personally lead our forces down and purge the Zhu Family Village so that our reputation for valor will not be lost. Children, off with their heads!"

"Wait," said Song Jiang. "Didn't you hear what these two

brothers just said? Shi Qian the Flea on a Drum has always been light-fingered. It was his behavior that provoked the Zhu Family. In what way have these two brothers shamed our stronghold? I've heard many people say that the Zhu Family Manor is hostile to us. Cool down, brother. We have many men and horses, but we're short of money and grain. Although we're not looking for trouble with the Zhu's, since they've started the provocations, this is a good chance to go down and nab them. When we defeat the manor, we'll capture enough grain to last us four or five years. We're not seeking an excuse to harm them, but those oafs are really much too rude. You are the highest leader here, brother. Why sally forth on minor matters? I have no talent, but with a contingent of men and horses, and the help of some of our brothers, I'd like to attack the Zhu Family Manor. If we don't wipe it out, we won't return. For one thing, only vengeance will restore our prestige. Secondly, we must pay those pipsqueaks for their insults. Thirdly, we'll get a lot of grain for the use of our fortress. And fourthly, we can ask Li Ying to come up and join our band."

"A very good idea," said Wu Yong. "We in the fortress shouldn't destroy men who are like our own hands."

"I'd rather you decapitated me than hurt one of our brothers," said Dai Zong.

At the urging of all the leaders, Chao Gai finally pardoned Yang Xiong and Shi Xiu. They thanked him and kowtowed.

"Don't be angry," Song Jiang said to them soothingly. "It's a rule of our stronghold, and we must obey. Even I could be decapitated if I violated it. I could expect no forgiveness. Pei Xuan, the Ironclad Virtue, has recently been made provost marshal, and rules regarding rewards and punishments have been promulgated. Don't hold it against us, please."

Chao asked Yang Xiong and Shi Xiu to take seats after Yang Lin, and all the rank and file bandits were summoned to join in congratulating the new chieftains. Cows and horses were slaughtered and a celebration feast was laid. Living quarters were allocated to Yang and Shi, and ten bandits were appointed to each as attendants.

The banquet ended that evening, and the next day they feasted again. Then the leaders conferred. Song Jiang directed Ironclad Virtue to compile a list of men to go down the mountain, and he invited the other leaders to accompany him in a raid on the Zhu Family Manor. He was determined to demolish it. It was agreed that Wu Yong, Liu Tang, the three Ruan brothers, Lü Fang and Guo Sheng would remain to hold the fortress, in addition to Chao Gai. Those guarding the shore, the gates and the taverns would also remain at their posts. Newly arrived Meng Kang, who had been appointed boat builder, would replace Ma Lin as the supervisor of war vessels. A written announcement was drawn stating that the leaders participating in the raid on the Zhu Family Manor were divided into two units. The first included Song Jiang, and would head a body of three thousand foot soldiers and three hundred cavalry. When armored and equipped, this would go first, as the van.

The second unit would include Lin Chong, and would also head three thousand foot soldiers and three hundred cavalry. This body would follow, as reinforcements.

Song Wan and Zheng Tianshou would continue holding the small forts at the Shore of Golden Sands and Duck's Bill Shore, respectively, and be responsible for supplying the attackers with grain and fodder.

Chao Gai saw the raiders off and returned to the stronghold.

Song Jiang's party made straight for the Zhu Family Manor. Nothing untoward happened on the way, and they soon were approaching Lone Dragon Mountain. When they were about a *li* or so away, they pitched camp. Song Jiang's tent was in the middle, and he sat there conferring with Hua Rong.

"I hear the roads to the manor are very tricky," he said, "and that it's difficult to move up on them with soldiers. I'll send a couple of men to scout out which paths are best. Then we can advance and engage the foe."

"I've been idle for a long time, brother," said Li Kui. "I haven't killed a single person. Let me go in first."

"Not you, brother," said Song Jiang. "If we needed a shock assault, I'd send you. But this is careful, delicate work. You're not suitable."

Li Kui laughed. "That friggin manor. Why trouble yourself? I'll take two or three hundred of the lads, and we'll carve our way in and cut all the wretches down. What do you need scouts for?"

"You're talking rot. Get out of here, and don't come till I call you."

Li Kui left, muttering to himself: "All that fuss about swatting a few flies."

Song Jiang summoned Shi Xiu and said: "You've been here before. I'd like you and Yang Lin to scout around."

"Since you've come with a large force, they're of course on their guard at the manor. How should we disguise ourselves?"

"I'll dress up as an exorcist," said Yang Lin, "and conceal a knife in my clothes. I'll carry a prayer wheel as I walk along. The moment you hear the sound of it, come up to me and stay close."

"I sold fuel in Qizhou," said Shi Xiu. "I'll tote a load as if I was selling again. I also will have a concealed weapon. In an emergency I can use the carrying-pole as well."

"Good. We'll work out the details, and prepare tonight. We'll get up at the fifth watch and go."

The next morning, Shi Xiu left first with his load of fuel. Before he had gone twenty *li*, he encountered a complicated maze of paths which seemed to go round in circles through thick groves of trees. He couldn't figure them out. Shi Xiu set down his load. Behind, he heard the hum of an approaching prayer wheel. Yang Lin, a broken straw hat on his head, wearing an old priest's robe and twirling a prayer wheel, was coming towards him with stately tread. No one else was in sight, so Shi Xiu spoke to him:

"These paths all twist and turn. I can't remember which was the one I took with Li Ying the other day. It was nearly dark and they knew the way and travelled fast. I wasn't able to get a good look."

"Stay off the paths, then, and stick to the main road."

Shi Xiu shouldered his load again and continued on. He saw a village ahead, and several taverns and butcher shops. He walked up to the gate of one of the taverns. He noticed that racks of weapons stood in front of every shop, and that all the men in them wore golden vests with the word "Zhu" emblazoned on the backs. People on the streets were similarly dressed. Shi Xiu respectfully hailed an old man who was passing by and bowed.

"May I ask you about a local custom, grandpa? Why are there weapons at every door?"

"Where are you from, stranger? If you don't know, you'd better leave quickly."

"I'm a date-seller from Shandong. I've lost my capital and can't go home. Now I sell fuel. I'm not familiar with your local ways."

"Go quickly. Get out of sight. There's going to be a big battle here soon."

"How can that be, a nice place like this?"

"You really don't know? Well, I'll tell you. This is called Zhu Family Village. It's ruled by Lord Zhu, whose manor is up on that cliff. He's offended the bold fellows in Liangshan Marsh, and they've come with men and horses to kill us all. But the paths to our village are too complicated, and they're camped outside. The manor has directed every able-bodied young man to get ready. The moment the order comes, they're to rush to the aid of our fighters."

"How many people have you here in this village, grandpa?"

"Nearly twenty thousand. And we can count on help from the villages to our east and west. The eastern one is ruled by Heaven Soaring Eagle Li Ying. The western one belongs to Squire Hu. He has a daughter called Ten Feet of Steel who's a terror with weapons."

"In that case, you've nothing to fear from Liangshan Marsh!"

"That's right. If we ourselves had just arrived, we too could

314

be easily captured."

"What do you mean, grandpa?"

"We have a jingle that goes:

A fine Zhu Family Village,
Its paths twist round about,
Getting in is easy,
But just try getting out!"

Shi Xiu began to weep. He flopped to the ground and kowtowed. "I'm a poor trader who lost his capital on the road and can't go home, and now I'm selling fuel," he cried. "This is awful. I've landed in the middle of a battle and can't escape. Pity me, grandpa. I'll give you this load of fuel, only show me the way out!"

"I don't want your fuel for nothing. I'll buy it from you. Come with me. I'll treat you to some food and wine."

Shi Xiu thanked him, shouldered his load, and went with the old man to his house. His host poured out two bowls of white wine, filled another with rice gruel, and set them before him. Again Shi Xiu expressed his thanks.

"Grandpa," he begged, "tell me how to get out of here."

"You just turn whenever you reach a white poplar. Take the path that starts from there, whether it be narrow or broad. Any other path leads to a dead end. No other tree will do. If you take a wrong path, you'll never get out, whether you go left or right. The dead-end trails are strewn with hidden bamboo spikes and iron prongs. You're liable to step on them, and you're sure to be captured. You wouldn't have a chance of getting away."

The young man kowtowed and thanked him. "What is your name, grandpa?"

"Most people in this village have the surname of Zhu. Only my family is named Zhongli. We've always been here."

"I've had enough food and wine. Some day I'll repay you well."

While they were talking, they heard a clamor outside. A voice shouted: "We've caught a spy." Startled, Shi Xiu and

the old man hurried into the courtyard. They saw seventy
or eighty soldiers escorting a man with his hands tied behind
his back. Shi Xiu recognized Yang Lin. He had been stripped
naked. Shi Xiu groaned inwardly.

"Who is that?" he made a pretense of asking the old man.
"Why is he bound?"

"Didn't you hear them say he's a spy sent by Song Jiang?"

"How was he caught?"

"He's a bold rascal. He came alone, disguised as an exorcist priest, barging into the village. Since he didn't know the
way, he could only follow the main road. Left or right would
have taken him into dead ends. He'd never heard the secret
of the white poplars. Someone saw him wandering off on
a wrong turning, and thought he looked suspicious. So he
reported to the manor, and they sent men to nab him. The
rogue pulled a knife and wounded four or five of them. But
they were too many, and he was overpowered. Now he's been
recognized as a robber. They say he's called Yang Lin the
Elegant Panther."

Down the road a voice exclaimed: "The Third Son of the
manor has come on patrol."

Through a crack in the courtyard wall Shi Xiu saw twenty
foot soldiers with red-tasseled spears, followed by five mounted
men, all with bows and arrows. Behind, another four or five
riders on white horses were gathered protectively around a
young warrior on a snow-white steed. In full armor, he carried a
bow and arrows, and gripped a lance. Shi Xiu recognized him,
but feigned ignorance.

"Who is that young gentleman passing by?"

"Lord Zhu's third son, Tiger Cub. He's engaged to Ten
Feet of Steel of the Hu Family Manor, west of here. Of the
three sons, he's the most terrific fighter."

Shi Xiu again thanked the old man and said: "Please point
out which road I should take."

"It's late already, and a battle may be raging ahead. You'll
be throwing your life away."

"Save me, grandpa, I beg you."

"Spend the night here. Tomorrow, if things are quiet, you can leave."

Shi Xiu thanked him, and remained. Four or five mounted men were going from door to door and exhorting the populace: "If you see a red signal lantern tonight, use might and main to catch the Mount Liangshan bandits and claim the reward."

When they had gone, Shi Xiu asked: "Who was that official with them?"

"He's our local sheriff. Tonight they're planning to capture Song Jiang."

Shi Xiu gave this some thought. Then he borrowed a torch, said good night, and retired to sleep in a thatched hut in the rear.

Song Jiang and his forces were encamped outside the village. Neither Shi Xiu nor Yang Lin had returned. Ou Peng was sent to the village entrance to check. After a while he reported back.

"People are saying they've caught a spy. Those paths are very complicated. I didn't dare to go further in."

Song Jiang grew angry. "I can't wait for a report any longer. Now the word is they've caught a spy. That means our two brothers have been trapped. We'll attack tonight, regardless. We'll fight our way in and rescue them. How do the rest of you feel about it?" he asked the other leaders.

"I'll go first," said Li Kui. "Just to see what it's like."

Song Jiang ordered all men to arm themselves and put on their gear. Li Kui and Yang Xiong would be the vanguard. Li Jun would command the rear. Mu Hong would take the left flank, Huang Xin the right. Song Jiang, Hua Rong and Ou Peng would lead the central contingent.

Amid waving flags, pounding drums and braying gongs, the raiders, shouting and brandishing swords and axes, marched rapidly on the Zhu Family Manor.

It was dusk when they reached Lone Dragon Cliff. Song Jiang urged the forward contingent to attack the manor. Li Kui, stripped to the buff and brandishing two steel battle-axes,

宋公明一打祝家庄

rushed ahead like a streak of fire. But at the manor, he found the drawbridge raised and not a light showing anywhere. Li Kui was going to jump into the moat and swim across, but Yang Xiong stopped him.

"No, don't. If they've closed the manor gates, they must have some scheme. Wait till brother Song Jiang arrives, then we'll decide what to do."

To Li Kui this was unbearable. He smote his battle-axes and shouted up the cliff: "Lord Zhu, you friggin crook, come out! Your master Black Whirlwind is here, waiting!"

There was no response from the manor.

Song Jiang, followed by Yang, arrived with his men. The manor was quiet. He reined in his horse and looked. Not a weapon or a soldier was in sight. Warily, he thought: "I'm wrong. The Heavenly Books say clearly: 'Avoid rashness in the face of the enemy.' I didn't foresee this. I thought only of rescuing our two brothers, and moved my troops up through the night. I didn't expect that when I got in deep, right up to their manor, that the foe's army wouldn't show. They must be up to something."

He ordered his three contingents to withdraw at once. Li Kui objected.

"We've come this far. You mustn't retreat," he cried. "You and I will fight our way in. All of you, follow me!"

Before the words were out of his mouth, the manor knew about it. A signal rocket arched through the sky. On the cliff thousands of torches suddenly flared. Arrows showered down from the gate-house above the wall. Song Jiang hastily withdrew his forces along the road on which it had come. The rear guard under Li Jun set up a shout.

"We're cut off! They've laid an ambush!"

Song Jiang directed his men to seek other roads. Li Kui, flourishing his axes, dashed about, looking for adversaries, but he couldn't find a single enemy soldier. Another signal rocket soared from the cliff. Before the sound of it had died away, thunderous shouts rang from all sides.

Song Jiang, on his horse, gazed around. Enemy troops were

lying in wait in every direction. He ordered his men to fight their way towards the main road. Soon, he again heard cries of consternation. When he asked the cause, the men said: "These paths all wind in circles. No matter how we turn, we keep coming back here."

"Advance to where you see torches and people's dwellings," he said.

Before long, the vanguard once more set up a cry. "We can't head for the torches. The paths are strewn with bamboo spikes and iron barbs and blocked with sharp-pronged branches like deer antlers."

Song Jiang groaned. "Heaven has forsaken me."

Just then there was a stir in the left flank contingent under Mu Hong. A messenger reported: "Shi Xiu is here." In a moment, Shi Xiu, twirling his blade, rushed up to Song Jiang's horse.

"Don't be alarmed, brother," he said. "I know how to travel these paths. Pass the word, quietly: Take any path, whether narrow or broad, which starts at a white poplar."

Song Jiang issued the appropriate order. When they had proceeded another five or six *li*, he saw ahead a large concentration of enemy men and horses. He shouted for Shi Xiu and asked: "Why are there so many of those rogues up there, brother?"

"They use a lantern as an assembly signal."

Hua Rong peered from his saddle. He pointed and said to Song Jiang: "You see that lantern with a candle in it among the trees? Whichever way we go, east or west, it moves in that direction, and their troops gather at the lantern to meet us. It's their signal, all right."

"How can we deal with the lantern?"

"Easy," said Hua Rong. He fitted an arrow to his bow, urged his mount forward, and let fly. He hit the red lantern squarely, knocking it out.

With no lantern to guide them, the ambushing foe was thrown into confusion. Song Jiang told Shi Xiu to lead the way, and they fought their way out of the village.

There were shouts on the mountain ahead and a wildly dancing row of torches. Song Jiang ordered a halt. He sent Shi Xiu to investigate. Before long, Shi returned and reported:

"It's another contingent from our fortress, come to reinforce us and scatter the enemy troops."

Song Jiang urged his men forward into the fray, forcing a passage away from the village. The Zhu Family Manor soldiers dispersed and withdrew.

CHAPTER 18
Song Jiang's Second Attack on the Zhu Family Manor

The forces of Lin Chong and Qin Ming joined up with Song Jiang's men, and they all halted outside the village. By then it was daylight. They pitched camp on high ground and counted their men and horses. Huang Xin, Suppressor of the Three Mountains, was missing. Startled, Song Jiang asked about him. The men who had been with him the night before explained.

"When Commander Huang received your order, he went to seek a path. But two hooks shot out of the reeds and tumbled his horse. Half a dozen men seized the commander and pulled him away. We couldn't rescue him."

Song Jiang was enraged. He wanted to kill Huang's soldiers for not having reported this earlier. Lin Chong and Hua Rong finally cooled him down. The others were upset.

"We haven't taken the manor," they said, "and we've lost two brothers besides. What are we going to do?"

"The three villages have an alliance," said Yang Xiong. "But Li Ying, who rules the east village, was wounded by Tiger Cub Zhu the other day, and he's resting at home. Why don't you go and consult with him, brother?"

"I'd forgotten about that," said Song Jiang. "He knows the terrain and the situation well." He ordered that two bolts of silk, two sheep and two jugs of wine be prepared as gifts, along with a good riding horse, complete with saddle and bridle. He set out to deliver them personally, leaving Lin Chong and Qin Ming to guard the camp.

Hua Rong, Yang Xiong and Shi Xiu and three hundred

cavalrymen mounted and went with him towards the Li Family Manor. At the walls, they found the gate-house closed and the drawbridge raised. Soldiers lined the ramparts. Within the gate-house, a battle drum thundered. Song Jiang shouted from his horse.

"I am Song Jiang, a warrior from Mount Liangshan, here to call on your lord. I have no other purpose. You needn't be on guard against me."

When Du Xing saw that Yang Xiong and Shi Xiu were among the party, he opened the manor gate, came across the moat in a small boat and hailed Song Jiang respectfully. Song Jiang dismounted and returned the courtesy. Yang Xiong and Shi Xiu drew near.

"This is the brother who introduced us to Lord Li," they said to Song Jiang. "He is known as Demon Face Du Xing."

"Ah, Steward Du. Could I trouble you to tell Lord Li that Song Jiang of Liangshan Marsh has long known of his fame, though we have never had occasion to meet. Because we are in conflict with Zhu Family Manor, we are passing by here. I would like to present him with some colored silk, a fine horse, two sheep and some wine — trifling gifts — and request the pleasure of meeting him. I want nothing else."

Du Xing took this message into the manor. Li Ying was seated in bed in his hall with a quilt draped over his shoulders, recovering from his wound. Du Xing told him what Song Jiang had said.

"He's a rebel from Liangshan Marsh. How can I receive him?" Li replied. "Though groundless, I would become suspect to the authorities. Say that I am sick in bed, that I can't get up and meet him. I hope to have the honor another day. As to the gifts, I cannot presume to accept them."

Du Xing again crossed the moat. "My master sends his respects," he said to Song Jiang. "He was hoping to welcome you in person, but because of his wound he is ill in bed and is unable to greet you. He will make a special point of it some other day. The gifts which you so graciously present, he dares not accept."

"I know what's in your master's mind. I want to see him because I've been unsuccessful in my attack on the Zhu Family Manor. He won't see me because he's afraid they would resent it."

"No, that's not the reason. He's really ill. Although I'm originally from Zhongshan, I've been here many years, and I know something of the local situation. The Zhu Family Manor is in the center, the Li Family Manor to the east, the Hu Family Manor to the west. They have a solemn alliance to help one another in time of danger. Because the Zhu's wounded my master, he hasn't gone to their aid. But the Hu's probably will. They're not much to worry about, except for their woman general, who's called Ten Feet of Steel because of the two shining swords she wields. She's a remarkable warrior. She and Tiger Cub of the Zhu Family are engaged, and one of these days they'll marry. When attacking the Zhu Family Manor the east needn't concern you, but watch your west.

"The manor has two gates, one facing the front of Lone Dragon Cliff, the other facing the rear. It's no use assaulting only the front gate. Both gates must be attacked simultaneously. That's the only way you can break in. The paths to the front gate are twisted and complicated. They wind round and round and are of different widths. Only those with white poplars at their starting points are through paths. The rest are dead-ends."

"What if they cut all the poplars down?" said Shi Xiu. "How will we be able to travel?"

"The stumps will still be there, won't they? Those will be your markers. Attack only in daylight. Don't try to advance at night."

Song Jiang thanked Du Xing and returned to camp with his party. Lin Chong and the others met them on the way, then all went to the camp and conferred. Song Jiang told of Li Ying's refusal to meet him, and of the advice given by Du Xing.

"With the best intentions in the world we send him gifts, and the oaf doesn't even come out to greet brother!" Li Kui blurted. "Give me three hundred men and I'll crack open his friggin manor and drag the varlet over by the head and make him pay our brother his proper respects!"

"You don't understand, brother," said Song Jiang. "He's virtuous and law-abiding. He's afraid of the authorities. How could he meet us?"

Li Kui grinned. "Shy, like a child."

Everyone laughed.

"Nevertheless, two of our brothers have been captured, and we don't know whether they're alive or dead," said Song Jiang. "I hope you brothers will do your utmost and join with me in another attack on Zhu Family Manor."

The other leaders rose to their feet. "Give the orders. We'll obey. Who do you want to go first?"

"If you're afraid of children, why not send me?" cried Li Kui.

"You're not suitable for the van, not this time," said Song Jiang. While Li Kui fumed with lowered head, he selected Ma Lin, Deng Fei, Ou Peng, and the Stumpy Tiger. "You four and I will go first," he stated.

For the second contingent he chose Dai Zong and seven others, and told them to prepare to attack via water. The third group was to be led by Lin Chong, Hua Rong, Mu Hong and Li Kui, and would be divided into two columns to serve as reinforcements.

The order of battle decided, the leaders ate, then put on their armor and mounted their horses.

Since Song Jiang himself was leading the van which would launch the first assault, it flaunted a large red banner inscribed with the word "Marshal". He, the other four leaders, a hundred and fifty cavalrymen, and a thousand foot soldiers marched rapidly on Zhu Family Manor.

Before Lone Dragon Cliff Song Jiang drew rein and stared at their objective. Two white banners floated over the ramparts. Brightly embroidered on them were the rallying calls: *Fill in the Marsh and nab Chao Gai. Level the Mountain and catch Song Jiang.*

Angrily, Song Jiang vowed: "If I don't take Zhu Family

一丈青单捉王矮虎

Manor I'll never return to Mount Liangshan!"

The other leaders were equally enraged. When the second contingent arrived, Song Jiang left them to attack the front gate, while he and his unit went round to the cliff's rear. There, the manor was as solid as a wall of bronze, and heavily fortified.

While he was examining it, an enemy force came charging from the west, shouting fiercely. Song Jiang left Ma Lin and Deng Fei to hold the rear gate. With Ou Peng and Stumpy Tiger and half the men, he went forward to meet the foe. Riding towards him down the slope were about thirty horsemen. In their midst was the girl warrior known as Ten Feet of Steel, astride a black-maned steed and whirling her shining swords. Followed by four or five hundred armed vassals, she was coming to the aid of Zhu Family Manor.

"A formidable-looking adversary," said Song Jiang. "That must be the famous daughter of the Hu Family. Who dares to give her battle?"

Wang the Stumpy Tiger was a lecherous fellow. When he heard that the warrior was a lady, he immediately hoped to capture her for his own. With a yell, he urged his mount forward, his lance levelled. Both armies shouted. The girl smote her horse and galloped towards Stumpy Tiger, flourishing her blades. A superb artisan with the double swords and an outstanding veteran with the single lance clashed in scores of rounds.

Song Jiang soon could see that Wang was no match for the girl. The short-legged man had longed to catch her quickly, but by the tenth round his hands were trembling and his legs were paralyzed with fatigue, and his skill with the lance was faltering. If they weren't in a battle to the death, Wang would gladly have yielded.

Ten Feet of Steel was an intelligent, sensitive girl. "That's a crude varlet," she thought. She closed in, swinging both blades. It was too much for Stumpy Tiger. He turned his horse and fled, pursued by the girl warrior. She hung up her right sword, stretched forth her lovely arm, and plucked Wang from the saddle. The vassals rushed forward, grabbed him by the feet, and dragged him off, a prisoner.

With levelled lance Ou Peng hurried to his aid. Ten Feet of Steel urged her mount forward to meet him, swords at the ready. They fought. Ou Peng was descended from generations of military men, and was first-rate with the iron lance. Song Jiang observed his skill admiringly. But despite Ou Peng's excellence, he was unable to gain the slightest advantage over the girl.

Deng Fei had seen from afar the capture of Stumpy Tiger Wang, and now witnessed the failure of Ou Peng to vanquish the girl. He galloped towards the contestants, shouting and brandishing his iron chain. The warriors of the Zhu Family Manor, who had been watching for some time, feared for the girl's safety. Quickly, they lowered the drawbridge and opened the gate. The Dragon, leading three hundred men, rode lickety-split, lance in hand, to seize Song Jiang.

Ma Lin galloped, with twin swords, to head off the Dragon. Deng Fei was worried about Song Jiang. Keeping close to him, he watched the clashes raging on both sides amid wild shouts. Song Jiang realized that Ma Lin couldn't defeat Zhu the Dragon, and Ou Peng clearly was making no headway against Ten Feet of Steel. Song Jiang was growing extremely anxious when a troop of horsemen appeared, riding in rapidly from an angle. He looked, and was delighted to recognize Qin Ming. When the Thunderbolt had heard the noise of battle at the manor, he had decided to join in.

"General Qin," Song Jiang called, "help Ma Lin!"

Qin Ming had a low flash point. The Zhu Family had captured his disciple Huang Xin, and his temper hadn't improved. He clapped his steed forward and unlimbered his wolf-toothed cudgel, riding directly at the Dragon. With raised lance, the Dragon advanced to meet him. This left Ma Lin free to lead a body of men after Stumpy Wang's captors. Ten Feet of Steel promptly abandoned Ou Peng to attack Ma Lin. Man and girl both used double swords, and their clash on horseback was like jade snowflakes swirling in the wind.

Song Jiang stared, positively dazzled.

The Dragon and Qin Ming fought ten rounds or more, but the Dragon was no match for the Thunderbolt. Arms instructor in the Zhu manor, Luan Tingyu, mounted and rode forth with his hammer. Ou Peng cantered towards him. But Luan, instead of coming on directly, swerved as Ou Peng gripped his lance, and appeared to flee. Ou Peng gave chase. Luan threw his hammer, hit Ou Peng squarely and knocked him from his mount.

"Children, to the rescue," roared Deng Fei. He charged at Luan, swinging his iron chain.

Song Jiang shouted for his men to get Ou Peng back in the saddle. The Dragon, being bested by Qin Ming, smote his horse and ran. Luan left Deng Fei to engage Qin Ming. They fought nearly twenty rounds, with no result. Luan feinted, then galloped into the wilds, with Qin Ming, brandishing his cudgel, hot on the trail. Luan raced his steed into the deep grass. Unaware that this was a ruse, Qin Ming pounded after him. Men of the Zhu Family Manor were lying in ambush. When Qin Ming appeared, they pulled taut a rope across the path and sent horse and rider tumbling to the ground. Yelling, they grabbed him. Deng Fei galloped heedlessly to save the Thunderbolt. He saw the trip rope rising before him, and pulled frantically on the rein to turn his steed.

"Get him," cried voices on either side. Hooked ropes landed on Deng Fei like a tangle of hemp, and he too was captured, still seated on his horse.

Song Jiang groaned. The rescued Ou Peng mounted once more.

Ma Lin sped from Ten Feet of Steel to protect Song Jiang. He rode south, chased by the girl, Luan and the Dragon. He knew he couldn't get away, and was reconciling himself to being taken when he saw a bold fellow on horseback galloping towards him from due south, followed by about five hundred men, mounted and on foot.

Song Jiang recognized the rider as Mu Hong the Unrestrained. From the southeast came another three hundred fighters, preceded by two racing gallants — Yang Xiong the Pallid and Shi Xiu the Reckless. From the northeast came another bold fellow, who shouted: "Let that man alone!" It was the master bowman Hua Rong.

The rescuers converged from three directions. Song Jiang was overjoyed as they joined to do battle with Luan and the Dragon and his men. Concerned for the two, the manor command directed Tiger to hold the gates, while the young gentleman Tiger Cub sallied forth on a fiery steed, holding a long lance and leading five hundred infantry and cavalry. These plunged into the fray.

Before the manor Li Jun, Zhang Heng and Zhang Shun crossed the stream which served as a moat, but were prevented from advancing by a shower of arrows. Dai Zong and Bai Sheng, on the opposite bank, could only shout in frustration.

Daylight was fading. Song Jiang instructed Ma Lin to escort Ou Peng safely from the village. Then he ordered that the gongs be beaten as the signal for his gallants to converge and fight their way out. He whipped up his horse and made a circuit of the combat area, worried lest any brothers had become lost.

Suddenly, he saw Ten Feet of Steel galloping towards him. He had no time to defend himself. He smote his steed and raced east, with the girl in close pursuit. Eight hoofs drummed the ground like inverted bowls as the two animals sped deep into the village. Ten Feet of Steel was catching up, and was preparing to strike when a voice boomed from the slope.

"Why is that friggin female chasing my brother?"

Song Jiang looked. Li Kui the Black Whirlwind, whirling his battle-axes, was striding towards them, leading seventy or eighty brigands. The girl reined her mount, turned and headed for the woods. But from the glade a dozen horsemen came directly at her. Foremost among them was Panther Head Lin Chong.

"Where do you think you're going?" he shouted at Ten Feet of Steel.

The girl charged him with flying swords. Lance levelled, he met her and they fought more than ten rounds. Lin Chong feinted and deliberately let the girl close in. Parrying her blades with his lance, he stretched forth an arm as strong as an ape's, grabbed her and, with the twist of a waist as sinewy as a wolf's, yanked her over to him. Song Jiang cheered heartily. Lin told his men to bind the girl and cantered over to Song Jiang.

"Are you hurt, brother?"

"No, I'm all right," Song replied. He instructed Li Kui to go into the village and bring out the remaining leaders. "Tell them we'll confer at the edge of the village. It's getting late. They're to stop fighting."

Li Kui and his party left. Lin Chong, protecting Song Jiang, proceeded to the village entry, with Ten Feet of Steel mounted and under guard. The Liangshan leaders won no gains that evening. All hastened to the edge of the village.

The Zhu Family forces returned to the manor, leaving behind countless dead. They put their prisoners in cage carts. If they could capture Song Jiang, they intended to deliver the whole lot to the authorities in the Eastern Capital and claim the reward. The Hu Family had already turned Wang the Stumpy Tiger over to the Zhu Family Manor.

Song Jiang, having regathered his forces, went to the encampment at the edge of the village. He directed that Ten Feet of Steel be brought forth, and ordered twenty veteran brigands and four mounted chiefs to seat the bound girl on a horse.

"Take her to Mount Liangshan tonight and deliver her to the care of my father, Squire Song, then report back to me. We'll decide what to do with her when I return to the fortress."

The leaders thought Song Jiang wanted the girl for himself, and took special care in escorting her. They sent the wounded Ou Peng on ahead in a cart to recuperate in the stronghold. The escort party set out immediately. Song Jiang brooded in his tent. He didn't sleep all night. At dawn he was still seated there.

CHAPTER 19
Song Jiang's Third Attack on the Zhu Family Manor

That day a scout reported: "Military Advisor Wu Yong is coming with the three Ruan brothers, Lü Fang and Guo Sheng, and five hundred men."

Song Jiang welcomed them outside the camp and led Wu Yong to his tent. When they were seated, Wu had wine and food laid, and toasted Song Jiang and congratulated his commanders.

"Chieftain Chao Gai has heard that you had some difficulty during your first assault. He sent me with these five leaders to lend a hand," Wu Yong said. "How have you been getting on?"

"It's hard to put it briefly. Those rogues of the Zhu Family have a pair of white banners over their manor gate which read: *Fill in the Marsh and nab Chao Gai. Level the Mountain and catch Song Jiang.* What brass! In our first assault, because we didn't know the terrain, we lost Yang Lin and Huang Xin. Near dusk we tried again, and Ten Feet of Steel took Stumpy Tiger Wang, Luan Tingyu wounded Ou Peng with his hammer, and trip ropes unhorsed Qin Ming and Deng Fei. Both were seized. That's how bad it's been. If Lin Chong hadn't captured Ten Feet of Steel, we'd be deflated completely. We can't seem to make a dent in this place. I'll vanquish the Zhu Family Manor and rescue our brothers, or die in the attempt. I couldn't go back and face brother Chao Gai, otherwise."

Wu Yong smiled. "Heaven has ordained that the Zhu

Family Manor shall fall. This is a good opportunity for us. I think we can bring it about very soon."

Song Jiang was amazed. "What do you mean?"

"Shi Yong, Yang Lin and Deng Fei know the major of the Dengzhou garrison, Sun Li the Sickly General," said Wu Yong. "He and Luan Tingyu, the weapons instructor in the Zhu Family Manor, both learned from the same teacher. Sun Li is here with seven men to join our band. As an entrance gift he's offering a plan, in which he'll take part, for attacking the manor from within and without. He's on his way here to see you."

Song Jiang soared out of his dark mood to the highest joy. He ordered that wine be prepared and a feast be laid, and waited for his guests.

Sun Li told his entourage to find a place to rest. He brought the Xie brothers, the two Zou's, Sun Xin, Mistress Gu and Yue Ho, to call on Song Jiang. After courtesies were exchanged, Song Jiang wined and dined them. Of that we'll say no more.

Wu Yong quietly notified his forces of secret signals. On the third day, they would do this . . . on the fifth day they would do that. . . . The plans finalized, Sun Li and his party, with their cart, and people on horse and on foot, advanced towards the Zhu Family Manor.

To Dai Zong, Wu Yong said: "I want Ironclad Virtue Pei Xuan, the Master Hand Xiao Rang, Hou Jian the Long-Armed Ape and the Jade-Armed Craftsman Jin Dajian. Tell them to bring their tools and come down the mountain tonight. I need them."

Dai Zong departed.

A soldier posted outside the camp entered and reported: "Hu Cheng, from the Hu Family Manor in the west, is here with gifts of cattle and wine. He asks to see you."

Song Jiang said to invite him in. Hu Cheng approached the tent in the center of camp, kowtowed, and offered a sincere plea.

"My sister is young and untutored. In a moment of rudeness she offended you and your generals captured her. I'm here to beg forgiveness. It is because she has been pledged to a son of the Zhu Family that she displayed a misplaced valor and landed in captivity. If you will release her, whatever you require you have only to command and I will deliver."

"Please be seated," said Song Jiang. "That Zhu Family are boors. They're always picking on the people of our mountain stronghold. For that reason we've come with armed forces to avenge ourselves. We have nothing against the Hu Family. Your sister and her men seized our Stumpy Tiger Wang. And so we returned the compliment and captured her. Give Wang back to us and you can have your sister."

"Though we didn't expect it, the Zhu Family have already taken him."

"Where is he now?" Wu Yong asked.

"Locked up in their manor. I don't dare ask for him."

"If you don't return the Stumpy Tiger, how can we release your sister?" Song Jiang said.

"Don't talk like that, brother," Wu Yong urged. "Let me say a few words. Sooner or later the Zhu Family is going to have an alarm. Don't send people from your manor to help them. If any of them try to take refuge with you, tie them up and bring them here. When you do that, we'll return your sister. She's not in this camp. We sent her to our mountain fortress the other day and entrusted her to the care of Squire Song. You needn't worry. We have a plan."

"I wouldn't dare go to the aid of the Zhu Family. Should any of their people seek refuge with me, I'll bind them and bring them here to you."

"If you do that," said Song Jiang, "it will be worth more to us than any gold or brocade."

Hu Cheng thanked them and left.

We'll tell now of Sun Li who changed his banner to read: *Sun Li Major of the Dengzhou Garrison.* He arrived at the rear gate of the Zhu Family Manor with his company of men and horses. The soldiers on the walls, seeing the banner, reported to their leaders.

"He's like a brother to me. Since childhood we learned to

play with weapons from the same teacher," Luan Tingyu said to the three sons of the Zhu Family. "I wonder what he's doing here."

Luan opened the manor gate, lowered the drawbridge, and rode out with twenty men to welcome him. Sun Li and his company dismounted. They exchanged greetings.

"I thought you're with the Dengzhou garrison," said Luan. "What are you doing in these parts?"

"The high command has transferred me here to Yunzhou Prefecture to defend the cities and towns against the bandits of Liangshan Marsh. We were passing by and I knew that you were with the Zhu Family Manor, so I came to see how you are. We intended to approach your front gate, but the village entry was full of troops and cavalry. I didn't want to disturb them. I came along the paths through the hamlets to the rear gate to pay my respects."

"We've had one clash after another with those bandits the last few days. We've already caught several of their leaders. When we get Song Jiang, their chief, we'll turn them all over to the authorities. How fortunate we are that you've come to protect us! You'll be like 'flowery stitches on brocade', like 'rain to parched sprouts'."

Sun Li smiled. "I have no talent. But I can assist you to nab those rogues, so that your worthy goal will be achieved."

Luan was delighted. He led them into the manor, pulled up the drawbridge and bolted the gate. Sun Li and his party changed into fresh clothes and were presented in the main hall to Lord Zhu and his three sons. After courtesies were exchanged, Luan addressed Zhu:

"My brother Sun Li is known as the Sickly General. He was major of the Dengzhou garrison, but the high command has just transferred him here to protect Yunzhou."

"I too shall be under your supervision," said Lord Zhu.

"Scarcely that, with my lowly rank. I shall be looking forward to constant enlightenment by you, and your instructions."

The three sons invited the guests to be seated.

"You must be weary, after several days of fighting," Sun

Li said to them.

"There's been no decisive battle as yet," said the Dragon. "But you brothers must be tired from your long journey in the saddle."

Sun Li instructed Mistress Gu and Mistress Yue to go to the rear chambers and pay their respects to the female members of the household. Then he summoned Sun Xin, Xie Zhen and Xie Bao, and presented them.

"These three are my brothers," he said. He pointed at Yue Ho. "This is the officer sent from Yunzhou to fetch me." Indicating Zou Yuan and Zou Run, he said: "These two are army officers from Dengzhou."

Zhu and his three sons were clever. But Sun Li had come with women and children, luggage and carts. What's more, he was an old friend of Luan Tingyu. Why should they suspect him? They ordered that cows and horses be slaughtered and a feast be laid, after which the guests were wined and dined.

A day or two later a soldier of the manor reported: "Song Jiang is sending another force against us."

"I'll go and take that robber personally," said Tiger Cub. He left the manor, lowered the drawbridge and led forth a hundred mounted men.

Ahead were five hundred fighters, on horse and on foot. The chieftain in their lead was equipped with a bow and 'arrows. Twirling his lance, he urged his beast forward. It was Hua Rong.

When Tiger Cub saw him he spurred his mount, levelled his lance and charged. Hua Rong galloped towards Tiger Cub. Before Lone Dragon Cliff they fought a dozen rounds, with neither vanquishing the other. Hua Rong executed a feint, turned and moved off. Tiger Cub was about to give chase when one of his cohorts recognized his opponent.

"Don't pursue him, general. He might strike you a sneak blow," the man called. "He's a crack archer."

Tiger Cub reined his animal to a halt, then led his party back into the manor and raised the drawbridge. Hua Rong and his contingent were last seen riding away. Tiger Cub dismounted in front of the main hall and went to the rear chambers for food and drink.

"Did you catch any robbers today, young general?" Sun Li asked.

"Among those louts was some Hua Rong or other, a first-rate man with the lance. We fought fifty rounds, then he withdrew. I wanted to go after him, but my soldiers said he's fantastic with the bow and arrow. So I brought my company back."

"Though I'm not very capable, in a day or so I'll nab him and a few of his gang."

At the feast that day Sun Li had Yue Ho sing a few ballads, to the pleasure of the assembled diners. In the evening the gathering broke up, and all retired for the night.

A manor soldier suddenly reported, around noon of the fourth day: "Song Jiang's forces are coming at us again."

The three sons of the Zhu Family donned their armor and went outside the manor gate. They could hear the crash of gongs and the thunder of drums in the distance. The shouting foe, banners waving, had spread out in battle formation. Lord Zhu took his seat in the tower atop the gate. To his left was Luan Tingyu, to his right was Major Sun Li. The three sons and the men Sun Li had brought were arrayed before the gate.

From the enemy position Panther Head Lin Chong shouted imprecations. Stung, the Dragon yelled for the drawbridge to be lowered. He took his lance, mounted, and rode forth with two hundred foot soldiers and cavalry. They galloped, shouting, towards Lin Chong. In the gate-house the big drums pounded, and the two sides winged arrows against each other.

Lin Chong raised his long, serpent lance and engaged the Dragon in combat. Thirty rounds they fought, with neither being the victor. On each side gongs crashed, and both contestants withdrew.

The Tiger was enraged. Sabre in hand, he climbed into the saddle and raced upon the field, shouting his challenge: "Song Jiang, fight to a finish!"

Before the sound of his voice had died away, a rider emerged from the opposite ranks. Mu Hong the Unrestrained had come to do battle. The two fought for thirty rounds, again with no result. Tiger Cub was furious. Seizing his lance he flew onto his horse, and galloped forth with two hundred cavalrymen.

Yang Xiong the Pallid, astride his steed, lance in hand, charged from the Song Jiang position to meet him. Now the two sides were locked in slashing combat and Sun Li could restrain himself no longer.

"Get my ridged rod," he called to his brother Sun Xin. "And my armor, helmet and robe."

He put on his equipment and led out his own horse, known as the Piebald Steed. Heaving the saddle on its back, he tightened the three girths, hung the tiger-eyed, ridged steel rod from his wrist, grasped his lance, and mounted. To the accompaniment of crashing gongs from the Zhu Family Manor, Sun Li rode onto the field.

Lined up opposite on the other side, their animals reined in motionless, were Lin Chong, Mu Hong and Yang Xiong. "I'll take those rogues," Sun Li exclaimed as he cantered forward. Pulling his beast to a halt, he shouted: "If there's a good fighter among you thieving scoundrels let him come forward and battle with me to the death!"

A rider galloped out, bridle bells tinkling. Everyone stared. It was Shi Xiu the Rash. The gap between the horses narrowed, and the two lances met. Fifty rounds the contestants fought. Sun Li feinted, letting Shi Xiu close in and thrust. Agilely, he dodged, yanked Shi Xiu from the saddle, carried him under one arm to the front of the manor, and dumped him on the ground.

"Tie him up," he shouted.

Meanwhile, the three sons had thrown Song Jiang's forces into disarray, scattering and driving them off.

The three sons gathered their men and returned to the foot of the gate tower. They clasped their hands together and bowed to Sun Li respectfully.

"How many robbers have been captured so far?" Sun Li asked.

"The first one we caught was Shi Qian," Lord Zhu volunteered. "Then we took the spy Yang Lin. Later we captured

Huang Xin. Ten Feet of Steel of the Hu Family Manor caught
Stumpy Tiger Wang. Two more were taken on the battlefield
— Qin Ming and Deng Fei. Today, you, sir, captured Shi Xiu.
The lout burned down my inn. That makes a total of seven."

"Don't hurt any of them. Build seven cage-carts, quickly.
But give them food and wine, keep them in good health. It
would look bad if we starved them. Later, when we've taken
Song Jiang, we'll deliver them all to the Eastern Capital.
Everyone will know your fame, and will sing the praises of the
three sons of the Zhu Family."

Lord Zhu thanked him. "We are fortunate to have your help,
Major. The Liangshan Marsh gang is doomed."

He invited Sun Li to a feast in the rear hall. Shi Xiu was
locked in a cage-cart.

Hear me, gentle reader: Shi Xiu's skill with weapons was
in no way inferior to Sun Li's. But to fool the Zhu Family he
let himself be taken. This caused the manor people to trust the
major completely. Sun Li secretly instructed Zou Yuan, Zou
Run and Yue Ho to check the number of doors in the rear
building. At the sight of them, Yang Lin and Deng Fei were
pleased. Seeing that no one was around, Yue Ho softly told
the prisoners of the latest developments. Mistresses Gu and
Yue, in the compound's interior, looked over the entrances and
exits of the living quarters.

On the fifth day, Sun Li and the others strolled around the
manor. Shortly after breakfast a soldier reported: "Song Jiang
has divided his forces into four columns and is advancing to
attack."

"Even if he had ten columns, what would it matter?" said
Sun Li to the Zhu Family. "Tell your underlings not to be
alarmed, but just get ready. First, conceal a party with hooks
and snares. We want live prisoners. Dead ones are no use."

The men of the manor donned their armor, and Lord Zhu
went with a group to watch from the gate tower. To the east
they could see a body of men and horses approaching, led by
Panther Head Lin Chong. Behind him were Li Jun and Ruan
the Second, and five hundred fighters on horse and on foot.

From the west another five hundred were coming, with Hua Rong in the lead, followed by Zhang Heng and Zhang Shun. Due south were five hundred more, commanded by Mu Hong the Unrestrained, Yang Xiong the Pallid, and Black Whirlwind Li Kui. In every direction infantry and cavalry were advancing, battle drums pounding in unison, shouts rising to the skies.

"Those villains are coming at us in force today," said Luan Tingyu. "We mustn't underestimate them. I shall take a company through the rear gate and deal with the foe to the northwest."

"I shall go through the front gate and fight the eastern foe," said the Dragon.

"I'll also go through the rear gate and take on the enemy attacking from the southwest," said the Tiger.

"I'm going via the front gate to grab Song Jiang," said the Tiger Cub. "He's the chief robber."

Pleased, Lord Zhu rewarded them with cups of wine. All mounted and sallied forth with troops of three hundred cavalry each. Those remaining to guard the manor stood in front of the gate towers and cheered.

Zou Yuan and Zou Run had already hidden big axes and were standing near the door of the building which held the prisoners. The Xie brothers, also with concealed weapons, stayed close to the rear gate. Sun Xin and Yue Ho were in position on either side of the front gate. Mistress Gu, after having assigned soldiers to protect Mistress Yue, paced with a pair of daggers before the hall, ready to strike at the signal.

Three volleys thundered on the manor drums, a cannon boomed, the front and rear gates swung open, the drawbridges were lowered, and the army surged forth. Four Zhu Family contingents marched to engage the foe.

Sun Li and a dozen men promptly occupied the front bridge. On the gate tower, Sun Li unfurled the original banner. Yue Ho, lance in hand, entered, singing. At the sound of his voice, Zou Yuan and Zou Run whistled several times, shrilly. Swinging their axes, they cut down the few dozen soldiers guarding the temporary prison and broke open the cage-carts. The seven released captives seized lances from the weapons racks. When she heard their shouts, Mistress Gu charged into the inner chambers and slaughtered all the women with her daggers. Lord Zhu recognized his danger and ran to jump into a well, but Shi Xiu hacked him down with one blow of his sabre and cut off his head.

The ten or more bold fellows separated to kill the manor soldiers. Near the rear gate the Xie brothers set fire to the haystacks. Black smoke funneled into the sky. When the attackers saw this, they redoubled their forward drive.

Tiger, seeing the manor ablaze, hastened back. "Where do you think you're going," shouted Sun Li, and blocked his passage over the bridge. Tiger understood. He turned his steed and galloped towards Song Jiang's position. But Lü Fang and Guo Sheng, waiting with barbed lances, tumbled horse and rider. Brigand fighters swarmed all over him and chopped him to mincemeat. The soldiers in front of the manor scattered, and Sun Li and Sun Xin escorted Song Jiang in.

To the east, the Dragon found he was no match for Lin Chong. He raced his horse to the rear of the manor. But when he reached the back drawbridge he saw the Xie brothers, inside the gate, throwing the bodies of slain vassals into the flames. He pulled his mount hastily around and sped north. Suddenly, he was confronted by Li Kui. Black Whirlwind bounded towards him, whirling his axes and cutting the animal's legs from under it. The Dragon fell helplessly to the ground. With one swing Li Kui split his skull open.

When these happenings were reported to Tiger Cub, he didn't dare return. He hurried to the Hu Family Manor. On the orders of Hu Cheng, vassals seized and bound him. As they were taking him to deliver him to Song Jiang, they met Li Kui, who cut off Tiger Cub's head with a single sweep of his ax. The vassals fled and Li Kui charged towards Hu Cheng. Obviously, it was a bad situation. Hu Cheng raced his steed into the wilderness. Abandoning his home, he rode for his life. He finally took refuge in the prefecture of Yanan. In later years, when order was restored, he became a general.

Black Whirlwind went on killing smoothly. He charged into the Hu Family Manor and slaughtered the old squire and the whole family, young and old. He instructed his men to load the squire's horses with the forty or fifty bundles of loot he collected, then put the manor to the torch and started back with his prizes.

Song Jiang was by then seated in the hall of the Zhu Family Manor, listening to the reports of his chieftains' achievements. They had captured nearly five hundred men and an equal number of good horses, in addition to innumerable cattle and sheep.

Song Jiang was very pleased, although when he thought of Luan Tingyu he sighed regretfully. "What a pity that gallant fellow was killed."

A brigand entered and announced: "Black Whirlwind has burned down the Hu Family Manor and cut off their heads. He's returned to present his booty."

"But Hu Cheng had already surrendered. Who told him to kill those people? Why has he burned their manor?"

Stained with blood, his two axes stuck in his sash, Li Kui entered and hailed Song Jiang respectfully. "I've killed the Dragon and cut down the Tiger Cub," he said. "That lout Hu Cheng got away, but I made a clean sweep of Squire Hu and the entire family. I've come to be commended."

"People saw you kill the Dragon, but why did you kill the others?" demanded Song Jiang.

"I got into the swing of it. I was heading for the Hu Family Manor when I ran into Tiger Cub, brother of that Ten Feet of Steel. I finished him off with one chop. Too bad that oaf Hu Cheng got away. But I killed every single person in his manor."

"You rogue! Who told you to go there? You knew that Hu Cheng came with gifts of cattle and wine the other day and surrendered. Why didn't you listen to me? Why did you take it on yourself to kill his whole family in deliberate violation of my order?"

"Maybe you've forgotten, but I haven't. He also sent his friggin woman to kill you the other day, yet now you're all sympathetic! You're not engaged to his sister. Why should you care about her brother and father?"

"Iron Ox, you're raving! What would I want with her? I have something else in mind. How many live ones have you taken, you swarthy devil?"

"Who's got the patience? Any live one I met, I cut down."

"You've disobeyed my orders. That's a beheading offence! It wipes out the credit you deserve for killing the Dragon and the Tiger Cub. The next time you violate an order I won't forgive you!"

Black Whirlwind grinned. "So I don't get any credit. But all that killing was a real pleasure."

Military Advisor Wu Yong was seen approaching with a company of mounted men. On reaching the manor they drank to Song Jiang and congratulated him. Song Jiang conferred with Wu Yong. He wanted to annihilate the village attached to the manor. But Shi Xiu reminded him of the old man who had been of such help in telling the secret of the paths.

"There are many good people like him in the village. They shouldn't be harmed."

Song Jiang instructed Shi Xiu to fetch the old man. Not long after, Shi Xiu brought him to the manor. The oldster kowtowed to Song and Wu Yong. Song Jiang rewarded him with silks and a bag of gold and told him he could remain in the village permanently.

"If it weren't for your kindness we would have obliterated your village," Song Jiang said, "and every family in it. But now, thanks to your meritorious conduct, they all shall be spared."

The old man could only kowtow again.

"I've been worried about you ordinary folk for several days," Song Jiang continued. "Today, we've taken the Zhu Family Manor and rid you of an oppressor. Each family shall receive a load of rice, as a sign of our concern."

He put the old man in charge of distribution. At the same time, he had the manor's surplus grain loaded onto carts. Gold and silver and other valuables he gave as rewards to the leaders and men of his forces. All cattle, sheep, donkeys, horses, and the like were driven off for use in the mountain fortress.

As a result of the capture of the Zhu Family Manor, the brigands obtained five hundred thousand loads of grain. Song Jiang was very pleased.

The chieftains big and small assembled their fighters. Several new leaders were added: Sun Li, Sun Xin, Xie Zhen, Xie Bao, Zou Yuan, Zou Run, Yue Ho and Mistress Gu. Seven gallant men had been rescued.

Sun Li, with his own horses and the valuables he had brought from home, took his wife Mistress Yue and followed the main force up the mountain. Local villagers, supporting the old and carrying small children, burned incense and lit festive lanterns, kowtowed and gave thanks, as they saw them off.

Song Jiang and the leaders mounted. The army, divided into three contingents, marched through the night on the return trip to the mountain stronghold.

We'll speak now of Li Ying the Heaven Soaring Eagle who had been resting and recovering from his arrow wound. He kept the gates of the manor closed and did not go out, but he frequently sent men in secret to get news of the Zhu Family Manor. He was both startled and glad to learn that Song Jiang had conquered it.

A vassal entered and reported: "The prefect has come with forty or fifty men to inquire about the Zhu Family Manor."

Li Ying hurriedly ordered Du Xing to open the gate, lower the drawbridge and escort them in. He bound his injured arm in white silk and went out to welcome his callers and invite them into the main hall. The prefect dismounted, entered the hall, and seated himself in the center. His clerk sat by his side. Next were two sheriffs and several captains. At the foot of the platform were many bailiffs and prison guards. Li Ying kowtowed to the prefect and stood before him.

"The slaughter of the Zhu Family, how did that come about?" the prefect demanded.

"Their son the Dragon wounded me in the left arm with an

arrow. I've kept my gates closed and have not ventured out. I have no knowledge of the affair."

"Lies! A complaint accuses you of complicity with the Liangshan Marsh bandits. You lured out the Zhu forces so that the bandits could break into the manor. The other day you received from them saddle horses, sheep, wine, silks, gold and silver. How can you deny it?"

"I'm a law-abiding man. I'd never accepted their gifts."

"I can't believe that. I'm taking you to the prefecture. There, you can confront your accuser and have this out."

At a word from the prefect, the guards seized Li Ying, and the sheriffs and captains tied his arms. The entourage swarmed around the prefect as he mounted his horse.

"Who is the steward Du Xing?" asked the prefect.

"I am that humble person," said Du.

"Your name is also in the complaint. Take him along."

Du was promptly fettered. The party left the manor. With Li Ying and Du Xing under restraint, they marched without halt along the road.

Before they had gone thirty *li*, Song Jiang, Lin Chong, Hua Rong, Yang Xiong and Shi Xiu suddenly emerged from the edge of the forest and blocked their way. "The gallants of Liangshan Marsh are here together," shouted Lin Chong.

The prefect and his party didn't dare put up a fight. Abandoning Li Ying and Du Xing, they fled. "After them," yelled Song Jiang. Brigands pursued them for a while, then returned.

"We'd have killed that friggin prefect if we'd caught up with him," they reported, "but he got away."

They untied the ropes and opened the fetters on Li Ying and Du Xing, and led forward two horses for them to ride.

"Won't you come and take refuge in our Liangshan Marsh for a time, sir?" said Song Jiang.

"I can't do that," said Li Ying. "You're the ones who tried to kill the prefect. It has nothing to do with me."

Song Jiang smiled. "Do you think the authorities would

accept such an argument? Even if we went off without you, you'd still be implicated. You're not willing to become an outlaw, but at least stay in our mountain fortress a few days. As soon as we hear you're in no danger, you can come down again."

Li Ying and Du Xing had no choice, surrounded as they were by a whole army. Divided into three contingents, the force wound its way to Mount Liangshan.

Chao Gai and the others, beating drums and blowing flutes, came down the mountain to welcome them with wine. All repaired to Fraternity Hall and seated themselves fanwise.

Li Ying was introduced to the leaders. After courtesies had been exchanged, he said to Song Jiang: "Du Xing and I have seen you back to your stronghold, General, and have met the leaders. I don't mind staying here for a time, but I'm concerned about my family. I'd like to go down and see."

Wu Yong laughed. "No need, sir. Your family is already here. And your manor has been burned to the ground. What would you go back for?"

Li Ying looked sceptical, until he saw carts and people advancing up the path. They were vassals from his manor and members of his family. He hastened to them.

His wife said: "After you were taken by the prefect, two sheriffs came with four constables and a patrol of three hundred soldiers. They wrapped our belongings into bundles and made us get into carts. They took along all our hampers and livestock, and put the manor to the torch."

Li Ying uttered a cry of lamentation. Chao Gai and Song Jiang apologized. "The truth is that we have long heard of your excellence," they said, "and so we evolved this scheme. We beg your forgiveness."

Since they put it that way, Li Ying had no choice but to comply.

"Please ask your family to rest in a wing of the rear hall," said Song Jiang.

Li Ying observed that many of the chieftains had their wives and children with them. He told his spouse: "We can only obey him."

Song Jiang then invited Li to the front part of the hall for a chat. Everyone was pleased. In a jocular tone, Song said to Li Ying: "I'd like you to meet the two patrol sheriffs and the prefect."

Out stepped Xiao Rang, disguised as the prefect, and Dai Zong and Yang Lin, who had assumed the roles of the sheriffs. Pei Xuan had been the clerk, Jin Dajian and Hou Jian had been the captains. Song Jiang also summoned the four constables. They were Li Jun, Zhang Shun, Ma Lin, and Bai Sheng.

Li Ying gaped at them, speechless.

Song Jiang instructed the lesser chieftains to slaughter cows and horses quickly for a feast both of apology to Li Ying and of celebration over the addition of twelve new leaders: Li Ying, Sun Li, Sun Xin, Xie Zhen, Xie Bao, Zou Yuan, Zou Run, Du Xing, Yue Ho, Shi Qian, Ten Feet of Steel and Mistress Gu. The women leaders had a table of their own in the rear hall with Mistress Yue and the female members of Li Ying's family.

All brigands, large and small, were rewarded, and merry pipes and drums sounded in the hall. The bold fellows drank and dined until late. When the festivities ended, the new leaders retired to the quarters assigned to them.

The chieftains were invited to another feast the following day to seek their aid in another matter. Song Jiang called forth Stumpy Tiger Wang and said: "When we were on Clear Winds Mountain I promised you a wife. I haven't forgotten, but I haven't yet fulfilled my pledge. Today, my father has a daughter he'll give to you in marriage."

Song Jiang requested Squire Song to bring the Hu Family girl to the feast.

"My brother Wang Ying is a good fighter. Of course, his skill can't be compared with yours," Song said to her apologetically. "But I've promised him a bride, and I still haven't produced one. You, sister, are now my father's ward.

I'd like all these leaders to serve as match-makers and give you in marriage to Wang Ying. Today is an auspicious day."

Ten Feet of Steel saw how deeply Song Jiang felt his chivalrous obligations. She was unable to refuse. The bride and groom kowtowed their thanks. Chao Gai and the other leaders were pleased. They all praised Song Jiang for his virtue and loyalty. Everyone feasted the entire day, and many toasts were drunk in congratulations.

CHAPTER 20
Huyan Zhuo Deploys an Armored Cavalry

The outlaw forces in Liangshan Marsh grew steadily in strength. They destroyed the city of Gaotang and killed its prefect Gao Lian, cousin of Marshal Gao Qiu.

The neighboring prefectures of Dongchang and Kouzhou immediately dispatched written reports to the emperor. Officials who had escaped from Gaotang also brought news of this to the capital. Marshal Gao Qiu thus learned that his cousin had been slain.

At the fifth watch the next day he went to the imperial ante-hall and waited for the morning bell. Hundreds of officials in ceremonial robes thronged the inner hall, waiting to attend the audience. At the third section of the fifth watch, the emperor entered the imperial chamber. Three times the ceremonial staff tapped, and civil and military officials formed in separate ranks as the emperor seated himself on the throne.

"Let those with business present their petitions," intoned the chief of ceremonies.

Marshal Gao stepped forward and spoke. "Of late Chao Gai and Song Jiang, leaders of the bandits in Liangshan Marsh in Jizhou Prefecture, have committed a series of terrible crimes, plundering cities and robbing government granaries. In savage hordes they slaughtered government troops in Jizhou and ran riot in Jiangzhou and Wuweijun. Most recently, they wiped out the entire city of Gaotang and walked off with everything in the granary and treasury. They are like a canker in our vitals. If we don't quell them quickly they will grow so strong that we shall be unable to control them. I beseech Your

Majesty to act."

The emperor was shocked. He ordered Gao to assemble an army, arrest the culprits, thoroughly purge the Marsh, and kill all such persons.

"We don't need a large army to deal with those petty outlaws. If Your Majesty will grant me a certain man, he will take care of them," said Gao.

"If you consider him so useful, he must be good. Have him go at once. Let us hear news of victory soon and we shall raise him in rank and reward him well. He will be given a high and important post."

"He is the direct descendant of Huyan Zan, the general from Hedong who won fame at the start of the dynasty. His name is Huyan Zhuo. He wields two steel rods and is a man of peerless courage. At present he is garrison commander of Runing Shire, and has under him many crack soldiers and brave officers. With the services of this man we can restore order to Liangshan Marsh. If given good officers and skilled troops and placed at their head, he will swiftly clean out the lair and return victorious."

The emperor directed the Council of Military Affairs to send an emissary to Runing immediately to fetch Huyan Zhuo. When the imperial court was concluded, Gao personally selected an official from the Council to serve as the emissary. He was sent forth that same day, and a time limit set for his return.

Huyan was conducting business in his military headquarters in Runing when an officer at the city gate entered and announced: "An emissary has come with an imperial edict ordering you, General, to the capital for a special mission."

With several prefectural officials Huyan went to the gate and conducted the emissary to military headquarters. Huyan read the edict and had a feast laid for the emissary. Then he donned his helmet and armor, saddled his horse and gathered his weapons, and left Runing with an escort of thirty or forty. They travelled through the night and soon reached the capital after an uneventful journey. Huyan Zhuo dismounted before the Chancellery of Imperial Defense and went in to see Marshal Gao.

Gao Qiu was holding court. The gate-keeper announced: "Huyan Zhuo, summoned from Runing, is at the gate." Very pleased, Gao directed that he be brought in. After asking Huyan solicitously about himself, Gao rewarded him.

Early the next day, Gao presented Huyan to their sovereign. The emperor could see that he was no ordinary man, and the imperial countenance smiled. He presented Huyan with a fine horse known as the Ebony Steed Which Treads in Snow. Pitch black in color except for snowy white hoofs, it could cover a thousand *li* in a single day. This beast was given to Huyan as his mount.

After thanking the emperor, Huyan Zhuo returned with Gao Qiu to the chancellery, where they discussed how to take Liangshan Marsh.

"I've spied out that place, Your Excellency," said Huyan. "They've many officers and men, and they're well equipped with fine horses and weapons. An adversary not to be despised. But I have two men I can guarantee to lead my vanguard, while I follow with our main force. We definitely will win a great victory."

Gao was delighted. "Who are these men?" he asked.

"I have in mind a district garrison commander in Chengzhou, a man named Han Tao," said Huyan. "Originally he's from the Eastern Capital. He's passed the Second Degree Military Examination and wields a datewood lance eighteen feet long. Everyone calls him the Ever-Victorious General. He can lead the vanguard. The other man I want is a district garrison commander in Yingzhou. His name is Peng Qi, and he also hails from the Eastern Capital. His family have been military people for generations. He uses a three-pointed two-edged lance. His skill with weapons is extraordinary, and he's known as the Eyes of Heaven General. This man can be second in command."

Marshal Gao was very pleased. "With Han and Peng in the van, we need have no fears about those impudent bandits," he exclaimed.

He wrote out two summonses and directed the Chancellery of Imperial Defense to dispatch messengers from the Council of Military Affairs with them immediately to Chenzhou and Yingzhou to fetch Han and Peng. In less than ten days the garrison commanders arrived in the capital. They went directly to the chancellery and presented themselves to Gao and Huyan.

The next day Gao and his entourage went to the training ground and watched imperial troops practising and drilling. Then Gao returned to the chancellery and conferred with the Council of Military Affairs on important matters of military strategy.

He asked Huyan and Han and Peng: "How many men have the three of you together?"

"About five thousand cavalry," said Huyan. "Ten thousand, if you include the infantry."

"Go back to your respective cities and pick three thousand of your best cavalry and five thousand foot soldiers. Assemble, set forth, and clean out Liangshan Marsh."

"Our cavalry and infantry are crack troops," said Huyan. "Both men and horses are in fine fettle. Your Excellency need have no worry about them. But we're short of clothing and armor. We don't want to cause delay and inconvenience, but we must request more time to prepare."

"If that's the case, go to the capital armory and pick out as much as you need in the way of clothing, armor, helmets and weapons. I'll issue the order now. We want your forces well equipped so that they can cope with the enemy. The day you're ready to march I'll send officials to check you over."

Huyan took the order and went with some of his people to the armory. There he selected three thousand sets of steel armor, five thousand sets of horsehide armor, three thousand bronze and iron helmets, two thousand pikes, one thousand swords, countless bows and arrows, and over five hundred cannon, and loaded them all onto carts. The day the three men were leaving the capital Gao issued them three thousand battle chargers and all the grain their forces would require, and gave them personal gifts of gold and silver, silks and satins.

Huyan, Han Tao and Peng Qi submitted written guarantees of victory, and took their leave of Marshal Gao and officials from the Council of Military Affairs.

They mounted their horses and rode back to Runing. The journey was uneventful. When they arrived, Huyan directed Han Tao and Peng Qi to return to their respective cities, raise their armies and bring them to Runing.

In less than half a month the three columns were complete. Huyan issued the equipment he had drawn from the imperial armory — clothing, armor, helmets, swords, pikes and saddles. He also had chainmail made, plus various other items of military ware, and distributed these as well among the three columns.

They were ready to go. Gao sent two officials from his chancellery to review them. The officials handsomely rewarded the three commanders, and Huyan marched forth with his three columns. Han Tao led the van, Huyan commanded the main force in the middle, Peng Qi and his men brought up the rear. The three columns of infantry and cavalry were a splendid sight as they hastened grimly towards Liangshan Marsh.

To the mountain stronghold came a far-posted scout with a report of the approaching troops. Chao Gai and Song Jiang, together with Military Advisor Wu Yong, magic expert Gong-sun Sheng, and the various other chieftains had been feasting daily in celebration with Chai Jin. When they heard that Two Rods Huyan Zhuo of Runing was leading an army of infantry and cavalry to attack, they conferred on strategy.

"I've heard of him," said Wu Yong. "He's a direct descendant of Huyan Zan, the general from Hedong who helped establish the dynasty. His skill with weapons is superb. When he wields those two steel rods of his no one can come near him. We must use our most competent and courageous officers. To capture him we'll have to apply first force and second guile."

Before the words were out of his mouth, Black Whirlwind

Li Kui spoke up. "I'll nab the wretch for you!"

"You'd never do it," said Song Jiang. "I have a plan of my own. We'll ask Qin Ming the Thunderbolt to fight the first bout, Panther Head Lin Chong the second, Hua Rong the third, Ten Feet of Steel the fourth, and Sickly General Sun Li the fifth. These bouts must come one right after the next, like the spokes of a spinning wheel. I myself will head ten brothers who will command our main divisions. On the left will be Zhu Tong, Lei Heng, Mu Hong, Huang Xin and Lü Fang. On the right will be Yang Xiong, Shi Xiu, Ou Peng, Ma Lin and Guo Sheng. Our water approaches will be defended by boats under the command of Li Jun, Zhang Heng, Zhang Shun and the three Ruan brothers. Li Kui and Yang Lin will lead two columns of infantry and lie in ambush as reinforcements."

Shortly thereafter, Qin Ming went down the mountain with a unit of men and horses. They set up a battle position on a broad plain.

Although it was already winter, the weather was pleasantly warm. The next day, they saw in the distance the approaching government troops. The van, led by Ever-Victorious General Han Tao, made camp and built surrounding palisades. There was no fighting that night.

The two armies faced each other at dawn the following day. Horns blared, and the thunder of drums shook the heavens. On Song Jiang's side Qin Ming the Thunderbolt rode forth from the arch of pennants, his wolf-toothed mace athwart his mount. On the opposite side at the arch of pennants appeared Han Tao, leader of the van. Holding his lance crosswise, he gave his horse rein and shouted at his foe.

"We heavenly hosts have arrived! But instead of surrendering, you dare to resist! You're asking to die! I'll fill in your Marsh and pulverise your Mount Liangshan! I'll capture you rebellious bandits, take you to the capital, and have you smashed to bits!"

Qin Ming was a hot tempered man. Without a word, he clapped his steed, and rode straight at Han Tao, flourishing his mace. Han Tao kicked up his horse, levelled his lance, and galloped to meet him. They fought over twenty rounds, and Han Tao began to weaken. He turned to go. From behind him came Huyan Zhuo, commander of the main contingent. He saw that Han Tao was being bested, and he charged forth on the snowy-hoofed black steed the emperor had given him, roaring and waving his steel rods.

Qin Ming recognized him, and prepared to do battle. But Lin Chong the Panther Head cantered up, calling: "Rest a while, commander. Let me go three hundred rounds with this fellow, then we'll see."

Lin Chong levelled his serpent-decorated lance and charged Huyan. Qin Ming wheeled his mount to the left and rode out of sight behind a bend. The new adversaries were evenly matched. The lance and rods interwove in flowery patterns for more than fifty rounds, but neither man could vanquish the other.

Hua Rong appeared for the third bout. At the entrance to the field of combat he called: "Rest a while, General Lin Chong. Watch me capture the lout."

Panther Head turned his horse and departed. Huyan had seen enough of his high-powered use of weapons. He let him go and returned to his own position, while Lin Chong disappeared around a bend with his men. Huyan was already among his rear column when Hua Rong emerged with lance at the level. Peng Qi the Eyes of Heaven General, astride a glossy brown piebald that could run a thousand *li* in a day, rode towards Hua Rong. Holding crosswise his three-pointed, two-edged, four-holed, eight-ringed weapon, Peng shouted: "Traitorous robber! You're devoid of all morality! Let's fight this one to a finish!"

Hua Rong was furious. Without a word, he clashed with Peng Qi. More than twenty rounds they battled. Huyan could see that Peng was weakening. He gave his horse rein and engaged Hua Rong.

Before they had fought three rounds, the girl warrior Ten

Feet of Steel rode out for the fourth round. "Rest a while, General Hua Rong," she cried. "Watch me take this oaf!"

Hua Rong led his contingent off to the right and departed round a bend. Even before the battle between Peng Qi and Ten Feet of Steel approached a decisive stage, Sun Li the Sickly General, who would fight the fifth bout, had already arrived. He had reined his horse at the edge of the field of combat and was watching the two contestants.

They fought in a cloud of dust with murderous intensity, one with a long-handled sabre, the other with a pair of swords. For over twenty rounds they battled. Then the girl separated her blades and rode off. Peng Qi, eager for glory, gave chase. Ten Feet of Steel hung her swords on the pommel of her saddle. From inside her robe she pulled out a red lariat bearing twenty-four gold hooks. She let Peng Qi draw near, then suddenly twisted around and flung the rope. The noose landed squarely on him before he could ward it off, and he was dragged from his horse. Sun Li yelled a command, and his men rushed forward and grabbed the fallen rider.

Huyan, enraged, galloped to the rescue. Ten Feet of Steel clapped her steed and met him. The seething Huyan would have swallowed her down in one gulp, if he could. They battled more than ten rounds, Huyan increasingly frantic because he couldn't defeat the girl.

"What a spitfire," he fretted. "After all this fighting, she's still so tough!"

Impatiently, he feinted and let her close in, then raised his steel rods and started to bring them down. The swords were still in their resting place when the rod in Huyan's right hand was only a hair away from the girl's forehead. But Ten Feet of Steel was clear of eye and swift of hand. A sword sprang into her right fist, flew up and warded off the blow with a clang of metal and a shower of sparks.

The girl galloped back towards her own position. Huyan raced in pursuit. Sun Li promptly levelled his lance, intercepted Huyan and engaged him in fierce combat. Song Jiang moved up with his ten divisions and deployed them in battle formation. Ten Feet of Steel and her contingent, meanwhile, had ridden away down the slope.

Song Jiang was very pleased that Peng Qi the Eyes of Heaven General had been taken. He rode to the front to watch Sun Li and Huyan do battle. Sun Li sheathed his lance and went at Huyan with the steel rod ribbed like bamboo, which had been hanging from his wrist. Now, both were wielding rods of steel. Even their style of dress was similar. Sun Li wore a five cornered iron helmet bound in place by a red silk band around his forehead, a white-flowered black silk robe flecked with jade green, and darkly gleaming gold embossed armor. He rode a black stallion, and wielded a bamboo-shaped steel rod with dragon's eyes. Truly, a bolder picture than Yuchi Gong, that hero of old.

As to Huyan Zhuo, he wore a high pointed five-cornered helmet bound round the forehead by gold-flecked yellow silk, a black robe with sequins of seven stars, and darkly gleaming armor of over-lapping leaf. He rode the snowy-hoofed black stallion given him by the emperor, and wielded two octagonal steel rods polished bright as water. The one in his left hand weighed twelve catties, the one in his right thirteen. He indeed resembled his ancestor Huyan Zan.

Left and right over the field of combat they fought for more than thirty rounds, with neither man the victor.

When Han Tao saw Peng Qi captured, he quickly gathered the rear column and led them forward in a headlong rush. Song Jiang, afraid that they would break through, pointed his whip, and his ten commanders moved their divisions up to meet them, the last two spreading out in an enveloping pincers. Huyan hurriedly wheeled his columns around and each engaged their adversaries.

Why didn't the Liangshan warriors win total victory? Because of Huyan's "Armored Cavalry". Both horses and men wore chainmail. The battle steeds were draped to their hoofs, the soldiers protected to the eyes. Although Song Jiang's animals were equipped with some cover, this consisted mainly of red-tasseled net masks, copper bells, and plumes. The arrows sped by his archers were easily deflected by the chainmail. And all three thousand of Huyan's cavalry were armed with bows. They spewed flights of arrows which discouraged the men of Liangshan from coming any closer.

Song Jiang hastily had the horns sound the call to withdraw. Huyan also pulled his forces back twenty *li*, where they made camp.

The Song Jiang army encamped west of the mountain and settled their horses. At Song Jiang's command, his swordsmen hustled Peng Qi forward. Shouting for them to fall back, Song Jiang rose and untied his captive's bonds, then escorted him into the headquarters tent. He seated Peng Qi as a guest and kowtowed. Peng Qi at once returned the courtesy.

"I am your prisoner. By rights I should be killed. Why are you treating me with such courtesy, General?"

"Most of us are hunted men who have taken temporary shelter in the Marsh. The imperial court has sent you, General, here to arrest us. The proper thing for me would be to submit and be bound. But I fear for my life. And so I've criminally clashed with you. I beg your forgiveness for my presumptuousness."

"I have long known of your fraternal devotion and righteousness, of your aid to the endangered and your succor to the needy. But I never expected such chivalry! If you will spare my miserable life, I will serve you with every breath in my body!"

That day Song Jiang had the Eyes of Heaven General Peng Qi escorted to the mountain fortress to be introduced to Chao Gai and given refuge there. After rewarding his three armies, he conferred with his commanders on the military situation.

Meanwhile, Huyan Zhuo discussed with Han Tao' how to vanquish Liangshan Marsh.

"Today, those louts moved forward in a quick covering action when they saw us coming at them," said Han Tao. "Tomorrow, we ought to hit them with our entire cavalry. That way, a big victory, will be guaranteed."

呼延灼擺布連環馬

"Exactly what I had in mind. I just wanted to make sure you agreed."

Huyan then ordered that all three thousand of the cavalry be stretched out in a single line, divided into troops of thirty, and that all the horses in each troop be connected together by chains. On nearing the foe, the men were to use arrows at a distance and their lances when they got close, and drive relentlessly ahead. The three thousand armored cavalry would become one hundred platoons, each locked in solid formation. Five thousand infantry would follow as support.

"Don't challenge them in person, tomorrow," Huyan admonished Han Tao. "You and I will stay behind with the reinforcements. When the fighting starts, we'll rush them from three sides."

It was decided they would go into action the next day at dawn.

The following day Song Jiang set five troops of cavalry to the fore, backed by the ten divisions, with two contingents to left and right lying in ambush.

Qin Ming rode forth and challenged Huyan. But the imperial troops only shouted, and no one appeared. The five Liangshan cavalry units spread out in a line. Qin Ming was in the center, Lin Chong and Ten Feet of Steel were on the left, Hua Rong and Sun Li were on the right. The ten divisions under Song Jiang stood to the rear, a dense mass of men and horses. About a thousand imperial foot soldiers were arrayed opposite. Although they beat their drums and yelled, not a single man rode out to joust.

Song Jiang grew suspicious. He quietly gave the order for his rear forces to withdraw, then rode up to Hua Rong's contingent to look. Suddenly, a volley of cannon fire erupted from the opposite side. The thousand imperial foot soldiers separated into two sections and platoons of linked cavalry poured through in an enveloping three-sided phalanx. Arrows winged from both flanks. The middle bristled with long lances.

Startled, Song Jiang ordered his archers to reply. But how could they withstand this assault? Every animal in the thirty-horse platoons galloped together, unable to hold back even if it wanted to. From all over the hills and plains the linked cavalry charged.

Song Jiang's forward five cavalry units were thrown into a panic. They couldn't stem the tide. The rear divisions, also unable to make a stand, broke and ran. Song Jiang raced away on his horse, guarded by his ten commanders.

A platoon of imperial linked cavalry closed in after them. Li Kui, Yang Lin and their men rose out of their ambush in the reeds and drove them off. Song Jiang fled to the water's edge. Li Jun, Zhang Heng, Zhang Shun and the three Ruan brothers were waiting with war boats. Song Jiang hurriedly boarded one of craft and ordered them to rescue the chieftains and get them into the boats, quickly.

A platoon of linked cavalry rode right up to the river and showered the craft with arrows, but shields blocked the arrows and no one was hurt. The boats were rowed hastily to Duck's Bill Shore, where everyone disembarked. In the fort there a count was made. They had lost more than half their effectives. Fortunately all of the chieftains had been saved, although several of their mounts had been killed.

Shortly thereafter, Shi Yong, Shi Qian, Sun Xin and Mistress Gu arrived. "The imperial infantry swarmed all over us," they reported. "They levelled our inns and houses. If our boats hadn't rescued us, we would have been captured."

Song Jiang consoled them and took stock of his commanders. Six had arrow wounds — Lin Chong, Lei Heng, Li Kui, Shi Xiu, Sun Xin and Huang Xin. Innumerable lesser chieftains had also been struck by arrows or otherwise wounded.

When Chao Gai learned of this, he came down the mountain with Wu Yong and Gongsun Sheng. They found Song Jiang frowning and depressed.

"Don't fret, brother," Wu Yong said soothingly. "Both victory and defeat are common fare for the soldier. Why worry? We'll work out a good plan to deal with that linked cavalry."

Chao Gai ordered the naval forces to strengthen the shore

stockades, repair the boats, and guard the beaches day and night. He urged Song Jiang to return to the mountain stronghold and rest. But Song insisted on remaining at the fort on Duck's Bill Shore. He agreed only that the wounded commanders should go up and recuperate.

Song Jiang, in the Duck's Bill Shore fort, conferred with Wu Yong on how to achieve a breakthrough on the battlefield. But they could not think of anything.

A spy entered and reported: "The Eastern Capital has sent a cannoneer, Ling Zhen, Heaven-Shaking Thunder. He's set up guns near the river and he's getting ready to bombard our forts."

"It doesn't matter," said Wu Yong. "Our mountain stronghold is surrounded by a marsh which is full of creeks and ponds. It's a long way from the river. Even if he has guns that can reach the sky, he'll never hit it. We'll just abandon this fort on Duck's Bill Shore and let him shoot. Then we'll talk some more."

Song Jiang left the fort and returned to the mountain stronghold. Chao Gai and Gongsun Sheng escorted him to Fraternity Hall.

"How are we going to crack the enemy?" they asked.

Almost before the words were out of their mouths, they heard the boom of artillery at the foot of the mountain. Three cannon balls were fired. Two landed in the river. A third scored a direct hit on the Duck's Bill Shore fort.

Song Jiang watched glumly. The other leaders blanched.

"If Ling Zhen could be inveigled to the river we could nab him," said Wu Yong. "Then we could discuss what to do about the enemy."

"We'll send Li Jun, Zhang Heng, Zhang Shun and the three Ruan brothers in charge of six boats. Zhu Tong and Lei Heng will be on the opposite shore," said Chao Gai. And he told what each would do.

The six naval leaders received their orders and divided into two units. Li Jun and Zhang Heng took forty or fifty good swimmers in two fast craft and slipped across through the reeds. Backing them were Zhang Shun and the three Ruan brothers with another forty or so men in a fleet of small boats. On reaching the shore, Li Jun and Zhang Heng and their men, shouting and yelling, charged up to the cannon mountings and knocked them over.

Soldiers hurriedly reported this to Ling Zhen, who at once took two Fireball cannon and his lance, mounted his horse, and hastened to the scene with a thousand soldiers. Only then did Li Jun and Zhang Heng and their men leave. Ling Zhen chased them as far as the reedy shore, where a line of forty small craft, manned by a hundred or more sailors, were moored.

Li and Zhang went aboard, but didn't cast off. When Ling Zhen and his force came in sight, everyone on the boats shouted and jumped into the water.

Ling Zhen's men seized the boats. Zhu Tong and Lei Heng, on the opposite shore, began yelling and pounding drums. Ling Zhen ordered his soldiers to board the craft and go across and get them.

When the boats reached the middle of the river, Zhu Tong and Lei Heng struck a gong loudly. Forty or fifty swimmers rose from beneath the waves and pulled the plugs from sterns. Water flooded the craft. Strong hands capsized many of the boats, dumping the soldiers into the river.

Ling Zhen made haste to go back, but his craft's rudder had already been removed under water. Two of the chieftains clambered aboard. With one quick rock, they turned it bottom up. Ling Zhen landed in the water. He was grabbed by Ruan the Second from below and dragged ashore. There, other chieftains who were waiting had him bound and taken up the mountain.

Over two hundred soldiers were captured. More than half of the remainder had been drowned. The few who escaped with their lives reported to Huyan Zhuo. He hastily mustered his forces and galloped to the rescue. But the boats had already crossed to Duck's Bill Shore. It was too far for arrows. Besides, the raiders were gone.

CHAPTER 21
Song Jiang Breaks the Linked-Up Cavalry

The next day there was a meeting of the leaders in Fraternity Hall. As they drank Song Jiang discussed with them the problem of the linked cavalry. No one could think of how to cope with it. Finally, Gold-Coin Spotted Leopard Tang Long rose to his feet.

"Though I have no talent, I'd like to suggest a plan," he said. "But we need a certain weapon and a cousin of mine."

"What kind of weapon, and who is this cousin?" asked Wu Yong.

"My ancestors have always been armorers," Tang Long said to the chieftains. "Because of this skill my father was raised by Border Area Governor Old General Zhong to be head of the Yanan garrison. The linked cavalry method won victories for the previous emperor. The only way you can beat it is with barbed lances. I have a drawing of such a lance, passed down to me by my family, which can serve as a likeness. I can make one for you, but I don't know how to use it. Only my cousin, an arms instructor, knows. The art has been handed down from generation to generation. They never teach it to any outsider. My cousin can ply the lance ahorse or on foot. When he goes into action, he's like nothing human."

"You don't mean Xu Ning, Arms Instructor of the Metal Lancers?" Lin Chong interrupted.

"The very man."

"I'd forgotten until you mentioned him. His skill with metal and barbed lances is indeed unique. We met many times when I was in the capital and tested our military arts against one another. We developed a deep mutual respect and affection.

But how can you get him to come up here?"

"Xu Ning has a matchless ancestral treasure. It protects his family from evil spirits. I often saw it when I went with my father to visit Xu Ning's mother in the Eastern Capital. It's a suit of goose-feather armor hooped in metal. Known as 'lion's fur', it's light and snug-fitting, and no blade or arrow can pierce it. Many high officials have begged to see it, but Xu Ning always refuses. He cherishes it like his life. He keeps it in a leather box which he hangs on the central beam of his bedroom. If we can get hold of that armor, he'll have to come whether he wants to or not."

"No problem at all," said Wu Yong. "We'll ask our talented brother Shi Qian, Flea on a Drum, to attend to it."

"If it's there, I'll get it, by hook or crook," Shi Qian avowed.

"Do that, and I guarantee to bring Xu Ning up the mountain," said Tang Long.

"How?" Song Jiang demanded.

Tang Long leaned close and whispered in his ear. Song Jiang laughed.

"Very shrewd."

Shi Qian concealed on his person certain tools and implements as he left Liangshan Marsh. He followed a winding road until he reached the capital. He spent the night at an inn and the next day quietly entered the city. He inquired where he might find Arms Instructor Xu Ning.

"Go through the gate of the battalion compound," a man instructed, pointing. "He lives in the fifth house. It has a black gate in the corner of the wall."

Shi Qian went into the city, had some dinner, then quietly approached the home of Xu Ning in the compound of the Metal Lancers Battalion. He looked around but couldn't find any suitable place to hide. Night was falling, and he took up a position inside the compound gateway. Soon it was dark. There was no moon in the winter sky.

He noted a big poplar behind an Earth God Temple. He shinnied up, sat astride a limb, and watched silently. Xu Ning

returned and went into his house. Two people with lanterns
closed and locked the compound gate, then went back to their
homes. In a drum tower the beat of the first watch sounded.
Through the chill overcast the stars appeared lustreless. Dew
turned to frost. All was still.

Shi Qian slid down from his tree, stole to Xu Ning's rear
gate, and effortlessly scaled the courtyard wall. He crossed
a small garden to the kitchen and peered in. Two serving
girls were still cleaning up in the light of a lamp. Up the
decorative pole he went, and over to the upcurved eave of
a corner of the roof. Lying in this concealment, he looked
into the window of the upper storey. Xu Ning and his wife
were seated beside a stove. The woman held a child of six
or seven in her arms.

It was their bedroom. Sure enough, there was a big leather
box tied to the beam. Near the door hung a bow and arrows
and a dagger. On a clothes rack were garments of various
colors.

When both husband and wife were in bed, the two serving
girls lay down on pallets outside the bedroom door. A night
lamp had been lit upon the table. Soon the four were asleep.
The girls had worked hard all day, and were exhausted. They
snored lustily.

When he was sure they were asleep, Shi Qian on the beam extended
his long reed and puffed out the lamp. Softly, he untied the leather
box. He was about to come down when the wife, hearing a noise,
awakened.

"What's that sound up on the beam?" she called to Plum
Fragrance.

Shi Qian promptly squeaked like a rat.

"Can't you hear, mistress?" said the girl. "Those are rats,
fighting."

Shi Qian emitted a series of squeaks like a whole battle,
slipped down, stealthily opened the door at the head of the
stairs, agilely swung the box to his back, went down the stairs,
opened the house door, and stepped out. The various guards
were departing, and the battalion compound gate was open,

it having been unlocked at the fourth watch. He mingled with the crowd and left swiftly, not stopping until he reached his inn outside the city.

It was still not yet light. He knocked on the door and went to his room to get his luggage. He tied this and the box to a carrying pole, paid his bill, left the inn and headed east. Only after covering more than forty *li* did he stop at an eating house and make himself some food.

Suddenly a man came in. Shi Qian looked up. It was none other than Dai Zong the Marvellous Traveller. Dai observed that Shi Qian had got what he had gone for. The two conversed in low tones.

"I'll take the armor to our mountain fortress," Dai Zong said. "You follow slowly with Tang Long."

Shi Qian opened the leather box, took out the metal-bound goose feather armor and wrapped it in a bundle, which Dai Zong tied to his body. The Marvellous Traveller left the inn, performed his magic rites, and sped off to Liangshan Marsh.

Shi Qian tied the empty leather box openly to one end of his carrying pole. He finished eating, paid the bill, shouldered the pole, and set out. When he had gone about twenty *li*, he met Tang Long. They went into a tavern to confer.

Only at dusk did Xu Ning remove his official robe. He gave it to his orderly. Carrying his metal lance, Xu slowly returned. At the gateway of the battalion compound, a neighbor spoke to him.

"Your house has been robbed! Your wife has been waiting for you all day!"

Startled, Xu Ning hurried home. The serving girls met him at the door.

"The thief must have slipped in when you left at the fifth watch," they said. "All he took was that leather box on the beam."

Cries of anguish burst through Xu Ning's lips from the depths of his vitals.

"Who knows when that thief crept into our room," exclaimed his wife.

"Anything else wouldn't have mattered," said Xu Ning.
"But that goose feather armor has been a family heirloom for
four generations! It's never been lost. Marshal Wang the
dilletante offered me thirty thousand strings of cash, but I
hadn't the heart to sell it. I thought I might need it in battle
again. Because I was afraid that something might happen to
it, I tied it on the beam. Many people asked to see it, but
I said it was gone. If I raise a hue and cry about it, they'll
surely laugh at me. Now it really is gone. What can I do?"

That night he couldn't sleep. "Who could have stolen it?"
he wondered. "It must have been someone who knew I had
the armor."

His wife thought a while and said: "The thief must have
already been in the house when the lamp went out. Someone
who became enamored of it and tried to buy it from you probably sent a high-class housebreaker to steal it when you
wouldn't sell. Get people to ask around quietly and find out
where it is. Then we'll decide what to do. Don't 'disturb the
grass and alert the snake'."

Xu Ning listened in silence. He rose the next morning at
dawn and sat brooding in the house.

At breakfast time, there was a knock at the courtyard gate.
The orderly went to see who it was. He returned and announced: "Tang Long, son of the head of the Yanan garrison,
is calling to pay his respects."

Xu Ning directed that he be invited in. On seeing Xu Ning,
Tang Long kowtowed.

"I trust all has been well with you, cousin," he said.

"I heard my uncle had returned to Heaven," Xu Ning replied. "I was tied down by official duties and your home
is far away, so I never went to offer my condolences. I haven't
had any news of you, either, cousin. Where have you been?
What brings you here?"

"It's a long story. I've had bad luck since my father died,
and wandered to many places. Today, I've come directly from
Shandong to the capital to see you."

"Cousin, stay a while," said Xu Ning. He ordered that wine and food be brought for his guest.

Tang Long took from his pack two, long thin gold bars like scallion leaves, weighing twenty ounces, and presented them to Xu Ning.

"Before he died, my father asked me to give you these as a remembrance. There wasn't anybody I could trust to deliver them, so I've come today to hand them to you myself."

"How very kind of uncle to think of me. I've done absolutely nothing to show my esteem. I'll never be able to express my gratitude."

"Don't talk like that, cousin. Father was a great admirer of your skill with arms. He was sorry we lived so far apart and couldn't see each other. That's why he's left you these momentoes."

Xu Ning thanked Tang Long and accepted the gold bars. He had wine served and entertained him. But his brows were knit and he looked glum all the while they were drinking.

Finally, Tang Long rose and said: "You don't seem very happy, cousin. Is something troubling you?"

Xu Ning sighed. "Of course you don't know. It's a long story. Last night we were robbed."

"Did you lose much?"

"Only the goose-feather metal-hooped armor known as 'lion's fur', left to me by my ancestors. But it's a remarkable suit, and last night it was taken. I'm very upset."

"I've seen that armor. It really is beyond compare. My late father often praised it to the skies. Where were you keeping it?"

"In a leather box tied to the main beam in the bedroom. I can't imagine when the thief slipped in and got away with it."

"What's the leather box like?"

"It's of red sheepskin, and the armor inside is wrapped in fragrant silk quilting."

"A red sheepskin box?" Tang Long appeared startled. "Does it have cloud head sceptres stitched in white thread on the surface, with a lion playing with an embroidered ball in the middle?"

"Cousin, where have you seen it?"

"Last night I was drinking wine in a village tavern about forty *li* from the city. I saw a sharp-eyed thin swarthy fellow carrying it on a shoulder pole. I wondered what was in it. As I was leaving the tavern I asked him: 'What's that box for?' He said: 'Originally it held armor. But now it's only got a few garments.' That must be your man. He evidently has hurt his leg, because he walks with a limp. Why don't we go after him and catch him?"

"If we can do that, it will be a blessing from Heaven!"

"Let's not delay then. We'll go at once."

Xu Ning quickly changed into hemp sandals, fastened his dagger, took his halberd, and left the city with Tang Long through the east gate. They strode swiftly along the winding road. Ahead they saw a tavern with a white circle on its wall.

"Let's have a bowl of wine," Tang Long suggested. "We can inquire here."

They went in and sat down. Tang Long asked the host: "Has a sharp-eyed dark thin fellow carrying a red sheepskin box passed this way?"

"There was a man like that last night. He seemed to have a bad leg, and was limping."

"Did you hear that, cousin?" Tang Long exclaimed.

Xu Ning was beyond speech. The two paid for their wine and hurried through the door. Further on, they came to an inn. A white circle marked its wall. Tang Long halted.

"I can't go another step," he said. "Why not spend the night here, and continue the chase early tomorrow morning?"

"I have official duties. If I'm not there for roll call I'll surely be reprimanded. What can I do?"

"You needn't worry about that, cousin. Your wife will explain, of course."

At the inn that night they again made inquiries. The attendant told them: "Last night a thin swarthy fellow put up here. He slept late and didn't leave till mid-morning. He asked about the road to Shandong."

"That means we can catch him," said Tang Long.

The two men rested at the inn and departed before dawn, continuing along the winding road. Whenever they saw a white chalk circle on a wall, Tang Long called a halt for food and wine, and to ask the way. At each place they were told the same thing. Xu Ning was anxious to retrieve his armor, and he hastened along with Tang Long.

As daylight again began to wane, they saw ahead an ancient temple. In front of it, Shi Qian had rested his load and was sitting under a tree.

"Good," exclaimed Tang Long. "There, cousin, beneath that tree, isn't that your red sheepskin box?"

Xu Ning looked, then rushed forward and seized Shi Qian. "Impudent scoundrel," he roared. "How dare you steal my armor!"

"Stop, stop. Quit your yelling. Yes, I took your armor. What are you going to do about it?"

"Vulgar beast! You have the nerve to ask me that!"

"See if there's any armor in that box."

Tang Long opened the container. It was empty.

"What have you done with my armor, rogue?" Xu Ning demanded.

"Now listen to me. My name is Zhang. I'm an eldest son and I come from Tai'an Prefecture. A wealthy man in our prefecture knows Old General Zhong of the Border Garrison and learned from him about your goose feather armor and that you don't want to sell. So he hired me and another man called Li the Third to steal it. He's paying us ten thousand strings of cash. When I jumped from that pole in your yard I sprained my leg and I can't walk fast. So I've let Li go on ahead with the armor and have kept only the box. If you pressure me and take me before the court, I won't say a word even if I'm beaten to death. But if you forgive me, I'll go with you and get it back."

Xu Ning hesitated for several moments, unable to decide.

"There's no danger of him flying away, cousin," said Tang Long. "Let's go with him and recover your armor. If he doesn't produce it, you can always state your case to the local magistrate."

"That's quite true, cousin," Xu Ning agreed.

The three men continued along the road and spent the night at an inn. Xu Ning and Tang Long kept an eye on Shi Qian. But Flea on a Drum had bandaged one leg as if it were sprained, and Xu Ning, thinking he couldn't walk very fast, wasn't especially watchful. The following morning they rose and went on. Shi Qian frequently bought them food and drink, by way of apology. They travelled all day.

The next morning Xu Ning was growing increasingly anxious. Was Shi Qian really leading them to the armor? During their march they came upon three or four horses hitched to an empty cart by the side of the road. Behind it stood the driver. A merchant stood to one side. When he saw Tang Long, he dropped to his knees and kowtowed.

"What are you doing here, brother?" Tang Long queried.

"I had some business in Zhengzhou," the merchant replied. "I'm on my way back to Tai'an."

"Excellent. We three would like a ride. We're going to Tai'an, too."

"I wouldn't mind even if there were more of you, to say nothing of only three."

Very pleased, Tang Long brought him over to Xu Ning.

"Who is this?" Xu Ning asked.

"I met him last year when I went to a temple in Tai'an to burn incense. His name is Li Rong and he's a righteous man."

"Since Zhang can hardly walk, I suppose we'd better ride." Xu Ning told the driver to start, and the four men got in the cart.

"Tell me the name of your rich patron," Xu Ning demanded of Shi Qian.

Flea on a Drum stalled for a few minutes, then said: "He's called Lord Guo."

"Do you have a Lord Guo in Tai'an?" Xu Ning asked Li Rong.

"Yes. He's a very wealthy man who hobnobs with big officials," Li Rong replied. "He supports a whole bevy of hangers-on."

Xu Ning said to himself: "Since there is such a person, I needn't be suspicious."

Li Rong chatted about play with weapons, and sang a few songs. The day passed quickly and pleasantly.

Soon they were only little more than two stages from Liangshan Marsh. Li Rong had the driver take the gourd and buy some wine and meat for his three passengers. Li filled a ladle and offered it to Xu Ning, who drained it at one go. Li called for more. The driver, pretending that his hand slipped, let the gourd drop, spilling its contents on the ground. Li shouted at him and ordered him to buy more wine.

Suddenly, Xu Ning began to drool from the corners of his mouth, and fell headlong in the cart. Who was Li Rong? Actually, he was Yue Ho the Iron Throat. He and the other two jumped down and hurried the horses on. They went directly to the tavern of Zhu Gui, the Dry-Land Crocodile, where they all carried Xu Ning to a boat and ferried him across to the Shore of Golden Sands. Song Jiang had already been informed, and had come down the mountain and was waiting with the other leaders.

Xu Ning by then awakened from the drug, and he was given an antidote. When he opened his eyes and saw the men standing around him, he was astonished.

"Cousin," he said to Tang Long, "why have you duped me into coming here?"

"Listen to me, cousin," said Tang Long. "I had heard that Song Jiang accepted bold men from all over. And so in Wugang Town I pledged myself a blood brother to Li Kui the Black Whirlwind and joined the forces in the stronghold. Now Huyan Zhuo is using linked cavalry against us on the battlefield and he's got us stymied. I proposed barbed lances, but you're the only one who knows how to wield them. So I thought of this scheme: Shi Qian was sent to steal your armor, and I tricked you to take to the road. Then Yue Ho, disguised as Li Rong, put a drug in your wine when we were crossing a hill. Please come up to our mountain stronghold and become one of our leaders."

"Cousin, you've ruined me!"

Song Jiang advanced, wine cup in hand, and said apologetically: "I'm here in this marsh only temporarily, just waiting for an imperial amnesty so that I can repay our country with my utmost loyalty and strength. I'm not covetous, I don't like killing, and I never perform unrighteous or unchivalrous deeds. I devoutly hope you will sympathize with me, Inspector, and join me in acting in Heaven's behalf."

Lin Chong also sought to mollify him. Cup in hand, he said: "I'm here, too, brother. Please don't refuse."

"You duped me into coming," Xu Ning said to Tang Long. "The authorities are sure to arrest my wife. What can I do?"

"Don't let that worry you, Inspector," said Song Jiang. "I personally guarantee her safety. In a few days you will be reunited."

Chao Gai, Wu Yong and Gongsun Sheng all apologized to Xu Ning, and a feast was laid in his honor. The most agile of the young brigands were selected to learn the use of the barbed lance. Dai Zong and Tang Long were dispatched to the Eastern Capital at all possible speed to fetch Xu Ning's family.

By then the barbed lances manufactured under the supervision of Lei Heng were ready.

In Fraternity Hall, the chieftains requested Xu Ning to demonstrate the barbed lance. He was a fine figure of a man. Tall, broad-shouldered and thick at the middle, he had a round fair face adorned by a mustache and goatee. After selecting his trainees, he went outside the Hall, picked up a barbed lance and showed how it was done. The spectators cheered.

"If you're using this weapon on horseback," he said, "you must swing from the waist. Advance in seven moves — three hooks and four parries. Then, one stab and one cleave. A total

of nine changes. If you're on foot, the best way is to advance
eight steps and parry four times. This will open the door. At
the twelfth step, change. At the sixteenth, turn completely
around, alternately hooking and stabbing. At the twenty-
fourth, push your opponent's weapon up, then down. Hook
to the east and parry to the west. At the thirty-sixth, making
sure that you're well covered, seize the tough and fight the
strong. This is the correct method of using the barbed lance.
We have a jingle that goes:

> Four parries, three hooks, seven in all,
> Nine changes in total weave a magic spell,
> At step twenty-four parry forward and back,
> At step sixteen do a big turn as well."

As Xu Ning demonstrated, stage by stage, the chieftains
watched. The fighters were delighted by the way he plied the
lance. From then on, he taught the deftest of them day and
night. He also showed infantry how to hide in brush and grass
and snag the legs of horses, instructing them in three secret
methods.

In less than half a month, he had taught five to seven hundred
men. Song Jiang and the other leaders were extremely pleased.
They made preparations to break the foe.

Huyan Zhuo, since the capture of Peng Qi and Ling Zhen,
had been riding forth with his cavalry every day to the edge
of the river and hurling challenges. But the brigand leaders
near the shore only continued holding the various beach heads
and installing sharp stakes under the water. Huyan was able
to send scouts along the roads west and north of the mountain,
but he had no way of getting to the stronghold.

Inside the brigand fortress Ling Zhen was directed to manufacture several types of cannon, and a day was set for the
attack against the enemy. The men who had been learning the
use of the barbed lance were by now quite adept.

"I'm neither clever nor far-sighted," Song Jiang said to the
other chieftains. "I wonder whether my idea will meet with
your approval."

"We'd like to hear it," said Wu Yong.

"Tomorrow we won't use our cavalry, but will fight entirely on foot. The military tactics of Sun and Wu are very suited to wooded and watery areas. We'll take the infantry down, divide them into ten units and lure on the enemy. When they charge with their cavalry, we'll withdraw into the reeds and brush. Our men with the barbed lances will already be there lying in ambush. For every ten of these will be an equal number with big hooked poles. The lances will bring down the horses, the poles will snag the riders. We'll prepare similar ambushes on the open plain and in the narrow defiles. How does that plan strike you?"

"I think that's how we ought to do it," said Wu Yong. "Conceal our soldiers and seize their officers."

"Barbed lances and hooked poles together. Exactly the way," said Xu Ning.

Song Jiang then formed ten infantry units, with two leaders in command of each to go down the mountain and lure the foe. Naval craft to serve as reinforcements were put under the command of nine chieftains. Six cavalry units were also dispatched under six chieftains. Their function was to shout challenges at the enemy from the side of the mountain. Ling Zhen and Du Xing were to have charge of the cannons.

Xu Ning and Tang Long were given leadership of the men with the barbed lances. The main army was under Song Jiang, Wu Yong, Gongsun Sheng, Dai Zong, Lü Fang and Guo Sheng. They issued all general orders and commands. The remaining chieftains were to defend the various forts.

That night at the third watch the barbed lancers crossed the river, spread out and went into ambush. At the fourth watch the ten infantry units moved across. Ling Zhen and Du Xing took with them Fiery Wind cannon and mountings, and set them up on a height. Xu Ning and Tang Long, as they crossed to the opposite shore, each carried a trumpet in a bag.

Dawn found Song Jiang and the main army lined up along the river. They beat drums, shouted and waved their banners. When news of this reached Huyan Zhuo in the headquarters tent of his central army, he directed Han Tao of his vanguard to go out and scout. Then he ordered that the horses of his armored cavalry be linked together. He put on his armor, mounted his snowy-hoofed black steed, took up his double rods, and rode forth towards Liangshan Marsh with his men and horses.

He saw Song Jiang with a large force on the other side of the river and spread his troops out in battle formation. He conferred with Han Tao, who said: "They have a detachment of infantry, I don't know how large, due south of here."

"Who cares how large! Charge them with our linked cavalry!"

Han Tao galloped forth with five hundred horsemen. But to the southeast another force of infantry appeared. Han Tao was about to send part of his cavalry against them, when to the southwest he saw still another detachment, waving pennants and shouting. He pulled his entire unit back.

"There are three bandit detachments to the south," he told Huyan. "They've all got Liangshan Marsh banners."

"For a long time those rascals have refused to come out and fight," Huyan mused. "They must be up to something."

Before the words were out of his mouth, to the north was heard the boom of cannon. Huyan swore, "Ling Zhen has gone over to the bandits! They've got him to bombard us!"

While they were all watching south, three more units welled up in the north. "Those bandits surely are hatching some scheme," Huyan said to Han Tao. "We'll divide our army in two. I'll fight north with one column, you fight south with the other."

They were about to do this when four more enemy units appeared to the west. Huyan began to grow panicky. Northwards, a volley of cannon fire erupted, and projectiles landed upon the bluffs. They were shot from one large and forty-nine smaller cannons, which is why the battery was called Mother and Sons. The shells burst with an overpowering roar. Huyan's soldiers, confused before the combat even started, dashed wildly amid the cavalry and troops led by Han Tao.

The ten brigand infantry units ran east when chased east, and west when chased west. Huyan was furious. He advanced north with his army. Song Jiang's men plunged into the reeds. Huyan came tearing after them with a large contingent of linked cavalry. The armored steeds, galloping in tandem, could not be checked. They crashed in among the dry reeds, tall grass and tangled thickets. A shrill whistle rent the air, and barbed lances on both ends of the linked lines snagged the horses' legs and brought them tumbling to the ground. The animals in the middle whinnied in fright. Long poles snaked out of the reeds and hooked the riders.

Huyan, realizing he had been tricked, gave his horse free rein and raced back south after Han Tao. To the north behind him Fiery Wind cannon thundered. Here, there, all over the hills and plain, brigand infantry gave chase. Linked armored cavalry rolled and fell everywhere amid the reeds and grasses, and everywhere were caught.

Han Tao and Huyan knew they had been duped. They rode madly about after their mounted men, seeking an escape route. But every path was thick as flax with the banners of Liangshan Marsh. No path was safe, and they headed northwest.

Before they had gone five or six *li* they were confronted by a strong unit with two bold fellows in the lead — Mu Hong the Unrestrained and Mu Chun the Slightly Restrained. Both carried halberds, and they shouted: "Defeated generals, stand where you are!"

Huyan, enraged, charged the two, brandishing his rods. They fought four or five rounds, then Mu Chun withdrew. Fearing a trap, Huyan did not pursue, but rode due north along the road.

Another powerful band came down the slope and blocked his way. It was led by Two-Headed Snake Xie Zhen and Twin-Tailed Scorpion Xie Bao. They raced towards him, each gripping a steel fork. Flourishing his rods, Huyan clashed with them in combat. They fought six or seven rounds, and the two brothers retreated. Huyan chased them less than half a *li* when from both sides suddenly twenty-four men with barbed lances surged forth. Huyan had no more heart for battle. He turned his mount and hurried off, northeast.

Again he was stopped, this time by Stumpy Tiger and Ten Feet of Steel, husband and wife. The road clearly was perilous, but the thorns and brambles on all sides were even worse. He kicked up his steed, brandished his rods, and charged through his interceptors. Stumpy Tiger and Ten Feet of Steel were unable to catch him. He rode pell-mell northeast, his army in ruins, his men scattered like raindrops and stars.

Song Jiang's trumpets sounded a return to the mountain, where each warrior came forward to claim his reward. Of the three thousand linked armored steeds, a troop and a half — brought down by the barbed lances — had their hoofs damaged. These were stripped of their armor and kept for eating purposes. But the mounts of more than two troops were in fine condition. These were led up the mountain to be fed and cared for and used as brigand mounts. All the armor-bedecked cavalrymen were captured alive and taken to the stronghold.

Five thousand imperial infantry, pressed fiercely on three sides, tried to flee back into the midst of their main army, but were all brought down by the barbed lances and caught. Those who ran to the river were rounded up by the naval chieftains, put on boats, ferried across, and escorted up the mountain under guard. The men and horses previously captured by the imperial forces were recovered and returned to the fortress. Huyan's palisades were dismantled and new forts were built along the banks. Two inns were again erected to serve as eyes for the brigands, and as before Sun Xin, Mistress Gu, Shi Yong and Shi Qian were put in charge.

Liu Tang and Du Qian brought Han Tao to the stronghold, a bound captive. Song Jiang personally untied him and invited him into the Hall. He apologized and had a feast laid in his honor. Peng Qi and Ling Zhen, at Song's behest, urged him to join them. Han Tao promptly became a chieftain of Liang-shan Marsh. Song Jiang had him write a letter to his family, then dispatched men to Chenzhou to bring them to the fortress, where they and Han Tao were reunited.

Song Jiang rejoiced. He had broken the linked cavalry, captured many men and horses, and collected large quantities of armor and weapons. Every day he and his cohorts feasted in celebration. But as usual they guarded all approaches against possible attack by imperial soldiers.

CHAPTER 22
Three Mountains Bands Attack Qingzhou

Huyan, having lost so much of his imperial army, dared not return to the capital. He rode alone on his black steed with the snowy hoofs, his armor hanging over the pommel as he hastened from the scene of his disaster. Without money, he had to take the gold belt from around his waist and sell it for silver.

"It happened so suddenly," he said to himself. "Who can I look to for refuge?" Then he remembered. "Murong, the prefect of Qingzhou is an old friend. Why not go to him? His sister is an imperial concubine. If, through her influence, I can be given another army, I may still get my revenge."

Towards evening of his second day on the road, he was hungry and thirsty. He dismounted at a village inn by the roadside and tied his horse to a tree near the front door. He went in, placed his rods on a table, sat down, and told the host to bring wine and meat.

"We've only wine here," said the host. "But they just slaughtered a sheep in the village. If you want meat, I'll buy you some."

Huyan opened the ration bag at his waist and took out some of the silver he had exchanged for his gold belt. He gave this to the host.

"Get a leg of mutton and boil it for me. And mix some fodder and feed my horse. I'll spend the night here. Tomorrow, I'm going on to Qingzhou."

"There's nothing against staying here, sir. But we don't have a good bed."

"I'm a military man. Any place I can rest will do."

The host took the silver and went off to purchase the mutton. Huyan removed his armor from his horse's back and loosened its girth straps, then sat down outside the door. He waited a long time. At last the host returned with the sheep leg. Huyan told him to boil it, knead three measures of flour for griddle-cakes, and draw two drams of wine.

While the meat was cooking and the griddlecakes were on the pan, the host heated water for Huyan to wash his feet and led the horse to a shed in the rear. The host chopped grass and boiled fodder. Huyan warmed some wine and imbibed a while. Soon the meat was ready, and Huyan invited the host to eat and drink with him.

"I'm an officer of the imperial army," Huyan said. "Because I've had a setback in arresting the bandits of Liangshan Marsh, I'm going to join Prefect Murong of Qingzhou. Take good care of my horse. It was given to me by the emperor, and is called the Ebony Steed Which Treads in Snow. I'll reward you handsomely later on."

"Thank you, Excellency. But there is something I must tell you. Not far from here is Peach Blossom Mountain. On it is a band of robbers. Their leader is Li Zhong the Tiger-Fighting General. Second in command is Zhou Tong the Little King. There are about six or seven hundred of them, and they rob and pillage. Sometimes they raid this village. The authorities have sent soldiers to capture them time and again, but always without success. You must sleep lightly during the night, sir."

"I'm a man of matchless courage. Even if those knaves came in full force it wouldn't matter to me. Just make sure to feed my horse well."

He dined on meat and wine and griddlecakes. Then the host spread a pallet and Huyan lay down to sleep.

Because he had been depressed for several days, and because he had drunk a few cups of wine too many, Huyan reclined without taking his clothes off. Around the third watch he awakened. He heard the host, to the rear of the house, lamenting. Huyan jumped up, seized his twin rods and went into the back yard.

"What's the trouble?" he demanded.

"I went out to add some hay and I found that the fence had been knocked down. Someone has stolen Your Excellency's horse! Look, there — torch light three or four *li* off in the distance. They must be heading for that place."

"What place are you talking about?"

"The robbers you see on that road are bandits from Peach Blossom Mountain!"

Huyan was startled. He ordered the host to lead the way, and they gave chase for two or three *li* along the edges of the fields. But the torches had vanished. There was no telling where they had gone.

"This is terrible," said Huyan. "I've lost the emperor's gift horse!"

"Go into the prefecture tomorrow and report the theft," advised the host. "They'll send soldiers to catch the robbers. That's the only way you'll get the animal back."

Sunk in gloom, Huyan sat until daybreak. Then he set out for Qingzhou, instructing the host to carry his armor. It was dark by the time they reached the city, and they put up at an inn for the night. Early the following morning Huyan presented himself at the prefectural court and kowtowed before Murong.

The prefect was astonished. "I heard that you had gone to catch the bandits in Liangshan Marsh, General," he said. "What are you doing here?"

Huyan related what had transpired.

"Although you lost many men and horses, it was not through lack of diligence," said Murong. "The bandits tricked you. It wasn't your fault. The area under my administration has often been raided by them. Now that you're here you can first clean out Peach Blossom Mountain and retake the steed presented you by the emperor. Then you can capture the robbers on Two-Dragon Mountain and White Tiger in one fell swoop. I'll report your exploits to the emperor, and you'll again be given command of an army and can get your revenge. How will that be?"

Huyan again kowtowed. "I'm deeply grateful for your concern. If you'll be kind enough to do this, I'll repay you with
my life."

Murong invited him to accept temporary quarters in a guest-
room, where he could change his clothes, eat and rest. The
prefect told the host who had been carrying Huyan's armor to
return home.

Three days passed. Huyan, anxious to retrieve the imperial
gift horse, entreated Murong to give him soldiers. The prefect
mustered two thousand infantry and cavalry, which he put
under Huyan's leadership, and presented him with a black-
maned charger. Huyan thanked him, donned his armor, mounted, and marched off with his men to recapture his horse,
heading straight for Peach Blossom Mountain.

On the mountain Li Zhong the Tiger-Fighting General and
Zhou Tong the Little King, having obtained the Ebony Steed
Which Treads in Snow, feasted and celebrated every day. A
scout who watched the road reported: "Soldiers and horses
from Qingzhou heading this way."

Zhou Tong rose and said to Li Zhong: "Brother, hold the
fort. I'll go and drive back the government forces."

He mustered a hundred brigands, took his lance, mounted,
and rode down to meet the foe.

Huyan Zhuo approached the mountain with two thousand
infantry and cavalry and spread out in battle position. Riding
forth, he shouted: "Robbers, come and be bound!"

Zhou Tong the Little King deployed his men in a single line
and cantered out with levelled lance. Huyan gave his mount
rein and advanced to do battle. Zhou Tong spurred his animal.
Soon the two horses drew together.

The riders fought six or seven rounds. Zhou Tong wasn't
strong enough. He pulled his steed around and headed up the
slope. Huyan chased him a while. But he was afraid of being
tricked. He rode hastily down the mountain and set up a
camp. There he waited for the next opportunity to fight.

Zhou Tong returned to his stronghold. "Huyan Zhuo is a highly skilled warrior," he told Li Zhong. "I couldn't stop him. I had no choice but to come back. If he pursues right to our fort, what can we do?"

"I hear that Sagacious Lu the Tattooed Monk is in the Precious Pearl Monastery on Two-Dragon Mountain with a large band of men. With him, what's more, is some fellow called Yang Zhi the Blue-Faced Beast, and a newly arrived pilgrim Wu Song. They're all formidable fighters. I'll send a letter requesting their aid. If we get out of this danger thanks to their efforts, I'll be glad to pay them tribute every month."

"I've known about those brave fellows for some time. I'm just afraid that monk still remembers the first time we met, and won't want to help."

Li Zhong laughed. "Never mind. He's a good man, very forthright. When he learns of the fix we're in, he'll sure come with warriors to the rescue."

"Yes, that's true."

The letter was written and two competent brigands were picked to deliver it. They rolled down the rear slope and struck out for Two-Dragon Mountain. They reached the foot of it in only two days. The brigands on guard there questioned them closely on the nature of their business.

Three chieftains sat in the main hall of the Precious Pearl Monastery. Sagacious Lu the Tattooed Monk was first in command. Yang Zhi the Blue-Faced Beast was second. Third was Wu Song the Pilgrim.

In the building at the entry gate were four lesser chiefs. One was Shi En the Golden-Eyed Tiger Cub. The son of the warden of Mengzhou Prison at the time Wu Song killed General Zhang and his entire family, he and his father had been made responsible for apprehending the culprit. Rather than do this, Shi En had abandoned his home and fled. For some time he was a wanderer. Later, his parents died, and he heard that Wu Song was on Two-Dragon Mountain. He had hurried to join him.

Another lesser chief was Cao Zheng the Demon Carver. He had been with Sagacious Lu and Yang Zhi when they took Precious Pearl Monastery and killed Deng Long. He too subsequently joined the band.

The third was Zhang Qing the Vegetable Gardener. The fourth was Sun the Witch. These two, husband and wife, had sold dumplings stuffed with human flesh at Crossroads Rise on the Mengzhou Road. They had joined in response to repeated letters from Sagacious Lu and Wu Song.

Cao Zheng, hearing that there was a letter from Peach Blossom Mountain, carefully questioned the messengers, then went up to the hall and reported to the three chieftains.

"When I left Mount Wutai I put up in Peach Blossom Village, and there I gave that prick Zhou Tong a good drubbing," Lu recalled. "Then Li Zhong came and recognized me. He invited me up to their mountain for a day of drinking. He pledged me his blood brother and wanted me to stay and be their chieftain. But the stinginess of those two annoyed me. I collected some of their gold and silver drinking vessels and left. Now they send messengers pleading for aid. Let them come up. We'll hear what they have to say."

Cao Zheng soon returned with the two emissaries. They hailed the chieftains respectfully and said: "Murong, prefect of Qingzhou, has recently been entertaining Two Rods Huyan Zhuo, who failed in an attack on Liangshan Marsh. The prefect has sent him to clean out our mountain strongholds on Peach Blossom, Two-Dragon and White Tiger, so that he may be given another army and take Liangshan and get his revenge. Our leaders beseech you great chieftains to come with armed forces and save us. When all this is over, we will be glad to pay tribute."

"We defend our own mountain and fortress. As a rule we don't go to anyone's rescue," Yang Zhi said to Wu Song and the Tattooed Monk. "But if we don't help, we'll damage the prestige of the gallant fraternity, for one thing. For another, if we let that lout capture Peach Blossom Mountain, he'll look

on us with contempt. Let's leave Zhang Qing, Sun the Witch,
Shi En and Cao Zheng to hold the fort. Then we three can
take a little trip."

He mustered five hundred foot soldiers and sixty cavalrymen.
Each donned his armor and equipment, and all headed for
Peach Blossom Mountain.

When Li Zhong heard the news from Two-Dragon Moun-
tain, he led three hundred brigands down as reinforcements.
Huyan Zhuo rushed his entire complement to block their path.
He deployed his men and, brandishing his rods, rode out against
Li Zhong.

Li was from Dingyuan in Haozhou Prefecture, where his
family, for generations, had earned their livelihood by their
skill at arms. Because of his stalwart physique, he was known
as the Tiger-Fighting General. But in his clash with Huyan
he discovered he had met his match. After ten rounds or so,
he could see it was going badly. He parried his adversary's
weapons and fled.

Huyan, with a low opinion of Li's fighting ability, chased him
up the mountain. Zhou Tong the Little King was at mid-point
on the slope. He promptly threw down stones like goose eggs.
Huyan hurriedly turned his mount and returned to the foot
of the mountain. He found his government soldiers shouting
in alarm.

"What are you yelling about?" he demanded.

"There, in the distance. A body of men and horses racing
this way!" exclaimed the rear guard.

Huyan looked beyond them. A big fat monk on a white
horse was leading a contingent, trailed by a rising cloud of
dust. It was Sagacious Lu the Tattooed Monk.

"Where is that prick who was beaten at Liangshan Marsh?"
he was roaring. "How dare you come here and bluster?"

"I'm going to kill you first, bald donkey," Huyan responded,
"to work off the rage inside me!"

Lu twirled his iron Buddhist staff, Huyan waved his rods,
the horses met, the opposing forces shouted. The two men

fought forty or fifty rounds with neither emerging the victor.

"This monk is fantastic," Huyan marvelled to himself.

On both sides trumpets blared and the contestants withdrew to rest. But after a short interval, Huyan grew impatient. Again he rode his steed into the arena. "Come out, thief of a monk," he cried. "Let's fight to a finish!"

Lu was about to meet the challenge when Yang Zhi said: "Rest a bit longer, brother. Watch me nab this oaf!"

Waving his sabre, he rode forth and clashed with Huyan. Forty or fifty rounds they fought with neither vanquishing the other.

Huyan was filled with admiration. "Where did they get two like these?" he wondered. "Truly remarkable. They never learned such jousting in the greenwood!"

Impressed by Huyan's superb skill with arms, Yang Zhi broke off the engagement, turned his horse and galloped back to his position. Huyan didn't give chase, but also turned his mount around. Both sides withdrew their forces.

"This is our first venture here," Sagacious Lu said to Yang Zhi. "We'd better not camp too close to them. Let's pull back another twenty *li*. We'll come out and fight again tomorrow."

With their men, they crossed to a nearby hollow and there set up a camp.

Huyan brooded in his tent. "I expected taking this gang of cheap robbers would be as easy as snapping bamboo," he thought. "Who knew I'd run into such adversaries. What rotten luck!"

He could see no way out of his dilemma. Just then a messenger arrived from Prefect Murong.

"The General is ordered to return at once with his soldiers and defend the city," the man said. "Bandits from White Tiger Mountain under Kong Ming and Kong Liang are on their way to raid the prison. To prevent anything from happening to the prefectural government, the General is requested to hurry back with his forces."

This was just the excuse Huyan was looking for. He set out for Qingzhou with his infantry and cavalry that very night.

The next day Sagacious Lu, Yang Zhi and Wu Song led their brigands, waving banners and yelling, down the mountain. To their astonishment, there was not a sign of their foe. Li Zhong and Zhou Tong came down with men from their own mountain and invited the three chieftains to their stronghold. There, they slaughtered sheep and horses and spread a feast in their honor. At the same time they dispatched scouts to find out what was happening on the road beyond.

As Huyan was leading his contingent back to the city he saw a body of men and horses already on the outskirts of Qingzhou. At their head were Kong Ming the Comet and Kong Liang the Flaming Star — sons of Squire Kong who lived at the foot of White Tiger Mountain. In a quarrel with a local rich man, they had slaughtered him and his entire household. Next, they gathered six or seven hundred men, occupied White Tiger Mountain, and took to pillage and plunder. Prefect Murong arrested their uncle Kong Bin, who lived in the city and threw him into jail. They had been heading for Qingzhou to get him out. Now, they found themselves confronted by Huyan Zhuo and his contingent.

The two sides spread out and engaged in battle. Huyan rode to the front of his position. Prefect Murong, watching from a tower on the city wall, saw Kong Ming, with levelled lance astride a charger, attack Huyan. They met and fought over twenty rounds. Huyan wanted to display his prowess before the prefect. He noted that Kong Ming, whose skill with arms was not exceptional, was now entirely on the defensive. Huyan drove in close and snatched him off his horse.

Kong Liang and his men turned and fled. Murong, from the tower, shouted for Huyan to go after them. The government soldiers pressed hard and captured more than a hundred of the foe. Badly defeated, Kong Liang and the rest of his forces ran in all directions. Towards evening, they put up in an ancient temple.

After capturing Kong Ming, Huyan led him into the city and presented himself before the prefect. Murong was delighted. He directed that a rack be placed around the prisoner's neck, and that he be confined in the same jail as his uncle Kong Bin. The prefect rewarded the troops and entertained Huyan. He asked about the brigands on Peach Blossom Mountain.

"I thought I had only to stretch out my hand and take them, as easily as catching turtles in a jug," said Huyan. "But unexpectedly a band of robbers came to their rescue. Among them was a monk and a big blue-faced fellow. I fought them both, but couldn't defeat either. Their skill is out of the ordinary. It's not the usual style of robbers in the greenwood. So I was prevented from capturing the bandits."

"That monk," said Murong, "is Lu Da, who was a major under Governor-General Zhong of the Yanan border region. Later, he shaved off his hair and became a monk, and he's now known as Sagacious Lu the Tattooed Monk. The big fellow with blue tinged complexion was once a aide in the palace in the Eastern Capital. He's called Yang Zhi the Blue-Faced Beast. Their third leader is Wu Song, known as the Pilgrim. He's the Constable Wu who killed the tiger on Jingyang Ridge.

"These three occupy Two-Dragon Mountain, from where they rob and plunder. We've sent troops to catch them several times, but they killed four or five of our officers. We haven't caught one of them to this day!"

"Their skill is superb. So that's who they are — Palace Aide Yang and Major Lu. They certainly deserve their reputation! But don't worry, Excellency. You have me here. I'll nab every one of them and turn them over!"

The prefect was very pleased. He gave a feast in Huyan's honor, then invited him to rest in a guest-house. Of that we'll say no more.

Kong Liang was leading the remnants of his beaten unit along the road. Suddenly, a band of men and horses emerged from among the trees. The bold fellow at their head was Wu Song the Pilgrim. Kong Liang rolled from his saddle and kowtowed.

"I trust all has gone well with you, sir warrior!"

Wu Song hastily returned the salutation. He raised Kong Liang to his feet.

"I heard you two brothers had occupied White Tiger Mountain and formed a righteous gathering," he said. "Several times I intended to pay my respects. But I wasn't able to leave our stronghold, and the road to your place is difficult, so I couldn't get to see you. What brings you here today?"

Kong Liang told how his brother was captured while trying to rescue their uncle Kong Bin.

"Don't be upset, friend," said Wu Song. "I have six or seven brothers with me in our band on Two-Dragon Mountain. The other day Li Zhong and Zhou Tong on Peach Blossom Mountain were strongly attacked by government troops from Qingzhou, and they asked for our assistance. Lu and Yang went with some of our forces and fought Huyan Zhuo all day. For some reason, he and his men suddenly left in the night. The Peach Blossom Mountain people feasted Lu and Yang and me and presented us with a snowy hoofed steed. I'm taking our first contingent back to our stronghold. Lu and Yang are following and will soon be here. I'll tell them to raid Qingzhou and save your uncle and brother. How will that be?"

Kong Liang thanked Wu Song. After a considerable wait, Sagacious Lu and Yang Zhi arrived with their cavalry. Wu Song introduced Kong Liang.

"I once met Song Jiang in his manor and put him to a lot of trouble," Wu said. "Today, for the sake of chivalry, we can combine the forces of the three mountain strongholds, attack Qingzhou, kill the prefect, capture Huyan Zhuo, and divide the money and grain in the storehouses for the use of our various bands. What do you say?"

"Just what I was thinking," asserted Sagacious Lu. "Let's notify Peach Blossom Mountain, and ask Li Zhong and Zhou Tong to bring their men. The three bands can strike Qingzhou together."

"It's a sturdily built city, its armed forces are strong, and Huyan Zhuo is a courageous fellow," mused Yang Zhi. "I don't mean to disparage us, but if you want to succeed you'd better take my advice."

"Let's hear your strategy, brother," said Wu Song.

"A large force is needed to take Qingzhou,"said Yang Zhi. "We know that the famous Song Jiang, called the Timely Rain in the gallant fraternity, is in Liangshan Marsh. Huyan Zhuo is his enemy. Our Two-Dragon Mountain band will co-operate with the Kong brother's band. We will wait here till the men from Peach Blossom Mountain arrive, and go with them to assault the town. Brother Kong Liang, you must travel at top speed to Mount Liangshan and beseech Song Jiang to join our attack. That is the best plan, because you and he are great friends. What do you brothers think?"

"Sounds all right to me," said Sagacious Lu. "I've heard a lot of good things about Song Jiang, though I'm sorry to say we've never met. People chatter about him so much they've nearly made me deaf. He must be quite a man, to be so famous. I went to see him when he was with Hua Rong in Fort Clear Winds. But by the time I got there, he was gone. Never mind. Kong Liang, you want to rescue your brother. You'd better hurry and ask Song Jiang's help. We'll stay here and start the battle against those pricks."

Kong Liang directed his men to remain with Sagacious Lu. He took only one companion. Disguised as a merchant, he set out swiftly for Liangshan Marsh.

Sagacious Lu, Yang Zhi and Wu Song went to their mountain strongholds and fetched Shi En and Cao Zheng and about two hundred fighters. On Peach Blossom Mountain when Li Zhong and Zhou Tong received the news they brought their entire force, except for forty or fifty left to hold the fort. All contingents converged outside the town and prepared for the assault. Of that we'll say no more.

On leaving Qingzhou, Kong Liang followed a winding road till he came to the tavern on the edge of Liangshan Marsh run by Li Li, who was called Hell's Summoner. There he stopped to buy some wine and ask the way. Kong Liang and his companion were strangers to Li. He invited them to be seated.

"Where are you from?" he queried.

"Qingzhou," said Kong Liang.

"Who is it you wish to see in the Marsh?"

"A friend of mine, on the mountain."

"Important chieftains live in that fortress on the mountain. How can you go there?"

"It's a chieftain I'm seeking — Song Jiang."

"In that case I have an obligation to you." Li Li ordered his attendants to serve wine.

"We've never met," said Kong Liang. "Why so courteous?"

"Anyone seeking a chieftain in the fortress is sure to be one of our kind, an old friend. He must be properly received and his arrival reported."

"I am Kong Liang, from a manor at the foot of White Tiger Mountain."

"I've heard brother Song Jiang mention you. We'll escort you to the stronghold today."

The two drank ceremonial cups of wine. Li Li opened a window overlooking the water and shot a whistling arrow. From the reeds on the opposite side of the cove a brigand propelled a boat. It stopped beside the tavern. Li Li invited Kong Liang on board. The craft was sculled to the Shore of Golden Sands, and the men began to climb.

Kong Liang was impressed by the bristling array of weapons at each of the three gates through which they had to pass. "I heard that the stronghold was well equipped," he said to himself, "but I never thought it was on such a scale!"

Brigands had gone ahead to report, and Song Jiang came down to greet him. Kong Liang hastily knelt and kowtowed.

"What brings you here, brother?" Song Jiang asked. Kong Liang burst into tears. Song Jiang said: "If you're in any danger or difficulty, don't hesitate to speak. We'll help you, no matter what it is. Brother, please rise."

"After we parted, my old father died. My brother Kong

Ming quarreled with a well-to-do neighbor and killed him and his entire family. The authorities were hot on his trail, so we went up White Tiger Mountain and formed a band of six or seven hundred. We lived by robbery and pillage. Murong, the prefect of Qingzhou, arrested Kong Bin, our uncle whose home was in town, and threw him into prison with a heavy rack around his neck. My brother and I staged a raid to rescue him, but outside the walls we were met by Huyan Zhuo who wields two rods. Brother fought, and Huyan captured him. They took him into Qingzhou and put him in prison also. There's no guarantee they won't kill him.

"I was chased and had to run. The next day, I met Wu Song. He introduced me to his companions. One was Sagacious Lu the Tattooed Monk. The other was Yang Zhi the Blue-Faced Beast. We were like old friends the moment we met. We discussed the rescue of my brother. Wu Song said: 'We'll ask Lu and Yang to get Li Zhong and Zhou Tong from Peach Blossom Mountain, and join the forces from three strongholds in an attack on Qingzhou. You hurry to Mount Liangshan and request Song Jiang to help save your uncle and your brother.' That's why I'm here. I pray, for the sake of my departed father, that you rescue them. I'll be eternally grateful."

"It will be easy. Don't worry. Come pay your respects to our leader Chao Gai. We'll talk it over together."

Song Jiang presented Kong Liang to Chao Gai, Wu Yong, Gongsun Sheng, and the other chieftains. He related that Huyan Zhuo had gone to Qingzhou and cast his lot in with Prefect Murong and had recently captured Kong Ming, and that Kong Liang was seeking his rescue.

Chao Gai said: "Since the two brave brothers out of chivalry and righteousness, desire to rescue their uncle, and since you, brother Song, are their friend, we should indeed assist them. But you've ridden forth on expeditions many times, brother. This time you hold the fort and let me go."

"You're our highest leader. We mustn't lightly put you to any trouble," said Song Jiang. "This is a personal matter. Kong Liang has come all this distance to see me. He'd be embarrassed if I didn't go personally. I'd prefer to handle this alone with a few of our brothers."

Immediately, chieftains high and low pushed forward and volunteered. "We'll give our all," they cried. "Only take us along!"

Song Jiang was very pleased. That day a feast was given for Kong Liang, and Song Jiang direct Pei Xuan to muster men for the expedition and divide them into five contingents. The vanguard was to be led by Hua Rong, Qin Ming, Yan Shun and Stumpy Tiger Wang. The second unit was under Mu Hong, Yang Xiong, Xie Zhen and Xie Bao. The chief generals Song Jiang, Wu Yong, Lü Fang and Guo Sheng commanded the central force. The fourth contingent was headed by Zhu Tong, Chai Jin, Li Jun and Zhang Heng, while the unit bringing up the rear was under Sun Li, Yang Lin, Ou Peng and Ling Zhen.

When the five battalions were mustered they had fighters on horse and on foot totalling three thousand, under twenty commanders. The other chieftains remained with Chao Gai to hold the fortress. Song Jiang took his leave of Chao Gai and went down the mountain with Kong Liang and the brigand force.

Their march was uneventful, and they harmed none of the prefectures and counties along the way. They soon reached Qingzhou. Kong Liang went on ahead and informed Sagacious Lu. The Tattooed Monk and his companions prepared a welcome. When Song Jiang and his central battalion arrived, Wu Song led Sagacious Lu, Yang Zhi, Li Zhong, Zhou Tong, Shi En and Cao Zheng forward to greet him. Song asked Sagacious to be seated.

"I've long known of your fame, brother," said the monk, "but I never had the chance to pay my respects. I'm very happy to meet you today."

"I don't deserve such courtesy," Song Jiang protested. "In the gallant fraternity your virtue is well known, Reverend. To be able to look upon your benevolent face is the greatest joy of my life!"

Yang Zhi rose and bowed. "I passed through Liangshan Marsh earlier," he said, "and the chieftains were kind enough to ask me to stay. But I stupidly declined. Today, you call here within sight of our mountain lair. Nothing under Heaven could please me more!"

"Everyone in the gallant fraternity has heard of Yang Zhi. My only regret is that we hadn't met sooner!"

Sagacious Lu ordered that wine be served, and introductions were made all around.

The next day Song Jiang asked about the situation in the prefectural town.

"After Kong Liang left, we had four or five clashes, with no clear result," said Yang Zhi. "Qingzhou's mainstay is Huyan Zhuo. If we capture him, we can push into that town like hot water through snow."

Wu Yong laughed. "He can be taken, but by guile, not by force."

"How do you propose to do it?" Song Jiang asked.

Wu Yong softly outlined his plan. Song Jiang was delighted. "Very shrewd!"

That day he issued his instructions, and the next morning they proceeded to the walls of Qingzhou. They surrounded the town, beat their drums, waved their pennants, shouted, and shook their weapons. Murong was informed, and he hurriedly summoned Huyan Zhuo.

"Those bandits have brought help from Liangshan Marsh. What are we going to do?" demanded the prefect.

"Don't worry, Your Excellency," said Huyan. "By coming here they've lost their favorable terrain. It's only in the marsh that they can act up. Now that they've left their lair, we can nab them as fast as they come. They've nowhere to deploy. Please go up on the ramparts, Prefect, and watch me slaughter those rogues!"

Huyan quickly donned his armor and mounted his charger. He shouted for the gates to be opened and the drawbridge to be lowered. He rode forth at the head of a thousand infantry and cavalry, and spread them out in battle formation. From Song Jiang's contingent a horseman emerged. He was carrying a wolf-toothed cudgel. In a stentorian voice he cursed the prefect.

"Grafter! People-injuring thief! You've destroyed my home,

and today I'm going to get my revenge!"

Murong recognized Qin Ming. "You were an officer of the imperial court," he shouted. "The state treated you well. How dare you rebel! When I capture you I'll have you smashed into ten thousand pieces! Nab that outlaw for me, first!" he yelled to Huyan.

Flourishing his rods, Huyan rode towards his objective. Qin Ming gave his steed full rein and galloped to meet Huyan, waving his wolf-toothed cudgel. They were a well-matched pair, and they fought nearly fifty rounds with neither vanquishing the other.

Murong felt the contest was lasting too long. He was afraid Huyan would lose. Hurriedly, he had the gongs summon his troops back to the town. Qin Ming did not pursue the departing foe, but returned to his own position. Song Jiang instructed his commanders to withdraw fifteen *li* and make camp.

Inside the town, Huyan got off his horse and reported to the prefect. "I was about to take that Qin Ming," he said. "Why did you sound retreat, Your Excellency?"

"You'd fought many rounds. I feared you were tired, so I called our forces back to rest, temporarily. Before he and Hua Rong rebelled, Qin Ming was commanding general here. The knave is not to be underestimated."

"I'll take that treacherous bandit, Your Excellency, rest assured. When I fought him just now he was getting clumsy with his rods. Next time, watch me smash him!"

"I know what a hero you are. But tomorrow, I want you to break open a gap in the enemy lines so that I can send out three men. I shall dispatch one to the Eastern Capital to ask for assistance, and two to neighboring districts and prefectures to raise troops to help capture the bandits."

"Your Excellency is indeed far-sighted."

The prefect wrote out a request for assistance, selected three officers, and made the necessary arrangements.

Huyan returned to his quarters, removed his armor and rested. Before dawn the next day an officer entered and reported: "On a hill outside the north gate three horsemen are observing the town. The one in the middle is wearing a red gown and is riding a white steed. The man on the right is Hua Rong. We don't recognize the man on the left, but he's dressed as a Taoist."

"That man in red is Song Jiang. The Taoist must be his general, Wu Yong. Don't alert them. Muster a hundred cavalry and bag all three."

Huyan hastily put on his armor and mounted. Rods in hand, leading his hundred horsemen, he had the north gate quietly opened and the drawbridge lowered, and rode swiftly towards the hill. Song Jiang, Wu Yong and Hua Rong continued staring at the town. Huyan raced up the slope. Only then did the three turn their mounts and walk them slowly away.

Before a grove of withered trees they again reined in. In hot pursuit, Huyan had just raced to the edge of the grove when shouts rang out and horse and rider dropped into a concealed pit. From both sides fifty or sixty men snared Huyan with hooked poles, hauled him out, and tied him up. Others extracted his horse.

By then the rest of Huyan's troop came charging up. Calmly fitting arrows to his bow, Hua Rong brought down the first five or six. Those behind halted abruptly, yanked their steeds around and, yelling, galloped off.

Song Jiang returned to camp and took his seat. Knife-wearing attendants pushed Huyan Zhuo before him. Song immediately rose and ordered that his bonds be removed. He personally conducted Huyan to a chair and greeted him respectfully.

"Why are you doing this?" Huyan asked.

"Would I be ungrateful to the imperial court?" Song Jiang retorted. "I was hard pressed by corrupt officials and forced to commit a crime. I've had to seek refuge in this marsh while awaiting an imperial pardon. I never expected to stir into action so mighty a general, for whom I have such great admiration. It was very wrong of me, and I beg your forgiveness."

"I am your prisoner. Ten thousand deaths would be too light a punishment. Yet you treat me with such courtesy!"

"Never would I presume to harm you. Heaven is my

witness."

"Is it your wish, respected brother, that I should go to the Eastern Capital and ask for a royal pardon to bring to your mountain?"

"You couldn't possibly do that, General! Marshal Gao is a narrow-hearted villain. He forgets a man's large accomplishments and remembers only his small failings. You've lost a lot of troops, money and grain. He'd surely hold you culpable. Han Tao, Peng Qi and Ling Zhen have all joined our band. If you don't scorn our mountain stronghold as too humble, I'd be happy to relinquish to you my place as chieftain. When the court has use for us and issues its imperial pardon, we can once again serve our country with our utmost efforts."

Huyan hesitated for several minutes. But, firstly, since he was one of the stars of Heavenly Spirits, he naturally was of the same chivalrous mentality. And, secondly, he was overwhelmed by Song Jiang's courtesy and reasonableness. With a sigh, he knelt.

"It's not that I lack loyalty to the government. But your exceeding gallantry leaves me no choice but to agree. I'll follow you faithfully. The situation being what it is, there's no alternative."

Song Jiang was very pleased. He introduced Huyan to the other chieftains and directed Li Zhong and Zhou Tong to return his mount the Ebony Steed Which Treads in Snow. Then the chieftains conferred on how to rescue Kong Ming.

Wu Yong said: "If Huyan can trick them into opening the gates, we'll take the town easily. It will also put an end to any thought he may have of rejoining them."

Song Jiang went to Huyan and said: "It's not loot I'm after, but Kong Ming and his uncle are imprisoned in Qingzhou. We can't save them unless you get the town to open the gates."

"Since you've been kind enough to accept me, of course I'll do my best."

That night ten chieftains disguised themselves as government troops and rode forth with Huyan at their head. At the town moat they halted.

"Open the gates," shouted the general. "I've escaped and returned!"

Soldiers on the wall recognized Huyan's voice and hastily reported to Murong. The prefect had been brooding over the loss of the general. Now, hearing that he had come back, Murong was delighted. He jumped on his horse and rode to the town wall. He saw Huyan with about a dozen mounted men. He couldn't make out their faces in the dark, but he knew the general's voice.

"How were you able to return?" Murong called.

"Those knaves trapped my horse and took me to their camp. Some of my commanders sneaked this mount to me, and we got away together."

Murong ordered his soldiers to open the gates and lower the drawbridge. As the chieftains entered the town, he came forward to greet them. With one blow of his cudgel, Qin Ming knocked the prefect from his saddle. The Xie brothers set the town to the torch. Ou Peng and Stumpy Tiger Wang dashed up the wall and killed or scattered the defenders.

Song Jiang and the main force, seeing that Qingzhou was on fire, surged in. He transmitted an urgent order that the townspeople were not to be harmed, but to empty the town's treasury and grain stores. Kong Ming and his uncle and Kong Bin's family were rescued from the prison. Song Jiang directed that the fires be extinguished. The prefect's entire family, young and old, were killed, and all their possessions distributed among the marauders.

At daybreak a count was made of those families whose homes had been damaged by the fires, and they were given grain as relief payments. The money and grain taken from government stores came to nearly six hundred cartloads. Over two hundred good horses were also captured. A great feast of celebration was held in the main hall of the prefectural government, and the leaders of the three mountain strongholds were invited to go together to the fortress on Mount Liangshan.

Li Zhong and Zhou Tong sent people to Peach Blossom Mountain with orders to collect men and horses, and as much money and grain as possible, and then set fire to the stronghold and abandon it. Sagacious Lu dispatched Shi En and Cao Zheng to Two-Dragon Mountain. There, with Zhang Qing and his wife Sun the Witch, they assembled the brigands, loaded their money and grain, and burned down their stronghold in Precious Pearl Monastery.

In a few days time, the forces from the three mountains completed their preparations, and the entire body, led by Song Jiang, set out for the Mount Liangshan fortress. Song put Hua Rong, Qin Ming, Huyan Zhuo and Zhu Tong in the van to clear the way. Not a single prefecture or county was harmed during the march. Villagers, carrying their babes and supporting their old folk, burned incense and kowtowed in greeting.

The cavalcade reached Liangshan Marsh several days later. Chieftains of the water forces met them with boats, and Chao Gai and the leaders of the infantry and cavalry were awaiting them when they landed on the Shore of Golden Sands. They climbed together to the big stronghold, entered Fraternity Hall and took their seats.

A big feast was laid to celebrate the addition of twelve new chieftains: Huyan Zhuo, Sagacious Lu, Yang Zhi, Wu Song, Shi En, Cao Zheng, Zhang Qing, Sun the Witch, Li Zhong, Zhou Tong, Kong Ming and Kong Liang. Lin Chong rose and thanked Sagacious Lu for his aid in the rescue.

"I've thought about you a lot after we parted in Cangzhou," said the monk. "Has there been any news of your wife?"

"After I took over from Wang Lun, I sent someone home to fetch her. He found that Marshal Gao's wicked son had kept after her so hard that she finally killed herself. Her father was very depressed, and took ill and died."

Yang Zhi related how he met with Lin Chong when Wang Lun was still in control of the lair. All agreed that this had been fated. It was no accident. Chao Gai told the story of the capture of the birthday gifts on Yellow Earth Ridge. Everyone laughed heartily.

More feasts were given for several successive days. Of that we'll say no more.

The fortress had been strengthened by many men and horses,

and Song Jiang was exceedingly pleased. He ordered Tang Long to oversee all metalwork and manufacture many kinds of weapons and armor. Hou Jian, who he put in charge of banners and clothing, added flags and pennants of every size and shape, embroidered with dragons, tigers, bears and leopards, and decorated with golden standards, white tassels, crimson fringes and black covers. On all sides of the mountain broad glacis were constructed. On the western and southern roads two taverns were rebuilt, both to receive visiting gallants and to listen for and quickly report the approach of government troops. Zhang Qing and his wife Sun the Witch, who originally had been innkeepers, were given charge of the tavern on the west. The south side tavern remained under Sun Xin and his wife Mistress Gu. Zhu Gui and Yue Ho continued to run the tavern on the east side, and Li Li and Shi Qian the one on the north. More barricades were set up in each of the three passes, and chieftains assigned to their defense. All were abjured to perform strictly their defined duties.

CHAPTER 23
Chao the Heavenly King Is Hit by an Arrow in Zengtou Village

Song Jiang and his forces went back to Liangshan Marsh. As they were about to ford the river at the edge of the marsh, a big fellow on the road near the reeds saw Song Jiang and kowtowed. Song hastily dismounted and raised the man to his feet.

"What is your name, sir, and where are you from?"

"My family name is Duan, my given name Jingzhu. Because of my red hair and yellow beard, I'm called the Golden Dog. My family are from Zhuozhou Prefecture, and I earn my living rustling horses in the north. This spring I stole a splendid animal north of the Spear Range. It's white as snow, without a single hair of a different color. From head to tail it's ten feet long, and stands eight feet high from hoofs to back. It can cover a thousand *li* in a day. It's famed throughout the north as the White Jade Lion That Glows in the Night. It belonged to a prince of the Tartars. When it was put out to graze at the foot of Spear Range, I nabbed it. In the gallant fraternity the Timely Rain is famous, but I never had a chance to meet you. I wanted to present you with the horse as a mark of my respect. But while passing through the village of Zengtou, southwest of the prefectural town of Lingzhou, it was seized from me by the fifth son of the Zeng family. I told him it belonged to Song Jiang of Liangshan Marsh, but the churl was very insulting, and I dared say no more. I got away as quickly as I could. I've come here specially to inform you."

Song Jiang took a liking to the thin rough-looking fellow. In spite of his odd appearance, he was clearly not an ordinary person.

"Come with us to the stronghold," he said. "We'll talk about it there." He took Duan in his boat and they crossed to the Shore of Golden Sands.

Chao Gai, the Heavenly King, and the other chieftains, escorted the returning leaders to Fraternity Hall. Song Jiang introduced Fan Rui, Xiang Chong and Li Gun to the chieftains. Duan and the three greeted them with respect. Drums beat clamorously, and a feast was held in celebration.

More and more men were joining the mountain citadel. Bold fellows from all over came like the wind. And so Song Jiang instructed Li Yun and Tao Zongwang to supervise the building of new dwellings, and to construct additional forts on every side.

Duan spoke again of the merits of the horse. Song Jiang sent Dai Zong the Marvellous Traveller to the village of Zengtou to inquire about it. In four or five days Dai returned.

"Zengtou has something over three thousand families," he told the chieftains. "One is known as the Zeng Family Establishment. It is headed by Zeng the Elder, who comes originally from the land of the Tartars. He has five sons, called the Five Tigers of the Zeng Family. Their names, in order of age, are: Tu, Mi, Suo, Kui and Sheng. Their instructor is Shi Wengong, and his assistant is Su Ding. The village is defended by six or seven thousand men and stockaded camps. They've built more than fifty cage carts, boasting there is no room on this earth for both us and them. They say they will capture all of our chieftains, that we are enemies.

"The thousand li horse known as the Jade Lion is ridden by the instructor Shi Wengong. Even more infuriating, the wretch has composed a rhyme which he's taught all the kids in the village. It goes like this:

When our horses' bridles jingle
God and demons with fear tingle.
Iron carts plus iron locks,
Prisoners nailed in iron stocks.
Liangshan Marsh we'll cleanly flush,

Chao Gai to the capital we'll rush,
And capture Timely Rain — that's Song,
And his war mentor Wu Yong.
Five Zeng tigers boldly stand,
Famed far and wide throughout the land.

Chao Gai was enraged. "How dare those animals be so unmannerly!" he fumed. "I'm going down there personally. If I don't capture those rogues I won't return!"

"You're the leader of our fortress, brother," said Song Jiang. "You mustn't lightly take action. Let me go."

"It's not that I want to steal your thunder," said Chao Gai, "but you've gone many times. You must be weary from combat. This time I'm going. Next time, brother, it will be your turn."

Song Jiang pleaded in vain. The furious Chao Gai selected five thousand men and twenty chieftains and set forth. The remainder stayed with Song Jiang to guard the stronghold. Chao divided his forces into three brigades and went down the mountain, ready to march on Zengtou Village.

Song Jiang, Wu Yong and Gongsun saw them to the Shore of Golden Sands. While they were drinking a sudden wind snapped the pole supporting Chao Gai's standard. Everyone blanched.

"An evil omen," said Wu Yong. "Choose another day for your expedition, brother."

"The wind snaps your standard, brother, just as you're about to set forth. It's not auspicious for military action," said Song Jiang. "Wait a bit longer and then deal with those knaves. There'll still be time."

"The movement of wind and clouds is nothing to be alarmed about," retorted Chao Gai. "Now is the time, in the warmth of spring. If we wait until they build up their strength and then attack, it will be too late. Don't try to stop me. I'm going, come what may!"

Song Jiang couldn't dissuade him. With his troops, Chao Gai ferried across the river. Sunk in gloom, Song returned to the fortress. He sent Dai Zong down to watch developments and report.

Chao Gai with his five thousand men and twenty chieftains neared the village of Zengtou. Confronting them was a stockaded camp. The following morning Chao went with the chieftains for a closer look. Clearly, the village was strongly fortified.

Suddenly, from a grove of willows seven or eight hundred men emerged. At their head was a bold fellow — Kui, fourth son of the Zeng family.

"You bandits from Liangshan Marsh are all rebels," he shouted. "I've been meaning to turn you over to the authorities and claim the reward, and now Heaven sends you right into my arms! Get off your horses and be bound. What are you waiting for!"

Chao Gai was very angry. As he turned his head he saw one of the chieftains riding forth to do battle with Kui. It was Lin Chong, the first to form the chivalrous band on Mount Liangshan.

The two horses met, and the warriors fought more than twenty rounds, with neither vanquishing the other. Kui realized he was no match for Lin Chong. He wheeled his mount and, lance in hand, rode for the willow grove. Lin Chong reined in his steed and did not pursue. Chao Gai led his forces back to camp. There, they discussed strategy for attacking the village.

"Let's go tomorrow and provoke a battle," Lin Chong proposed. "We'll see what their strength actually is, then we can talk some more."

The next morning they marched with five thousand men to the broad plain outside the entrance to Zengtou, took up positions, beat their drums and shouted. Cannon thundered from the village and a large body of men rode forth, led by seven bold fellows in a single line. In the middle was the instructor Shi Wengong. To his left was his assistant Su Ding; to his right the eldest son, Tu. Continuing to the left were Mi and Kui; further right were Sheng and Suo. All were clad in armor from head to foot. An arrow fitted to his bow, Shi sat the thousand-*li* Jade Lion horse. He held also a crescent-bladed halberd.

After three rolls of the drums, several cage carts were pushed out from the Zeng family position and placed to the fore. Tu pointed at his adversaries.

"Rebellious bandits," he shouted, "do you see these carts? If we simply kill you, we won't be real men. We're going to nab every one of you, lock you in the carts and deliver you to the Eastern Capital, just to show you how tough we Five Tigers really are! Surrender now, while you still have the chance, then we'll see!"

Chao Gai, enraged, levelled his lance and galloped towards Tu. To protect him, the other chieftains also charged, and the two sides were soon locked in combat. The Zeng family forces retreated step by step into the village. Lin Chong and Huyan Zhuo slew mightily to east and west, providing close cover for Chao Gai. But Lin could see that the prospects were poor. He hastily pulled back and reassembled his men. Both sides were strewn with casualties. Chao Gai returned to camp very depressed.

"Don't take it to heart, brother," the chieftains urged. "Worry will only injure your health. Brother Song Jiang also has setbacks at times in battle, but he wins in the end. The fighting was confused today. Both sides suffered casualties. But we haven't lost. No need to feel bad!"

Chao Gai said: "I'm not in a good mood, that's all." He remained in camp for three days. Though each day his troops went to challenge the foe, not a man came forth from Zengtou.

On the fourth day, two monks called on Chao Gai. They were escorted by several of the brigand soldiers. Chao received them outside his tent. The two dropped to their knees and kowtowed.

"We are custodians of the Fahua Monastery east of Zengtou," they said. "Those Five Tiger sons constantly harrass our monastery, demanding gold and silver and money. There's nothing they won't do. We know their layout in detail, and we've come to show you how to get inside and take their fortifications. If you can eliminate them it will be a blessing."

Chao Gai was very pleased. He invited the monks to be seated, and had them served wine.

"Don't believe them, brother," Lin Chong advised. "How do you know it isn't a trick?"

"We are men who have renounced the material world. We wouldn't dare to deceive," protested the monks. "We've long known of the righteous behavior of the men of Liangshan Marsh. You never harm the common people wherever you go. We've come to join you. Why should we want to fool you chieftains? Besides, the Zeng family forces could hardly defeat your great army. Why be suspicious?"

"You needn't doubt them, brother," said Chao Gai. "We'll miss a big opportunity. I'll go myself, tonight, to see."

"Please don't, brother," Lin Chong urged. "Let me raid the village with half our men. You wait outside with reinforcements."

"If I don't go personally, would our forces be willing to attack? You remain with half our troops as reinforcements."

"Who will you take with you?"

"Ten chieftains and twenty-five hundred men."

That evening a meal was prepared and eaten. The bells were removed from the horses' bridles, the men wore stick gags, for a swift night march. Silently, they followed the two monks to the Fahua Monastery. It was very ancient. Chao Gai dismounted and went inside. There was no one around.

"Why are there no monks in a monastery of this size?" he queried.

"Those animals of the Zeng family caused so much trouble that most of them were compelled to return to secular life. Only the abbot and a few retainers remain. They're living in the courtyard where the tower is. Stay here temporarily. A little later, we'll lead you into the stockade of those rogues."

"Where is it?"

"There are four stockades. The Zeng brothers are in the northern one. If you take that, the others won't matter. The

remaining three will quit."

"When shall we go?"

"It's now the second watch. We'll go at the third, and take them by surprise."

From Zengtou, they heard the measured beat of the watchman's drum. Later, they heard the drum sounding the half-watch. After that, they listened no more.

"The soldiers are all asleep," said the two monks. "We can go now."

They led the way. Chao Gai and the chieftains mounted and, with their men, left the monastery and followed. Before they had gone five *li*, the two monks had disappeared into the shadows.

The van was afraid to continue. The paths on all sides were tortuous and difficult. No homes or people could be seen. The forward troops became alarmed and informed Chao Gai.

Huyan Zhuo ordered a retreat. They had marched less than a hundred paces when on every side gongs crashed and drums pounded. Resounding yells shook the ground. Torches everywhere sprang to light.

Chao Gai and the chieftains hurriedly led their men in a withdrawal. They had just traversed two turns in the road when they ran into a troop of enemy cavalry, who showered them with arrows. One struck Chao Gai in the face, and he fell from his horse.

Huyan Zhuo and Yan Shun galloped off at top speed. Liu Tang and Bai Sheng behind them, put Chao back on his steed and fought their way out of the village. At the village entrance Lin Chong rushed up with reinforcements. Only then were they able to stem the foe. A wild melee continued until dawn, when both sides retired to their bases.

Lin Chong made a count of the troops. The three Ruan brothers, Song Wan and Du Qian had escaped by crossing the stream. Of the twenty-five hundred men who had gone in with Chao Gai only twelve or thirteen hundred were left. They had followed Ou Peng back to camp.

The chieftains came to see Chao Gai. An arrow was stuck in his cheek. They pulled it out. Blood flowed, and he fainted. On the arrow was the name of the instructor Shi Wengong. Lin Chong directed that a salve made for metal weapon wounds be applied. Chao Gai had been hit by a poisoned arrow. The venom was working, and he was unable to speak.

Lin Chong ordered that he be placed on a cart, and that the three Ruan brothers, plus Du Qian and Song Wan, escort him back to the mountain fortress. The fifteen chieftains remaining in the camp conferred.

"Who would have thought when brother Chao Gai the Heavenly King came down the mountain that such a thing would happen," they said. "The wind snapped the pole of his standard, and this was the fulfilment of that bad omen. We'll simply have to return to the stronghold. Zengtou Village can't be taken in a hurry."

"We'd better wait for orders from brother Song Jiang before pulling our troops out," Huyan Zhuo said.

The chieftains were morose, the men had no heart for battle. All wanted to go back to the fortress. That night at the fifth watch, as the earliest faint light began to appear, the fifteen chieftains were still sunk in gloom. For indeed, a snake cannot travel without a head, a bird without wings cannot fly. The chieftains sighed. They had no assurance that either an advance or a retreat would succeed.

Suddenly, a picket guarding the road rushed in and reported: "Five enemy columns heading this way. Their torches are without number!"

Lin Chong immediately mounted. Torchlight had turned the hills on three sides as bright as day. Shouting foe were rapidly advancing. The chieftains did not resist. At Lin's orders, they broke camp and withdrew.

The Zeng family forces pursued them fiercely. The two sides fought a running battle for sixty *li* before the brigands could break free. They counted their men. They had lost nearly seven hundred. It was a heavy defeat.

They hurriedly resumed the march in the direction of Liang-shan Marsh. Halfway there, they were met by Dai Zong, who transmitted a command: They were to bring their troops back to the stronghold. There, new plans would be formulated.

The chieftains complied. On their arrival, they went to see Chao Gai. He was no longer able to eat or drink, and his whole body was swollen. Song Jiang wept by his bedside. He personally applied poultices and fed Chao medicines. The chieftains all kept vigil outside the tent. By the third watch of the third day a great weight seemed to be depressing Chao's body. He turned his head to Song Jiang.

"Preserve your health, brother," he said. "Let whoever captures the bowman who slew me become the ruler of Liang-shan Marsh." Chao Gai closed his eyes and died.

To Song Jiang it was as if he had lost one of his parents. He cried until he was faint. The chieftains helped him out of the tent. They urged him to look after the stronghold's affairs.

"Don't grieve so, brother," Wu Yong and Gongsun Sheng advised. "Life and death are man's destiny. Why take it so hard? There are important matters awaiting your attention."

Song Jiang ceased his weeping. He directed that the body be laved in fragrant water, dressed in burial garments and hat, and displayed in Fraternity Hall. The chieftains performed sacrificial ceremonies. A coffin and inner casket were built and, after an auspicious day was selected, placed in the main hall. A spirit curtain was hung and a memorial tablet put before it, in the center. The inscription read: *Memorial Tablet of the Venerable Chao the Heavenly King and Leader of Liangshan Marsh.*

All the chieftains, from Song Jiang on down, dressed in deep mourning. The junior officers and the rank and file wore mourning head kerchiefs of white. The fatal arrow, broken in a vow of vengeance, lay before the altar. A long white banner was raised. Monks were invited to the citadel from a nearby monastery to offer prayers for the departed. Every day Song Jiang led the outlaws in mourning. He had no heart to attend to the affairs of the fortress.

Lin Chong, with Gongsun Sheng and Wu Yong, discussed the matter with the other chieftains. They decided to make Song Jiang their leader and take their orders from him. The following morning, bearing flowers, lanterns and candles, Lin Chong and the others invited Song Jiang, the Defender of Chivalry, to be seated in the Hall of Fraternity.

"Hear us, brother," said Wu Yong and Lin Chong. "A country cannot be governed without a sovereign, a household cannot be ruled without a master. Chao Gai, leader of our mountain stronghold, has gone to Heaven. There is no one to make decisions. Your name, brother, is world renowned. We wish to choose an auspicious day and invite you to become our leader. We will obey your commands."

"Remember the dying wish of Chao the Heavenly King: 'Let whoever captures the bowman who slew me become the ruler of Liangshan Marsh,'" said Song Jiang. "You all know about it, you mustn't forget. I haven't avenged him, or wiped out this debt. How can I accept?"

"That is what Chao said," Wu Yong admitted. "But we still haven't caught the culprit, and the stronghold cannot be without a leader. If you don't take over, brother, who else would dare? Who will command our forces? His wish was as you say. Why don't you accept temporarily? We'll work something out later."

"Putting it that way is reasonable. I'll accept the post for the time being. When Chao Gai is avenged, when someone captures Shi Wengong, no matter who, he must become our ruler."

Li Kui the Black Whirlwind shouted: "Not only are you right for leadership of Liangshan Marsh, brother — you'd make a fine emperor of the Song Dynasty!"

"You're talking wildly again, you wretched oaf. Stop your raving or I'll cut your tongue out!"

"Why should you do that? I'm inviting you to become emperor, not the head of some little group worshipping a local god!"

Wu Yong intervened. "The scamp has no sense of proportion. Don't trouble yourself with the likes of him. Please deal with important affairs."

Song Jiang burned incense and sat in the chair of the supreme leader. On his left was Wu Yong, on his right was Gongsun Sheng. The row to the left was headed by Lin Chong, Huyan Zhuo headed the row to the right. All paid their respects and took their seats. Song Jiang addressed them:

"I have accepted this post temporarily. I am completely reliant on your support, brothers. We must be of one heart and mind, united in our efforts, as close as bone and marrow, acting together to carry out Heaven's will. Today our fortress has many men. It's no longer like it was before. I'm asking you brothers to command six sets of fortifications. Fraternity Hall shall be known from now on as Loyalty Hall. We shall have four sets of land fortifications, front and back, left and right. On the rear of the mountain will be two small forts. On the front of the mountain will be three fortified passes. We'll also have a fort on the water at the foot of the mountain, plus a small fort on each of the banks. We shall ask you brothers to take charge."

From the day Song Jiang assumed the leadership of the stronghold in Liangshan Marsh, every chieftain, large and small, was happy and content. All gladly acceded to his directions.

CHAPTER 24
Wu Yong Cleverly Tricks the Jade Unicorn

One day Song Jiang conferred with the chieftains. He wanted to avenge Chao Gai and lead troops against the village of Zengtou. But Wu Yong was opposed.

"The mourning customs of the people must be respected, brother," he advised. "You must wait a hundred days before going into battle. It won't be too late."

Song Jiang heeded his words and remained in the stronghold. Every day he had prayers offered for Chao Gai's safe passage into Heaven.

One day he invited a monk whose Buddhist name was the Beatified and who was a member of the Longhua Monastery in Daming the Northern Capital. The Beatified, on his way to Jining, had been passing through Liangshan Marsh, and had been asked to the fortress to conduct services for the departed. During a vegetarian meal, Song Jiang, in the course of conversation, inquired whether the Northern Capital had any places or people of note.

"Surely you've heard of the Jade Unicorn of Hebei?" the monk retorted.

Song Jiang and Wu Yong suddenly remembered. "We're not yet old. We shouldn't be so forgetful at our age," Song exclaimed. "There's a rich man in the Northern Capital called Lu Junyi. His nickname is the Jade Unicorn. He's one of the Three Remarkable Men of Hebei Province. He lives in the capital city and is highly skilled in the martial arts. With cudgel and staff he has no equal. If we could get him to join our stronghold, we'd need have no fear of any government troops or police sent to catch us."

Wu Yong laughed. "Why so despondent, brother? You want him up here? There's nothing hard about that!"

"He's the head of one of the leading families of Daming. How can we induce him to become an outlaw?"

"I've been thinking of this for some time, though for the moment I'd forgotten. I have a plan that will bring him up the mountain."

"You're not known as the Wizard without cause. Will you tell us, please, Military Advisor, what your plan is?"

"With the aid of this facile three-inch tongue of mine, I shall go fearlessly to the Northern Capital and persuade Lu Junyi to come to our mountain," Wu Yong avowed. "It will be as easy as taking something out of a bag. You just put your hand in and you've got it. All I need is a rough courageous companion to go with me."

Before he had finished speaking, Li Kui the Black Whirlwind shouted: "Take me, brother Military Advisor."

"Desist, brother," Song Jiang cried. "If someone was needed for arson or murder, pillaging homes or raiding towns, you would be just right. This is a careful delicate operation. You're much too violent."

"You all scorn me because I'm ugly. That's why you won't let me go."

"It's not that. Daming is full of police. If anyone should recognize you, you'd be finished."

"That doesn't matter. No one is better suited for what the Military Advisor wants."

Wu Yong intervened. "I'll take you if you'll promise me three things. If you don't, you'll just have to stay here in the stronghold."

"I'll promise you not three, but thirty!"

"First, you're like wildfire when you're drunk. From today on, you've got to quit drinking. You can begin again when we get back. Second, you'll go as a Taoist acolyte serving me. When I tell you to do something, you do it. Third, — and this is the most difficult — starting tomorrow you're not to say another word, you're to become a mute. If you promise these three things, I'll take you along."

"I can promise not to drink, and to act like an acolyte. But if I can't talk, I'll stifle!"

"If you open your mouth you'll get us into a muddle."

"Of course, it's easy. I'll keep a copper coin in my mouth. That'll do it."

The chieftains laughed. Who could persuade Li Kui to remain behind?

That day a farewell feast was given in Loyalty Hall. In the evening, all retired. Early the next morning Wu Yong gathered a bundle of luggage and directed Li Kui, disguised as an acolyte, to tote it down the mountain on a carrying-pole. Song Jiang and the other chieftains saw them as far as the Shore of Golden Sands. They urged Wu Yong to be careful, and to keep Li Kui out of scrapes. Wu Yong and Li Kui took their leave. The others returned to the stronghold.

The two travelled four or five days, stopping at inns in the evening and rising at daybreak, when they cooked breakfast and continued their journey. Li Kui was a constant irritation to Wu Yong. After several days, they arrived at an inn on the outskirts of the city. They spent the night there, and when Li Kui went down to the kitchen to cook their evening meal he hit the waiter so hard the fellow coughed blood.

The waiter went to their room and complained to Wu Yong. "That mute acolyte of yours is too rough, I was just a little slow in lighting the stove and he gave such a punch I spit blood!"

Wu Yong apologized and handed the man a dozen strings of cash for his pains. He berated Li Kui. Of that we'll say no more. They rose the next morning at dawn, cooked breakfast and ate. Wu Yong summoned Li Kui to the room.

"You pleaded to be taken along, and all you do is aggravate me. We're going into the city today. It's no place for fooling around. I don't want you to cost me my life!"

"I wouldn't dare!"

"Now remember this signal. If I shake my head, you're not to move."

Li Kui promised. The two left the inn and set out for the city in disguise. Wu Yong wore a black crinkled silk head kerchief that came down to his eyebrows, a black Taoist cassock trimmed in white, and a multi-colored girdle. His feet were shod in square-toed cloth shoes, and he carried a pole with a bronze bell which shone like gold. Li Kui's bristly brown hair was wound up into two coils on either side of his head. His black tiger body was clad in a short brown gown. A multi-colored short-fringed sash bound his bear-like waist. He wore a pair of open-work boots for climbing mountains. On a pole with a curved end a strip of paper dangled, reading: "Fortunes told. One ounce of silver." At that time robbers marauded throughout the land, and every prefecture and county had to be defended by troops. Since the Northern Capital was the leading city in Hebei, it was garrisoned by an army under the personal command of Governor Liang. It was a neatly laid out metropolis.

Wu Yong and Li Kui swaggered up to the gate. The forty or fifty soldiers on guard were gathered around an officer seated in a chair. Wu Yong approached and bowed.

"Where are you from, scholar?" one of the soldiers asked.

"My name is Zhang Yong. This is Li, my acolyte. I'm a wandering caster of horoscopes. I've come to this great city to tell fortunes." Wu Yong produced his false license and showed it to the soldier.

"That acolyte has wicked eyes," some of the other soldiers said. "Shifty, like a thief."

Li Kui, who overheard, was ready to burst into action. Wu Yong hastily shook his head, and Li Kui lowered his gaze.

"It's a long story," Wu Yong said apologetically. "He's a deaf mute, but he's terribly strong. He's the son of one our family's bondmaids. I had to take him along. He has no manners at all. Please forgive him."

Wu Yong strolled on through the gate, with Li Kui plodding at his heels. They walked towards the center of the city. Wu Yong rang his bell and chanted:

Gan Luo won fame early, Zi Ya late,
Peng Zu and Yan Hui, each a different life span,
Fan Dan was poor, Shi Chong rich,
Fortune varies for every man.

"Fortune, destiny, fate. I predict life, I foretell death, I know who shall rise high and who shall fall low," cried Wu Yong. "I'll tell your future for one ounce of silver." Once more he vigorously rang his bell.

Fifty or sixty laughing children trailed behind. Singing and giggling, they passed the gate of Magnate Lu's storehouse. Soon Wu Yong returned and marched by again, followed by the hooting youngsters.

Lu was seated in the office, watching his stewards check merchandise in and out. Hearing the noise, he asked the man in charge for the day: "What's all that racket outside?"

"It's really very funny," the man replied. "Some Taoist fortune teller from out of town is walking the streets offering his services. But he wants an ounce of silver. Who would give that much! With him is an acolyte, a sloppy looking fellow who walks like nothing human. Kids are following them and laughing."

"He wouldn't venture to make such large claims if he wasn't a man of learning. Invite him in."

The steward went out. "Sir priest," he called. "The magnate asks you in."

"Who is he?"

"The magnate Lu Junyi."

Wu Yong told Li Kui to come along, raised the door curtain, and entered the office. He instructed Li Kui to sit down on a goose-necked chair and wait. Then he approached Lu and bowed.

Lu bowed in return. "Where are you from, sir priest? What is your name?"

"My name is Zhang Yong. I call myself the Mouth That Talks of Heaven. I'm from Shandong, originally. I can cast horoscopes for emperors, I can predict births and deaths, high position or poverty. For an ounce of silver I can tell your fortune."

Lu invited Wu Yong to a small alcove in the rear of the hall. They seated themselves as host and guest. After tea was served, Lu ordered the steward to bring an ounce of silver.

"Please, sir priest, tell me my humble fate."

"When were you born?"

"A gentleman asks only about misfortune, not fortune. So you needn't talk of prosperity. Just tell me what else is in store," said Lu. "I'm thirty-two." He stated the year, month, day and hour of his birth.

Wu Yong took out an iron abacus, calculated a moment, then slammed it down. "Fantastic!" he exclaimed.

Startled, Lu demanded: "What lies ahead for me?"

"I'll tell you frankly, if you won't take it amiss."

"Point out the road to the lost traveller, sir priest. Speak freely."

"Within the next hundred days, bloody tragedy will strike. Your family wealth will be lost, and you will die at the sword."

Lu Junyi laughed. "You're wrong, sir priest. I was born in the Northern Capital and grew up in a wealthy family. No male ancestor ever broke the law, no female widow ever remarried. I conduct my affairs with decorum, I do nothing unreasonable, I take no tainted money. How can I have incurred a bloody fate?"

Wu Yong's face hardened. He returned the silver piece, rose, and walked towards the door. "People always prefer to hear what pleases them," he sighed. "Forget it. I'm willing to point out a smooth road, but you take my good words as evil. I'll leave you now."

"Don't be angry, sir priest. I was only joking. I'd like to

hear your instructions."

"If I speak directly, don't hold it against me."

"I'm listening carefully. Hold nothing back."

"Your fortune has always been good, magnate. But your horoscope conflicts with this year's fate god, and the result is evil. Within a hundred days, your head shall be separated from your body. This has been destined. There is no escape."

"Isn't there any way to avoid it?"

Wu Yong again calculated on the abacus. He said: "Only if you go to a place one thousand *li* southeast of here. Although you may suffer some shocks and alarms, you will not be injured."

"If you can arrange that, I'll gladly reward you!"

"I'll tell you a four line prediction verse. You must write it on the wall. When it comes true, you'll appreciate my mystic powers."

Lu called for a brush pen and ink slab. Wu Yong sang these four lines and Lu wrote them on the white calcimined wall:

A boat sails through the reeds,
At dusk a hero wanders by,
Righteous to the very end,
Out of trouble you must fly.

Wu Yong collected his abacus, bowed and turned to go. Lu Junyi urged him to stay, at least until the afternoon.

"Thank you for kindness," said Wu Yong, "but I must get on with my fortune telling. I'll come and pay my respects another day."

Lu saw him to the gate. Li Kui took up the pole with the curved end and went out. Wu Yong bid Lu farewell. Followed by Li Kui, he departed from the city and returned to the inn. There he paid their bill and collected his luggage. Li Kui carried the fortune telling sign.

"The main job has been done," Wu Yong exulted, after they had left the inn. "Now we must hurry back to the stronghold and prepare our welcome for Lu Junyi. Sooner or later, he'll come."

To return to Lu Junyi, every evening at dusk he stood in front of his hall and gazed unhappily at the sky, sometimes muttering unintelligibly to himself. One day he impatiently summoned his stewards. Before long, they all arrived.

The chief steward was named Li Gu. Originally from the Eastern Capital, he had come to join a friend living in Daming. But the man was nowhere to be found and, after a time, Li Gu fell, frozen, outside the magnate's gate. Lu Junyi saved his life and took him into the household. Because Li Gu was diligent, could write and calculate, Lu put him in charge of household affairs. Within five years he rose to the post of chief steward. He managed all matters of both household and outside business, and had forty or fifty clerks working under him.

These now followed Li Gu into the hall and respectfully greeted the magnate. Lu looked them over and asked: "Where is that man of mine?"

The words were scarcely out of his mouth, when a person came before him. Over six feet tall, he was twenty-four or five years of age, was adorned with a thin mustache and goatee, and had a slim waist and broad shoulders. The kerchief on his head was twisted into the shape of a papaya, with his hair coming up through a hole in the middle. His white gown had a round silk collar of filagreed silver thread. Around his waist was a girdle woven of fine spotted red thread. His feet were shod in brown oiled leather boots. A pair of gold rings shaped like animals dangled from the back of his head. His neckerchief was of fragrant silk. A fan inscribed by a famous calligrapher was tucked slantwise at his waist. Over one ear hung an all-season flower.

The young man was a native of the Northern Capital. After losing his parents as a child, he had been adopted by the Lu family. Because he had pure white skin, Lu engaged a skilled tattooist to decorate his body. The result was kingfisher blue added to white jade. No one could match the young man in beauty of physique. Not only was he gorgeously tattooed, but he could blow and strum musical instruments, sing and dance, and play word games. There was nothing he didn't know, nothing he couldn't do.

He could speak various dialects, knew the special jargon of many different trades. As for the fighting arts, no one could touch him. Hunting in the outskirts of the city, he could bring down any game with his bow. He used only three short arrows, and never missed. Wherever his arrow struck, there his quarry fell. Returning to the city in the evening, he seldom brought back less than a hundred birds. In archery contests, he cleaned up all the prizes.

His mind, too, was quick and agile. You had only to mention a problem and he gave you the answer. His name was Yan Qing. People of the Northern Capital were fond of quips, and they called him the Prodigy. He was Lu Junyi's most trusted adviser.

The men Lu summoned greeted him respectfully and stood in two lines. Li Gu headed the line on the left, Yan Qing headed the line on the right. Lu the Magnate addressed them.

"Last night a fortune teller predicted that unless I took refuge a thousand *li* southeast of here, I would suffer a bloody disaster within a hundred days. I remember now that southeast of here in Tai'an Prefecture, there's a temple on Mount Taishan called the Golden Temple of the Match-Heaven God. This god governs births and deaths and man's disasters. I shall go there and burn incense to expiate my sins and avoid the calamity. At the same time I can do a bit of business and admire the scenery. Li Gu, I want you to get me ten large carts and load them with our Shandong local products. Pack your luggage, because you're going with me. Yan Qing, you stay and look after the household and our storehouses. Li Gu will turn over his duties to you. I'm leaving in three days."

"Master, you're making a mistake," said Li Gu. "Everybody knows fortune tellers are slick talkers. You shouldn't listen to that fellow's claptrap. Remain at home. What's there to be afraid of?"

"My fate has been determined. Don't try to stop me. Once disaster strikes, it's too late to be sorry."

"Please listen to my humble opinion, master," said Yan Qing. "The road to Tai'an runs pass Liangshan Marsh, which is infested with bandits under Song Jiang. Though they rob and pillage, government soldiers and police can't get near them. Wait until times are more settled, if you want to burn incense. Don't believe that fortune teller's wild story. He's probably a plant from Mount Liangshan, sent to stir you up so that they can trick you into joining them. It's too bad I wasn't home last night. With two or three phrases I could have exposed the fellow and made him a laughing stock."

"You're both talking rot. Who would dare to deceive me! Those oafs in Liangshan Marsh — what do they matter? I can scatter them like grass, in fact I'll go and nab them. My prowess with weapons will show them what a real man is like!"

Before he had finished speaking, a woman emerged from behind a screen. It was his wife Jia.

"Husband," she said, "I've been listening to what you've been saying. 'Better to stay at home than even one *li* roam,' as the old saw goes. Ignore that fortune teller. Why put your vast family affairs aside and expose yourself to shocks and alarms in a den of tigers and lair of dragons just to do some business? Stay at home, be calm and content, relax quietly, and naturally nothing will go wrong."

"You don't know anything about it, woman! My mind is made up. I don't want to hear any more from any of you!"

Yan Qing said: "Basking in the reflection of your good fortune, master, I have been able to learn a little skill with weapons. I don't mean to boast, but if you take me with you and any bandits happen along, I should be able to knock off forty or fifty. Leave Chief Steward Li to look after things at home and let me accompany you."

"Li Gu knows trade practices I don't understand. He'll save me a lot of trouble. That's why I'm taking him and leaving you here. I have others to keep the accounts. All you have to do is take charge of the manor."

"My feet have been bothering me quite a lot lately," said Li Gu. "It's hard for me to walk any distance."

Lu was very angry. "Soldiers are trained for months for the sake of a few days of battle. I want you to go with me on this trip, and you've got all kinds of excuses. The next man who defies me is going to get a taste of my fists!"

Li Gu, frightened, looked towards the mistress. But she only walked sadly into an inner room. Yan Qing was even less inclined to speak.

Silently swallowing his humiliation, Li Gu went to pack the luggage. He got ten drivers, ten large carts, and forty or fifty animals to haul them. He loaded on the luggage, and had the merchandise securely tied in place.

Lu Junyi put his own affairs in order. The third day, he burned paper prayers, dispersed money to the male and female members of his family, and gave instructions to each. That evening he directed Li Gu to finish up quickly and prepare to leave the city first with two servants. Li Gu went off. The magnate's wife, seeing the carts, wept.

At the fifth watch the following morning, Lu rose, washed, and put on a complete set of new clothes. He gathered his weapons and went to the rear hall, where he burned incense in farewell to his ancestors. He instructed his wife: "Take good care of things at home. At the latest I'll be back in three months; at the earliest, only forty or fifty days."

"Be careful on the road, husband. Write to us when you can, so that we'll know how you're getting on."

Yan Qing came forward and bowed, in tears. Lu had orders for him as well.

"Be diligent in all things. Don't go running off to roister in houses of pleasure."

"Since you'll be away, master, I certainly won't slacken."

Staff in hand, Lu left the city. He was met by Li Gu.

"You and the two servants go on ahead," Lu directed. "When you find a clean inn have them prepare food, so that it's ready for the drivers and porters when they get there, and we won't be delayed."

Li Gu also carried a staff. He set off with the two servants. Lu and other servants followed with the carts. They passed splendid mountains and elegant waterways, travelling broad roads and level plains.

"I couldn't have enjoyed such scenery if I remained at home," Lu thought pleasurably.

After travelling forty *li* or more he was met by Li Gu, and they had a pastry lunch. Li Gu went on again. Another forty or fifty *li* and they reached an inn, where Li Gu had arranged quarters for the night for all.

Lu went to his room, leaned his staff, hung up his felt hat, removed his knife, and changed his shoes and stockings. It goes without saying that he rested and dined. The company rose early the next morning and cooked breakfast. When everyone had eaten, the animals were hitched to the carts and the march resumed.

They proceeded in this manner for several days, stopping at dark and continuing at dawn. Again, they put up at an inn for the night. The following morning they were preparing to go on when one of the waiters addressed Lu Junyi.

"I must tell you, sir, that less than twenty *li* from here the road passes an entry to Liangshan Marsh. The lord of the mountain is Song Jiang. Although he doesn't harm travellers, rather than suffer frights and alarms it's best to go by quietly."

"So that's how it is," Lu exclaimed. He told a servant to fetch his trunk. Lu unlocked it and took out a bundle from which he extracted four white silk banners. He ordered the waiter to bring four bamboo poles and attach the banners, one to each. On them, Lu wrote this series of lines:

> *From the Northern Capital Lu the Bold*
> *Transports merchandise a long, long way,*
> *Determined is he to catch the robbers,*
> *Fully his manliness to display.*

Li Gu and the others groaned. "Are you a relative of Song the mountain lord, sir?" asked the waiter.

"I'm a magnate from the Northern Capital. What relation would I be to those crooks! I've come specially to nab that lout Song Jiang."

"Speak softly, sir," begged the waiter. "Don't get me involved. This is no joke. Even with ten thousand men, you'll never get near Song Jiang!"

"Bullshit. You oafs are probably all in cahoots with him!"

The waiter was beside himself with despair. The drivers and porters were dumbfounded. Li Gu and the other servants knelt at the magnate's feet.

"Master, have pity on us. Save our lives, go back. Rather that than prayers for our departed souls!"

"What do you know!" Lu barked. "Would those little finches dare contend with an eagle? I've always wanted to show my prowess with arms, but I've never met a foe worthy. Today, I have my chance, here and now. Why wait! In those bags on my cart I've got some good hemp rope. The bandits I don't kill I'll knock down with my halberd. You tie them up and put them on the carts. If necessary abandon the merchandise. We'll use the carts for transporting prisoners. I'll deliver their chief to the capital and claim the reward. That will satisfy my wish of a lifetime. If a single one of you refuses to go along with me now, I'll slaughter you right here!"

The four banners were affixed to the four leading carts. The remaining six carts followed. Li Gu and the rest, weeping and sniveling, had no choice but to obey the magnate. Lu took out a halberd head and tied it to his staff tightly with three strong knots. He hastened the carts forward in the direction of Liangshan Marsh. Li Gu trembled with every step he took on the winding mountain road, but Lu pushed on relentlessly.

They marched from early morning till almost noon. In the distance they saw a big forest, with trees larger than a two-man embrace. When they reached the edge of the forest a shrill whistle pierced the air, terrifying Li Gu and the two servants. They didn't know where to hide.

Lu Junyi ordered that the carts be pulled to one side, under guard. The drivers and porters, bemoaning their fate, crawled beneath the carts.

"When I knock the robbers down, you tie them up," Lu shouted.

Before the words were out of his mouth, four or five hundred outlaws emerged from the edge of the forest. Behind them the crashing of gongs could be heard. Another four or five hundred brigands cut off Lu's retreat. Cannon boomed in the woods, and out leaped a bold warrior.

"Do you recognize the mute acolyte, Magnate Lu?" he called, brandishing a pair of axes.

Lu suddenly understood. "I've often thought of capturing you robbers," he cried, "and I'm here today to do it. Bring that knave Song Jiang down the mountain to surrender. Any tricks and I'll kill you all. I won't spare a one!"

Li Kui laughed. "Magnate, you've fallen for a clever ruse by our Military Advisor. Come and take your place in a chieftain's chair."

Enraged, Lu twisted his halberd and charged. Li Kui met him with axes swinging. Before they had fought three rounds Li Kui jumped from the combat circle, turned, and headed for the forest. Lu pursued, halberd level. Li Kui ran into the wood, zigzagging left and right. In a towering fury, Lu plunged in after him. Li Kui flew into a grove of pines. By the time Lu got there, his adversary was gone.

He was turning away when a group of men appeared from the side of the grove and a voice called: "Don't go, Magnate. Do you know me?"

Lu looked and saw a big fat monk, dressed in a black cassock and carrying án iron Buddhist staff by its lower end.

"Who are you, monk?" the magnate shouted.

The man laughed. "I'm Sagacious Lu the Tattooed Monk. I'm here on orders from brother Song Jiang to welcome you and lead you up the mountain."

"Bald donkey," Lu exploded, "how dare you be so rude!" Twisting his halberd, he rushed the monk.

Sagacious met him with whirling staff. Before they had fought three rounds, the monk parried Lu's halberd, turned and ran. Lu gave chase. At that moment Wu Song the Pilgrim stepped forth from among the brigands. He charged, brandishing two swords. Lu abandoned his pursuit of Sagacious and battled with Wu Song. They had fought less than three rounds when the Pilgrim hastened away.

Lu Junyi laughed. "I won't chase you. You louts aren't worth it!"

But then someone on the mountain slope called out: "You don't understand, Magnate. Haven't you heard that man fears falling into the water, just as iron fears falling into the fire? Our Military Advisor has made his plan. How can you escape?"

"Who are you, rogue?" Lu yelled.

The man laughed. "Liu Tang the Red-Haired Demon."

"Petty crook, don't try to get away," the magnate fumed. He dashed at Liu, halberd in hand.

They had just battled three rounds when a voice off at an angle shouted: "Gallant Mu Hong the Unrestrained is here!" And Liu Tang and Mu Hong, each with a halberd, attacked Lu Junyi.

Before they had gone three rounds, Lu heard footsteps behind him. "At you!" he exclaimed. Liu Tang and Mu Hong fell back a few paces, and Lu whirled to face the adversary in his rear. It was Li Ying the Heaven-Soaring Eagle. From three sides Lu's foes assailed him. But he was completely unruffled, in fact the more he fought the stronger he became.

As they were belaboring each other, gongs crashed on the mountain top. The three chieftains feinted with their weapons and swiftly withdrew. Reeking of sweat from his exertions, Lu did not pursue. He returned to the edge of the forest to seek his carts and drivers. But the ten carts, their drivers and all the animals had vanished. Lu groaned.

He clambered to a high point and looked around. Far in the distance at the foot of a slope he saw a group of brigands driving the carts and animals before them. Li Gu and the others, tied in a line, followed. To the beat of drums and gongs, they were being led to a grove of pines.

Lu's heart burst into flames, rage engulfed him like smoke. Halberd in hand, he chased after the procession. When he was not far from the slope two bold fellows shouted at him: "Where do you think you're going?" One was Zhu Tong the Beautiful Beard, the other Lei Heng the Winged Tiger.

"Small-time robbers," Lu yelled back. "Return my carts and drivers and animals!"

Zhu Tong twiddled his beard and laughed. "How can you be so dense, Magnate? Our Military Advisor often says: 'A star can only fly down, it can never fly back.' The way things stand, you might just as well come with us to the fortress and take your place in a chieftain's chair."

Infuriated, Lu charged the two with levelled halberd. Zhu Tong and Lei Heng met him with their own weapons. Before they had fought three rounds the former constables turned and fled.

"I'll never get my carts back unless I knock one of those bandits over," thought Lu. He pursued them recklessly around the bend of the slope. But the two had vanished. Instead, he heard the sound of clappers and flutes wafting down from the mountain top. He looked up. Fluttering in the breeze was an apricot yellow pennant on which was embroidered the words: *Righteous Deeds on Heaven's Behalf.* And there beyond, beneath a gold-spangled red silk umbrella, was Song Jiang, with Wu Yong to his left and Gongsun Sheng to his right. They were accompanied by a column of sixty or seventy men. All politely hailed Lu Junyi.

"Magnate, we trust you've been well!"

Lu grew very angry, and he cursed them by name. Wu Yong tried to soothe him.

"Calm yourself, brother. Song Jiang has long known of your virtue, and holds you in the greatest respect. He sent me to call at your gates and lure you up the mountain so that we might perform righteous deeds for Heaven together. Please don't take it amiss."

"Presumptious bandits," yelled Lu. "How dare you trick me!"

From behind Song Jiang emerged Hua Rong with bow and arrow. "Magnate," he called, "don't force a showdown between us. Let me demonstrate my archery."

Before he had finished speaking, the arrow whizzed straight into the big red tassel atop Lu's broad-brimmed felt hat. Astonished, the magnate turned and fled. On the heights, drums shook the ground. From the east side of the mountain, led by Qin Ming the Thunderbolt and Panther Head Lin Chong, came a body of yelling mounted men, banners waving. A similar troop, also shouting and waving banners, charged out from the west side of the mountain, led by Two Rods Huyan Zhuo and Metal Lancer Xu Ning. Lu was so frightened he didn't know which way to go.

It was growing dark. Lu's feet hurt, and he was hungry. Frantically seeking an escape route, he hurried along a small mountain path. At dusk, mist veiled the distant waters, fog locked the deep mountains. The moon and stars were dim, the vegetation a pale blur. Lu was reaching the ends of the earth, if not the limits of the sky.

He looked around. There was nothing but reeds here, and misty water. Lu raised his face to the sky and sighed. "I wouldn't listen to good advice, and now I'm in a terrible mess!"

A small boat slid out from among the reeds, sculled by a fisherman. "You're very brave, sir traveller," the fisherman called. "This is the entry to Liangshan Marsh. What are you doing here in the middle of the night?"

"I've lost my way and can't find a place to spend the night. Save me!"

"This region is very broad, but there is a market town. It's over thirty *li* if you go by land, and the road is tortuous and difficult to follow. By water, though, it's only four or five *li*. Give me ten strings of cash and I'll take you there in my boat."

"Get me to an inn in the market town and I'll give you plenty of silver."

The fisherman rowed up to the shore and helped Lu on board, then shoved off with his iron-tipped bamboo pole. When they had gone four or five *li*, they heard the sound of an oar in the reeds ahead. A small craft flew out. On it were two men. The one in the prow, buff naked, gripped a long punting pole. The one in the stern was wielding a sweep oar. Pole held athwart, the man forward sang this song:

> *Though poems and books I cannot read,*
> *And in Liangshan Marsh I dwell,*
> *I shoot fierce tigers with snarebows and arrows,*
> *Fresh baited hooks bring me fish as well.*

Lu Junyi, startled, didn't dare utter a sound. From reeds on the right, two more men rowed out on another small boat. The man in the stern plied a creaking sweep oar. The man in the bow held horizontally a long punting pole. He sang this song:

> *My favorite pastime is killing men,*
> *A rogue I've been since the day I was born,*
> *Thousands in gold means nothing to me,*
> *I'm determined to nab the Jade Unicorn.*

Lu the Magnate groaned. Now, from the middle reeds a third boat came skimming towards him. The man in the prow was holding an iron-tipped wooden pole upside down, and he was singing this song:

> *A boat sails through the reeds,*
> *At dusk a hero wanders by,*
> *Righteous to the end,*
> *Out of trouble you must fly.*

The men on all three craft hailed Lu respectfully. The one in the center was Ruan the Second. Ruan the Fifth was on the boat to left, Ruan the Seventh was on the boat to the right. The three craft approached. Lu was very alarmed. He knew he couldn't swim.

"Land me on the nearest shore," he urged the fisherman.

The man laughed. "By the blue sky above and the green waters below, I was born on the Xunyang River, came to Liang-shan Marsh, and have never concealed my name. Meet Li Jun the Turbulent River Dragon! If you don't surrender, Magnate, you'll be throwing your life away!"

Lu was astonished. "It's either you or me!" he shouted, and he lunged at Li's heart with his halberd. Li saw the blade coming. Hands on the sweep oar, he flipped over in a back somersault and landed ka-plonk in the water. The boat spun around in a circle and the halberd fell overboard.

Suddenly, at the stern, a man shot up from under the water with a shout. It was White Streak in the Waves Zhang Shun. Treading water, he grasped the rudder and gave a quick twist. The boat turned turtle, and the hero landed in the drink.

Zhang Shun wrapped an arm around Lu's waist and swam with him towards shore. They soon reached the bank. Fifty or sixty men were waiting with lighted torches. These gathered round, removed Lu's dagger and stripped him of his wet clothes. They were about to bind his arms when Dai Zong the Marvel-lous Traveller transmitted an order.

"Lu the Magnate is not to be harmed," he shouted.

An attendant gave Lu a silken embroidered tunic and gown to wear. Eight brigands brought a sedan-chair, assisted Lu into it, and set forth. Seen in the distance were twenty or thirty red silk lanterns, illuminating a mounted troop which was ap-proaching to the accompaniment of drums and music. At the head was Song Jiang, Wu Yong and Gongsun Sheng. They were followed by many chieftains.

All dismounted. Lu Junyi hastily got down from his sedan-chair. Song Jiang knelt. The other chieftains, in rows, did the same. Lu also dropped to his knees.

"Since I have been captured, I request an early death."

Song Jiang laughed. "Please sit in your sedan-chair, Magnate."

The chieftains resumed their saddles. To the sound of music, the procession climbed through the three fortified passes and went directly to Loyalty Hall. There, the hosts dismounted and led Lu into the hall. It was brightly lit by lanterns and candles.

"Your fame, Magnate, has long thundered in my ears," said Song Jiang. "Being able to meet you today is one of the greatest good fortunes of my life. My brothers behaved rudely a little while ago. We beg your forgiveness."

Wu Yong stepped forward and said: "The other day, on orders from brother Song Jiang, I called at your gates disguised as a fortune teller. My aim was to lure you up the mountain so that you might join us in our mutual endeavors to act on Heaven's behalf."

Song Jiang invited Lu Junyi to be seated in the highest chieftain's chair. Lu's reply was courteous.

"I've no talent, knowledge or ability, and I've offended your prestige. Ten thousand deaths would be a light retribution. Why do you make sport of me?"

Song Jiang smiled. "Who would dare? Because of our genuine respect for your great virtue, Magnate, we have hungered and thirsted for your arrival. We pray you do not scorn our humble mountain fortress. Be our leader. We will unquestioningly obey your every command."

"Then let me die immediately, for I cannot accede to your wish."

"Let's talk about it again another day," Wu Yong suggested.

Wine was brought for the magnate. Lu had no way out, and he drank several cups. Lesser brigands conducted him to the rear hall to rest.

CHAPTER 25
Song Jiang Attacks Zengtou Village at Night

The following Spring Guan Sheng and several other brigands, returning to the mountain lair, had just crossed over from the Shore of Golden Sands.

A man came running towards them, panting and exhausted. They all recognized him. It was Duan Jingzhu the Golden Dog.

"Didn't you go up north with Yang Lin and Shi Yong to buy horses?" asked Lin Chong. "Why have you come back in such a flurry?"

"I went north with Yang Lin and Shi Yong to buy horses," Duan said, "and I picked over two hundred strong, well-sinewed, fine-coated steeds. But on the way back, while passing through Qingzhou Prefecture, we were set upon by a gang of robbers, headed by Yu Baosi, known as the Spirit of the Dangerous Road. There were more than two hundred of them. They stole all our animals and took them to Zengtou Village. I don't know where Shi Yong and Yang Lin have gone. I fled through the night and am hastening to the stronghold to report."

Lin Chong agreed that it was necessary to discuss the matter with Big Brother. They all forded the river and repaired to Loyalty Hall, where they met Song Jiang. Guan Sheng introduced Shan Tinggui and Wei Dingguo to the various chieftains. Li Kui told how, after going down the mountain, he killed Han Bolong, met Jiao Ting and Bao Xu and, with them, broke into Lingzhou. Song Jiang was very pleased with the addition of these four brave men.

But he grew very angry when Duan related the robbery of the horses. "They did this sort of thing to me before," he cried, "and now they've behaved discourteously again! I've been un-happy day and night because I haven't avenged the death at their hands of Chao Gai the Heavenly King. If I still don't avenge him now, I'll be the butt of ridicule and shame!"

"Spring is here," said Wu Yong, "the ideal season for battle. When we attacked them before, we failed to utilize the terrain. This time we must be clever."

"I hate them to the marrow of my bones. I'll get my revenge or, I swear, I'll never return!"

"Shi Qian can fly over eaves and skim atop walls. Send him in to scout around. When he comes back, we'll confer."

Flea on a Drum was dispatched to Zengtou. Two or three days later, Yang Lin and Shi Yong, who had escaped, arrived at the fortress. They said that Shi Wengong had been boasting in Zengtou that there was no room on this earth for both him and the outlaws of Liangshan Marsh. Song Jiang was in favor of mustering their troops immediately.

But Wu Yong said: "Wait till Shi Qian comes back and reports. It will be time enough, then."

Song Jiang, filled with rage, was thirsting for revenge. He couldn't contain himself. He sent Dai Zong to fly to the village and report back quickly with all the news he could find. In only a few days Dai Zong returned.

"Zengtou wants to avenge itself for Lingzhou," he said. "They're raising an army and setting up a big emplacement at the village entrance, with headquarters in the Fahua Monastery. Banners mark their outposts for hundreds of li around. I don't know how we can get in there."

The following day Shi Qian returned and reported: "I made very detailed inquiries. They've built five forts. More than two thousand men are guarding the entrance, under Shi Wengong. This is the main fort. The north fort is commanded by Zeng Tu, with Su Ding as his lieutenant. Zeng Mi, the second Zeng son, is in charge of the south fort. Zeng Suo, the third son, commands the west fort. The east fort is under Zeng Kui, the fourth son. The central position, in the village itself, is held by the fifth son Zeng Sheng and the father Zeng Nong. Yu Baosi the Spirit of the Dangerous Road is a huge fellow with an enormous girth. He's feeding those horses he stole inside the monastery grounds."

Wu Yong summoned the chieftains to a conference. "Since they've got five forts," he said, "we'll divide into five columns and attack each separately."

Lu the Magnate rose. "I have not yet shown my gratitude for being rescued and brought here. I would now like to go forward and give my all. Would that, I wonder, meet with your respected approval?"

Song Jiang was delighted. "If you're willing to go down the mountain, Magnate, you may lead the vanguard."

"The Magnate has arrived only recently," Wu Yong intervened. "He has no battle experience, the mountain paths are tortuous and ill-suited for riding. Rather than lead the vanguard, he would be better at the head of a contingent in ambush on the plain. When he hears the sound of our central unit's cannon, he can reinforce us."

Wu Yong was afraid that Lu would capture Shi Wengong and Song Jiang would feel constrained to fulfil the dying wish of Chao Gai that leadership be given to whoever caught his killer. Song Jiang, on the contrary, hoped that Lu would make the capture precisely so that he could turn over command of the stronghold to him out of respect to Chao Gai. But Wu Yong was adamant. He directed Lu to go with Yan Qing and five hundred infantry to paths upon the plain and await the signal.

Wu Yong divided the outlaw forces into five columns. Against the fort due south of Zengtou would go three thousand cavalry under Qin Ming the Thunderbolt and Hua Rong, seconded by Ma Lin and Deng Fei. The fort east of the village would be attacked by three thousand infantry under Sagacious Lu the Tattooed Monk and Wu Song the Pilgrim, with Kong Ming and Kong Liang as their lieutenants. Yang Zhi the Blue-

Faced Beast and Nine Dragons Shi Jin, seconded by Yang Chun and Chen Da, would lead three thousand cavalry against the fort north of Zengtou. Sent against the fort to the west were three thousand infantry under Zhu Tong the Beautiful Beard and Lei Heng the Winged Tiger. Zou Yuan and Zou Run were their seconds in command. The central fort would be attacked by five thousand troops under commander-in-chief Song Jiang, Military Advisor Wu Yong, and Gongsun Sheng, accompanied by Lü Fang, Guo Sheng, Xie Zhen, Xie Bao, Dai Zong and Shi Qian. Bringing up the rear would be a five thousand man unit of mixed infantry and cavalry under Li Kui the Black Whirlwind and Fan Rui the Demon King Who Roils the World, with Xiang Chong and Li Gun as their lieutenants. The remaining chieftains would stay to guard the mountain stronghold.

The five columns led by Song Jiang advanced rapidly. Scouts reported their approach to Zeng Senior, who summoned Shi Wengong and Su Ding for a military conference.

"All we have to do is dig a lot of concealed pits and we'll catch their toughest commanders and fiercest men," said Shi. "That's the best way to deal with those scruffy bandits!"

Zeng Senior ordered his vassals out with mattocks and shovels to dig pits all round the entrance to the village, and cover them over with mats and earth. Then he had soldiers lie in ambush near the pits and wait for the arrival of the enemy. He had a dozen or so pits also dug around the northern approach to the village.

While Song Jiang's army was on the march Wu Yong sent Shi Qian ahead to scout. A few days later, Flea on a Drum returned and reported: "Pits have been dug north and south of Zengtou, I don't know how many, to trap us."

Wu Yong laughed. "Nothing remarkable about that!" He led the troops on until they were quite near the village.

Around noon that day the advance unit saw a rider passing by. Bronze bells tinkled on his horse's neck, and pheasant plumes were tied to its tail. The rider wore a black hat and white robe, and he carried a short spear.

Men of the vanguard wanted to give chase, but Wu Yong stopped them. He ordered them to make camp where they were, dig a deep moat on all four sides, and lay out a perimeter of iron spikes. Each of the five columns was directed to do the same.

For the next three days no one came forward from the Zeng-tou forts to give battle. Wu Yong once again sent Shi Qian, this time disguised as a junior officer manning one of the ambushes, to find out why. Flea on a Drum made a mental note of the concealed pits, how far they were from the various forts, and how many of them there were in total. In a single day, he had all the information required, in detail, and he returned and reported.

The next day Wu Yong instructed the vanguard infantry to divide into two units, equipped with mattocks. He also directed that one hundred carts be loaded with reeds and dry brushwood and be concealed among the central column.

That night he ordered that the infantry columns first attack the forts to the east and west of Zengtou at mid-morning the following day. The cavalry under Yang Zhi and Shi Jin should spread out in a straight line before the northern fort. If the foe there beat drums and waved banners, they should put on a display of might, but under no circumstances advance. Wu Yong's orders were transmitted.

Shi Wengong was hoping that Song Jiang's forces would attack the south fort and fall into the concealed pits. The road before it was narrow. Where else could they go?

At mid-morning the next day the sound of cannon was heard up ahead. Pursuit troops gathered at the south gate. Then a messenger arrived from the east fort.

"A monk with an iron staff and a pilgrim brandishing a pair of long knives are attacking us front and rear," he reported.

"They must be Sagacious Lu and Wu Song of Liangshan Marsh," said Shi Wengong. He sent part of his soldiers to support Zeng Kui.

From the west fort another messenger arrived. "A big fellow

with a long beard and a robber with a face like a tiger, with banners reading *Beautiful Beard Zhu Tong* and *Winged-Tiger Lei Heng,* are pressing us hard," he said.

Shi Wengong sent a portion of his men to aid Zeng Suo. Once more cannon boomed ahead. Shi had no more troops to spare. He could only wait for his adversaries to advance and tumble into the pits, at which time his soldiers hiding behind the hills would come out and help Shi nab them.

But Wu Yong swept forward around the hills in two flanking movements. The infantry guarding the fort was afraid to leave it. The soldiers flushed out of ambush were driven towards the fort by Wu Yong's pursuing troops, and large numbers of them fell into the pits.

Shi Wengong was about to sally forth when Wu Yong pointed with his whip. Gongs crashed and from the midst of the outlaw forces a hundred carts were pushed out and set ablaze. The conflagration of reeds, brushwood, sulphur and nitrate concealed the sky with smoke and flames. By the time Shi and his soldiers emerged their road was blocked by burning carts. They could only avoid them and hastily retreat. Gongsun waved his sword and conjured up a mighty wind which blew the flames into the south gate of the fort. Several buildings and part of the stockade burst into blaze and were destroyed.

A victory had been won. Trumpets summoned the outlaws to reassemble. They returned to their camps and rested. That night Shi repaired his gate and both sides secured their positions.

The next day Zeng Tu said to Shi Wengong: "If we don't kill their leaders it will be hard to wipe those bandits out." Telling his tutor to defend the fort, he donned his armor, mounted, and rode out at the head of his troops to challenge his adversaries to battle.

When Song Jiang heard who it was, he proceeded to the front, escorted by Lü Fang and Guo Sheng. He saw Zeng Tu under an arch of banners, and he burned with hatred. He pointed at him with his whip.

"Who will take that scamp for me and get me my long-

宋公明夜打曾頭市

awaited revenge?"

Lü Fang the Little Duke clapped his steed and rode against
Zeng Tu, holding upright his crescent-bladed halberd. The
antagonists met amid a clash of weapons. They fought over
thirty rounds. From beneath the arch of pennants Guo Sheng
could see that Lü Fang was weakening. He had fought well for
the first thirty rounds, but his movements had become clumsy,
and he was forced on the defensive.

Fearful that Lü Fang would be defeated, Guo Sheng suddenly
mounted and, twirling his own crescent-bladed halberd, flew
onto the battlefield and joined in the attack on Zeng Tu. The
three horsemen locked in combat.

A panther's tail, with spots like gold coins, dangled from the
head of each of the halberds. Both were lifted as the two
outlaws closed in to seize their opponent. Zeng Tu had a quick
eye. He raised his lance and entangled the tails, but the crimson
tassel on his own weapon was also caught. He couldn't pull
them apart. All three men were wrenching to free them.

Hua Rong, watching from the outlaws' position, was afraid
his two companions would suffer. He rode forward, his left
hand grasping his bow, his right hastily fitting a long slim arrow.
He bent the bow and let fly at Zeng Tu. At that very moment
Zeng Tu had extricated his lance, while the halberds were still
entangled and, quicker than it takes to say, was thrusting at Lü
Fang's neck. The arrow struck him in the left arm, knocking
him from his saddle. Lü Fang and Guo Sheng's halberds swiftly
took his life.

A dozen horsemen galloped back and reported to Shi Wengong, who reported in turn to the central fort. Zeng Senior wept
aloud. The warrior beside him, his son Zeng Sheng, was
enraged. A man of superb skill with arms, he wielded a pair
of swords with such deadliness that no foe dared come near him.
He ground his teeth in fury.

"Prepare my horse," he yelled. "I'm going to avenge
brother!"

His father couldn't stop him. In full armor, he took his

swords, mounted, and rode to the front fort.

"You mustn't underestimate the enemy," Shi Wengong warned him. "Song Jiang has many intelligent bold officers. In my humble opinion we should continue holding our five forts while secretly dispatching an emissary to Lingzhou to request that the throne be petitioned immediately for a relief army. One half of it should be sent to attack Mount Liangshan, the other to defend Zengtou. That will take the heart out of the bandits. Their only thought will be to rush back to their stronghold. Then, though I am a person of no talent, I shall be glad to join with you and your brothers in pursuing and exterminating the brigands. We're sure to attain great distinction."

Before he had finished speaking, assistant instructor Su Ding arrived from the north fort. He agreed with Shi's proposal. "That scoundrel Wu Yong is full of tricks," he said. "He mustn't be considered lightly. Defense is the best course. When the relief army arrives, we can discuss long-range plans again."

"They killed my brother," Zeng Sheng shouted. "He must be avenged! Why should we wait! Delay will only give the enemy time to gather strength and make them harder to defeat!"

Neither Shi nor Su could dissuade him. Zeng Sheng mounted and, with a few dozen horsemen, flew from the fort to challenge the foe.

Song Jiang was notified. He instructed the advance force to give battle. Qin Ming, on receiving the order, started to go out, brandishing his wolf-toothed cudgel, against Zeng Sheng. But suddenly Li Kui, axes in hand, rushed forward without a word to anyone and occupied the center of the arena.

One of the enemy recognized him. "That's Li Kui the Black Whirlwind," he said.

Zeng Sheng directed his archers to shoot. Ordinarily, Li Kui went naked into combat, and he relied on the shields of Xiang Chong and Li Gun for cover. But this time he rushed out alone, and an arrow struck him in the leg. He fell like a collapsing Mount Taishan. The horsemen behind Zeng Sheng galloped forward to seize him, while Qin Ming and Hua Rong raced from the opposite side, followed by Ma Lin, Deng Fei, Lü Fang and Guo Sheng. Since Song Jiang's men outnumbered him, Zeng Sheng was afraid to continue the engagement. He and his soldiers returned to the fort. Song Jiang called his forces back to camp.

The next day, Shi Wengong and Su Ding opposed any further combat. But they had no affect on Zeng Sheng. "Brother must be avenged," he insisted. Shi had no choice but to don his armor and mount. His horse was the famous White Jade Lion That Glows in the Night which he had taken forcibly from Duan Jingzhu. Song Jiang rode out with his chieftains to meet him.

Shi raced fiercely towards them. Qin Ming, eager for first honors, flew forward. The animals met and weapons clashed. After twenty rounds Qin Ming faltered, and he rode back towards his original position. Shi, pursuing, thrust with his lance. He hit Qin Ming in the leg, and the Thunderbolt fell from his saddle. Lü Fang, Guo Sheng, Ma Lin and Deng Fei raced to his defense. Although they managed to rescue Qin Ming, the enemy inflicted casualties. They withdrew and made camp ten *li* from the fort.

Song Jiang ordered a cart for the Thunderbolt and had him escorted back to the mountain fortress to rest. Then he conferred with Wu Yong. They sent word to the stronghold for Guan Sheng the Big Halberd, Xu Ning the Metal Lancer, Shan Tinggui and Wei Dingguo to come and lend a hand.

Song Jiang burned incense and prayed, and cast divining sticks. Wu Yong looked at the omens and said: "Since this place is penetrable, enemy soldiers will surely slip into camp tonight."

"We'd better prepare, then."

"Don't let it trouble you, brother. Simply order the chieftains of three camps to combine them into two, one east, one west, and place Xie Zhen on the left and Xie Bao on the right of this one. Let the remainder conceal themselves in ambush on all sides."

This was done. That night, the sky was clear and the moon

was bright. There was no wind or clouds.

Shi Wengong, in his fort, said to Zeng Sheng: "The bandits today lost two commanders. They must be frightened and depressed. This would be a good time to raid their camp."

Zeng Sheng immediately ordered Su Ding in the north fort, Zeng Mi in the south, and Zeng Suo in the west, to come at once with their soldiers and join in the attack. Around the second watch, they stealthily posted pickets, removed the bells from their horses and the clanking armor from the men, and crept into Song Jiang's central camp. No one was in sight. The camp was empty.

Realizing they'd been tricked, they turned to beat a hasty retreat. But from the left came Two-Headed Snake Xie Zhen and from the right came Twin-Tailed Scorpion Xie Bao, with Hua Rong appearing in the rear, and all closed in together. In the darkness, Zeng Suo was skewered by Xie Zhen's steel trident, and tumbled dead to the ground.

Torches were applied to Shi's fort to the rear and wild shouts rose as outlaw troops smashed into the stockade from the east and the west. A savage melee raged through half the night. Shi Wengong clawed out an escape route and fled.

Zeng Senior's agitation doubled on learning of the death of his son Suo. The next day he asked Shi to write a letter of surrender. The instructor, who was also very frightened, did so, and dispatched it by emissary to Song Jiang's camp. Song Jiang opened it and read:

> *Zeng Nong, lord of Zengtou Village, bows his head and respectfully greets Song Jiang, commander-in-chief: My sons in a moment of rashness wrongly offended your prestige. When Chao Gai the Heavenly King came with troops and reasonably demanded our submission, one of my underlings dared to snipe at him with bow and arrow. We also criminally stole your horses. There aren't words enough to express my apologies. All of this was against my wishes.*
>
> *Now that dog of a son is dead, and I sent this emissary to request peace. If you will end the fighting and retire your*

troops, I will return all of your horses and highly reward your forces with gold and cloth. It is my sincere desire to avoid casualties on both sides. I pray you give this matter your consideration.

By the time he finished reading, Song Jiang was in a rage. "He killed my brother Chao Gai," he fumed. "Why should I quit! I'll raze that village to the ground!"

The emissary, lying prostrate, trembled uncontrollably. Wu Yong hastily intervened.

"You're wrong, brother," he said. "We contended with them because they abused us. But now they are asking for peace. Can we abandon principle because of a moment of anger?"

A reply was written and ten ounces of silver given to the emissary, who returned to the village. Zeng Senior and Shi Wengong opened the missive and read:

Song Jiang, commander-in-chief of Mount Liangshan, sets his hand in reply to Zeng Nong, lord of Zengtou: Since ancient times a country without credibility must perish, a man without virtue must die, wealth gained without rectitude must be confiscated, generals without courage must suffer defeat. Originally there was no enmity between Liangshan Marsh and Zengtou Village. Each stayed within its own boundaries. But your evil deeds aroused our hostility. If you seek peace you must return the horses you stole on two occasions, turn over the thief Yu Baosi, and reward our soldiers with money and cloth. Let your generosity demonstrate your sincerity. If you change your mind, we shall have to take other measures.

Zeng Nong and Shi were both shocked and depressed. The next day Zeng Nong dispatched an emissary with another message: "If you want Yu Baosi, please send a man as hostage."

Song Jiang and Wu Yong dispatched Shi Qian, Li Kui, Fan Rui, Xiang Chong and Li Gun as an earnest of a desire for negotiations. Just before they left, they were told what to do in the event of an emergency, and urged to act promptly. The five departed.

Guan Sheng, Xu Ning, Shan Tinggui and Wei Tingguo arrived from the mountain stronghold. After a reunion with the other chieftains they were stationed in the central column.

Meanwhile, Shi Qian and the four bold fellows met with Zeng Senior. "Big Brother has ordered us here to discuss peace," said Flea on a Drum.

"If Wu Yong sends five men he must be up to some trick," said Shi Wengong.

Li Kui angrily grabbed Shi and commenced to beat him. Zeng Senior hurriedly intervened.

Shi Qian said: "Li Kui may be crude, but he has Big Brother's fullest trust. He was specially chosen. You have no need for suspicion."

Zeng Senior was very anxious for peace. Ignoring Shi, he served the five wine and invited them to rest in the camp in the Fahua Monastery, and posted a guard of five hundred soldiers front and rear. He then appointed his son Zeng Sheng his negotiator and sent him to Song Jiang's camp with Yu Baosi.

After presenting themselves at the central column, they delivered the horses they had stolen, plus a quantity of gold and bolts of cloth.

"These are the latest horses you rustled," said Song Jiang. "Where is White Jade Lion That Glows in the Night that you snatched from Duan Jingzhu the previous time?"

"My instructor Shi Wengong has been riding it," said Zeng Sheng. "That's why we didn't bring it."

"You hurry up and write a letter, and say I want that horse back, quickly!"

Zeng Sheng penned a missive and sent a man with it to the fort. When Shi was informed, he said: "Any other horse he can have, but not this one!"

Several times the messenger shuttled back and forth. Song Jiang absolutely insisted. Finally, Shi dispatched a reply.

"If he really must have my horse, let him withdraw his army first, and I'll give it to him."

Song Jiang went into a huddle with Wu Yong. While they were conferring a man suddenly arrived and reported: "Armies from Qingzhou and Lingzhou are on their way!"

"When those rascals in Zengtou hear about this, they're sure to pull a switch!" Song Jiang averred.

He secretly ordered Guan Sheng, Shan and Wei to engage the Qingzhou army, and Hua Rong, Ma Lin and Deng Fei to engage the forces from Lingzhou. He also summoned Yu Baosi privately, reassured him and treated him with great kindness.

"If you're willing to perform meritoriously, I'll make you a chieftain in our mountain stronghold," said Song Jiang. "Vengeance against you for stealing our horses will be forgotten. I'll break an arrow in pledge. If you won't co-operate, Zengtou will soon be destroyed. It's up to you."

Yu decided to give in and accept orders. Wu Yong told him of his plan.

"Pretend to have escaped and run back to your fort. Say to Shi Wengong: 'I was in Song Jiang's camp with Zeng Sheng, negotiating peace. From what I heard, I now have the true picture. Song Jiang's only purpose is to get back his fine horse. He's not interested in peace. Once you return the animal, he's going to turn on us. He's heard that relief armies are on the way from Qingzhou and Lingzhou, and he's in a terrible flap. You must take advantage of this situation and act. It's too good to miss.' If Shi heeds your advice, we'll be ready for him."

Yu went to Shi's fort and spoke as directed. Shi led him to Zeng Senior and said that Song Jiang had no intention of making peace, and that this was a good time to attack his camp.

"But Sheng is there," the father protested. "If we change, they're sure to kill him."

"We'll smash into the camp and rescue him, come what may. Tonight we'll order all of our forts to muster their full complement of men and go with us against Song Jiang's camp. Once we cut off the snake's head, its body — the rest of the bandits — will be immobilized. When we return there will be time enough to kill Li Kui and the other four."

"An excellent plan, instructor."

Su Ding in the north fort, Zeng Kui in the east fort and Zeng Mi in the south fort were notified to join in the raid. Yu managed to slip into the fort in the Fahua Monastery and see Li Kui and the others. He surreptitiously told Shi Qian what was going on.

Meanwhile, Song Jiang said to Wu Yong: "I wonder how our plan is working out?"

"If Yu doesn't come back, that means they've fallen for it," said the military advisor. "Tonight, they'll probably raid our camp. We'll pull out first, and lie in ambush on both sides. At the same time we'll send Sagacious Lu and Wu Song with foot soldiers against their east fort, and infantry under Zhu Tong and Lei Heng against their west fort, while Yang Zhi and Shi Jin attack the north fort with cavalry. This method is called 'The Foreign Hunting Dog Waits for the Quarry in Its Den'. It never fails."

That night Shi Wengong set out with Su Ding, Zeng Mi, Zeng Kui and their soldiers. The moon was hazy, the stars were dim. Shi and Su were in the lead, Mi and Kui covered the rear. Bells had been removed from the horses and clanking armor from the men. All advanced quietly towards Song Jiang's camp.

They found the gates open and not a soul inside. It was completely still. The raiders knew they had been duped, and quickly departed. As they hurried back towards their fort they heard gongs clashing and cannon booming in Zengtou. Shi Qian, who had climbed into the bell tower of Fahua Monastery, had clangorously tolled the big bell. This was the signal for outlaw artillery to open fire on the East and West Gates of the village. With a roar, countless brigands poured through the blasted portals, slaughtering as they came. In the monastery, Li Kui, Fan Rui, Xiang Chong and Li Gun vigorously fought their way out.

Shi was anxious to return to the fort, but he couldn't find the road. The fort itself was a scene of mad confusion. Zeng Senior, on being informed that the men of Liangshan Marsh were charging murderously in from two directions, hung himself in despair.

Zeng Mi, hastening to the west fort, died from a thrust of Zhu Tong's halberd. Zeng Kui, fleeing to the east fort, was trampled to jelly in the chaos by horses' hoofs.

Pursued by Sagacious Lu and Wu Song, Su Ding rushed pell-mell through the North Gate, outside of which were innumerable concealed pits. He ran into Yang Zhi and Shi Jin, who killed him with arrows. The men and horses fleeing in his wake tumbled one on top the other into the pits, countless numbers dying in their fall.

Shi Wengong's White Jade Lion steed was fleet. He galloped through the West Gate into the wilderness. A black mist curtained the sky. Shi couldn't tell north from south. He rode on for twenty *li*, not knowing where he was.

A gong crashed in a wood and four or five hundred troops surged out. The commander at their head held a long staff, which he swung at the legs of Shi's mount. The magnificent stallion, before the blow could land, leaped over its attacker's head and galloped on.

Shi continued to race through the night. Dark clouds massed, chill vapors floated, a black mist spread, a fierce wind blew. In the emptiness, wherever he turned he was dogged by Chao Gai's spirit. Shi resumed his original road, and he ran into Yan Qing the Prodigy and Lu Junyi the Magnate.

"Where do you think you're going, wretched thief!" shouted Lu. With one thrust of the halberd into Shi's leg, he brought him from his saddle. Lu tied him up and marched him to Zengtou. Yan Qing led the famous steed to the main camp.

Song Jiang was both delighted and angry. While glad that Lu Junyi had distinguished himself, he was enraged to see Shi Wengong, who had slain Chao Gai the Heavenly King.

First he had Zeng Sheng decapitated and every member of the Zeng family slaughtered, old and young, without exception. Then he stripped the village of all gold, silver, valuables and grain and loaded them onto carts for delivery to the mountain stronghold, where they would be distributed as rewards among the chieftains and troops.

Meanwhile, Guan Sheng drove off the army from Qingzhou, and Hua Rong scattered the soldiers from Lingzhou, and they and their forces returned to the village. Not a chieftain, big or small, had been lost, and Song Jiang had regained the White Jade Lion That Glows in the Night, to say nothing of large quantities of booty.

Shi Wengong was locked in a cage cart, the outlaw troops were assembled, and all headed back for Mount Liangshan. None of the towns, villages or hamlets en route were molested.

On arriving at Loyalty Hall, they gathered before Chao Gai's spirit tablet. Xiao Rang the Master Hand, at Song Jiang's direction, wrote the memorial address. The chieftains wore mourning and wept. Shi Wengong's heart was cut out and offered as a sacrifice to the departed. The ceremony was completed.

CHAPTER 26
The Heroes of Liangshan Marsh Take Seats in Order of Rank

Song Jiang called for a feast of celebration. Each took his place in Loyalty Hall according to rank. There were exactly one hundred and eight of them.

"After my trouble in Jiangzhou I came up the mountain," said Song Jiang, "and later, thanks entirely to the support of you heroic brothers, I was made leader. Gathered here today we have a total of one hundred and eight chieftains. I am very happy. Since brother Chao Gai's death, on each of the occasions we led troops down the mountain we always returned intact. This is because Heaven defended us. It was not due to the talent of any man. Whenever one of us was captured by the enemy, whether imprisoned or wounded, he always came back safely. All of this was the work of Heaven. None of us can claim any credit. And here we are today, one hundred and eight of us gathered in righteous meeting. Truly an event rarely witnessed from ancient times to the present!

"These are days when armed soldiers roam, slaughtering at will and committing unpardonable crimes. I'm thinking of holding a great mass to thank the spirits of Heaven and Earth for their protective benevolence. We should pray first that they continue to preserve our health and security. Second, that the emperor will pardon our terrible crimes and allow us to serve our country loyally to the death. Third, that Chao Gai's ghost may soon become a spirit in Heaven so that in later reincarnations we may meet again.

"We should pray also that those who died by violence — the burned, the drowned, the murdered innocents — be allowed to cross over into Heaven.

"This is what I'd like to do. I wonder what you brothers think of the idea?"

"Excellent," said the chieftains. "A fine thing that can bring only good."

"Let Taoist mentor Gongsun Sheng conduct the mass," suggested Wu Yong. "Send men down to invite Taoist priests of high attainment to attend and bring the necessary paraphernalia. Have someone buy scented candles and paper horses, plus fruit and flowers, vegetables and other meatless dishes, and all things required for the sacrifices."

It was decided to hold the mass for seven days, starting the fifteenth of the fourth lunar month. The stronghold spent money freely and made full preparations. As the time drew near, four banners were hung in front of Loyalty Hall. Inside, three high altars were built, and idols of the Seven Precious and Three Clean Saints were set. On either side stood the Spirits of the Twenty-Eight Constellations and the Twelve Watches — for these were the true officiators over all important masses. Outside the hall were placed idols of the guardian generals Cui, Lu, Deng and Dou. Then the paraphernalia was laid out and the Taoist priests invited to begin. Including Gongsun Sheng, they numbered forty-nine.

It was a clear, bright day, pleasant and mild, with the moon white in the summer sky and the breeze gentle. Song Jiang and Lu Junyi lit the incense first, followed by Wu Yong and the other chieftains. Gongsun Sheng, officiating over the sacrifices, handed out the required texts and orders. He and the forty-eight Taoist priests would conduct mass thrice daily for seven days. Then they would disperse.

Song Jiang begged Heaven for a sign. He asked Gongsun Sheng to burn special prayers written on paper three times daily, so that their smoke would waft them to the Emperor of Heaven. And so, the third watch of the seventh day found Gongsun Sheng on the first tier of the altar, the other priests on the second, and Song Jiang and the chieftains on the third. The lesser commanders and officers stood below. All were earnestly entreating Heaven for a sign.

Suddenly, there was a sound like the ripping of fabric in the northwest corner of the sky. Everyone looked. They saw an object resembling an up-ended golden platter, narrow at both ends and broad in the middle. Known as Heaven's Gate, or Heaven's Eye, it was dazzlingly bright and resplendent as sunset clouds. A column of fire, shaped like a willow basket, twirled down from the center of the Eye towards the altar. It circled the altar once, then plunged into the earth near the southern end of the hall.

Heaven's Eye was closed by then, and the Taoist priests descended from their altar. Song Jiang ordered men to dig with shovels and mattocks where the fire had vanished. At a depth of three feet, they found a stone tablet. It was inscribed on both sides with mystic writing. Song Jiang ordered that the ashes of the paper prayers be scattered.

At dawn the next day, after the priests had their breakfast, he gave them gifts of gold and cloth. Only then did they examine the stone tablet. It was covered with weird squiggles, like tadpoles, which no one could decipher. But one of the priests, named Ho, was skilled in the occult.

"I have a set of books at home, handed down from my ancestors," he said, "which teaches how to read Heavenly writing. Since ancient times, it's always been this tadpole script, and I've learned how to decipher it. Let me have a look and I'll tell you what it says."

Pleased, Song Jiang handed over the tablet. The priest perused it for some time. Finally, he spoke.

"These are names of all of you gallant warriors. On one side it says: 'Act in Heaven's Behalf'. On the other: 'Complete Loyalty and Righteousness'. At the top are diagrams of the Great and Small Dippers. Below that are your names. If there's nothing unfavorable, I'll read them aloud, one by one."

"How fortunate that you can solve the mystery. We're extremely thankful. If you can enlighten us, we'll owe you our deepest gratitude. Please don't hesitate even if it contains criticism. Hold nothing back. We want to hear every word."

Song Jiang told Xiao Rang the Master Hand to take notes on yellow paper.

Ho the Taoist priest said: "The thirty-six lines on the front are names of stars of Heavenly Spirits. The seventy-two lines on the back are names of stars of Earthly Fiends." He gazed at them for several minutes, then told Xiao Rang to copy as he dictated.

When he had finished, the chieftains stared at the list in amazement. "Who would have thought," Song Jiang mused, "that a petty functionary like me would be the highest of all the stars. And you, brothers, originally were with me up in the sky together. Today, Heaven has indicated that it is right for us to be united in chivalry. We've reached our full number, and our ranks have been decided by Heaven, with a general division into higher and lower. We've been listed in order, under the star categories of Heavenly Spirits and Earthly Fiends. Each of you chieftains must keep to his particular rank. Let there be no squabbling. Heaven's edict must be obeyed."

"Who would dare go against Heaven's will!" said the chieftains.

Song Jiang rewarded priest Ho with fifty ounces of gold. He also gave some payment to the other priests. They collected their paraphernalia for the mass and departed down the mountain.

Song Jiang then conferred with Wu Yong and Zhu Wu. They decided to hang a tablet reading "Loyalty Hall" on the building of that name, put another sign on Unity Pavilion, and build stockades around all three passes in front of the stronghold. Behind the hall they would level a "V" shaped terrace up the slope, and construct a large pavilion at the apex, with building wings extending down on the east and the west. In the pavilion they would place the spirit tablet of Chao Gai. Song Jiang, Wu Yong, Lü Fang and Guo Sheng would occupy the east wing. Lu Junyi, Gongsun Sheng, Kong Ming and Kong Liang would occupy the west.

New pennants and banners were made. On the very top of the mountain an apricot-yellow banner was stretched reading: "Act in Heaven's Behalf." In front of Loyalty Hall were two banners. One said: "Defender of Justice from Shandong," the other: "Jade Unicorn from Hebei," meaning Song Jiang and Lu Junyi, respectively. In addition there were banners of dragons, tigers, bears and panthers rampant; pennants of blue dragons with white tigers, vermillion birds on black backgrounds; golden axes with white tassels, blue banners and black umbrellas, and large fringed banners of black. These were for the use of the armies.

There were also banners of the Four Stars in the Big Dipper, Central Heaven and the Four Directions, the Three Essentials and the Nine Elements, the Twenty-Eight Constellations, the Sixty-Four Diagrams, the Nine Heavens and the Eight Diagrams — in all a hundred and twenty-four Heaven-governing banners, all made by Hou Jian. Metal tallies and seals were forged by Jin Dajian.

When everything was ready, an auspicious day was chosen, and oxen and horses were slaughtered in sacrifice to the Spirits of Heaven and Earth. The signs "Loyalty Hall" and "Unity Pavilion" were hung, and the apricot-yellow banner "Act in Heaven's Behalf" was also put in place. To the pillars on either side of the entrance to the hall two vermillion vertical tablets were attached. Reading downward, and continuing from the right tablet to the left, they said: "Be ardently righteous and loyal always, never covet wealth or harm the people."

That day Song Jiang ordered a huge feast. He took up his tallies and seals of office and addressed the gathering. "Brothers," he said, "let each of you carry out your duties of leadership, and hearken without fail to orders. To do otherwise would harm our chivalry. Whoever wilfully disobeys shall be punished according to military law. None will be let off lightly."

He then read the chain of command. The two highest leaders were himself and Lu Junyi, the two chiefs of staff were Wu Yong and Gongsun Sheng. He also designated commanders, and their number, to the following posts: Money and grain control —

two. Main cavalry — five. Light cavalry and vanguard — eight. Distant scouting and picket cavalry — sixteen. Infantry, senior officers — ten. Infantry, junior officers — seventeen. Four forts, water defenses — eight. Four inns gathering information and welcoming new arrivals — eight. Chief scout — one. Delivery of secret messages, infantry — four. Central army, guards, cavalry — two. Central army, guards, infantry — two. Punishments and executions — two. Cavalry liaison among the three armies — two. Military supplies — one.

And one each to the following sixteen supervisory positions: dispatches and orders, military and civil awards and punishments, money and grain accounting, boat building, tally and seal making, manufacture of banners and robes, veterinary, doctor of medicine and surgery, weapons and armor making, manufacture of cannon, house construction, butcher, banquet supervisor, brewer, erector of walls and fortifications, and chief standard bearer.

The decree was dated "a lucky day of the fourth lunar month, in the second year of the Xuan Ho Period,* at the great meeting on Mount Liangshan, when assignment of duties was proclaimed." Each chieftain then received his appropriate tallies and seals and the feasting ended. Everyone was very drunk. The chieftains left to take up their posts. Those who had not yet been appointed retired to quarters before and behind the "V" terrace to await orders.

Song Jiang selected another auspicious day, burned incense, and ordered drums beaten to summon the chieftains. When all had assembled in the hall, he addressed them.

"This is no ordinary occasion. I have something to say. Since we have come together as the stars of Heavenly Spirits and Earthly Fiends, we must vow before Heaven to unite to the death without reservation, rescue one another from danger and aid one another in misfortune, while striving jointly to defend the country and preserve peace for the people."

---

* A.D. 1121.

The chieftains heartily concurred. They too lit incense and knelt together in the hall. Song Jiang continued.

"I was only a petty functionary, and have neither learning nor ability. But thanks to the protection of Heaven and Earth and the illumination of the sun and the moon, we brothers have gathered here on Mount Liangshan in the Marsh and formed a heroic host. There are now one hundred and eight of us, which conforms to the number ordained by Heaven and is pleasing to the hearts of men. From this day on, if any of us acts in a deliberately unvirtuous manner, or offends our code of chivalry, we pray that Heaven and Earth scourge him, that the spirits and men destroy him, that he never again be reincarnated in human form and remain forever sunk in the depths. We vow to serve our country in righteous loyalty, act in Heaven's behalf, defend our borders and secure our people. Heaven examine us, and by Your Luminance reply."

In chorus the chieftains swore their eternal unity. That day, they reaffirmed their fraternity in a blood oath. They imbibed heavily of wine before the convention finally disbanded.

This, reader, was the grand confluence of chivalry in Liangshan Marsh. The origin of these men and their assignments was preordained.